“I ı sorry,” he said. “I don’t know w. you are.”

Sh ighed. “I hoped you would—that you mi ..”

“W ” he asked.

“B ıse it would’ve made this easier if you were ex ıng me,” she replied.

Ex ng her? He hadn’t been expecting anything els ’t the bombs or the shootings being meant for Why the hell would he have expected her?

“M vhat easier?” he asked.

Wa a hit woman? A hired assassin?

He ed around for his holster and weapon—but ke his clothes, were nowhere in sight. Ne ’as any of his damn family.

He ught they weren’t going to leave him alo

“W have to tell you,” she said. Then she drew ın a deep breath, as if to brace herself, and co ıued, “That this is your son.”

BRIDEGROOM BODYGUARD

BY
LISA CHILDS

Published in Great Britain 2014
by Mills & Boon, an imprint of Harlequin (UK) Limited,
Eton House, 18-24 Paradise Road, Richmond, Surrey, TW9 1SR

ISBN: 978-0-263-91367-5

46-0814

Harlequin (UK) Limited's policy is to use papers that are natural, renewable and recyclable products and made from wood grown in sustainable forests. The logging and manufacturing processes conform to the legal environmental regulations of the country of origin.

Printed and bound in Spain
by Blackprint CPI, Barcelona

Bestselling, award-winning author **Lisa Childs** writes paranormal and contemporary romance for Mills & Boon. She lives on thirty acres in Michigan with her two daughters, a talkative Siamese and a long-haired Chihuahua who thinks she's a rottweiler. Lisa loves hearing from readers, who can contact her through her website, www.lisachilds.com, or snail-mail address, PO Box 139, Marne, MI 49435, USA.

With much love and appreciation for my daughters
Ashley & Chloe Theeuwes.
You are both exceptionally smart and strong and
beautiful young women. You have made
your mother very proud!

Chapter One

Someone put out a hit on Parker Payne.

The statement echoed inside Parker's head, but it wasn't the only echo. His ears rang yet from the blast of the explosion that had sent him to the hospital and two Payne Protection Agency employees to the morgue.

Guilt and pain clutched his heart. He was supposed to have been inside that SUV, not Douglas and Terry. But, totally unaware of the bomb that had been wired to the ignition, they had jumped inside his vehicle for a lunch run. He'd been rushing out to catch them to change an order, but he had been too late. Doug turned the key, and the SUV exploded into bits of glass and scraps of metal. Two good men died, leaving behind wives and children.

It should have been Parker. Not only did he have no wife or child to leave behind, but he was actually the one whom somebody wanted dead.

He fought against the pain and confusion of the concussion that had his head pounding and his vision blurred. So he closed his eyes and tried to focus on the conversation swirling around his hospital bed.

His mother fussed. "We should take this conversation into the hall so that Parker can get some rest." Her fingers skimmed across his forehead, like they had when he'd been a little boy with a fever or a scraped knee or when his father died. She had always been there for her kids even though she hadn't had anyone to be there for her.

He caught her hand and gently squeezed her fingers in reassurance. She had to be scared at how close she had come to losing a child. In the past two weeks, there had been several attempts on his brother Cooper's life and on his twin Logan's life. But most of those attempts had really been meant to end *his* life.

Logan bossed. "We need to find out who the hell put out the hit." Then his tone turned suspicious, so he must have been addressing one of his new in-laws, when he added, "Unless you already know. Your *contacts* must have told you who when they told you about the hit."

The guy cursed Logan, so he must have been the hot-headed Garek instead of the milder-mannered Milek Kozminski. "If I knew who the hell it is, I would have told you—the monster put my sister in danger."

Parker forced open his eyes, but he had to squint against the glare of the overhead lights and the sunlight streaming through the blinds. His head pounded harder, but it was more with guilt than pain. Stacy Kozminski-Payne had been through a lot recently, most of it because of him. He focused on his new sister-in-law. The tawny-haired woman stood between her husband and her brother, as if ready to stop a brawl. It was probably a position in which she would find herself for most of her marriage.

But then his twin did something Logan rarely did; he apologized. "Sorry, man. I know you would do anything to protect your sister."

Garek nodded in acceptance of the apology and continued, "The only thing I know for certain is that it's somebody who has a lot of money and influence."

"You and Milek need to reach out to all your contacts and see what you can find out." Logan resumed his bossing. As CEO of Payne Protection Agency and the oldest Payne sibling by ten minutes, he'd gotten good at giving out orders.

But the Kozminskis weren't known for taking orders well, so Parker waited for them to bristle. Instead Milek asked, "Are you really hiring us?"

Payne Protection Agency was a security firm that Logan had founded when he'd left the police department a few years ago. He'd coerced Parker into leaving the force, too, and joining him. Logan had always been very selective about who he hired—that was why Terry and Douglas had been such good men and their deaths such a tragic loss.

Through narrowed blue eyes, Logan studied his new brothers-in-law. Very new since he and Stacy had married only hours ago in Parker's hospital room so that he could be Logan's best man. "I need your help," he said. And Parker knew his twin so well that he knew that wasn't an easy admission for him to make.

Stacy knew her husband well, too, because she hugged him in appreciation and sympathy. And love. It was obvious how much she loved him. And Logan loved her just as much.

So much that Parker felt a pang of envy. God, he must have hit his head harder than he'd realized.

His arms winding around his wife, Logan continued, "We need to keep Stacy and Parker safe."

And finally Parker managed to fight back the pain and gather his strength. He struggled to swing his legs over the bed and sit up. "This isn't your fight, Logan," he said. "It's mine. So you're not giving out the orders this time."

He had never minded before that Logan was his boss as well as his brother, but he minded now—because he didn't want his boss or his brother getting killed. "I'm not hiring Payne Protection. I can take care of this myself." Now that he knew he was the intended target...

Logan turned to him as if surprised to find him still in the room. "Parker—"

"This is all about me," he said. "And you need to be all about your new bride. You and Stacy need to leave for your honeymoon."

Logan's arms tightened protectively around his bride, but he shook his head. "I'm not leaving while you're in danger."

"That's exactly why you have to leave," Parker pointed out. "Because when I'm in danger, so are you." With the same black hair and blue eyes and chiseled features, they were so identical that most people couldn't tell them apart unless they knew them. Logan was always serious, and Parker was usually a smart aleck.

Logan shook his head. "That's exactly why we need to all work together to find out who put out the hit on you."

"Probably a jealous husband," a male voice remarked as another man stepped into the hospital room.

"Cooper!" their mother exclaimed over her youngest son.

Even though he was two years younger than Parker and Logan, he could have been their triplet. He looked that much like them. "Damn it," Parker grumbled. "You should still be on your honeymoon."

And that was when it struck him that both his brothers were husbands now. Only he and his baby sister were single yet. And his mom. But she was widowed, so that was different.

He didn't want his new sisters-in-law to become widows, too. "You need to take Tanya and get on a plane and get the hell out of here. And take Logan and Stacy with you."

"Logan and Stacy?" Cooper stared at the woman wrapped up in his oldest brother's arms, and his dark brows arched in shock. Logan and Stacy had spent the past several years hating each other before finally but quickly realizing that they actually loved each other. And they hadn't come to that realization until Cooper and Tanya had left for their honeymoon.

"Parker is getting upset," his mother said. "And he needs his rest. Maybe having Logan and Stacy's wedding in his room was too much for him—"

"Wedding!" Cooper interjected.

Their mother shushed him. "You all need to take the explanations and orders into the hall." Her tone had grown sharper and her usually warm brown eyes were dark with concern and determination.

Her children and even the Kozminskis hurried to obey her, nearly bumping into each other in their haste to step out into the hall. She gently pushed Parker back against the pillows. "The doctor is keeping you overnight for observation," she reminded him, which was probably good since the concussion had affected his short-term memory. "So you really need to rest."

"Mom—"

"You'll need all of your strength to fight with your brothers," she said, dredging up the argument she had used when he'd been a kid reluctant to go to bed. She kissed his forehead before joining the rest of their dysfunctional family in the hall.

Finally Parker was alone. He was also exhausted. But when he closed his eyes, the explosion played out behind his lids. He saw the men through the windshield—just briefly—before the glass shattered and the metal shredded and their bodies…

With a groan of horror and pain, he jerked awake and discovered that he was no longer alone. A woman stood over his bed. She wasn't a nurse—at least not one employed at the hospital—because she didn't wear the green scrubs. She wore a suit with tan pants and a high-necked blouse beneath a loose tan jacket. So he might have thought she worked in hospital administration if not for the baby she balanced on one lean hip.

"You're Parker Payne," she said.

He tensed with suspicion. Why did she want to know? Then he pushed aside the suspicions. It wasn't as if she was trying to collect on that hit—unless hired assassins brought their babies along with them, too.

And if they did, he would rather she try to hit *him* than Logan or Cooper. "Yes, I'm Parker Payne."

She released a shuddery breath of relief. "You're not dead."

"Not yet." But it wasn't for want of people trying.

She shuddered. "I saw on the news what happened to you—or nearly happened to you. It was your vehicle…"

"I'm fine," he said with a twinge of guilt at the unfairness of that. Doug and Terry should be fine, too, but they were gone, leaving family behind just like Parker had been left when his police-officer father died in the line of duty.

At least if someone was actually successful at carrying out the hit, he wouldn't leave a child behind to mourn him like he had mourned. His family and friends thought he stayed single because he couldn't commit, because he was a playboy. But he was practical. Given the dangerous nature of his job, he wasn't a good risk for a husband or father. And he didn't want to put anyone through the pain he, his mother and siblings had suffered.

The woman studied him through narrowed eyes. Even narrowed, her eerie light brown eyes were so huge that they nearly overwhelmed her thin face. If her hair was down, the caramel-colored locks might have softened her face, but it was pulled tautly back and bound in a tight knot on the top of her head. Her voice low and soft, she asked, "Are you sure you're all right?"

He shook off his maudlin thoughts. He wasn't going to leave anyone behind because he wasn't going to die—at least not before he found out who was after him and made that person pay for all the pain he'd caused. Parker had rested long enough, so he swung his legs over the bed again and sat up. His vision blurred for a moment, but he blinked to clear it.

"Should I get someone?" she asked as she backed up toward the door. She jostled the baby on her hip, and the little thing giggled.

Parker focused on the baby. Dressed in tiny overalls and a blue-and-green-striped shirt, he was apparently a boy. With fuzzy black hair and bright blue eyes, he was also damn cute.

"You know who I am," he realized. "But I don't know who you are. Should I?" He usually never forgot a face—at least not a female one. But she wore no makeup and dressed so frumpy that she wasn't exactly the kind of woman he usually noticed…unless he was in the mood for the repressed-librarian type. And maybe he was in the mood now because he was tempted to see what she would look like with her hair down…

"My name is Sharon Wells," she told him, her soft voice questioning as if she wondered if he remembered it.

As if he should…

He moved his head to shake it, but even the slight movement sent pain radiating throughout his skull. He groaned.

"I should get someone," she said again with a nervous glance toward the hall. "You need help."

"No." He already had too many people trying to help him, trying to fix a problem he must have somehow created himself. The hit was on *him*—no one else. Who had he pissed off enough to want him dead?

Cooper was wrong about the jealous husband. Parker had never messed around with a married woman and never would; there were lines even he refused to cross.

"I don't need anyone," he said.

Now she glanced down at the baby she bounced gently on her hip. His arms flailed, and his chubby little face flushed with happiness. Even though they looked nothing alike, it was as if the child was a part of her because they were so connected.

"Sharon Wells…" He repeated her name but it didn't sound familiar even on his own lips. She wasn't Doug's or Terry's wife; he knew their names, their faces, which he would never be able to look at again without a rush of guilt and shame. If Sharon Wells was a relative of one of them, she must've been a distant one, because he'd met most of their families, too.

He pushed up from the bed and stood on legs that were embarrassingly shaky until he locked his knees.

He wasn't staying overnight in the hospital, not when he had a killer to track down. "I'm sorry," he said. "I don't know who you are."

She sighed. "I hoped you would, that you might..."

"Why?" he asked.

"Because it would've made this easier if you were expecting me," she replied.

Expecting her? He hadn't been expecting anything else—not the bombs or the shootings to be meant for him. Why would he have expected her?

"Make what easier?" he asked.

Was she a hit woman? A hired assassin?

He glanced around for his holster and weapon, but they, like his clothes, were nowhere in sight. Neither was any of his family.

He'd thought they weren't going to leave him alone...

"What I have to tell you," she said. Then she drew in a deep breath, as if to brace herself, and continued, "That this is your son."

He focused on the baby again. The little guy had fuzzy black hair and very bright blue eyes. The kid looked exactly like old baby pictures of him and Logan and Cooper. The baby certainly could have been a Payne. He could have been Parker's...

Maybe he did need longer to recover from the concussion because standing was so much of a strain that his head grew light, and his knees gave out. His already banged-up body struck the floor. Hard. The last thing he heard, before oblivion claimed him, was her scream.

Chapter Two

She shouldn't have screamed, but his falling was such a shock that it slipped out. And started a commotion. Ethan screamed, too—his was high-pitched and blood-curdling as he reacted to her fear. And people rushed into the room.

These were the people she had passed in the hall, the people posted like guards outside his room. But given the police reports she had seen about the explosion and the previous attempts on his brothers' lives, she understood the need for security. Yet they had all let her just walk past them. They had asked her no questions; they had only stared…at Ethan, their eyes round with shock.

They had immediately known what it had taken Parker much longer to realize—that she carried his son.

"What did you do to him?" one of his brothers angrily asked her as he crouched next to Parker on the floor. He looked so much like him that he could have been a twin. There were two men that good-looking in the world? It wasn't fair.

Then a third one rushed forward to help lift Parker back onto the bed. Were they actually triplets? This man's black hair was shorter—in a military brush cut, but other than that he looked so much like the other two it was uncanny. And Ethan looked like a miniature version of all of them. He must have been the spitting image of what they had looked like as babies.

Parker shrugged off his brothers' helping hands and stood up again, steadily, as if his strength had already returned. And given the way his heavily muscled arms stretched the sleeves of his hospital gown, he was strong.

"I'm all right," he assured his concerned family. "I just tried to get up too fast."

An older woman tore her concerned gaze from Parker to stare at the baby. "Or was it the shock?" Her hand trembled slightly as she reached out for one of Ethan's flailing chubby fists. When she touched him, he calmed down, his howls trailing away to soft hiccups. "Of finding out you're a daddy?"

Parker shook his head then flinched at the motion. *"Mom,"* he exclaimed with shock and exasperation. "I am *not* a daddy." He glanced at one of his brothers. "Is he yours?"

Of the group of people who'd rushed back into the room, a tawny-haired woman laughed while a blond-haired man snorted derisively.

Parker's brother's eyes widened in horror, and he glanced from Ethan to her. "I've never seen her before."

"Neither have I."

Sharon flinched. They had met a few times, albeit a while ago. How did he not remember her at all?

"You took one heck of a hit on the head," his brother reminded him. "The doctor said you might have some memory loss because of the concussion."

"Short-term memory loss," Parker clarified. "That means I might forget what happened minutes or hours ago, not months ago."

Sharon should have realized that a man like him wouldn't remember a woman like her. She had spent her life trying to be quiet and unobtrusive, so there was no wonder that so few people ever noticed her.

But then the older woman glanced up at Sharon, her brown eyes full of warmth and wonder. Her hair was auburn, with no traces of gray, so she didn't look old enough to have three thirtysomething-old sons, let alone a grandson. "How old is he?"

"Nine months."

Ethan turned back to her and reached up his free hand toward her hair. Because he loved to pull it, she always bound it tightly and high on the top of her head. But a tendril must have slipped out of the knot because he found something to yank, the fine hairs tugging on her nape. She flinched again over the jolt of pain.

Mrs. Payne chuckled. "The boys always pulled my hair, too," she said. "May I hold him?" She held out her arms as she asked, and the baby boy leaned toward her, almost falling into her embrace.

Panic flashed through Sharon at how easily he had been taken from her. That was what would happen when these people learned the truth. She would be cut out of Ethan's life as though she had never been a part of it.

"Mom." Parker drew the older woman's attention briefly from the baby she held with such awe. "Can you bring him out into the hall?" He turned toward the others. "And the rest of you leave with her. I need to talk to Ms. Wells alone."

Sharon's panic increased, making her pulse race. She lifted her arms to reach for Ethan, to take him back, but the woman was already walking out the door with the sweet baby. And Parker grabbed her outstretched arms, holding her back, as all the others left.

She hadn't really been alone with him before. She'd had Ethan. Even though he was a baby, he had been protection from Parker's wrath. He had to be furious. And he had every right to be. His son had been kept from him, and someone was trying to kill him.

But he wasn't the only one someone was trying to kill.

HOURS BEFORE, the explosion had knocked Parker on his ass, literally. Sharon Wells's announcement, that the baby was his son, had knocked him on his ass, as well, although he would have rather blamed it on the concussion. But he'd recovered quickly.

Sharon was the one trembling now, as he held her arms. A diaper bag hung heavily from one of her thin shoulders, bumping against her side. She stepped back and jerked free of his grasp; apparently she was stronger than she looked.

"I shouldn't have come here," she said. "This was a mistake…."

"Trying to pass that kid off as mine?" he asked. "That was a mistake."

And why had she done it? What had she hoped to gain? If she had been hoping to force someone to marry her, Cooper or Logan would have been the better bet; they cared more about honor than he did. But, damn his short-term memory, they were already married.

"He *is* yours," she insisted. She held his gaze, her strange light brown eyes direct and sincere. "You can get a paternity test to prove it. Since we're at the hospital, maybe they can rush the results."

He dropped his hands from her arms and stepped back. "You're serious…."

"It's just a cheek swab," she said. "It won't hurt him or else I wouldn't have suggested it."

Because she loved her son…

Their son?

He scrutinized her face. The women he usually dated wore makeup and dressed in clothes that flattered their figures. But with her enormous, unusual eyes and delicate features, she didn't really need makeup. She was actually quite beautiful. And his pulse quickened as attraction kicked in, tempting him to see just what her figure was like beneath her baggy suit.

Because of those eyes and that face and his sudden attraction to her, he knew he'd never met her before—much less been with her.

"There is no way that I am the father of *your* baby," he insisted. "I would not have forgotten you if we'd ever been intimate."

He wasn't the careless playboy everyone thought he was. He didn't have a slew of conquests whose faces he couldn't remember.

Her gaze dropped from his, and her face flushed. "But—but you have a concussion…."

He shook his head, and pain from making the motion overwhelmed him. But he kept his legs under him this time and remained conscious. And finally the confusion from the concussion receded, leaving him angry.

"There is no way that *your* child is mine."

"Take the paternity test," she urged him. "Ethan is your son."

Like everyone else, she must have believed that he was such a playboy that he wouldn't remember every woman he'd ever slept with, but his reputation was grossly exaggerated and mostly undeserved. Even with the women with whom he was involved, he always used protection. He couldn't have gotten *anyone* pregnant. So she had to be playing some angle with him, running some scheme.

Why? That paternity test she was urging him to get would only prove him right. So was she just buying some time? Was she just trying to distract him? What did she hope to gain? Did she want to collect the payout for his murder? From what Garek Kozminski had said, it sounded like a substantial amount.

Maybe he needed to search that diaper bag and make certain that she didn't have a weapon concealed. Or maybe a bomb. He reached for the strap of the bag, but his hand grazed her breast instead.

Her already enormous eyes widened with shock.

She wasn't the only one surprised. Her baggy suit hid some curves. Parker was as intrigued as he was suspicious of her.

"What—what are you doing?" she asked, her voice all breathy and anxious.

"You're trying to convince me that I made a baby with you and the concussion made me forget." No wonder she had taken the opportunity to show up now after hearing the news reports about his condition. "The effects of this concussion aren't going to last," he continued.

She nodded, either in agreement or because she was humoring him.

How far would she go to humor him? And to further whatever her agenda really was? He wanted to find out. "My memory can be jogged," he told her.

"I—I still don't understand," she stammered.

"Jog my memory," he challenged her, as he cupped her shoulders and pulled her closer.

Her eyes widened even more as she stared up at him. "Me? You want me to jog your memory?" she asked. "How?"

"Kiss me." But he didn't wait for her to take his bait; he reeled her in first. He tipped up her chin and lowered his mouth to hers.

Instead of jogging his memory, the kiss proved to him that he had never kissed her before—because it was all new. The silkiness of her lips, the warmth and sweetness of her breath as she gasped. He took advantage of that gasp to deepen the kiss, to slide his tongue inside her mouth.

His pulse raced and his head grew light again, but he didn't blame the concussion for that reaction. He blamed her. Because now she was kissing him back, her tongue sliding over his, her lips pressing against his. If her goal was just to distract him, she was doing a damn good job.

He skimmed his hands up her face to that frustrating knot on top of her head. And he tugged her hair free so that it tumbled down around her shoulders. When he had first seen her, he must have still been half-blind from the concussion. Because there was no other explanation for how he hadn't realized how beautiful she was....

She was every bit as beautiful—maybe even more beautiful—than any other woman he had ever dated. But he'd never dated her before.

It wasn't just the first kiss with her—it felt bigger than that. More monumental. It was as if the earth was shaking beneath his feet.

Or at least the building. The structure rumbled, and

the windows rattled. There were no earthquakes in Michigan—so it had to be another explosion.

Someone had set a bomb inside the hospital? Someone was so desperate to kill him that they were willing to risk the lives of more innocent people?

Of this woman? And her baby?

Smoke alarms blared, but the warning was too late. The bomb had already gone off. How many people had been hurt? And would more people be harmed trying to escape the hospital?

The commotion in the hall was so loud that it affected his throbbing head. Voices rose in fear and confusion. Footsteps pounded as if people stampeded in their panic. He glanced toward the window that had rattled. Flames reflected back from the glass. Was it too late to escape?

Or were they already trapped?

Chapter Three

The flames rose from the burning scraps of metal…of what used to be Sharon's car. She remembered where she'd parked it—between the Mini Cooper that had rolled over from the force of the blast and the SUV that was already blackened from the heat of the explosion.

She gasped as she peered out the window around Parker's broad shoulder. Her heart pounded erratically. Well, even more erratically than it had when he'd kissed her. She couldn't think about that kiss right now.

She could think only about what could have happened to Ethan and her if they had been in that car. She pressed her hand over her mouth to hold back a scream of terror. The little boy was so smart and so sweet and affectionate. His life had barely begun; it could not be lost now.

She had already determined that she would do whatever was necessary to keep him safe. But bringing him here had been a mistake. She turned away from the window and headed toward the hall.

But Parker caught her arm, stopping her. "Where do you think you're going?"

"I need to find Ethan," she said.

She needed to hold him, to make certain that the baby boy was all right. Loud noises terrified him; so did too many people, especially strangers. It was a miracle that he'd gone so willingly into Mrs. Payne's arms, but that had been before the explosion and the chaos.

"I need to be with—"

"Here he is," Mrs. Payne said as she walked back into the room with her grandson.

Just as Sharon had feared, he was crying. Tears streamed down his chubby cheeks. His screams must have escalated to hysteria because all he was doing now was gasping for shaky breaths.

She reached for him, and he nearly leaped into her arms, snuggling into her neck. His hands clutched her hair, pulling it around him. And she didn't even care. Her eyes stung with tears at the thought of losing him. She loved this little boy so much; she couldn't love him any more if he was actually hers.

"IT WAS HERS." Logan confirmed what Parker had already suspected when he'd realized that the explosion had been a car in the parking lot blowing up.

At least it hadn't been inside the hospital or close enough to the building to cause any structural damage. The windows had rattled and the floor had shaken, and the smoke from the parking lot had set off some of the alarms.

Logan added, "And the kid is yours."

Stunned, Parker tensed and paused with his hand on his gun. That baby was his? But that made no sense. Unless…

Like a hostage at a bank holdup, Logan lifted his arms. "Don't shoot me. I'm just the messenger."

Parker slid his gun into the holster he had strapped under his arm. God, it felt good to be out of that hospital gown. And in a few minutes, he would be out of the hospital, too. After the explosion in the parking lot and all the media trying to get past security, he doubted that the doctor would protest his leaving early.

"The tests came back already?" he asked as he tried to slow the rapid beat of his heart.

It had been just as she'd said—just a simple cheek swab. From the baby. And him. And Logan and Cooper.

"Mom sweet-talked someone in the lab into rushing the results," Logan replied.

Only a couple of hours had passed since the car exploded. The paternity test had been taken before the police arrived to talk to them. An officer had taken Sharon into a separate room, no doubt to question why and when someone would have put a bomb on her car. The police would have run the registration or vehicle number, if nothing had been left of the plate, to find out who owned it.

Parker had wanted to hear Sharon's answers, too. But those weren't the only answers he wanted from Sharon Wells.

"So who is she?" Logan asked.

"I have no idea," he replied honestly.

Logan gestured around the hospital room. "It's just you and me, Park. Tell me the truth."

"I have no idea," he repeated.

"So she was just a one-night stand?"

His temper rising, Parker grabbed the front of his twin's shirt. "She's not a one-night stand." Not his, and he doubted, from the innocent way she dressed, that she was anyone else's. He just wished he knew what exactly she was. A con artist? A killer? A kidnapper?

He hoped like hell she was none of those things. But

he couldn't let the sweetness of her kiss alleviate his suspicions about her.

"But you don't even know who she is," Logan pointed out.

"I'm going to change that," he said. When the police were done with her, he was going to take his turn interrogating her. Hopefully he hadn't lost his touch from his years with the River City Police Department. Of course, he had spent more time undercover than interrogating suspects. That had been more Logan's job, which he was proving with his inquisition of him.

"Since you've got a baby together, that would probably be a good thing," Logan remarked. He shook his head. "I can't believe you're a father…."

Neither could Parker. But he had no reason to doubt the test. The only one he doubted was Sharon Wells.

THIS HAD BEEN a mistake. Sharon had realized that even before Parker Payne had kissed her. She should not have come here. But she had been warned to trust no one else. So she hadn't told the police anything—not that she'd had much to tell them. She really had no idea who was trying to kill her or why. But she hadn't told the officers about the other attempts on her life.

And she had tried to pass this one off as her car being mistaken for someone else's—maybe even Parker Payne's. He was the one who someone was trying to kill—or so the news reports had claimed.

The gray-haired police officer opened the door of the vacant doctor's office he had used to question her and held it for her. She had her hands full with the diaper bag and the sleeping baby. Ethan had exhausted himself from crying, but even in slumber, he clung to her, strands of her hair clutched in his chubby little fists.

How could she love this child so much? He had never been part of her plan. She had never wanted to marry or have children; she had intended to focus only on her career.

"You're very lucky, miss," the officer told her.

How? Along with her car, Sharon had lost her purse and her suitcases. She sighed. "I know it was just a vehicle…"

She could replace the money and other lost items; she would not have been able to replace Ethan. But even though he hadn't been hurt in the explosion, she was still going to lose him.

To his father…

"The car wasn't the only thing lost," the officer informed her. "The bomb didn't go off until someone started the engine."

"But I had the keys," she murmured. But when she patted the pocket on the front of the diaper bag, she realized they weren't there. She must have left them dangling from the ignition.

"Security cameras picked up someone checking out cars in the lot, obviously looking for one to steal," the officer said.

"Someone was trying to steal my car?" Because she had left the keys and the purse and the suitcases…

How had she been so careless? She'd had her hands full with Ethan. But she'd also been scared to bring Parker Payne a baby he hadn't even known he had.

Shaking his head as if in pity of the dead carjacker, the officer said, "He picked the wrong car to steal."

And he'd died because of it—because of *her.* She

gasped as guilt and regret overwhelmed her. But then a strong hand gripped her shoulder, squeezing gently as if offering reassurance.

She glanced up at Parker Payne. He was dressed in a shirt nearly as blue as his brilliant eyes; it was tucked into a pair of faded jeans. She kind of missed the hospital gown.

"Did the security cameras pick up who planted the bomb?" Parker asked the officer.

The older man shook his head again with regret. "The bomber knew where the cameras were and avoided them. We're going to have the techs go over the footage again to see if they can find anything usable."

Parker nodded in approval.

She was surprised the officer had been so free with information about a police investigation. But then the older man clasped Parker's shoulder.

"Glad you're alive, Payne," he said. "Losing your father was hard enough."

A muscle twitched along Parker's clenched jaw, and he nodded again.

"You tired of working for your brother yet?" he asked. "We'd love to have you back on the force."

Parker arched a brow as if in skepticism of the older man's claim.

"Well, maybe not now," the officer amended, "but once you find out who's trying to kill you…"

"That'll be soon," Parker promised.

"We'll help," the officer said. He turned to Sharon. "But until that person is caught, you might want to stay away from Mr. Payne, miss. For your own safety…"

She had already discovered she wasn't safe anywhere, either.

"We'll protect her, too," Parker said. "It's what Payne Protection does."

His family ran a security firm; he acted as a bodyguard. But what happened when he was the one needing protection? Who protected him?

He stepped back to allow the officer to pass him, and she saw the others standing just down the hall. The brothers who looked so much like him and the other two men who looked like each other with their blond hair and light-colored eyes. All of the men watched him and her carefully, as if they didn't even trust *her* not to try to kill him.

But then, they were smart to trust no one—especially not her. She needed to tell him the truth. But when she turned back to him and found him staring in wonder at the sleeping baby she held, she realized that he already knew.

"He is your son," she said.

"I know." But he shook his head as if he was still in denial of being a dad. Or maybe that wasn't what he was denying....

He was denying *her.*

Pain clutched her heart, and even though it killed her to admit it, she added, "I am not his mother."

"I know."

Of course he knew. Despite the concussion, he would have remembered her had they ever been involved. But they would have never been involved. Even when they'd previously met, they hadn't been formally introduced; they had only glanced at each other in passing. Apparently he hadn't noticed her, but she had noticed him. It was impossible to not notice a man as devastatingly handsome and charming as Parker Payne.

But he wasn't her type any more than she was his. She would never have gone for a man with his reputation or with his good looks. The only men she had ever dated, and there had been only a few, had been as serious about their education and their careers as she had been.

Before her little man had come along. Before Ethan…

So what was she supposed to do now? Hand Parker Payne his son and walk away? That was what she had been instructed to do, but her car was gone now. Her purse and money, too. She had no means with which to walk away…even if she could bring herself to turn her little man over to strangers.

"You're coming with me," he told her, as if he had read her mind or, more likely, seen her indecision. "And you're going to tell me what the hell is going on…."

If only she knew…

But just as she hadn't immediately admitted that she wasn't Ethan's mother, she stalled on admitting her ignorance, too. She needed more time with the little boy—enough time to make sure he would be safe…without her.

Parker's hand moved to her elbow now, as he guided her toward his family and friends. "We need a diversion," he told them, "a way to get out of here and make sure that no one follows us."

One of his brothers nodded. "We'll distract whoever might be watching. Do you have a safe place to take them?"

Parker nodded.

But Sharon felt no relief. Parker might be able to keep them safe from whoever was after them. But who would keep her safe from him?

One of the light-haired men spoke. "I found out more information from my contacts."

Parker lifted a brow in question. "You know who ordered the hit on me?"

He shook his head. "No, but I know that you're not the only one. A hit was put out on someone else the same day as it was put out on you."

His eyes darkening with concern, Parker glanced toward his brother.

And the man shook his head again. "It's on a woman." His gray-eyed gaze focused on her. "A woman named Sharon Wells."

So she hadn't just been in the wrong places at the wrong times. It had not been coincidence or mistaken identity. Someone was definitely trying to kill *her.* Someone wanted both her and Parker Payne dead.

Chapter Four

Parker closed and locked the door behind Sharon Wells and the baby she carried—his baby. Then he slid his gun back into the holster beneath his shoulder. Before he'd brought her up from the garage in the basement, he had cleared the penthouse condo on Lake Michigan that his brother Logan used as a safe house. Parker had also made certain they weren't followed from the hospital.

"We'll be safe here," he assured her.

She trembled—maybe with cold or maybe with exhaustion from carrying the sleeping child. When he'd cleared the penthouse, he had also brought up the portable crib his mother had somehow conjured up at the hospital. He had set it up in a corner of the master bedroom. He reached out for the baby and carefully lifted him from her arms. But the child—even in his sleep—clutched her hair in his hands, binding the baby to her as if those tresses were caramel-colored ropes.

She was not his mother; she had finally admitted that. But there was definitely a bond between her and the baby. She gently pried open the little fingers so that her hair slipped free. And Parker held only the baby.

Ethan—she called him. His son's name was Ethan. He stared down in wonder at the little boy. His pudgy cheeks were flushed and drool trailed from the corner of his open mouth. His fuzzy black hair was damp, too. He had been held so tightly in Sharon's arms that the child had gotten too warm. She had held him as if she would never let him go. And now she visibly held her breath as she watched him handle the baby, as if afraid that Parker might drop him.

That he might hurt him…

A test had proved that somehow this child was his. Parker had vowed to never become a father, but now that he was, he would do anything for his son. He would die for him before he would ever let any harm come to him.

If Ethan had been in that car when it exploded…

Parker shuddered in horror over the thought. He could have lost his child before he had ever realized that the little boy was his. He never wanted to let him go now, but the little boy was already overly warm. And Parker was hot himself—with anger over Sharon Wells's deception. But she watched him as if he was the one who couldn't be trusted.

Very gently, so that he didn't awaken the boy, he laid him down in the crib. The child sighed softly as he relaxed against the thin mattress, his slumber deepening.

"We're safe here," he repeated. But he was reassuring himself now that nothing would happen to his little boy.

"You probably want to kill me yourself," she said, "for misleading you."

He snorted. "Misleading me?" He wrapped his fingers around her arm and tugged her farther from the crib so that he wouldn't wake the baby as the anger he had barely been able to contain boiled over in his voice. "That's all you think you've done?"

"I didn't lie to you," she insisted, those huge light

brown eyes wide with innocence and sincerity. “I never told you that I was Ethan’s mother—just that you are his father.”

He dropped his hand from her arm as he realized she hadn’t lied. She had never claimed to be the baby’s mother; he had only assumed that she was because she had brought the baby to him. Why hadn’t the boy’s mother? That woman—whoever she was—had kept her pregnancy from him.

“Why were you the one to bring me my son?” he wondered aloud.

While the baby’s mother hadn’t even told him that he was a father, this woman had brought him his baby. She had shared a secret that wasn’t even hers.

“I shouldn’t be mad at you,” he said as he turned back to the crib and studied the sleeping baby. “I should probably be thanking you instead.” If not for Sharon Wells, he might never have known he had a son.

“So you don’t want to kill me?” she asked, but she narrowed those eyes with suspicion as if she still couldn’t trust him. But given that someone was trying to kill them, she shouldn’t trust him or anyone else.

He shrugged. “I don’t know.” He was treating her as his family treated each other, making jokes to defuse a tense situation. “I could use the money for carrying out the hit. Maybe set up a college fund for Ethan…”

She smiled nervously, probably not completely certain he was kidding.

He wasn’t entirely kidding. He would have to set up a college fund; he would have to provide for his son’s present and his future. But he wouldn’t be able to do any of that if he was dead.

And why was there a hit out on Sharon, as well? She wasn't the baby's mother, so who exactly was she?

"Maybe you haven't lied to me," he said, "but you haven't been completely honest with me, either. You know a lot more than I do. You know who Ethan's mother is."

Color flushed her face, giving away her guilt.

"And I think you even know why someone's trying to kill us," he continued, "maybe even who…"

She shook her head and all that thick hair tumbled around her shoulders. He was so glad that he had pulled it free from that knot. Those caramel-colored waves softened the sharp angles of her thin face, making her beautiful. "I don't know why," she said, "or who…"

He stared into her eyes, trying to gauge if she was being honest. If only he were the interrogator that his brother, the former detective, was…

But he had been the undercover cop—the one more adept at keeping secrets than at flushing them out. He hadn't needed confessions; he had caught 'em in the act—in the commission of the crime.

Had Sharon Wells committed any crime?

"Who are you?" he asked.

It wasn't the question he should be asking. He should be asking who Ethan's mother was. But Sharon was the one with the bounty on her head—not whoever the baby's mother was. And for some reason Parker was more interested in Sharon than in whoever had kept his son from him.

"Who are you?" Parker asked again.

SHARON HAD EXPECTED his anger. She hadn't expected his suspicion. "I told you who I am. I would show you my driver's license to prove it, but it burned up when my car exploded."

But more than material possessions had blown up. Somebody had lost his life because of her, because someone else wanted her dead. And that man might not have been the only one who'd been hurt in the cross fire….

Parker crossed the enormous master suite to a desk near the window that overlooked Lake Michigan. The sun was setting now, streaking across the surface of the water. He lifted a piece of paper from a fax machine. "Here's a copy of your license."

Her face—looking pale and tense—stared back at her from the paper he held up. Then he replaced that with another photo—one of a burned-out and boarded-up apartment building. "And here's a picture of the address on your driver's license…."

Sharon stepped closer to him. "Did anyone die in the fire?" She reached for the picture, which was actually part of a newspaper article.

He caught her wrist. "You knew about this?" A muscle twitched in his cheek and his blue eyes were so intense, so filled with concern. "Were you and Ethan there when the building caught fire?"

His concern was for his son. But she was concerned for the baby, too. She had been entrusted with his safety, with his welfare. It wasn't a job for which she had asked, but it was one she had taken more seriously than her *real* job. And she had nearly failed. She glanced at that picture of destruction and shuddered.

"No," she replied. "We weren't there. But I saw it on the news."

Panic clutched her heart as she remembered that horrific moment when she had realized that it was her home on the news, her apartment complex burning, flames reflecting off the shattered glass on the blackened lawn.

"I know there were injuries," she said, "but I haven't seen any follow-up reports to see if everyone recovered."

That muscle twitched in his cheek again and he replied slowly, with reluctance, "Someone was killed…."

She sucked in a breath. "That's two people," she murmured. "Two people killed because of me…."

"Today two people were killed because of *me*." He slid his hand from her wrist up her arm and squeezed her shoulder, offering comfort and sharing her guilt. "Two friends—two family men—lost their lives because someone wanted *me* dead."

Tears stung her eyes, but she blinked them back. Long ago she had learned that crying was a waste of time. And she had never had anyone offer her a shoulder to cry on or arms to hold her. She had been left alone with swollen eyes and a red face.

"Why does someone want you dead?" he asked and then repeated his question again. "Who *are* you?"

"You have a copy of my license. You know who I am."

He shook his head. "I know your name and your old address. But that doesn't tell me why someone would want you dead. Are you involved with the wrong people?"

She hadn't thought so…until now.

"Do you have a crazy boyfriend?" he asked, firing questions at her like bullets. "A dangerous career? Do you lead a life of crime?"

She laughed at the wild image he painted of her. It could not have been further from the truth. He had to have been kidding again like he had when he'd acted as if he would consider killing her for the money.

From the little time she had spent around his family, she had noticed that they teased each other as a way of communicating. But what did she know about family? She had never really had one.

"You think this is funny?" he asked, his voice gruff with disapproval.

"Of course I don't," she said. With all the guilt and fear she felt, she was barely holding it together. If she let herself think about those people…

Tears stung her eyes, but she blinked them back. If she gave in to them, she wouldn't be able to stop. "I think this is surreal. None of this is my life. None of this has anything to do with me. I am only the messenger delivering your son."

He laughed bitterly. "You make yourself sound like FedEx, like you're just delivering a package."

That was what she had been told—how the baby had been referred to—as a package. She cringed now as she remembered Ethan's mother's careless words.

"And that's bull," he said, "because you have an undeniable bond with…" His throat moved as if emotion choked him. He visibly swallowed and continued. "…my son."

He had already claimed his child. Where did that leave Sharon? If she admitted everything to him, it would leave her alone again as she already had been for so much of her life. But she shrugged off the self-pity and focused on what was important: Ethan would have a parent who would love and protect him.

And if Parker were to protect his son, he had to find out who was trying to kill him and stop that person. So she had to tell him everything she knew—the little that it was.

"I have been taking care of him," she said, "pretty much since he's been born."

"You're a foster mother?" he asked.

She shook her head.

"A nanny?"

She sighed. That wasn't the job she had started out with, but it was the one she had wound up doing. "I'm a law student."

"So you work as a nanny on the side?"

"I work as a law clerk for a judge." And she watched realization dawn on his handsome face. He knew who the mother of his son was.

He cursed. But then he tensed and glanced toward his son, as if regretful of swearing in front of the child. Ethan slept on, though. "Judge Foster?"

He had slept with the woman but didn't address her by her first name?

She nodded.

And he shook his head. "She told me that she couldn't have kids…."

"She was actually having fertility treatments so that she could," Sharon said, flinching as she remembered the judge's mercurial mood changes. She had been so thrilled to get the position clerking for the infamous Judge Brenda Foster…until she'd actually had the job. But the job as clerk had turned into the nanny job when Brenda had been unable to keep any other nannies working for her.

He cursed again but under his breath. "I need to talk to her."

"Good luck," she murmured. "I haven't been able to reach her for the past two weeks."

"Two weeks?" he echoed in shock. "She hasn't seen her child in two weeks?"

With all the hours the judge worked and socialized, two weeks wasn't the longest she had gone without seeing her son. "She sent me and Ethan away with enough cash to stay in hotels for two weeks. She didn't want me using credit cards to buy anything."

"Because she didn't want you to get tracked down," Parker said, his blue eyes narrowing. "She must have known someone was after you."

Sharon shook her head. "Nobody was after me."

He clutched the paper in his hand so tightly that he crumpled it. "This newspaper article proves otherwise. And so does your car getting blown up in the hospital parking lot today."

Sharon shuddered as she faced the reality that someone definitely wanted her dead. Why?

"What else did the judge tell you?" Parker asked.

Sharon sighed. "Just that if I hadn't heard from her before those two weeks were over, I was to bring Ethan to you." It wasn't exactly what the judge had said, but he was already so angry with Brenda—and rightfully so—that Sharon didn't want to make the situation worse.

But then, she wasn't certain that it could get much worse…until she heard the creak of footsteps on the stairs. Parker heard them, too, because he reached for his gun. Obviously, he hadn't been expecting anyone.

He had promised that they would be safe here. But Sharon was beginning to fear that they wouldn't be safe anywhere—not with someone determined that they die.

The steps squeaked again. There was more than one person coming up the stairwell. While Parker was armed, he was outnumbered. And even if he had another gun,

Sharon had never touched one, let alone knew how to use one. She could only watch helplessly as he moved toward the stairs—putting himself between her and Ethan and the threat to all their lives….

Chapter Five

Curses echoed inside Parker's head. He had been so certain that he hadn't been followed. He'd been so certain that he had done everything necessary to keep his son and Sharon Wells safe. He hadn't even told his family where he was bringing them, just that he had a place.

As a head rose above the stairwell railing, the curses slipped through his lips. "Damn you, Logan! I could've shot you. . . ." His twin had admonished him many times for sneaking up on him. Why hadn't the lesson applied to himself?

"I wasn't sure if you knew about this place," Logan said. "But Mom was insistent that I find you."

And her head rose above the stairwell railing as she pushed past her oldest and rushed over to the youngest Payne. The new grandmother uttered a wistful sigh as she stared down at the sleeping baby.

She had known about her grandchild for only a few hours, but it was obvious she already loved him. Something gripped Parker's heart, squeezing it tightly, and he realized he loved the baby, too. Ethan was a part of him.

And a part of Brenda Foster. She had lied to him. She had tricked him. Those tactics had made her such an effective district attorney that she had been one of the youngest judges ever appointed to the bench. And her ruthlessness had made her both one of the most respected and most hated judges ever.

Parker had been flattered that such a successful woman had been attracted to him. But while he'd been her bodyguard, he had refused to act anything but professional with her. So she'd fired Payne Protection. He had been attracted to her combination of beauty and brains, and once he no longer worked for her, he had acted on that attraction.

And, unbeknownst to him, they had created a child. She hadn't just lied to him once; she had continued that lie with every day she had kept his baby's existence from him. What had compelled her to finally have Sharon Wells bring the baby to him?

What kind of trouble was she in? Because of her ruthlessness as a judge, she had made many enemies and had constantly received threats to her life. But why would those criminals threaten the life of the father of her child and her nanny?

"I'm actually glad you showed up," Parker begrudgingly admitted to his overprotective twin.

"What?" Logan reached for his gun and glanced around the condo as if looking for intruders hiding in the shadows. "Were you followed?"

"No. I was careful." If he hadn't been, he and Sharon would already be dead. "But I need to leave for a while. I need to go see someone."

And find out what kind of game she was playing....

This was about more than a criminal with a grudge or the hit would have been on Brenda. Not on her nanny and the father of her child.

"So I need you to protect Sharon and…my son…." He could say those words that he thought he would never say because he couldn't *not* claim that beautiful little boy as his. Like his mother, he already loved the child. "I need you to protect them while I'm gone."

"Where are you going?" Logan asked.

Sharon just stared at him because she obviously knew where. She knew that he would have to go to Brenda. He would have to see her and maybe have a few choice words with her…. He couldn't believe how she had lied and tricked him and cheated him out of Ethan's first months of life.

"I'm going to see Judge Foster," he admitted. "She's part of this whole mess." He wasn't going to share that she was also a part of Ethan. He wouldn't share that news with his family until he talked to the judge herself.

"Judge Foster fired us over a year and a half ago," Logan recalled. "What would she have to do with anything going on with you and Sharon?"

"I work for her," Sharon said. But like him, she didn't divulge any more information. Maybe she was following his lead; maybe she didn't want his family to know that Ethan wasn't her son.

Logan dragged his hand through his hair in frustration and warned him, "You can't just go traipsing off alone when you've got a bounty on your head."

"I'll be fine," Parker assured him. "Nobody's touched me yet." Not for lack of trying, though.

"He won't be alone," Sharon said. "I'm going with him."

Parker shook his head. "Nobody's touched me," he repeated. "But a lot of other people got hurt or worse because they were too close to me."

So there was no way he would let her go along, no way that he would put Sharon Wells in any more danger than she already was.

SHARON SHOULDN'T HAVE left the baby…because she worried that she might never see him again. But at least she knew that he had a family—a real family. They would protect him and take care of him—not out of obligation but love.

Mrs. Payne had clearly fallen for her grandson. He wasn't an inconvenience for her. Or evidence of her son's mistake.

That was all Sharon had been to her grandparents—proof of their perfect daughter's fall from grace. The mistake that had ruined and eventually claimed her life. After Sharon's young mother had died, they'd taken over responsibility for raising her. Not out of love but out of fear that their friends and colleagues would think less of them if they had given her up for adoption like they had once urged their daughter to do. Even if she hadn't overheard their heated debate about whether or not to keep her, she would have figured out how they'd felt about her.

"You should have stayed with Ethan," Parker said as if he'd read her mind. Or maybe he had seen the fear and doubt on her face.

But darkness had fallen. And he had shut off the car so not even the dash lights illuminated the interior. He had also parked down the street from the judge's house but put some distance between the car and the lamps that burned outside the gates.

Then he admonished himself. "I shouldn't have brought you here."

"You had to," she reminded him, "or you wouldn't

have gotten past the security system." He had tried calling the judge, but she hadn't answered any of her phones, not the one at the house or her office or her cell. Brenda either wasn't home or wasn't in any condition to let them in. Panic pressed on Sharon's lungs. What if something had happened to Ethan's mother?

He had family that would take care of him. But Sharon had taken care of him for the judge; the Paynes wouldn't need her help like Brenda had. She would no longer have any connection to the child she had come to love as if he was her own.

Parker groaned. "That damn security system..."

Payne Protection had installed the high-tech system that didn't use codes but fingerprint recognition. Sharon was surprised that Parker's print wasn't able to deactivate it. But then, Brenda hadn't wanted him to have access to her house because she hadn't wanted him to know about his son.

She had wanted a child but no husband. No family. While Sharon respected the woman, she hadn't understood her desire for a baby. All Sharon had ever wanted was a career—one as successful as Judge Foster's. But then she'd met Ethan and had fallen for him.

"I still shouldn't have brought you," Parker said.

"You would have had to cut off my finger, then." She shuddered at the repulsive thought.

Parker chuckled. "I think my brother's new in-laws might be able to find a less gruesome way to bypass it. I doubt there's a security system that a Kozminski can't compromise."

"But they would need time to do that, and I haven't heard from the judge in two weeks," Sharon reminded him.

"And that's out of the ordinary for her?" he asked.

Not wanting to criticize the judge, she hesitated. "She's always very busy. But usually she would just have me take Ethan back to my place if she wanted us out of the way. But this time she wanted us out of town for those two weeks," she reminded him in case he still suffered short-term memory loss, "and she wanted me to use cash for everything—for the hotel and for food."

"She didn't want anyone to be able to track you down," Parker said. "She was hiding you and Ethan. So she must have known you were in danger."

Sharon shook her head. "I wasn't in danger before those two weeks. I wasn't the reason that she sent me and Ethan away."

"But you work for her and she is always in danger," Parker said. "You could have gotten caught in the cross fire."

"I'm kind of invisible. People don't usually notice me." Ignoring the sting to her pride, she admitted, "You obviously didn't notice me since you keep claiming to have never seen me before."

"I claimed to not have slept with you," he clarified, "which is true."

Maybe it was true, but he made it sound impossible. Of course, it probably was. "And that you never saw me before, and that's not true."

"When didn't I notice you?" he asked.

"When you were Brenda's bodyguard," she said. "I was working in her office then." Even then she had done little law clerking and more coffee- and lunch-getting. "I saw you a few times." Those times had admittedly been brief, but his ridiculously handsome image had lingered in her mind.

His eyes glinted in the darkness as he stared at her. "No, I would have remembered…."

"Maybe it's the concussion," she said. But she knew it was her being unremarkable. She had learned long ago to be unobtrusive and quiet, but she'd still felt like such an inconvenience and disappointment to her grandparents.

He touched his head. "Maybe the concussion is why I brought you with me when I should have left you with Logan for protection."

"And you would get into the estate…how?" she wondered.

"The Kozminskis…"

"Won't be able to deactivate the system that quickly," she pointed out. "Do you really want to wait any longer to talk to her?"

Even in the darkness, she noticed the muscle twitch in his cheek. He had to be furious with Brenda for having tricked him into helping her conceive Ethan and then for keeping the little boy from him.

His voice was gruff when he replied. "No."

Then he opened the driver's door. He had done something to the dome light because it didn't come on, leaving her in the darkness.

She fumbled for the handle on her side, but as she did, the door opened. He wrapped his fingers around her arm and helped her from the car.

"I'm taking you with me," he said. "But you need to stay close to me."

Her breath caught at his words. She had no problem sticking close to his side—for warmth and protection. His tall, muscular body blocked some of the cold wind that whipped at her loose hair and penetrated the thin material of her suit. And his gun, clutched tightly in his free hand, offered some security as fear chilled Sharon even more than the wind.

Sharon was tall but she had to quicken her pace to match Parker's long strides down the street. As they stopped at the gate, she drew in a quick breath before reaching for the security panel. But Parker caught her hand, holding her back from touching it.

"What's wrong?" she asked. Her skin tingled and warmed from the contact with his. He didn't let her go, continuing to hold her hand.

Didn't he want to go inside? Hadn't that been the point of coming to Brenda's estate?

Parker glanced around the area, his gaze scanning the street before he peered through the wrought-iron gate at the dark mansion on the other side.

"I wish I had Cujo," he murmured.

"Cujo?" Just how badly had he been concussed that he was longing for a fictional dog?

"My sister-in-law's former K9 German shepherd," he explained. "He's great at sniffing out bombs."

"You think there could be one inside?" she asked, turning her attention to that large brick residence. "But nobody could have gotten past security."

He studied the panel now, as if trying to determine if it had been tampered with. Still holding her hand, he lifted it toward the panel.

She pressed her index finger to the glass. A light flashed as the machine read her print. The lock clicked, then a motor revved and metal rattled as the gate drew open. Parker stepped inside but held Sharon back with a hand on her shoulder.

"You can't leave me out here!" she said, her voice cracking with fear as she imagined being alone in the dark.

It brought back memories of another lonely night long ago. She had been in the dark that night, hidden away. She reached out and clutched his arm.

"Don't leave me!" She had said the same thing that night but she had been too late. "You need me to open the house door, too."

"I won't leave you here," he assured her. "But you have to be careful. We don't know what we're going to find inside."

Her stomach muscles tightened with fear and dread. "You think she's dead?"

"It would have been on the news," he said, "if the judge had been killed or even if she'd gone missing."

She shook her head. "She had taken a leave of absence from work."

"Brenda Foster?" he asked, obviously incredulous.

He wasn't the only one who had been surprised. Brenda had taken only a couple weeks off after having Ethan.

"I think she was writing her memoirs or some kind of book," Sharon said. "She told me that I would have to do some proofreading for her when she was ready. But she hadn't asked me to look at anything yet."

"How long had she been off work?" he asked.

"Her leave started two weeks ago," Sharon said, "so nobody at the courts would have been alarmed that they hadn't heard from her."

"Would anyone else?"

"Are you asking me about her boyfriends or lovers?" Irritation eased some of her fear. He had kissed her, but now he was questioning her about another woman's social life. Of course, he had only kissed Sharon to prove the point that she couldn't be the mother of his child and not because he had actually been attracted or interested in her enough to want to kiss her.

"I'm asking if anyone would have reported her missing if they hadn't heard from her."

Guilt clutched her at the realization that she had been so petty as to be jealous of another woman—a woman she had always respected. But Sharon was one of very few who'd actually been close to the judge. "I don't know…."

She didn't know who would report *her* missing, either. With the hours she worked, she had little time to socialize. Not that she had ever socialized much. She had been more focused on school and studying and work than on making friends.

"Probably me," she said. As Ethan's primary caregiver, she was closer to his mother than anyone else. "But she told me to go to you if I didn't hear from her—and to trust no one else."

"Not even the police?"

She shrugged and then shivered. "No one but you."

Parker turned back toward the mansion. He cursed and reluctantly admitted, "I should have let Logan send backup with me."

"But there's no hit out on Brenda," she reminded him. "There is no reason to think anyone's trying to kill her."

"There isn't," he agreed. "But I know that someone's trying to kill us."

"They don't know that we would come here," she said. "And you made sure we weren't followed."

"So I could leave you out here…."

"You need me to open the door," she reminded him.

So she got that far with him—to the massive double front doors. After she pressed her index finger to the security panel, they opened slowly and creepily as if a ghost played butler for them.

Parker stepped over the threshold first, his gun drawn. He'd turned on a flashlight that was attached to the barrel, which he swung in every direction he turned, as if ready to confront a threat. But the house was eerily quiet. He must have thought so, too, because he asked, "Doesn't she have *any* live-in staff?"

"No." She wanted Sharon on call 24/7 but she hadn't wanted her to live with her. "She prefers her privacy, so she just has a cleaning service."

But that had obviously been canceled because as they crossed the foyer, it was clear that no one had been in to straighten up. Brenda's stilettos had been abandoned on the marble floor and her coat lay a little farther inside the house at the foot of the double stairwell leading to the second story. Parker lifted his foot to the first step, but Sharon grasped his arm.

"She won't be up there."

"But it's late and all the lights are off."

Brenda wouldn't have been in bed yet, though, unless she had company, and in that case, there would have been lights on. "She would be working," she said, and she started across the expansive living room toward the double doors that led to the den.

But Parker caught her arm, jerking her aside before she could reach for the door handles. He swung the beam of the flashlight around the doors.

"What are you looking for?" she asked.

"Trip wires—anything that could trigger a bomb."

She shuddered.

"It's clear," he said.

But she didn't reach for the handle again, so he had to turn it. He pushed open the doors and swung the beam around the room. It glanced off books and papers. But they weren't on the bookshelf or the desk. They were strewn across the floor.

"Someone's ransacked the room," he said.

She shook her head. "No. Her chambers often look like this." Each of the books was open to a specific page. But as she stepped inside the room with Parker, she noted that these books were ripped apart.

"Someone was looking for something," he said. "Can you tell if anything's missing?"

"Her laptop." It wasn't on the desk or the floor in front of it.

"She must have taken it with her," Parker said. "She must have taken off."

Sharon stepped carefully over the books and papers to move around to the back of the big mahogany desk. If Brenda had taken the laptop, she would have put it in the case that she usually dropped behind her chair.

But she didn't find the bag behind the desk. She found something else instead—something she wished she had never seen. As she gave in to the fear and hysteria overwhelming her, screams burned her throat.

Chapter Six

Parker had known he shouldn't have brought Sharon along with him. But since there wasn't a hit out on Brenda, he hadn't thought they would be in danger in her mansion—as long as he made certain that they weren't followed. Now he knew why there was no hit on the judge.

She was already dead. On the floor behind her desk, her body sprawled across the toppled-over leather chair. Her neck was bent at an odd angle—not because of how she was lying but because her neck had been broken. Blood, trailing from her mouth, had dried into a thick, black pool beneath her head. Her face was ghostly white. She must have been dead for a while. It could have been days, or weeks….

Sharon trembled and shivered in his arms. She was in shock.

But at least she had finally stopped screaming. Her voice had grown hoarse and cracked before she had finally calmed down, before she had finally stopped punching her fists into his chest and collapsed against him.

He shouldn't have brought her here. He should have known it was a possibility that they might find the judge dead. But he was more surprised by what they hadn't found. Her bodyguard. While Brenda might not have let any other staff stay overnight, she would have kept the bodyguard—especially since she must have been aware that she was in danger.

Why else had she sent the baby away with Sharon? She must have loved her son—*their* son. Maybe Brenda Foster hadn't been as manipulative and selfish a woman as he had once thought she was. She had tricked and lied to him, but as long as she'd loved their son…

"I'm sorry," Sharon murmured, as she clutched at his shirt, which was damp from her tears. "So sorry…"

Why was she apologizing?

"I'm the one who should be sorry," he said. "And I am. I shouldn't have brought you here. You shouldn't have had to see your boss like this…."

She drew in a shuddery breath, fighting back more sobs. "But she was the mother of your son." Her voice cracked and the tears began to fall again. "Ethan…"

His son no longer had a mother. And the boy's father had been aware of him for only hours….

Now Parker was solely responsible for him? He had no idea how to take care of a baby, how to be a father. A twinge of panic struck his heart, but he ignored it. He would figure it out—with his family's help. So he pushed aside that worry and focused on the woman trembling in his arms. He had to be strong for her.

But instead of clinging to him, she began to tense and ease away from him.

"Are you all right?" he asked Sharon. "I need to make some calls."

She nodded and pulled completely away from him. Replacing his arms with hers, she wrapped them around herself—as if trying to hold herself together. "Of course. You have to call the police."

She must have noticed his hesitation because she gasped and asked, “You are calling the police, right?”

He wasn’t sure that he should and reminded Sharon, “Brenda told you to trust nobody but me.”

Those already enormous eyes widened as if she was scared that she had trusted the wrong man. “B-but you can’t just leave her here like this....”

Brenda Foster was beyond help. It was Sharon and Ethan about whom he was concerned. But the crime scene needed to be processed for evidence. So he reached for his phone. But his first call wasn’t to the police.

He had called a woman—a beautiful, young woman with auburn hair and brown eyes. She showed up before the police arrived. But he didn’t let her look at the body; he didn’t even let her past the security-system control panel at the door to the den.

And goose bumps rose on Sharon’s skin beneath the thin material of her jacket. What if Brenda had been wrong about him? What if she shouldn’t have trusted Parker Payne?

“Are you all right?” the woman asked Sharon, her brown eyes warm with concern.

Sharon must have looked as pale and sick as she felt. Seeing Brenda like that... It had brought back so many horrific memories that she had lost it. And she was barely hanging on to her composure now. She could only nod.

The woman turned toward Parker. “Did you call an ambulance?”

Parker glanced up from where he was studying the body—that horribly broken and lifeless body—behind the desk. “She’s been beyond medical help for a while now.”

“I’m not talking about the judge....” She gestured toward Sharon.

"I'm—I'm okay," she insisted. "I don't need an ambulance."

"She's in shock." The woman spoke again to Parker, as if Sharon wasn't even in the room.

Who were they to each other? Obviously the brunette worked in the security business, too, since she hooked a laptop to the security panel at the door, so familiar with the high-tech system that she must have handled it all the time.

Parker moved from behind the desk to join the woman at the door. But she didn't look at him; she was focused on the laptop instead. How could she ignore Parker Payne? How could any woman? He turned toward Sharon and studied her face. "Are you really all right?"

She nodded again. Physically, she was fine. Emotionally, she was a mess. But it wasn't just over finding another dead body. It was over the suspicion that had begun to niggle at her.

Why had Parker called this woman to mess with the security system? To cover his tracks?

And Sharon had left Ethan with his family. If Parker couldn't be trusted, could she trust any of the Paynes?

"I—I should get back to Ethan," she said. "He'll be afraid if he wakes up and I'm not there."

"Ethan?" The young woman's breath caught, and she stared at Sharon. "Is that…your baby's name?"

Parker hadn't told anyone that Sharon wasn't the boy's mother; he had told them only that he had to talk to the judge, for whom Sharon worked. He hadn't told them the reason *specifically,* only that Judge Foster might have some involvement or information about why someone wanted him and Sharon dead.

Judge Foster couldn't help them now. Not when she had already become a victim....

But whose victim?

"Ethan is my son," Parker told the woman. "You could have met him at the hospital if you'd been there...."

If they meant anything to each other, why hadn't she been at the hospital when he had been wounded in that explosion? He was obviously hurt that she hadn't come to see him, so this woman was important to him.

If Sharon had been involved with him, she would have rushed to his side. Heck, she wasn't involved with him, but she had rushed to the hospital as soon as she had seen the news of the explosion at Payne Protection. Of course, she had been trying to find him anyway because the two weeks had already ended with no word from Brenda.

Now she knew why....

"I was there," the woman replied.

Parker's brow furrowed. "You were? Then why didn't you come see me?"

She shrugged, but her thin shoulders were tense. "What do you want to know from the security system?"

He sighed before replying, "I want to know who was here last."

"Sharon Wells," she replied.

Sharon shuddered. She wished she hadn't come along with Parker; she would have rather cut off and given him her finger than see what she had behind the desk.

"Before tonight," Parker specified. "Who was the last one here?"

"Sharon Wells," she repeated. "Two weeks ago."

Parker turned toward her, and now he looked suspicious of her with the intensity of his blue-eyed stare. "You were the last one here?"

"Two weeks ago was when I packed up some of Ethan's stuff and took the cash Brenda gave me to use the past two weeks," she said. "But I couldn't have been the last one to see her…"

"Alive?"

Knowing what that meant, she shook her head. If she had been the last one to see the judge alive, she would have been the one who killed her. If that was what Parker thought, the police would think that, too.

Sirens blared as police cars, lights flashing, sped through the open gate and up to the house. If Sharon was arrested, she had no hope of ever seeing Ethan again.

Panicking, she clutched Parker's arm. "Brenda wasn't alone when I was here last," she said. "Her bodyguard was with her."

And there was no way she could have overpowered that gorilla to hurt Brenda. There was no way she could have hurt Brenda or anyone else. Parker had to believe her. But why would he when she had begun to doubt him?

Even now, she had only this woman's word that she was the last one who had come in or out of the house. She could have erased other names; she could have erased Parker's. Maybe he hadn't really needed her to let him inside the house; maybe he had brought her along only to help him cover his tracks. Maybe he'd been only using her this whole time as a scapegoat.

"Her bodyguard was with the two of you when the judge told you to hide for two weeks and then contact me if you hadn't heard from her?" he asked.

She nodded.

"Who is her bodyguard?"

The woman snorted. "Obviously not someone very good…"

"I—I only know his first name," Sharon said. "Chuck…" Would that be enough information for them to be able to track him down and prove that when Sharon left two weeks ago the judge had still been alive?

She turned toward the door as police officers burst through it—guns drawn. Why were they acting as if the killer was still at the scene? Was he?

Parker and the woman lifted their hands. "We're with Payne Protection," he said, identifying the two of them. "I'm the one who placed the 911 call."

A bald-headed officer nodded at him. "Hey, Park. Are you still protecting the judge?"

Parker shook his head. "If I had been, you wouldn't have been called here." He pointed behind the desk. "We found the judge dead."

"We?" the officer asked.

"Me and Sharon Wells." Finally he pointed to her; maybe he was pointing the finger *at* her. Was he going to try to place the blame on her?

"I'm Sharon Wells," she identified herself. "And I work—*worked*," she corrected herself, "for Judge Foster."

They began to look at her as Parker had, as if she was a suspect. But she couldn't have hurt her; she couldn't hurt anyone.

But Parker didn't know that about her; he didn't know her. He hadn't even remembered ever meeting her.

And the police didn't know her at all. Since, according to the security system, she was the last one to have seen Brenda alive, then she would be the most likely suspect in her murder.

Would the police be arresting her before they left the

judge's house? And if they arrested her, she didn't have anyone to bail her out. She might never see Ethan again. When she'd brought him to his father, she had known that never seeing him again might be a possibility, but she hadn't realized that she might not see him because she was behind bars for his mother's murder.

Chapter Seven

Parker could not help Sharon now. The police were questioning her the same way that he had—wondering why she was the last person to have seen her employer alive. Only she hadn't been the last person.

And he would prove that for her. But first he had to settle something else. So he hurried across the driveway to chase down the person who had tried sneaking away from the crime scene.

"Why didn't you come see me at the hospital?" Parker asked his sister. Nikki turned away from him again. But he grabbed her shoulder and turned her back.

She squirmed beneath his grasp and ducked away. But before she turned away from him again, he caught the shimmer of tears in her eyes.

"Niks, what's wrong?"

She shrugged. "Nothing…"

"Niks?"

He grabbed her again and didn't let her get away this time as he folded her into a hug. His little sister never cried; she was too tough for that—or at least too determined to prove to her brothers that she was every bit as tough as they were.

"I'm sorry," she said, "so sorry…"

That she hadn't visited him in the hospital?

"It's okay," he assured her. "I didn't mean to make you feel bad." And this was another reason that he had never had a long-term relationship; he wasn't sensitive enough to a woman's feelings.

"I feel bad because it was my fault," she murmured, her voice cracking with emotion.

Thoroughly confused, Parker had to ask, "What was your fault?"

"It was my fault that you nearly got blown up!" she exclaimed.

"You didn't put the bomb in my SUV," he said, unable to follow her logic or understand her guilt. He loved his sister, but he had never understood her as easily as he had his brothers.

"I sent you back out there to change my lunch order," she said, her voice cracking with the tears she fought so hard with furious blinking and sniffling. "If I hadn't, you wouldn't have been hurt...."

"I'm not hurt," he assured her. He ignored the pounding in his head; it had gone down to a dull thud anyway.

"You have a concussion," she said. "You can't even remember the mother of your child...."

She hadn't visited him in the hospital but she had obviously been apprised of everything that had happened there. His family had no secrets from each other.

"Oh, I remember her...." He glanced to where morgue technicians loaded Brenda Foster's body into the back of the coroner's van.

Poor Ethan. He was so young that he wouldn't even remember his mother.

"That's good," Nikki said with a deep breath of relief. "I'm glad your memory is back."

It had never really been gone. He couldn't blame the concussion for not remembering meeting Sharon at the judge's office. With the security at the courthouse, he hadn't had to assess any of them as threats, so he hadn't paid much attention to the people who had already gone through metal detectors and body screeners.

"I'm glad you're here," Parker said even though the information Nikki had recovered from the security system might hurt Sharon more than help her.

He glanced to where she sat in the back of a police car. According to Officer Green, Detective Sharpe had ordered them to bring her down to the police department so that he could personally interrogate her. Sharpe had just recently been promoted—though he hadn't earned it. So he was probably just trying to scare her; he needn't have bothered.

The poor woman had been absolutely terrified when she had found Brenda's body. There was no way she could have killed her. Physically, she wasn't strong enough. Emotionally, she was too sensitive and too empathetic to hurt anyone.

"Did you tell her that I'm your sister?" Nikki asked.

Parker couldn't remember if he had introduced them; he'd been preoccupied with finding the judge's body and with trying to find out who had killed her and how.

If her bodyguard had been there when the judge had sent Sharon and Ethan into hiding, why hadn't he protected Brenda? Why hadn't he even tried?

Parker wouldn't have failed a client like that. He would have died trying to keep her safe. But maybe he *had* failed a client. If he hadn't let Brenda fire him just so they could sleep together, she would still be alive. He wouldn't have let anyone hurt her.

And he wouldn't let anyone hurt Sharon, either.

"When they take her to the police department to give her statement," he told Nikki, "you need to go with her and make sure she stays safe." He didn't want his sister in danger, either, though, so he would call his brother Cooper for backup. After seeing how brutally Brenda had been murdered, Parker was going to heed the judge's warning to trust no one but him. And his family, of course.

"Where are you going?" Nikki asked.

"You tell me," he said. "Find out who this Chuck is who was supposed to be protecting the judge." Logan probably would have known. As the CEO of Payne Protection Agency, he was aware of the other security firms in the area. But those firms were no competition for Payne Protection—obviously.

"There was no Chuck with fingerprint access to the judge's home," Nikki said with a glance at the police car. "Could she have been lying?"

He shook his head. "No." He didn't think Sharon was capable of lying. He never should have doubted her—even for a minute. "Brenda must not have trusted the guy enough to give him access."

"Then why would she have had him protecting her?"

Because she had fired Parker…

Maybe it was his fault that she had been killed….

As Parker had suspected, Logan knew who the Chuck was that worked bodyguard detail. Charles "Chuck" Horowitz.

Parker stood outside the man's apartment; he was supposed to wait for Logan—since his twin had warned that Chuck was more of a mercenary than a bodyguard. His loyalty went to the person who paid him the most. But Parker did not need backup. He preferred that Logan protect his son and their mother. Parker could take care of himself.

Someone had been trying to kill him for two weeks and had not succeeded yet. And that was before Parker had realized the hit was on him. Now that he knew, he was ready.

An outside stairwell led to Chuck Horowitz's second-story combination apartment-office. Brenda had really dropped her standards when she had fired Payne Protection and hired this yahoo.

Glad that he had changed into dark clothes, Parker kept to the shadows as he climbed the stairs. He didn't need to make himself a target for all the people who would take up that hit for the money.

God, he hoped Sharon was safe. His brother Cooper had assured him that nothing would happen to her or Nikki. But while Cooper could protect her on the outside, if she was arrested…

There was nothing Cooper or Parker could do for her but help try to prove her innocence….

The defense lawyer should be able to prove that although Sharon was taller than Brenda, she wasn't strong enough to have so violently broken the woman's neck. Even the coroner should be able to conclude that it would take a very strong man to do something like that.

A twinge of regret and loss struck Parker's heart. One day Ethan might learn, either through the internet or gossip, how brutally his mother had died. Parker knew from experience that people never forgot tragic deaths like his father's. When the day came that Ethan heard about the murder, Parker wanted to be able to tell his son that he had caught and brought his mother's killer to justice.

He reached the narrow landing at the top of the stairs.

But before he could knock on the door, his cell phone vibrated in his pocket. He ignored it and reached for his gun instead. But it continued to vibrate, so he pulled out the cell. And after lowering his voice to a whisper, he answered it. "Damn it, Logan—"

His voice a shout, Logan burst out, "Don't go in there alone!"

"Do you have eyes on me?" He glanced around in the darkness. He wouldn't have put it past his twin to have assigned one of their bodyguards to tail him. It would actually explain why Logan hadn't fought him that hard when Parker had insisted on leaving the safe house.

"I just know you," Logan replied, which really didn't answer Parker's question. "I know that when you're mad you get hotheaded—too hotheaded to wait for backup."

Parker *was* mad. He was mad that someone was trying to kill him. He was mad that someone was trying to kill Sharon. And he was mad that innocent people had died in their places.

"I don't need backup, big brother." Logan would never let him forget that he had entered the world a whole ten minutes before him. "I got this."

"Before he got kicked out of the league some years ago, Chuck Horowitz was a mixed-martial-arts champion. He could kill you with his bare hands."

Parker's guts tightened—not with fear but with certainty. Brenda had been killed with someone's bare hands. An MMA champ would have easily been able to kill her. He'd just thought the bodyguard had failed to protect her. But had he actually murdered her?

Parker tightened his grip on his gun. "A bullet will stop him."

"Wait for me," Logan ordered again. "I'm on my way there."

"I told you to stay with Ethan and Mom." He had no way of knowing if Chuck Horowitz was even in his apartment.

"Candace is protecting them," Logan assured him. Because of her military and police background, Candace was not just their best female bodyguard but also one of their most competent bodyguards overall.

But Parker didn't feel all that reassured. He glanced down toward the dark street. Not even street lamps glowed in this area of town. But yet he caught a glint of something in the enveloping darkness. Either a glint of eyes… or perhaps of metal…like a gun. "You don't have Candace tailing me?"

"Not since you left the judge's mansion."

So he had had the female bodyguard protecting him and Sharon. If only he had known that, he could have left her outside so the poor woman wouldn't have had to see her employer's corpse….

Parker cursed his twin.

"Hey, it was for your protection."

"It would have been better protection if I had known…." Like now. "Is there anyone following me now?"

"I don't know," Logan said. "You've been driving to make sure you wouldn't have a tail…."

Apparently that hadn't worked with Candace. But then, she had a lot of experience as a security expert and, before then, police and military experience. Someone else would have had more trouble following him…unless…

"But *you* know where I am," Parker pointed out. So Logan could have sent someone ahead of him—someone who watched him now from the darkness.

"And I'm almost there," Logan said. "So wait for me..."

What if Chuck Horowitz was the judge's killer? Then he probably hadn't just killed the judge; he had been trying to kill Sharon and Parker, too, which meant he had mistaken Logan and Cooper for Parker more than once already. That wasn't a risk Parker was willing to take. He didn't want Logan taking a bullet meant for him.

So he clicked off his cell and slid it back into his pocket. Then he gripped the gun with both hands and kicked open the door to Chuck Horowitz's office/apartment. Better to take the man by surprise than give him a chance to react or arm himself.

Using the flashlight on the barrel, Parker swung it around the tiny apartment. The place was trashed—really trashed. The couch was overturned and gutted, stuffing strewn across the dirty carpet. Holes had been smashed through the drywall. There had been a hell of a struggle within those walls. If this was what Chuck had done to his own place, maybe Parker should have waited for backup.

But then the beam of his flashlight glanced across a pair of glazed-over eyes. Dead eyes. Parker trained the light on the man tied to the chair behind his desk. From the bloating and the stench, which Parker only noticed now as it overwhelmed the stale odor of cigarette smoke, it was obvious this corpse had been here awhile.

Chuck Horowitz had been tied up and beaten. But Parker noticed something else about him—the scratches on his hands and arms and the side of his face. The mercenary bodyguard hadn't gotten those scratches from whoever had beaten him to death.

He had probably gotten those from the woman he had killed. Brenda had fought him even though she would have known that she couldn't have overpowered him. What she had done was get his DNA under her nails; she had been smart and resourceful as she had provided evidence for police to arrest her killer and for prosecutors to win the trial against him.

But they wouldn't be able to prosecute a dead man. Shortly after he had killed the judge, someone had killed Chuck Horowitz. But before they'd done that, they had torn his place apart looking for something—and they had tortured him to find out where that something was.

What had his killer wanted? Chuck had already killed the judge—undoubtedly for money. Hadn't that been enough?

From the destruction of the apartment and the corpse, Parker suspected that Chuck's killer hadn't found whatever he had been looking for. Maybe that killer thought he or Sharon had whatever they wanted. Did they have something in their possession that they weren't aware they had? Or did they know something that somebody didn't want them knowing? Was that why someone had put out a hit on them, too?

He heard the click of a gun cocking, and then another light, on high beam, flashed in his face—blinding him so that he couldn't see whoever had sneaked into the apartment behind him. But he didn't need to see to know that it wasn't his brother—Logan wouldn't have pulled a gun on him.

And if Logan had sent backup for him, whoever it was wouldn't have pulled a gun on Parker, either. But a hired killer would....

Chapter Eight

Sharon couldn't stop shaking, but she was no longer in shock. She was angry. Parker Payne was supposed to be the one person she could trust, but he had let the police take her down to the station. And he had just disappeared.

How could he desert her like that when she had needed him?

Because he didn't need her. She wasn't the mother of his son. She had no information to lead him to the person who had offered money for his murder. And hers…

She had nothing to offer Parker Payne. So he had offered her nothing. He hadn't even acknowledged her when the police car had driven off with her in the backseat. Of course, he had been preoccupied with the auburn-haired woman.

"I have answered all of your questions," she told the detective who sat across the table from her in the small, windowless interrogation room. "You have no reason to hold me here."

When the officer had questioned her at the hospital, he had used an office with a window. It hadn't been so confining and suffocating.

"You were the last one to see the Honorable Brenda Foster alive," the detective said—again. He had kept repeating it as if that statement alone would force her to confess to something she hadn't done.

And Brenda Foster honorable? Sharon wasn't so sure about that. After working for her awhile and listening to her brag about how she had tricked Parker into fathering her child, Sharon had learned that her idol had had clay feet. Now Brenda had a broken neck. Sharon grimaced as an image of the woman's dead and grotesquely contorted body flashed through her mind.

Her head pounded, too, with stress and exhaustion. Maybe that was part of why she kept shaking. "Her bodyguard was the last person to see her alive," Sharon repeated for the umpteenth time.

"A man whose last name you don't even know," the detective said with the snide little smirk he had been flashing her for the past couple of hours. He was older than her but not by much, so he had apparently made detective young enough that it had gone to his head. "That's quite convenient."

Nothing about this had been convenient for Sharon. Maybe it was the fatigue or the headache, but her tenuous control over the anger she had been feeling snapped. "It's quite convenient that you're forgetting I have rights, Detective Sharpe. Rights that you haven't read me because you have no evidence to put me under arrest."

His smirk widened. "Now I can tell that you've been working for a judge for a while. So then you should know that I can hold you as a material witness—"

"I didn't witness anything." This time. "And I haven't just worked for a judge."

His voice rising with excitement, he leaned across the small, scratched-up metal table. "Oh, you and Judge Foster were more than employee and employer?" He obviously thought he had found a salacious motive for the judge's murder. A lover's quarrel…

Sharon couldn't believe that such an idiot had made detective. He had to know that there was no physical way that she could have broken her boss's neck. So with her temper rising even higher, she pulled out a card she had never played before. "I haven't just worked for a judge," she repeated. "I am the granddaughter of a judge."

He leaned back and lifted a brow. "Really?"

"I am Judge Wells's granddaughter." It wasn't something he had ever freely or happily admitted, but it was an irrefutable fact. Like Judge Foster, police officers had respected Judge Wells for his tough sentences.

The guy leaned forward again and he got *that* look on his face—that look of horror and concern—that told her he knew her story. Even as young as he was, he had heard it. "I'm sorry…."

Not that she was Judge Wells's granddaughter. He was sorry for the rest of it.

"That must have been tough tonight, seeing the judge's corpse…." He shuddered for her.

It had been more than twenty years, but she still occasionally had the nightmares. She had no doubt that she would have one tonight…if she ever slept. She nodded.

"But that doesn't mean that you couldn't have killed her."

She lifted her hands. "I couldn't have. Physically, I couldn't have, and you know that."

He shrugged. "Maybe you used a weapon. Did you really have nothing with you when the officers brought you in?"

She shook her head. "I have no idea what kind of

weapon could have done that to Brenda." Now she shuddered for herself and for her dead employer.

"If that were true, why did you hide your things from the officers at the scene?" he asked.

"What things?" she asked. "I didn't bring anything with me." Thanks to the car explosion, she had nothing left.

The detective sighed, as if frustrated with her. "Miss Wells—"

"You're wasting your time with me when you should be finding Judge Foster's bodyguard," she said. "He was the last one to see her alive—because he was with her when I left her house."

And Chuck had been such a burly man that he wouldn't have needed a weapon to kill Brenda or even a man twice her size. Had Parker gone after him? Was that why he hadn't come to the police department with her?

If he had tracked down Chuck on his own, he could wind up as brutally murdered as Brenda had been. Despite the heat of the stale air in the small room, her blood chilled, and she shivered in reaction.

"You need to find that man right now," she said. Before Parker found him—unless it was already too late.

The detective touched his ear, where he must have been wearing a radio piece. "It's too late," he said, as if he had read her mind.

"What's too late?" she asked, fearfully. Had Parker already found him?

"He's dead."

She gasped as her heart kicked against her ribs. "Who's dead?"

"The bodyguard—Chuck," he said.

Her breath shuddered out in relief. That relief was

short-lived, though, when she realized that just because the bodyguard was dead didn't mean that Parker was alive.

The detective hadn't missed her initial reaction. "That makes you happy? I guess it would since a dead man can't refute your statement."

"Are you going to accuse me of killing him, too?" she wondered aloud. "I don't even know his last name."

"Parker Payne knows it," he said. "He was at the man's apartment when we found his corpse."

That was where Parker had gone. He had tracked down the bodyguard. But what had happened when he'd found him?

She remembered and repeated the detective's choice of word. "Corpse?"

"The coroner thinks Chuck Horowitz died around the same time the judge must have."

So someone had killed them both? She shuddered.

The man leaned forward again, and his eyes narrowed speculatively. "What do you know about Parker Payne, Ms. Wells?"

"That the judge trusted him," she said.

"Do you?" the detective asked.

She had thought she could. But now she wasn't so certain. "If the bodyguard was killed weeks ago, then Parker didn't have anything to do with it."

"Do you know what he was doing weeks ago?"

No. She had been in hiding. If the news was to be believed, though, he had been getting shot at and nearly blown up. "But I think you know."

The detective shrugged. "Payne Protection has definitely been filing a lot of police reports recently."

"Then you know that Parker is in danger." Just like

she was, but if he didn't know about the hit on her, she wasn't going to draw Detective Sharpe's attention to it. Brenda had warned her to trust no one but Parker. Now she was going to trust no one—not even Parker.

"Or maybe he *is* the danger. I thought you just needed to watch out for him because he's a playboy, but maybe you need to watch out for him because he's a killer," the detective warned her.

She shook her head. "He's not shooting at himself or trying to blow himself up."

"But he could have killed the judge," the detective persisted. "He could have also killed the bodyguard."

"And gone back tonight?" she asked. "Why?"

Detective Sharpe shrugged again. "Your grandfather never told you about the criminals who returned to the scenes of their crimes?"

"Parker Payne is no criminal." Her instinctive defense of him laid to rest those doubts she'd kept having about him. While her mind found reasons why she shouldn't trust him, her gut trusted him instinctively. Her heart trusted him.

The detective cocked his head as if considering the veracity of her statement; he obviously didn't know and respect Parker like the older officer who had spoken with her at the hospital or the bald-headed officer at the judge's house.

"I would have agreed with you," Sharpe admitted, "but he has recently started associating with some known criminals."

She shrugged now. She had no idea with whom Parker associated. "I wouldn't know—"

"The Kozminskis," he said, as if she had asked. "They were at the hospital earlier when the bomb went off in the parking lot. They were with their new brother-in-law—Logan Payne."

They must have been the blond men with the light-colored eyes who had found out that someone had put out a hit on her as well as Parker.

"The Kozminskis have long criminal records," Detective Sharpe continued, "starting with stints in juvie for theft and murder…."

"I don't know the Kozminskis." But if they were any part of the reason for her interrogation, she didn't like them very much. "I have nothing to do with any of this. Not only am I physically incapable of doing—" an involuntary shudder struck her with the memory of Brenda's corpse "—what was done to the judge, but I have no motive to hurt her. Now that she's dead I have no job."

No mentor to help her pass the bar. Not that Brenda had been much help on Sharon's previous attempts. She had even suggested that Sharon give up on law and continue as Ethan's nanny. Now she wouldn't even be able to do that—and that was the far greater loss to Sharon.

The detective snorted. "You have the biggest motive, Ms. Wells."

"Unemployment?" she scoffed.

"Inheritance."

The detective had obviously lost it. "What inheritance?" The judge hadn't even paid her that well.

"When the judge's murder was reported on television, her lawyer contacted us about her child. He thought the child would be with you…."

"He—he's with…friends." Given the detective's opinion of the Paynes and the Kozminskis, she didn't dare be more specific, or else he might send a police car to pick up Ethan, too.

"The judge's will made you the guardian of her son and the trustee of the estate he'll inherit from her—a sizable estate from which you'll draw a sizable salary for his care." His smirk was back. "That gives you a very big motive for her murder."

"I am Judge Wells's granddaughter," she reminded the dim-witted detective. "I don't need money." And maybe that was why Brenda hadn't paid her very much. The judge had known what Sharon had inherited when her grandparents had passed away a few years ago—a lot of money. But they had never given Sharon what she had really wanted from them: their love.

"I would never kill anyone...."

"Not even for that little boy?" he asked. "The judge must have really trusted you with him to appoint you as his guardian in her will."

Sharon had lied to the detective...because Ethan was the one person for whom she would kill. She would do anything to protect that little boy.

She shrugged. "I never really knew what Judge Foster was thinking or what she was involved in. You will need to investigate *her* life to find out who killed her. Not mine." Because Sharon had never really had much of a life. She had studied and she had worked. "So unless you're going to press charges, I'm leaving, Detective."

She stood up and walked to the door. She tried to turn the knob, but it was locked in place. He had locked her inside the interrogation room, the small, windowless room. All those memories that had already rushed over her once that evening rushed back again, overwhelming her.

Her legs weakened, and her shaking body dropped to the floor. She briefly registered the hardness of the concrete beneath her before she passed out.

PARKER'S HEART BEAT a frantic pace as he watched the paramedics wheel Sharon's unconscious body into the hospital, where he had been pacing the emergency room while he waited for her arrival. "You were supposed to protect her!" he yelled at his sister as soon as she ran in behind the paramedics.

As Cooper followed Nikki inside, he shook his head. "Back off. She couldn't go into the interrogation room with her."

"She was hurt in the interrogation room?" he asked. "Who the hell was interrogating her?"

"Sharpe," Nikki reminded him.

Parker's temper flared with frustration with himself and with the detective. That little weasel wouldn't have made detective if his mother wasn't the chief's little sister. "I'll kill him."

The jerk already thought Parker was a killer. He had actually had a police officer following him from the judge's house to the bodyguard's apartment. Parker had nearly shot the damn kid who'd been too scared at Chuck Horowitz's crime scene to identify himself as a police officer. If not for Logan showing up behind the kid…

"Don't go making any threats," Logan advised as he showed up behind Parker now.

"But what the hell did he do to her?"

Nikki and Cooper both shrugged. His younger brother replied, "He had her in the interrogation room for a long time."

"And she was already in shock from the crime scene," Nikki added, her dark eyes flashing with frustration. "She should have gone from the judge's house to the hospital, not to the police station."

Detective Sharpe stepped through the doors behind

Nikki and Cooper. But before Parker could reach for his scrawny little neck, Logan pulled him back. "No threats. Calm down," his older brother advised. "Or he will have the authority to arrest you this time."

"Let him," Parker growled. Then he whirled on Sharpe. "What the hell did you do to her?"

The man's eyes widened. "What did *I* do? It's what *you* did—bringing *Sharon Wells* to a murder scene!"

"I didn't know it was a murder scene," he said. "Any more than I knew that there was a murder scene at Chuck Horowitz's house."

The man nodded with a patronizing smile pasted on his pallid face. "That's what all the criminals say…."

"Okay, maybe you should hit him," Logan remarked. "You're way out of line here, Sharpe."

Parker didn't care what the jerk said about him. He cared about Sharon. "What did you mean about Sharon? What do you know about her?"

"You don't know who she is?" Sharpe asked smugly.

Parker really wanted to hit him. "Just tell me what you know…" He bit off the insult he wanted to add; it wouldn't get him anywhere when the man thought so highly of himself. "…about Sharon."

"She's Judge Wells's granddaughter…."

Judge Wells? The name sounded vaguely familiar. Maybe Parker had testified before him in a drug-arrest case back in the days when he'd worked undercover vice for River City P.D. He shrugged. "I don't remember much about him."

"Guess you only pay attention to the female judges."

He really, really wanted to hit him now, but he restrained himself. "How old is this Judge Wells?" After all, he was her *grandfather.*

"He's dead."

"Then how would I know the guy?"

"Ooooh." The word slipped out of Nikki with a sudden nod of understanding.

"Your sister knows," Sharpe said, "and she's younger than you are."

He turned toward Nikki; he would rather hear it from her than the defective detective anyway. "What do you know, Niks?"

Nikki shuddered. "It was a tragic story…."

"Oh," Logan said. "I remember…."

"Where was I?" Parker wondered.

"We were kids when it happened," Logan said. "It's just that people seemed to bring it up every time they talked about the judge…."

Like people had brought up their father's murder every time they talked about any other Payne. Yeah, they never forgot tragic deaths.

"Who died?" Parker asked.

"Sharon's mother," Nikki said. "She was really young. She was just a teenager when she had Sharon. The story goes that the judge and his wife didn't approve, so she ran away from home. She was working nights at a gas station—" her forehead creased as she searched her memory "—or a convenience store when she was murdered."

"That's awful," Parker said. Like Ethan, Sharon had also lost her mother when she was young. She would be able to identify with the little boy even more than she already seemed to.

Nikki shuddered again. "What was worse is that the girl couldn't afford a babysitter, so she brought Sharon to work with her. She was there when her mother was murdered."

"How old was she?" Old enough to remember?

"I think three or four," Nikki said. "When customers came in, her mother would have her crawl into a cupboard behind the counter. The killer didn't know she was there or she probably would have been killed, too."

Horror gripped Parker. "Do you think she saw what happened?"

"She picked the killer out of a line-up." Logan chimed in with the detail that he, as a former detective, would of course remember best.

"At three or four years old?" he asked in disbelief. He knew that young witnesses weren't always the most reliable. But then, the face of her mother's killer was probably one Sharon would never forget—even more than twenty years later. "Did she testify?"

"It didn't go to trial," Logan said. "The killer didn't know there was a witness, so he confessed."

At least she had been spared a trial. But the horror she must have witnessed…and finding Brenda murdered so violently had probably brought back all the old nightmares. He had to talk to her doctor. But would her doctor talk to him?

Parker was nobody to her. He wasn't family. He wasn't even her friend or he wouldn't have left her alone to deal with the police. But he hadn't known….

He'd had no idea how upset she must have been. He couldn't keep his anger to himself, though, so he reached out for Sharpe. But Logan dragged him back. "You know all this about her and you still interrogated her in some little room? You sadistic blowhard! You have to know that she couldn't have hurt her employer."

"Maybe she wasn't strong enough to have broken the judge's neck," the detective admitted. "But we know that she was the last one to go past the security system. We don't know if she was alone."

"She wasn't," Parker said. "The bodyguard was with Brenda."

"I meant Ms. Wells," he said. "She may have brought someone with her—someone who killed the judge for her."

He was an even bigger idiot than Parker had thought. "Really? So she willingly put herself through witnessing another murder? That's ridiculous."

"It really is," Logan added. "Have you ever even cleared a case, Sharpe?"

Finally color flushed the man's pasty face, giving Logan his answer.

"She has no motive, either," Parker pointed out.

"The judge made her trustee of the estate with a generous income."

Nikki laughed. "She's Judge Wells's granddaughter. I hardly think she needs money."

The color deepened in Sharpe's face. "But she doesn't just get money out of the deal. She gets the kid, too."

"What?" Parker asked.

"Brenda Foster's will awards Sharon Wells custody of the kid."

"But the kid has a father," Parker pointed out. He was Ethan's father. But he wasn't about to announce that in front of Sharpe and provide the man with his own motive for killing Brenda.

Sharpe shook his head. "Birth certificate states father unknown. She probably used a sperm donor."

Now Parker's face was the one that flushed with embarrassment. He had been a sperm donor—but an unwitting one. He had even insisted on using a condom, but Brenda must have compromised it somehow.

"But if someone can prove he's the boy's father," Parker persisted, "as the sole parent, he would become the boy's guardian."

Sharpe shrugged. "It would probably go to court. He'd have to fight for custody. I doubt he would have killed the judge because it probably just complicates his life."

So Parker was off the hook for murder. And fatherhood?

But he wanted his son. He wanted to fight, but he didn't want to fight a woman who had already been through too much in her life. Could Sharon even handle a fight?

Hell, she couldn't handle any more attempts on her life. Parker would deal with the custody issue after he'd dealt with whoever wanted him and Sharon dead.

Chapter Nine

If someone can prove he's the boy's father...

The words she had heard as she'd walked out to join the others in the waiting room still rang in Sharon's ears now, as she stared down at the sleeping baby.

Why had they been waiting for her? She was scarcely more than a stranger to them. But when they had turned toward her, she'd seen it on all of their faces—that overly solicitous concern that told her they knew. They knew what had happened to her mother. And they thought that witnessing it had made Sharon fragile.

Weak.

And passing out in the interrogation room had only proved their opinion of her. Would Parker use that against her in court when he fought her for custody of his child?

"Didn't he even wake up?" Sharon asked the boy's grandmother. She had been gone so long, away from the baby for far longer than she had wanted to be away.

"He woke up," Mrs. Payne said with a sigh. "And he cried most of the time you were gone. He only fell back to sleep a short while ago."

So he had cried for hours without her?

When Parker exercised his parental rights, she would be away from Ethan for far longer than a few hours. She would be cut out of the rest of his life. And he wouldn't remember her any more than he was likely to remember his dead mother.

Tears stung her eyes, but she blinked them back. Too many of the Paynes already thought she was weak.

But Mrs. Payne must have caught her action because she rubbed her back, as she probably had the crying baby's to soothe him to sleep. "While he's sleeping, you should get some rest. You must be exhausted."

She had been exhausted a couple of sleepless nights ago. She was beyond exhausted now. But she worried that if she slept, she wouldn't see Ethan again. "I—I just want to watch him sleep…."

To assure herself that he was all right, that he wasn't gone like his mother, like the bodyguard, like all those people who had died for no reason that she could fathom…

She and Parker had come no closer to learning why someone wanted them dead; they had only found more dead. The tears threatened again. She blinked harder but one slipped through her lashes and rolled down her cheek to drop onto the sleeping baby. Her breath caught, but he only sighed.

Next to her, Mrs. Payne had tensed, but she relaxed with the child. "It's like he knows you're here. He recognizes his mother's presence."

But Sharon wasn't his mother. And she was probably only his guardian for now…until a judge decided the biological father's rights overruled hers.

She shook her head. "No, I—I'm not…"

Why hadn't Parker told his family right away? He'd been upset with her for letting him believe she was the baby's mother. Why had he let his family believe it even after he'd learned the truth?

"Judge Foster was Ethan's mother," Sharon said. "And I worked for her—first as her law clerk and then as her nanny." Brenda had kept telling her that she didn't have the aptitude to be a lawyer, and Sharon's failed attempts at passing the bar supported that supposition.

All those years she had spent in school and studying…

And she'd found what she loved by default. She had found Ethan because Brenda hadn't been able to keep any other nanny working for her.

"You love him like he's yours," Mrs. Payne observed. "And he loves and relies on you like you're his mother."

She nodded. "I do love him—very much." And if she hadn't been afraid that she wouldn't be able to keep him safe on her own, she might not have brought him to Parker. But she wasn't equipped to protect him from fires and bombs.… Eventually he would have been hurt just from being around her. Maybe the best thing for the boy would be for her to turn down the guardianship and let the Paynes have him.

"Are you going to fight me?" Parker asked.

She was so tired that she hadn't even heard him climb the stairs to the top-floor master bedroom, where he'd set up that portable crib what seemed like so long ago.

"Fight you?" Mrs. Payne asked. Her brow furrowed as she turned toward her son, clearly puzzled.

It wasn't her place to tell the woman what her son had not, but Sharon found herself explaining, "Judge Foster gave me guardianship of Ethan in her will."

She was sorry that the woman was dead, but she still resented how she had treated her son—more like a possession than a person. But then, Brenda Foster had been too busy to get to know the little boy, to appreciate how smart and affectionate he was.

Mrs. Payne continued to stare at her son. "Then why would *she* fight *you?*"

He furrowed his brow now, obviously as confused as she had been with him. "Because there is no way that I am going to give up my son."

Pain struck Sharon's heart. "So because I'm not his blood relative, you would cut me out of his life?" Then anger surged within her and the heat of it dried up her tears. "I've been with him pretty much every day since he was born, and you expect me to just give him up? To just walk away?"

That was what her grandparents had expected her mother to do—to give up her baby to strangers. To just give her up and walk away and forget all about her.

But maybe they'd been right. Maybe if her mother had, she would still be alive—since she would have been in college and not working at a convenience store in a bad area of the city.

"Nobody's asking you to do that," Mrs. Payne said.

Sharon stared at Parker; he wasn't asking. But it was what he expected.

"A judge might," Parker said.

"A judge might not care that he has your DNA," Sharon replied. "You didn't even know about him until I brought him to you."

"You're probably regretting that now," he remarked, his blue eyes glittering with sarcasm and resentment. He had every right to be angry that she had been awarded guardianship over him—but she was not the one he should be angry with.

She had actually regretted not telling him earlier. She'd thought the judge was wrong to keep him from his child. But then she remembered her excuse for doing that. "According to Brenda, you never wanted to be a father."

"That's why she tricked me."

There were other reasons why Brenda had admitted that she had chosen Parker as the father of her baby: because he was smart and handsome and protective and had the kind of charisma that drew everyone to him. But Sharon didn't want to tell him that and add to his argument for custody.

"You have said before—a lot—that you never wanted to be a father," Mrs. Payne agreed.

Parker sucked in a breath. "Mom, whose side are you on?"

She pointed toward the sleeping baby. "I'm on my grandson's side. I don't want him to have to give up either one of you. And if you take each other to court, you might both lose him."

Sharon sucked in the breath now. That hadn't occurred to her.

"If you both prove the other unworthy of parenthood, the judge might put Ethan into the foster-care system," Mrs. Payne pointed out. "Doesn't a judge still have to approve this guardianship?"

There had been so much going on with the attacks and the murders that Sharon hadn't considered that there was more to the process than just Brenda granting her guardianship of Ethan.

What if a judge didn't approve? Given her history as a woman with a traumatic past, she might not be considered emotionally stable enough to be a guardian.

"And just because you're his father doesn't mean you'll automatically get him," Mrs. Payne continued. "You've never had any interest in children or in being a father—"

"That was before I knew that I am a father," Parker replied defensively.

Sharon reached out and grasped Parker's arm; his muscles tensed beneath her touch. She was tense, too. "We can't lose him to the system."

Too many kids got lost in the system. Her grandfather had definitely made certain she was aware of what could have happened to her if he and her grandmother hadn't been gracious enough to take custody of her after her mother's murder.

Parker narrowed his eyes and studied his mother. "So you must have a plan for your grandson since you have a plan for everyone. What do you propose we do?"

"Propose," Mrs. Payne said. "Marry her."

Sharon must have fallen asleep; she had to be dreaming. Because there was no way that anyone would have suggested that she—shy, quiet Sharon Wells—marry a devastatingly handsome playboy like Parker Payne. But it didn't matter whether or not it was a dream because it would never become reality. Parker Payne would never ask her to marry him.

By the time he had gotten rid of everyone else, Sharon had fallen asleep in the middle of the king-sized bed in the master suite. And he found himself standing over her, watching her sleep.

She was exhausted. That was the excuse she had given for passing out during her interrogation, the reason she had given for checking herself out of the emergency room before the doctor had even seen her. The dark circles beneath her eyes proved her weariness.

But the way she murmured and twitched in her sleep betrayed her stress. And her fear. Finding the judge dead must have brought all those horrible memories rushing back to her.

He wanted to gather her into his arms and hold her close—to protect her. Maybe his mother was right. Maybe he should marry her. Not just so they would have a better chance at keeping Ethan but also so Parker could protect her.

He was no closer to finding out who wanted them dead. Certainly it involved the judge, but how had Brenda dragged him and Sharon into whatever mess she'd created?

He had lost touch with Brenda—probably shortly after she'd conceived Ethan. He needed to delve into her life more and find out what she'd been up to, and nobody knew her life better than Sharon did.

That was probably why Sharon was in danger. She had to know something that she wasn't even aware that she knew. And that something had put her life at risk.

Brenda had put her life at risk.

He had to protect Sharon. He leaned down and reached out for her, skimming his fingertips across her cheek. Her skin was so smooth, so silky. She was young—probably even younger than he'd realized when he had first seen her with her hair in a tight knot. Her severe suit had also made her look older. But now with the jacket discarded on the floor and her blouse all rumpled, she looked like a teenager who had dressed up in her mother's clothes for an interview.

But after witnessing what she had at such a young age, had she ever really had a normal life? She must have grown up so fast. By picking her mother's killer out of a line-up, she had been the one to bring him to justice. To get justice for her mother…

He wanted to get justice for Ethan—for *his* mother. But he also wanted to keep safe the woman whom Ethan probably saw as his mother, the woman who had actually been taking care of him. Sharon.

Marrying her wouldn't be enough to keep her safe, though. He had to find out who was after them before they wound up like Brenda and her bodyguard....

Dead.

A cry broke the eerie silence of the penthouse. It hadn't come from the baby, though. It had slipped through the parted lips of the woman. A whimper full of pain and fear followed it.

It pierced his heart. He cupped her cheek in his palm. "Sharon..."

She was exhausted, but he would rather wake her up than leave her in such a state.

"Sharon..."

Her thick lashes fluttered as if she struggled to wake. Or maybe it was the dream—the nightmare—that she struggled to escape. Finally her eyes—those enormous light brown eyes—opened, and she stared up at him.

But the fear didn't leave her face. It was as if it increased, as if she'd become more afraid. Was she afraid of him? Because of the custody thing or because of the suspicions that he'd seen on her expressive face back at Brenda's house?

She must have wondered if he had killed her boss. She might even wonder if he'd killed the bodyguard, too.

But then she reached out, as if trying to hold on to him—as if seeking his protection. And he heard it, too. The footsteps on the stairs. She knew he had gotten rid of everyone, that he had told them not to come back until he called for them.

Logan was the boss—as he always pointed out—but even he respected that this time Parker was giving the orders. The only one who might have disregarded his wishes was his mother, but she'd wanted to give them time alone—to think about her suggestion of marrying.

And while Logan might have thought about crossing Parker, he wouldn't disobey their mother. That was how *he* had wound up married.

His mother was so convinced that she was right that she was sure he would realize it, too, if she gave him enough time. So she wouldn't have let anyone disturb him.

He reached for his gun. But he didn't want any more dead bodies and not just because Sharon didn't need to see another one.

But because dead bodies meant dead ends.

If he killed whoever was coming after him and Sharon, he wouldn't be able to find out who had sent that person. He needed his would-be assassin capable of talking.

But if he didn't use the gun, he risked the person getting away or taking him down first. That meant he was putting Sharon and Ethan in danger.

He reached for the gun again, but then he pressed it into her hands. And he leaned close to whisper in her ear. "If it looks like he's getting the best of me, pull the trigger. I took the safety off…."

She gasped in protest of taking the gun. But he hadn't given her a choice.

He turned toward the stairwell. But he couldn't risk the intruder reaching the top and maybe firing wild shots around the room, taking them both out. So he vaulted over the railing and rushed down the steps.

Chapter Ten

The gun was heavy and cold in her hands. Sharon wanted to slide the safety back on and put it aside. But curses and grunts and groans emanated from the stairwell while Parker struggled with whoever had broken into the condo.

And then Ethan awoke with a startled cry, which quickly became screams of utter terror as the loud fighting in the stairwell continued.

"Shhh, sweetheart…I'm here," she assured him. "You're safe."

But was she lying to him?

She rose carefully from the bed, the gun grasped in her trembling hands. Keeping the barrel pointed away from the crib, she walked toward it and the screaming baby. "Shhh…"

He kicked his feet and flailed his arms, reaching for her. And she wanted to reach for him. But if she put down the gun…

If Parker needed her…

"You're okay, little man," she told the baby. But she wasn't so sure about his daddy. So she moved back toward the stairwell and peered over the side, over the barrel of the gun she held. The men were a tangle of arms and legs. She couldn't make out who was who.

But she did see the glint of metal in the beam of sunshine pouring through the skylights above the stairwell. While Parker had handed her his weapon, the intruder had brought one of his own.

A gun?

A knife?

She couldn't tell. Yet…

But if Parker needed her to defend him, she would shoot. She would not let Ethan lose his mother and his father….

FEAR AND REGRET chilled his blood as Parker stared down the barrel of a gun. He should not have given his weapon to Sharon—especially since she was now pointing his Glock at him.

"I come here to warn you and this is how you thank me," Garek Kozminski grumbled. "You break my neck on the damn stairs…."

Sharon gasped, no doubt as the memory of Brenda's corpse flashed through her mind as it just had his. The gun shook in her trembling hands. Not only was she scared, but the weapon was probably too heavy for her given how exhausted she was.

Why had he taken off the safety?

He elbowed Garek, who cursed in protest. "Show some sensitivity, man…."

"Show some appreciation," he retorted. "I've got important news."

When Parker had first realized that the man he'd attacked on the stairs was Logan's brother-in-law, he had been relieved. But now it occurred to him that Garek Kozminski wasn't someone he should trust. The Payne family tradition was law enforcement or protection; the

Kozminski family tradition was jewelry thieving. But that wasn't the only crime Garek had committed; he had also killed.

And if he'd done it once…

"Why didn't you go to Logan with your important news?" he wondered.

"I thought you were running this show," Garek replied. "That's what you said at the hospital."

It was….

"But how did you find *me?*"

Garek grunted and shoved, trying to lever Parker off him. But Parker wasn't ready yet to let the man up. He wanted to stay between him and Sharon. Although maybe that wasn't the safest place for him given that Sharon's grasp on the loaded gun was so shaky….

"I've been tailing you," Garek admitted.

"How?" He had been careful to avoid any tails or so he'd thought. But the rookie cop had followed him and apparently so had a criminal….

Garek shrugged. "Don't get all bent out of shape like your brother did when I tailed him. You guys are good at losing tails, but I'm better at—"

"Stalking?"

"I am not a stalker," he said, and now he was the one with wounded pride.

"Then why are you holding a knife?" Sharon asked, her voice sharp with suspicion.

As Garek flashed the blade in question, Sharon steadied the barrel of the gun. She was ready to shoot. Despite everything she had been through and her exhaustion, she was prepared to protect him—better than he had been protecting her.

"I cannot say exactly what this is," Garek began, "since

I am not allowed to possess any tools for breaking and entering. But hypothetically speaking, this looks more like a lock pick than a knife...." He glanced at it as if considering how much damage he could do with it. "It probably couldn't cause a wound much deeper than a paper cut."

Parker could have called him on that lie since it had sliced through his shirt and grazed his skin. But then he was worried that Sharon might shoot. Hell, maybe he should let her.

"I don't understand why you tailed me here and broke in," he said. And he had some big concerns about the man's motives. "Logan would have preferred you'd gone through him."

"I don't want Logan putting himself and my sister in the line of fire," Garek said. And that reply made more sense than him wanting to tell Parker directly. "She was nearly killed because she was with him when he was mistaken for you. My sister's already been through too much...."

And her brother had blamed Logan for that. Now he knew that Parker was really the one to blame. But then maybe he had reasoned that if he killed Parker, people would stop trying to kill his twin.

"Sharon has already been through too much, too," Parker said. And he glanced up again, but she—and the gun barrel—were both gone. She must have determined that Garek was no threat. Or she had decided that Ethan needed her more than Parker did because the baby's cries had subsided. "Don't hurt her."

"You think I came here to hurt you?" Garek asked, his voice gruff with more than wounded pride. "I came here to warn you, to help you..." He shoved off Parker and struggled to his feet, groaning as his body shifted.

Parker had hurt him, but probably more emotionally than physically. Maybe since their siblings had married, Kozminski had begun to feel as if they were family. Parker had begun to feel that way, too, until he had suddenly gained an instant family of his own with Ethan and…Sharon. He wasn't sure what she was, but before he had even known that the baby was his, he had witnessed that she and the boy were as connected as if they were mother and son.

His mother was right. *Damn her...*

"I'm sorry," Parker said. "I just have to be careful…."

"You have to be more careful now," Garek advised.

"Why? What have you learned?" What information did he have that was so important that he'd broken into the condo to share it?

"The reward for your murders has been doubled," Garek said. "And it was already a generous amount of money for a hit." He shook his head, as if he was dumbfounded. "Now it's an *obscene* amount of money."

Parker cursed.

And Sharon appeared at the top of the stairwell. Those enormous eyes wide with concern, she stared down at him. Apparently she had heard only his curses, not what Garek had said. "What's going on?"

He wished he knew. Why was someone so determined that he and Sharon die?

"You should tell her," Garek advised.

Parker wasn't sure she could handle knowing how badly someone wanted her dead. But then he remembered how her grip had steadied on the gun and how she had been ready to shoot to protect him.

"Tell me what?" she asked, and as she stepped closer

to the stairs, he noticed the baby in her arms. Ethan clung to her, his little fingers tangled in her hair.

While Parker was his father, *she* was the boy's security. Ethan couldn't lose her. The greatest thing Parker could do as the boy's father was to make sure he kept this woman safe. "Whoever wants us dead upped the ante."

He wasn't sure she would understand, but she nodded and sucked in an audibly shaky breath. And then with the boy balanced on one of her lean hips, she pulled the gun out with the hand on her other side. The barrel was pointed straight and steady down the stairwell.

Garek laughed. "So *she's* going to shoot you to collect?"

"I have money," Sharon said. "I'll pay you to leave us alone."

Garek tensed as he realized what she thought, that she had the same suspicion that Parker had briefly entertained. "I have never met two more ungrateful people," he murmured. "I come here to warn you and you both think that I came here to collect on the damn rewards."

"I'm sorry," she said. "But you're a Kozminski, right?"

He hesitated but nodded.

"Detective Sharpe warned me about you."

Garek sighed. "Of course he did."

"He warned me about Parker, too."

Garek laughed. "I knew the guy was an idiot. But you have nothing to fear from any one of the Paynes—they're all about law and order." But he notably didn't make that claim for himself. "You're safer with this guy than you would be with anybody else—probably even with the police right now."

Parker flinched as he remembered how the greed of a certain police officer had cost both him and Garek their fathers. Parker's dad had died and Garek's dad had gone to prison for killing him even though another man had pulled the trigger. Parker hadn't had time to deal yet with finding out how his father's partner had betrayed him before he'd found out that someone was trying to kill him.

And then he had found out he was a father….

No wonder his head was pounding now. It wasn't just because of the concussion or exhaustion…

He was overwhelmed.

No doubt so was Sharon. So many people had been telling her so many things. Was it any wonder that she might struggle over what to believe and whom to trust?

She said, "Detective Sharpe warned me that Parker's a playboy."

Garek laughed harder—so hard that the baby laughed with him. "Maybe Sharpe's not as big an idiot as I thought…."

"He's an idiot," Parker insisted to Sharon. Then he turned back to Garek. "And *you* have no room to talk in the playboy department."

He laughed again. "I'm not denying that…."

Parker couldn't deny his reputation, either. He had vowed to never marry, to never have children. But he'd had reasons. He had actually wanted to spare someone mourning him the way he and his mother and siblings had mourned the loss of their father. And even before the hit had gone out on him, his life had often been in jeopardy. As an undercover cop, he'd put his life on the line with every dangerous assignment. And when he protected someone, he again placed himself between that person and potential danger.

"Thanks for breaking and entering," Parker said, "to give us the heads-up."

Garek shrugged and winced. "Don't mention it. I'd stay to help protect you and all, but I'm a lousy shot. And I should probably stop by the emergency room and have them x-ray my ribs."

"Sorry about that," Parker said with a carefully light slap on Garek's shoulder.

"I would have called..."

But Parker had pulled the battery out of his phone so no one would have been able to hack the GPS and find out where he was. He pulled another phone from his pocket. "I replaced my cell with this one. It's an untraceable track phone." He gave the number to Garek. "Now you can call next time...."

"Let's hope there isn't a next time. You don't want the reward getting tripled." He grinned. "Or I might be tempted to collect." Then he turned and headed down the stairs to the basement garage.

Parker wasn't so sure that Kozminski was kidding. If double an already generous reward was obscene, then triple would probably prove irresistible.

After the door clicked behind Garek, Parker made sure it was locked and the alarm was engaged. Then he headed up the stairs to where Sharon waited for him. Instead of the gun, she held a bottle, which Ethan was eagerly sucking down. She arched her neck to indicate where she had left his weapon sitting on the nightstand next to the rumpled king-sized bed.

He only noticed how delicate her neck looked; how slender she was. Vulnerable. And beautiful...even as exhausted as she was.

She hadn't had much sleep, and it showed in the dark circles beneath her enormous eyes. After what they had just learned from Garek, she probably wouldn't be able to go back to sleep even if Ethan did.

"I'm sorry about that," he said.

She skeptically arched a brow. "Sorry that he made you tell me?"

"Yes," he admitted.

"Why?" she asked, and she bristled with pride. "Do you think I'm too weak or fragile to know what's going on? That the reward for our murders has been increased?"

He glanced again to where she'd put the gun. "You handled that pretty well."

Her mouth curved into a slight smile. "Don't patronize me. I could barely hold on to it. But that wasn't because I'm weak or fragile. It's because I don't like guns."

Probably with good reason. Had her mother been shot? Or worse…

And at a young, impressionable age, Sharon had seen that and survived. "I don't think you're weak or fragile," he assured her.

She narrowed her eyes and stared at him suspiciously. "Are you still patronizing me?"

"No," he said. "I know how strong you have to be when you lose a parent."

She gasped. "Oh, that's right…." Her face flushed a bright red with embarrassment. "I'm sorry…."

"You know about my dad?" he asked.

"Brenda told me that he died when you were a teenager," she said. "And then I saw on the news that it was just discovered that another man killed him than the one who'd been in prison for his murder."

"Garek's dad was the man in prison for his murder," he said, "until he died there."

Her brows lifted in surprise. "And his sister is married to your brother?"

Parker laughed. "They used to hate each other—or so they claimed. But Stacy always knew it wasn't her dad who had killed ours." A twinge of pain struck his chest over the betrayal that had led to his dad's death. "She was right. It wound up being another officer—his partner."

She nodded. "Brenda told me not to trust the police."

"I can't argue with her now," he said. "I'd like to say they can't be bought. But some of them can be more greedy than honorable." He wondered about Sharpe and that kid that Sharpe had sent to follow him. Why hadn't he identified himself as an officer when he'd pulled the gun on Parker? What might have happened if Logan hadn't shown up?

"And the reward to kill us is a lot of money?" she asked nervously.

He wasn't going to patronize her with a lie, so he answered honestly. "An obscene amount, according to Garek."

Her arm tightened around Ethan protectively, and she glanced around the condo as if looking for more intruders. He glanced around, too, just in case....

Since Garek had so easily followed him and broken in, someone else could, too. They really weren't safe anywhere. And because they were in danger, so was his son. And if something happened to either one of them or both, what would become of Ethan?

Would Parker's mother be able to get custody or would the baby go straight into the foster-care system? He had to protect his son and Sharon.

Her skin had grown pale, her eyes wide and dark with

fear. Her voice even trembled a bit when she asked, "What do we do now?"

Ignoring the twinge of panic striking his bachelor heart, he replied, "We get married."

Chapter Eleven

Sharon stared at herself in the oval mirror—unable to believe that was actually her reflection staring back at her. How was that her in the lacy, strapless white dress and veil? She had pulled back the veil so that she could see, so that the image would be clear.

But nothing was clear to her. Why did someone so desperately want both her and Parker dead? With the reward for their murders doubled, it was probably only a matter of time before one of the attempts was successful.

Her stomach pitched. She couldn't remember the last time she had eaten. She wasn't worried about marrying the notorious playboy Payne, either. She wasn't about to give him her heart. The only thing she really had to lose was Ethan. And her life.

"I've seen a lot of brides in this room, but I have never seen one look as scared as you do," a female voice remarked. "But then, you're the one marrying Parker."

Sharon turned to see the young auburn-haired woman who had been at Brenda's house and at the police station and at the hospital with her. The young woman had been nearly everywhere that Sharon had, so maybe she should have expected her to show up here. But still, she gasped in surprise.

And the woman wasn't alone; she had brought an enormous dog with her. As it sniffed around the bride's room, Sharon realized it was Cujo—the K9 dog that Parker had previously and wistfully mentioned. He had brought the dog to the wedding to sniff out any bombs. But the German shepherd was disinterested in everything in the room—even Sharon.

"I didn't mean to scare you more," the woman said.

Sharon remembered her solicitous look from the hospital; the woman obviously knew about her tragic past. And pitied her. "I'm fine," she said. "How about you?"

Was she upset that Parker was marrying another woman?

The young woman sighed before replying, "No. With all my brothers married, Mom's going to have no one left to manipulate into marriage but me."

"Brothers?"

She snorted in disgust. "Parker still hasn't told you that I'm his sister?" She thrust her hand between them. "I'm Nikki Payne."

Sharon clasped the proffered hand and firmly shook it. "I'm glad to meet you." Finally…

And she felt like a fool for that fleeting jealousy she had felt—and to which she'd had no right. She and Parker were nothing to each other even though they were about to become husband and wife.

"He should have introduced us at the judge's house," Nikki said. "But I was still a mess from him nearly getting blown up earlier."

It hadn't occurred to Sharon until now how the attempts on his life must have been affecting his family. "And here *I* thought I was the mess…"

"You were," Nikki said with the Payne directness. But

then she laughed. Was she only kidding? "But you had every right. Parker didn't even let me see the body, so it must have been bad." She slapped her hand over her own mouth. "God, I'm so crass."

"You're honest and straightforward," Sharon said. "I appreciate that—even though I haven't been that straightforward myself."

Nikki chuckled again. "You messed with Parker—letting him think you'd had his kid and that he didn't even remember you."

Was his sister angry about that? Sharon opened her mouth to apologize.

But Nikki continued, "That's great. For all the hearts he's broken, he deserved that!"

Sharon shook her head. "He didn't deserve to be kept in the dark about his son all this time."

"It wasn't your secret to tell," another woman remarked as she joined them in the bride's dressing room of the Little White Wedding Chapel that Parker's mother owned. After petting the dog that was overjoyed to see her, she held out her hand as Nikki had. "I'm Stacy Koz—Stacy Payne," she corrected herself with a chuckle. "Logan's wife."

Nikki laughed. "I still can't believe that one. I don't know which one is harder to believe, though—you and Logan getting married or Parker getting married…."

"Me and Logan," Stacy easily replied. "I saw Parker's house before it nearly blew up—it's a family house."

Nikki shook her head. "He uses it to fool women into thinking that he might actually get married."

"He *is* getting married," another woman chimed in as Mrs. Payne bustled into the room. "And very soon…"

"Where's Ethan?" Sharon asked, alarmed that the

woman who had taken her little man from her no longer had him.

"He's with his father," Mrs. Payne said.

And that reminded Sharon why she was marrying the playboy—so that Ethan wouldn't be taken away from her.

Mrs. Payne smiled. "All the guys are getting into their tuxes."

"I'm dressed now," Sharon pointed out. "I can take him back."

Mrs. Payne stepped forward and fussed with the veil, pulling it back over Sharon's face. "You're so beautiful. We can't have the baby messing with my new daughter's hair and veil."

My new daughter...

Sharon was grateful for the concealment of the veil now as it hid the tears that Mrs. Payne's sweet remark had springing to her eyes. She had claimed not just Ethan as family but Sharon, too. Sharon had never really had a family.

"I may step into the groom's quarters," Nikki said. "I'd love to see Parker wrestling a baby into a tuxedo."

"I already dressed Ethan," Mrs. Payne said. "And Logan is holding him while Parker dresses." She turned toward Stacy. "He looks very comfortable with a baby."

Stacy laughed. "You just talked us into getting married. Give us some time before you go looking for more grandbabies."

"You've already got one more than you thought you had," Nikki pointed out.

Mrs. Payne grinned. "Having him makes me want more."

Sharon had no intention of even consummating this

marriage, let alone procreating. "Mrs. Payne, are you sure we should be getting married in your beautiful chapel?"

"We already had one wedding at the hospital," she said with a glance toward Stacy.

Stacy smiled with pure happiness. "Logan couldn't wait another minute before making me his wife, and he wanted Parker to be his best man."

With the hit out on them, Parker and Sharon could wind up back in the hospital at any time—in a bed or the morgue.

"So we could get married somewhere else," Sharon suggested.

"It would break my heart if you got married anywhere else," Mrs. Payne replied.

But it would break Sharon's heart if something happened to the old church that the older woman had painstakingly restored and made into her livelihood.

But that didn't mean that there weren't other dangers out there. Sharon tentatively touched the lace gown. "And me in your beautiful gown?"

Stacy shook her head in amazement. "How has that same dress fit all the Payne brides? We're all different heights and sizes."

Stacy was shorter than Sharon and much curvier. "You wore this dress, too?"

Stacy nodded. "At the hospital. I was nervous to wear it, too, and changed quickly."

"It's Mom's magic dress," Nikki remarked.

Mrs. Payne gave an unladylike snort of derision. "It's a needle and thread and different-sized heels. And of course, beautiful brides that make it look so perfect...." She turned toward Nikki as if studying her to figure out the next round of alterations.

Nikki shook her head. "Oh, no! Don't even start looking at me like that…." She pointed at her mother and addressed Sharon. "See, I told you—"

"I was talking about the danger that Parker and I are in," Sharon reminded the others. "We've had people try to blow up the places we live or visit. I don't want anyone blowing up your chapel to get to us." And if the chapel blew up, the dress was sure to be destroyed…along with Sharon and her groom and everyone else in their wedding party.

"Cujo hasn't found any explosives. And all of the Payne Protection Agency is here," Nikki said. "You've never been safer than you are right now."

But as she walked down the aisle toward her groom standing at the altar, Sharon didn't feel safe. Not when she saw how tenderly he held the tiny boy who, also clad in a black tuxedo, was a perfect miniature of him. She felt a terror that she hadn't felt since she was a kid.

And if it wasn't fear for her life, was it fear for her heart? Was she afraid that she was going to lose it to the man she was about to marry?

God, she is beautiful….

Parker had been told that Sharon was wearing his mother's dress—the same dress that all the other Payne brides had worn. But his memory must have still been screwed up because he couldn't remember ever seeing anyone else in that concoction of white lace and silk. It looked as if it had been made for her alone—for her long, slender body. But it fitted and highlighted the curves that the ugly tan suit had hid.

She walked alone down the aisle on which so many other brides had clutched the arm of a father or a brother.

She had no one…but Ethan, who wriggled with excitement in his arms as he caught sight of the woman who had been more of a mother to him than his biological mother had. As she drew nearer, Parker forgot to breathe—until one of Ethan's flailing arms caught him in the jaw.

Even with the veil covering her face, the little boy knew who she was—and he wanted to be in her arms. And Parker was surprised that the boy wasn't the only one—Parker wanted her arms around him, too. But even more, he wanted to hold her—to keep her safe. He was so distracted by the sudden onslaught of wants and needs that the little boy managed to wriggle loose enough to lean toward Sharon.

As she lifted her arms to catch him, she nearly dropped the bouquet. But Nikki caught it before it hit the ground. Then, as she stood there with it clutched in her hands, Nikki's eyes widened in horror and she shook her head. "This doesn't count…." She slid back into the pew next to their mother, whispering, "This doesn't count, Mom…."

Light laughter rippled around the church at his sister's reaction. And usually Parker would have laughed the loudest before adding some additional comments. But he was too stunned by the beauty of his bride to be amused by anything.

But then Ethan tugged at Sharon's veil. And he laughed at the little boy's determination to get his hands in her hair. Parker reached out and lifted the veil over her face. It wasn't the time. He was supposed to do that at the end of the ceremony—before he kissed her. But he couldn't wait to see her face. And when he saw her face flushed with color, and her caramel-colored eyes sparkling, he couldn't wait to kiss her.

But he resisted temptation—just as Ethan resisted

letting go of the veil. Parker hadn't anticipated playing tug-of-war with his son on his wedding day—just like he hadn't anticipated his overwhelming desire for his bride.

"Be careful," Sharon advised in a soft whisper.

She was probably worried about the lace. But Parker was worried about *her.* Even though he had always been open and honest about his inability to commit, he had broken a lot of hearts. He didn't want to break hers. But she was looking at him—staring up at him—as if she was as fascinated with him as he was with her.

He had been unable to commit before because of his dangerous profession. But he had never been in as much danger as he was now and yet he was standing at an altar with this woman who held his son.

The minister cleared his throat and whispered, "Are we ready to begin?"

Parker managed to loosen Ethan's grip on the lace. His hands skimmed Sharon's bare shoulders as he pushed it behind her back. She shivered as if reacting to his touch, and her eyes darkened.

His stomach tightened with a desire more intense than he had ever felt before. He wanted his bride. He turned back to the minister and nodded. "We're ready…."

And he repeated vows he had sworn he would never utter—vows all about loving and honoring and cherishing until being parted by death. Her voice trembling, Sharon repeated back those vows to him.

Death…

Could he protect her from it? Could he protect himself?

His mother had thought of everything because Logan was thrusting a ring at him, which he slid onto Sharon's trembling finger. And then she produced one for him, which Ethan tried to grab from her hand. "No, little man," she admonished him. "That's not for you. You'd only put it in your mouth."

Chuckles emanated throughout the church again at her comments as she evaded the baby's attempt to grab the ring. Then she slid it onto Parker's finger. His skin tingled from her touch. Hell, he tingled all over from just her nearness. She was so beautiful....

He wanted to touch more than her hands; he wanted to touch her all over. Finally, the minister said the words Parker had been impatiently waiting for. "You may kiss your bride...."

He leaned down over the child she held and pressed his lips to hers. Her breath caught audibly, but then she was kissing him back—her silky lips sliding over his. Her mouth opened—maybe for air—but he deepened the kiss, consuming her as desire overwhelmed him. She tasted so sweet, so fresh and pure.

As if she had never been kissed before...

He wanted to kiss her forever. But the minister was clearing his throat again. Then a small fist smacked his cheek, bringing him to his senses, just as the guests began to clap and cheer.

Heat climbed into his face with embarrassment that he had forgotten all about the guests. They were all family—either by blood or the bond of working together at Payne Protection. There had been no one invited who wasn't related—who couldn't be trusted. Well, the Kozminski brothers were there, but his mother and Logan trusted them now. And they were family—by marriage.

As well as his protection, he could give Sharon family. He doubted he could give her his heart, though. He hoped she didn't expect it, that his kiss hadn't given her the wrong idea. He had decided so long ago that he would never let himself love anyone and he doubted he could change now. But then again, he had gotten married....

His mother had gone all out despite his pleas that she not do that. Besides the dress and the ceremony and the rings, there was a reception. Food, cake, dancing...

He folded his arms around his bride, holding her close, while music played softly around them. His hips brushed hers and his body tensed, aching for her. He wanted to be alone with her, away from all the watchful eyes of his family, which was also hers now. But maybe it was better if he wasn't alone with her....

She stared up at him, her eyes dark and dazed, as if she was as surprised and overwhelmed by her desire as he was by his. They definitely should not be alone.

But his mother walked up to them, a sleeping baby in her arms. "You two should leave now," she said. "I will take care of him for the night."

Sharon seemed startled at the thought, but Parker wasn't sure if it was because she was panicked over being separated from the child or over being alone with her new groom. "But what if he wakes—"

"He's going to have to get used to spending time with his grandma," said his mother.

He should have known this was where her matchmaking was leading. She had wanted her kids married so she could get grandkids. Well, he'd already done his part, albeit unintentionally.

"Mom, I appreciate everything you did to make this seem like a real wedding, but—"

"It *is* a real wedding, sweetheart," she said. And she patted his cheek with her open palm. "It is a real wedding. You have a license to prove it."

So the wedding had been real, but the marriage wouldn't be. He couldn't let anyone hurt Sharon—not even him. "Mom—"

She smacked his cheek again—a little harder—and leaned in closer to him to whisper, "The marriage has to look real, too, so a court can't challenge it."

What was she asking him to do?

"Just leave together," she suggested. Then she turned toward Sharon and patted her cheek, but gently. "You are as beautiful a bride as you are a person."

Sharon's face flushed at the compliment. But she shook her head, denying it.

But Parker realized his mother was right. Sharon's beauty came from the inside out. If he was alone with her, he might be the one in trouble. But as his brothers had already learned, there was no arguing with his mother. Amid a shower of birdseed and glittering confetti, she ushered them out the doors to the front steps of the church.

Parker kept close to Sharon—not just because he was so drawn to her, but because he had already nearly been shot on these very steps. Logan had thought that those shots had been intended for him, but they had actually been meant to kill Parker.

"We set up a perimeter around the church," Logan said. "Nobody could get near it. You're safe here."

"Maybe we should stay," Sharon murmured, turning back toward the baby clutched in his mother's arms. She started reaching back, but Parker clasped her hand in his and led her down the stairs. A car waited for them at the curb—someone had attached cans to the back bumper along with a sign that read Just Married.

Nikki stepped forward and pressed the keys into

Parker's hand. "It's safe," she assured him. "Cujo and I checked it out thoroughly."

He pointed toward the cans and the sign. "I see that…."

She grinned and then reached up and kissed his cheek. "Be safe…."

She turned toward Sharon and kissed her cheek, as well. "Be careful…."

Parker helped his bride inside the car, making sure her dress was all in before he closed the door. Then as he ran around the front of the car to the driver's side, more birdseed and confetti struck him—stinging his face. He laughed and ducked and slid behind the wheel. As he shut the door, more birdseed hit the window.

But his laughter died and his hand stilled as he slid the key into the ignition. Nikki had checked out the car, and he trusted her. But he wasn't just trusting her with his life; he was also trusting her with the life of his new bride.

"It's okay," Sharon said. And she put her hand over his and turned the key.

The motor sputtered and then turned over, revving as he gave it gas. He uttered a sigh of relief. His family had kept them safe. He waved at them as he pulled away from the curb. To keep other cars away from the church, a big truck blocked the end of the street. It pulled forward as he neared, and Candace waved from the driver's seat. Payne Protection had surrounded the perimeter. But once he passed her truck, he was on his own. He would have to make sure that they were not tailed. He wasn't bringing Sharon back to the condo, though. He had found another place—a place nobody else knew about.

So he had to make extra certain that they weren't followed. He had to stay focused on the mirrors, watching for cars. But his bride kept drawing his attention to the passenger's seat. She was quiet, probably because she was scared. Maybe she didn't trust him to protect her alone. Or maybe she was upset about leaving Ethan with his mother.

It was when he turned to assure her that everything was all right that he saw the black SUV. It wasn't behind them. It was coming right at them—blowing through a stop sign to slam into the passenger's side—into Sharon. The big SUV struck with such force that glass shattered and metal crunched and then the car spun, turning over and over—scattering those cans tied to the back of it across the road. Glass struck his face and metal smashed against his arm and his head. He fought to stay conscious.

But Sharon was not. Her eyes were closed and blood streaked down from a cut on her head. Was she unconscious or dead?

Glass crunched beneath shoes as someone rushed toward the car. He didn't believe it was someone coming to his aid—it was someone coming to make sure he could collect that reward for a double murder.

Parker reached for his gun, but the seat belt, which held him in as the car landed upside down, was now also holding down his jacket so he couldn't get to his holster. He had no way of defending himself and Sharon.

He may not have wanted to get married, but now that he had, he damn well wanted it to last more than a few short hours. And the whole purpose of marrying had been to protect his bride, not to get her killed. But it was probably already too late for him to save her.

Now he couldn't save himself, either.

Chapter Twelve

Gunshots blasted, rousing Sharon from unconsciousness. The windshield now lay in pieces that were scattered on the pavement beneath the upside-down car. She sucked in a quick breath of panic. The car had turned over—and over—glass and air bags exploding while metal crunched.

Ethan! Had his child seat protected him?

No, no...

Ethan hadn't been with them. Mrs. Payne had kept him for their *honeymoon.* How had she forgotten?

She must have hit her head. She lifted her fingers to it now and they came away sticky and stained with her blood. But the cut was the least of her concerns with someone shooting....

She had hesitated to turn toward Parker, terrified that he hadn't survived the accident. But she turned now, as more shots rang out, and she realized that he was the one shooting. That he had drawn his weapon from his torn jacket, and, bleeding and pinned in the car, he was defending them.

"You're awake," he said with a ragged sigh of relief. But then he asked, "Are you all right?"

She replied with honesty. "I don't know...."

"If you can move, you have to get out of your seat belt," he said. "We have to get out of here."

"How many are they?" she asked. She wasn't naive enough to believe the SUV hitting them had been an accident—it had been another attempt on their lives. And since the accident hadn't killed them…

So many gunshots rang out, ricocheting off the exposed undercarriage of Parker's vehicle. Maybe it had been a blessing that they had landed upside down because it was harder for the men to fire bullets inside the vehicle.

Before Parker answered her question, he fired again, and a man's body, dressed all in black, dropped to the pavement in front of the car. He joined another darkly clothed man already lying there in a pool of blood.

A scream burned in her throat, making her eyes water. But she held it in and tamped down the fear that threatened to overwhelm her. She had to be strong now.

So she steadied her trembling hands and reached for the seat belt. But the car door had crumpled against it despite the side air bag that had opened on her seat. If not for the air bag, she would have undoubtedly been crushed. She had to push her hand between the now deflated air bag and the jagged metal—wincing as the metal scraped her skin—before she found the mechanism and released her belt.

She dropped onto the roof of the car—which was littered with glass and blood. Whose blood? Just hers or Parker's, too?

Like her, she noticed, he had a cut on his head. But he must not have lost consciousness as she had, or they would have already been dead.

"My seat belt is stuck," Parker said. "You need to cut me loose."

Fear and helplessness overwhelmed her again. "How?"

"I have a knife in my jacket pocket," he said. "Can you reach it?"

She slid her hand inside his torn jacket. And as she did, he fired again. She flinched against the earsplitting noise. That was probably why he hadn't wanted to fight with the belt himself—he was too busy defending her. So she found the knife. And careful to not slice him with the blade, she hacked at the belt until it shredded and tore and finally freed her groom.

With a grunt, he dropped to the roof of the car with her. Because there wasn't much room in the crumpled space, their bodies touched everywhere. She waited for a rush of pain from all of her bumps and bruises and cuts, but she felt nothing but the heat of his body and the reassuring protection of his presence. With him—with her husband—she felt safe, no matter how much danger they faced.

"We have to get out of here," he said again. "But we have to be careful. We don't know how many are left...."

Left? Two of them already lay on the ground in front of the car. Were they dead or just hurt?

She didn't let herself care about their conditions. These were men who killed for money, who didn't care that they would leave a child alone in the world just as she had been left alone.

"Stick close to me," he ordered her as he crawled through the shattered windshield.

She moved to follow him, but the glass left in the frame caught the lace on her wedding gown—trapping her inside the wreckage. She couldn't follow him. And he wouldn't leave without her.

More shots rang out. Would Parker die defending her?

"JUST TEAR IT," Parker yelled at her, as he kicked away the weapons of the men lying on the ground. Their cartridges were spent or he would have grabbed them to replace his gun. He was about to run out of ammunition. He was down to his last clip, and when that was empty, they would be helpless to defend themselves.

"I can't rip it," she protested as if horrified. "It's your mother's dress."

The dress his mother had worn when she'd married his father. It should mean something to Parker, but he didn't care about it as Sharon seemed to. He cared only about Sharon.

But then she was sliding onto the pavement with him. She had freed herself the same way she'd freed him. She had been knocked out. She was bleeding. But she'd rallied.

How had he ever thought that she was fragile? She was definitely the strongest woman he'd ever known—and he had known some damn strong women. He tugged her down beside him, where he crouched behind the wreckage of the SUV that had struck her side of his car. Three armed men had climbed out of the wreckage and he'd dealt with them.

Regret flashed through him that he had taken lives. But the men had left him no choice. They would have killed him and Sharon if he hadn't killed them first. Ideally, he would have rather taken them alive, but he'd been trapped in his seat in an upside-down car. He wouldn't have been able to fight them, to overpower them—especially when he'd been outnumbered. Even now, he had no idea if there were more....

Then he noticed something. Their driver's head had gone through the windshield. He stared down at him, his eyes open but unseeing. He hadn't survived the crash like Parker and Sharon had.

"I didn't rip the dress," she murmured, as if he cared about the damn dress. "But I think I'm bleeding on it…." Her voice cracked with regret and fear…and probably the horrific memory of her mother's murder.

"Are you hurt?" he asked. When he'd asked her earlier, she hadn't known. He could understand that because he had no idea if he was hurt, either—if any of the shots fired at him had even struck him. Adrenaline rushed so quickly through his veins, it was all he could feel besides the concern for her safety.

"I don't think anything's broken," she said. "What about you? Are you hurt?"

He shrugged and winced as pain radiated from his shoulder to his neck. He probably had whiplash from the car flipping over, but it was the least of his worries now.

He heard footsteps—a lot of footsteps running on asphalt. More than one person was coming. Had there been another car of assassins following this car?

And his ammo was running low. He had lost at least one clip when he'd ripped his jacket to free his holster. The shells had dropped onto the roof and rolled away. He was going to run out of bullets. "Sharon, you said nothing's broken?"

"It doesn't feel like it," she said.

Which didn't offer him much reassurance. But she was a survivor. She wouldn't have survived twenty years ago if she hadn't been smart, and she wouldn't have survived all these recent attempts on her life if she wasn't resourceful.

"I want you to run," he ordered her.

"Where?"

"Toward the houses, through the yards—find an unlocked shed or a garage or basement—someplace to hide." Like her mother had hidden her all those years ago. He hated that he kept bringing up those tragic memories for her.

But she wasn't worried about herself because her only question was "What about you?"

"I'm going to cover you," he said. "And then I'll come find you." Unless he ran out of bullets before the assassins did....

But then someone from his family would find her. They would protect her as he wished he could. But he could only watch as she ran through the gathering darkness as night finally fell. But the darkness was no protection for her as her white dress glowed like a beacon, drawing all attention to her presence and the direction she had taken between the houses.

It was more likely that one of the assassins would follow her, that he would find her before she even had a chance to hide.

Damn it...

The sound of the footsteps, growing louder as the people came closer, drew his attention back to the street. He clutched his gun and raised the barrel and hoped like hell he had enough bullets left.

HER LUNGS BURNED as Sharon ran, and the skirt of the wedding gown tangled around her legs, nearly tripping her. Gravel stung the soles of her bare feet. She must have lost her shoes in the car—probably when she'd been hanging upside down. But she didn't dare stop as gunfire rang out again behind her. Should she go back and make sure that Parker was all right? Or would her presence only distract him?

He had defended them earlier. He had to be able to continue to defend himself. And then he would come for her once it was safe.

So she had to hide. She had to find a place where she would be safe until he came. He would be furious if she didn't, just like her mother would have been had Sharon come out of the cupboard where she had hidden her all those years ago.

Parker was a protector like her mother had been. She had worried more about Sharon's safety than her own. Parker was the same way; that was why he had stayed behind despite undoubtedly being outnumbered. And that was why he had told Sharon to hide.

She stopped running, but her bare feet slipped on the grass and she skidded across the lawn of someone's backyard. At least she assumed it was a backyard. It was so dark that she couldn't see much—and this house was dark, too. Nobody was home, or if they were home, they weren't awake anymore.

How late was it?

She could have tried the house, could have seen if one of the doors opened. But she didn't dare risk waking someone—someone who might be as armed as the assassins who'd just tried to kill her and Parker.

Instead, she continued through the backyard, tripping over flagstones and garden statues. And because they had such a garden, she wasn't surprised to see another shadow in the backyard—that of a shed.

She fumbled around in the dark, searching for the door with her hands. But all she found were the wooden walls, and jagged splinters dug deep into her palms. She winced, but that pain was nothing compared to her fear.

She wasn't afraid for herself; she was afraid for Parker. The gunfire had stopped. She hadn't run so far that she wouldn't still hear it if they were shooting.

What did that mean?

That he was already gone?

Pain and loss filled her, pressing down heavily on her chest so that she could hardly breathe—so that her heart could barely beat.

Her hands skimmed across trim. She had found the door. But she had to fumble around even more to find the knob. Her fingers jammed against the metal handle. She tugged on it; the door rattled but didn't budge.

Another clank echoed in the eerie silence. And she found the padlock holding it closed on the top of the door. The lock refused to budge, too, but the little hook through which the lock slid was loose. She dug a fingernail into the head of one of the screws and turned it. It was so stripped that it fell to the ground. Then she tore the hook from the wood and pulled open the door.

She hurried inside the shed, but not to hide. She wasn't going to cower and hide again. She had already done that too often in her life. This time she was going to fight. Finally. So she fumbled around in the windowless shed until she found something to use to protect herself.

And when she heard the footsteps coming toward her, she didn't wait for the person to shoot at her or grab her. Like swinging a bat at a ball, she swung the shovel out, hoping to make contact. Even with the shovel, she couldn't overpower a man. However, maybe she could knock him out.

But she missed.

The handle was caught, grabbed in a strong fist and wrenched from her hands, leaving her with no weapon. No defense.

This man was undoubtedly armed like the others had been. So, really, what defense was a shovel against a gun?

Chapter Thirteen

Parker held tightly to the shovel. And he exhaled a ragged breath of relief that the blade hadn't struck his head. She had swung it forcefully and wildly. And now she threw things that she pulled off shelves. But it was dark and most of them missed him.

"Sharon," he said. But she kept throwing things. So he dropped the shovel and grabbed her, pulling her flailing body into his arms. She swung her fists and feet, fighting him. "Sharon! It's me. It's Parker. It's your husband."

Her struggle stilled. And then she was crying and clutching at him. "You're alive!"

"Yes," he said. "And so are you..."

And he was clutching her back, pulling her closer so that he could feel her heart beat and her lungs breathe.

"You're alive...." He shouldn't have sent her running off alone. The minute he'd done it he had regretted it. And when he'd nearly shot his brother, he had realized that instead of sending Sharon to safety, he had sent her off alone to deal with whatever dangers awaited her in the dark. He hadn't realized that *she* might be the danger—with the deadly shovel she'd wielded.

Once he had identified the footsteps as belonging to his family, he had left them to run after his bride. He had been worried that he would find her cowering in fear. Once again, he had underestimated her. She was far stronger than he had given her credit for.

She pulled back and stared up at him, her eyes glistening in the darkness. "Who was running up when I left?"

"My family. They heard the crash and came running from the chapel," he explained. He should have known they would have heard it and the gunfire, too.

She kept staring up at him. "What about the gunshots I heard?"

He flinched, remembering how close he had come to hitting Cooper. "It was nothing." He wouldn't have fired at all but he had seen Cooper's gun before he had seen who was holding it. If he hadn't worried that a shot fired from it might hit Sharon as she ran away, he wouldn't have risked shooting so soon.

Sirens wailed as emergency units approached the scene. Parker wanted to keep his arms around Sharon, wanted to continue holding her. But she had been hurt; at the very least, she needed stitches for the cut on her head. Maybe a CT scan to make sure she didn't have a concussion. He had to bring her back to the ambulance.

"We have to go," he said.

She pulled back and nodded. "Of course..."

He led the way out of the shed, making sure he stayed between her and whatever might have been waiting for them in the dark. But she stumbled and fell against him. So he turned and lifted her up into his arms. And he carried her back to where all the lights flashed and sirens wailed.

What had taken them so long to come? Had no one reported the accident or the gunfire? Officers were there now, in full force, stringing yellow tape around the crime scene. He should have been carrying his bride over a threshold to a honeymoon suite; instead, he carried her across the crime-scene tape and headed toward the ambulance.

Paramedics were working on the men on the ground, but he didn't care about their injuries as he interrupted them. "My wife needs to be checked out," he said. "She was on the passenger's side of the car that took the initial impact of the crash."

The paramedic glanced up from the guy on the ground. The young man shook his head. "I can't stop working on this patient yet."

"He's beyond help," Parker pointed out. "She could have a head injury. She was unconscious for a while."

"Until the shooting started," she said. "But I'm fine now…."

"I still want you to check her out," Parker told the paramedic. "She has cuts and bruises, too." But hopefully no broken bones or concussion.

"You better do what he wants," Logan suggested. "He and his wife were the victims in this crash. The men you're treating tried to kill them."

Parker had thought he had killed the men. But if the paramedics were able to resuscitate them, he wished they would. He would like these guns-for-hire brought back to life to answer all the questions he had about who had ordered the hit on them.

But Sharon was more important.

The paramedic looked from him to Logan and back. "You're Paynes, right?"

His twin nodded. "I'm Logan Payne, and he's Parker. You should be aware that someone put out a professional hit on him and his wife, Sharon Wells."

The paramedic's eyes widened. "Sharon Wells?" As another paramedic continued to treat the man on the ground, he stood up and led Parker to the ambulance. He pointed to a stretcher in the back. "I'll check her out now."

Parker hesitated before releasing her. He liked the warmth and softness of her body in his arms, liked the reassuring beat of her heart against his and liked the whisper of her breath against his throat....

"Mr. Payne?" The paramedic questioned his reluctance. "I'll make sure she stays safe."

That was all he wanted—for her to be safe. That was one of the reasons, along with keeping Ethan out of the foster-care system, why he had married her. So he forced himself to lay her down onto the stretcher and walk away. But he didn't go far. He didn't trust the paramedic; he couldn't trust him or anyone else. So he kept his gaze on him as he rejoined his twin.

"Who's with Ethan and Mom?" he asked. He had to make certain that his son and the boy's grandmother were safe, too. They were probably the only members of his family who hadn't come running up to the scene of the accident. Except that it hadn't been an accident....

Someone had tried to kill him and Sharon. He blinked and could see behind his closed lids how the SUV had slammed into her side of the car. He'd thought he had lost her then.

"Candace is on protection duty," Logan replied. "She took them off to a safe house."

Nikki stepped over the crime-scene tape and joined them. "I let Mom know that you and Sharon are safe."

"I doubt we're safe," Parker said as he glanced back at the wreckage. The SUV driver had risked—and given up—his own life to try to take theirs. And the others had stepped right into the line of Parker's fire in order to try to shoot him and his new bride. These people were too desperate to kill him and Sharon to ever give up—especially since the person who wanted them dead kept raising the reward.

That amount of money might be enough to tempt anyone....

Parker pointed his sister toward the ambulance. "Stay close to Sharon. Make sure nobody harms her."

She nodded and hurried off, obviously happy to act as a bodyguard since Logan usually kept her tied to a desk at the office. He probably would have literally tied her to it if she hadn't fought him.

Even now, the oldest Payne caught their other brother's attention and pointed Cooper toward the ambulance, too. Parker was grateful for the extra protection on his bride.

"You should be in that ambulance, too," Logan remarked.

Parker nodded. He should have been protecting Sharon himself. "I wanted to talk to you where she couldn't overhear." She had already been through too much.

"I meant that you should have paramedics check you out, too," Logan clarified. "You were in that car." He glanced back at it and shuddered. "And you got shot at. Are you sure you weren't hit?" He patted Parker's torn jacket, checking for bullet holes.

Parker shrugged off his concern. "I'm fine."

"You're a hell of a shot," Garek Kozminski commented as he joined them. He had come running up with the others but must have made himself scarce when the police arrived.

Maybe Parker had been too good a shot since the paramedics had abandoned their efforts to resuscitate the men. But if he hadn't killed them, he and Sharon would not have survived. But if at least one of the men had been only wounded, he might have been able to learn who had put out the hit.

"Looks like a wall of Wanted posters at the post office," Garek remarked as he gazed around at the bodies lying on the pavement.

"You recognize some of these guys?" Logan asked.

"What, you think all criminals know each other?" Garek asked.

"No," Logan said. "There are too many criminals. But how do you know these guys are wanted?"

Garek shrugged. "I recognize a couple of them."

"From their Wanted posters?" Logan persisted.

Garek shrugged again noncommittally. "I'm not sure that they're wanted anymore. But if they're out already, they must have gotten some light sentences for what they'd done."

Some people thought he and his brother had received light sentences for the crimes they had committed. Parker glanced around for Garek's brother, Milek. They were usually together, but Parker hadn't noticed the more laid-back Kozminski. Maybe he had been worrying about trusting the wrong Kozminski. He glanced back at the ambulance, where the paramedic shone a light in Sharon's eyes. Nikki and Cooper stood close to the ambulance doors, watching her.

He breathed a slight sigh of relief.

"Well, you know Judge Foster didn't give them the sentences if they were light," Logan mused.

And Parker considered what he'd said. Criminals often held grudges against judges, so he could understand if one of them had killed Brenda. But why go after her nanny and her ex-bodyguard?

"We have a connection in the district attorney's office," Garek said. "Milek can talk to his ex-girlfriend. Amber is an assistant D.A."

Logan shook his head. "No, you should do it," he said, as if he was protecting Milek from having to talk to his ex. It must have been a hell of a breakup. "You know who they are…."

"True," Garek said. "I'll see if Amber can look into their cases and find out how they've been paroled already."

Logan nodded his approval of his brother-in-law's suggestion. Then he turned his attention back to Parker. "Now let's get *you* checked out."

"I'm fine," he assured him again.

"You nearly shot me," Cooper said as he joined his brothers. "So you meant to do that?"

"He nearly shot me, too," Logan said. "It's not personal. He's jumpy."

"He jumped on me," Garek chimed in. "Knocked me down the stairs and bruised my ribs." He grunted as if he was still in pain.

Parker felt no pain. Only concern. "Get back to Sharon," he told Cooper. "If anything happens to her, I'll mean to shoot you next time."

"Sharon sent me to get you," Cooper said. "She wants you to get checked out, too. She's worried about you."

"See," Logan said. "She thinks you need medical attention, too."

Parker shook his head. "I'm more worried about her. That's why I wanted to talk to you alone, Logan." The others didn't take his hint; they stayed to listen to what he'd wanted to discuss with his twin. "I want you to take her and Ethan away from here."

"The city?" Logan asked.

Given the amount of the reward, getting out of the city wouldn't be enough. "The state. Maybe even the country."

Garek nodded his approval and added, "But be careful which country you choose. It could be more dangerous than staying here."

Was there any place safe for them? Any place they could go where there wouldn't be people willing to kill them for money?

He had to catch the person who had put out the hit so that everyone learned that they wouldn't be able to collect any longer. Brenda was the key; she had done or said something that had put him and Sharon in danger.

But what?

Sharon knew her best, so she would be able to help him figure it out faster than if he tried on his own. But he would rather try on his own than continue to put her at risk like he had tonight. Marrying her hadn't been the answer. It had only let the would-be assassins know where to find them.

But how had they heard about the wedding? Only family and closely trusted friends had been invited. Who had let the word out?

"We'll figure out later where you'll take her and Ethan—" And for their safety, only Logan would know....

"And Mom," Cooper added. "She's not about to let her first grandchild out of her sight."

Parker was glad that his mother had the baby right now. If Ethan had been in that car, too...

He shuddered to think about what might have happened to the baby during the crash and after, with all those gunshots. It was a miracle that he and Sharon hadn't been hurt worse.

Sharon...

He turned back to the ambulance. But it was driving away, lights flashing. *What's going on?*

Had she been hurt worse than he'd thought?

Or was it worse than that?

That paramedic had acted strangely when Logan had told him who she was. He had obviously recognized her name. Had he heard about the hit? Was he going to try to collect?

Parker sprinted after the ambulance as it sped away. His legs burned as he ran, and thanks to the traffic and other first-response vehicles blocking the street, the ambulance slowed. He managed to catch up. He reached for the handle of the back door and his fingertips brushed over the metal seconds before the ambulance driver hit the gas and sped off again. Maybe the driver hadn't seen him.

Or maybe he had....

He stopped, gasping for breath. Cooper and Logan caught up with him. "Damn you!" he cursed his younger brother. "You were supposed to stay with her."

"Nikki's with her," Cooper defended himself.

That didn't make him feel any better.

"We can't trust anyone right now," Parker reminded them.

"You can't trust your own sister?" Cooper asked.

"He can't trust the paramedic," Logan said. "That's why I wanted you to watch her and Nikki." He cursed, too.

And Cooper added his own string of curses as he got angry with himself.

Garek Kozminski just shook his head as his brother,

Milek, drove up next to them. That was where he must have been; he'd gone back to get a vehicle since they had all run from the church. "And people think *our* family is dysfunctional," Garek told his brother.

"Milek!" Parker greeted the other Kozminski as he hurried around to the passenger's side of the vehicle. "You need to take me to the hospital right now."

"You're hurt?" Milek asked, his gray eyes wide with concern.

Parker shrugged. He didn't know and didn't care. "No. I have to make sure that ambulance really takes my… wife to the hospital."

"And if it doesn't?" Milek asked.

Parker reached a hand out the open window. "Hand me a weapon," he ordered his brothers.

Logan shook his head. "You can't leave. The police want to take your statement."

"Pretend to be me," Parker said. It wouldn't have been the first time they had taken each other's places. It wouldn't have been the first time someone had mistaken Logan for being him; that mistake had recently nearly cost Logan his life, though. Parker didn't want to put him in danger again. "Forget that—just tell them I had to go to the hospital. They can take my statement there."

Unless that wasn't where the ambulance was taking Sharon and Nikki. If it wasn't, then Parker would be too busy tracking down the paramedic to give anyone his statement. He couldn't lose his bride now….

Chapter Fourteen

Fear had Sharon's heart pounding fast and hard. She couldn't move her arms. She couldn't move her legs. She was trapped with no way to move, no way to escape. The walls were so close and the space so confining that she could barely breathe.

Hysteria rose with the fear, choking her as sobs threatened. But she couldn't cry because she couldn't lift her hands to wipe away her tears. And she couldn't betray her weakness again.

She had to be strong.

"Not much longer," a disembodied voice murmured reassuringly, "Mrs. Payne."

She tensed at the unfamiliar name. But it was hers now; it was what she had signed on the marriage license next to Parker's name. Sharon Wells Payne.

She was married now to a man everyone, most especially him, had always said would never marry. She was married to a notorious playboy. While she had dated over the years, it hadn't been all that often and never seriously. What had she been thinking to agree to this marriage?

What if he wanted to consummate it?

"Mrs. Payne," the voice said again, "please try to

relax. We need you to hold still so we can get accurate images."

She sucked in a breath, but it was shallow despite the oxygen being pumped into the MRI machine. And she held that breath until, finally, the machine released her, sliding her back out into the bright lights and warmth of the radiology room.

"Are you all right?" a woman asked.

But it wasn't the voice she had heard through the speakers inside the machine; it was her new sister-in-law. She hadn't left her side since joining her in the back of the ambulance. She even walked beside Sharon now as a medical tech pushed her, on the stretcher, back to a curtained-off area in the Emergency Unit.

"That must have been so hard for you," Nikki commiserated, "being in that small space."

Sharon swallowed to clear her throat; she was more choked up over the woman's sincere sympathy than her own fear. "I'm fine."

"The MRI will tell us that," Nikki said. "That's why the doctor insisted on it."

"That was because the paramedic overreacted," Sharon said. He hadn't needed to rush off to the hospital with the sirens blaring and lights flashing.

"He's not the only one," a man remarked, as he walked around the curtain with Parker. It was one of the two blond men. They looked as alike as Parker and his twin, but she didn't think it was the one who had broken into the condo. This man didn't exude the cockiness the other one had. "Your husband has been tearing apart this hospital looking for you. And that was after he tore apart the paramedic."

"You did what?" Sharon asked. But Parker only stared

at her as if he had never seen her before or as if he had thought he might never see her again.

Nikki smacked her brother's arm. "You didn't hurt that cute paramedic, did you?"

"I—I…" He paused and cleared his throat as if he'd been choking on emotion. "I thought he might have been trying to collect the reward."

"You thought he was going to kill me?" Now she understood his stunned look.

Parker nodded. "He got rid of Cooper and then took off with you and Nikki. He didn't even stop when I was chasing the ambulance."

His sister laughed. "You hate ambulance chasers, and now you've become one."

Parker hated lawyers? Sharon felt a twinge of regret before she reminded herself that she was not a lawyer yet. If she didn't pass the bar, she would never be a lawyer. But at the moment, the bar was the least of her concerns.

"He tried," the Kozminski brother answered for him. "But the police were chasing him. They caught us before we could leave the crime scene."

She had been at the hospital awhile—long enough for a doctor to examine her and long enough that she'd gotten on the schedule for the MRI.

"Did they arrest you?" she asked.

He shook his head.

"They want your statement, too," the other man replied. He extended his hand to her. "I don't believe we've officially met yet. I'm Milek Kozminski. I am the nice Kozminski—unlike my brother, Garek."

She shook his hand. "It's nice to meet you. And it was nice to meet your brother, too." She had appreciated his brother's warning, not that anything could have prepared her for the ambush after her wedding.

The wedding...

She glanced around for the bag of her personal belongings. "Nikki, your mother's dress—what happened to it?"

"It's here," Nikki assured her as she lifted the plastic bag from the end of the stretcher. "And it's fine. Stop worrying about the dress."

"But I know I bled on it, and I probably tore it, too. I tried not to—"

"She nearly got shot trying to save that damn dress," Parker remarked.

She gasped at his callous disregard for his mother's memories. "But it's your mom's dress. It's part of her history with your father."

A history that had been cut tragically short. They hadn't even made it to their twenty-fifth anniversary. But they should have had a golden wedding anniversary—and a seventy-five-year celebration after that. Sharon knew not to wish for an anniversary for herself—not with Parker.

"Technically, it's most likely my dress now," Nikki said. "Since all the other Paynes are married, that leaves only me to wear this thing. And since I'm not getting married—ever—Mom will have plenty of time to fix it."

"Never say never," Milek advised as he patted Parker's shoulder.

He had said never, and yet his hand had been steady when he had signed the marriage license.

"Thanks for the ride to the hospital," Parker told the other man.

"Is that my cue to leave?" Milek asked. He had obviously realized Parker was dismissing him.

"I really do appreciate all you and Garek are doing

for us," Parker said. "Can you check in with him and see what he's found out from your friend Amber—"

"Amber is not my friend," Milek interrupted him, his mild-mannered personality chilling to ice. Whoever Amber was, she was definitely not his friend.

Parker sighed. "I'm sorry. Your ex—the assistant district attorney. Garek is going to ask her about those men."

"Did any of them survive?" Sharon asked. Now that they were no longer shooting at her, she didn't wish them dead.

But Parker shook his head.

Was he upset that he had killed? Had he ever done it before? He had been a police officer and a bodyguard, so he probably had.

"Dead men can't talk," Nikki remarked with a sigh of disappointment.

"Those kind of men don't talk when they're alive, either," Milek said with another pat on Parker's shoulder. He really was the nice Kozminski. "I'll check in with Garek and see if he's found out anything from—" he swallowed hard as if he struggled to even say her name "—Amber and I'll let you know...."

"He has my new cell number," Parker said.

The other man left with a nod.

"Are you going to get rid of me, too?" Nikki asked.

"Sharon is going to need a change of clothes," Parker said. "She won't want to wear that wedding gown again."

She had nearly been killed in it, but she had also married a handsome groom in it. She had looked beautiful—for probably the first time in her life. The good memories would outweigh the bad.

"They'll probably keep her overnight," Nikki said. "The doctor's worried about her MRI results."

Sharon wasn't worried. And moments later the doctor pulled aside the curtain to confirm that she was fine. She could leave. But where would she go?

Her honeymoon was already over….

PARKER CARRIED HER across the threshold. Finally. And he didn't have to step over crime-scene tape. This place damn well better not become a crime scene, either. He had been beyond careful when he'd driven back toward the lakefront. He had changed vehicles twice and taken a circuitous route. The threshold over which he carried Sharon wasn't to the penthouse condo but to a small cabin.

A honeymoon cabin.

But he didn't anticipate a wedding night. His bride was so exhausted that he had unbuckled and carried her into the cabin without her waking up. The cabin was all open and therefore easy to secure. The only room inside it was the tiny bathroom; through the open door, he could see that it was empty—no killers hiding in the glass shower.

He turned back toward the living area. The big four-poster bed dominated the space. He carried her over to it and laid her onto the quilted comforter. But her arms remained locked around his neck.

"Don't let me go," she murmured sleepily.

"I'm right here," he assured her.

But she tightened her grasp around his neck and pulled him down with her onto the bed. "I only feel safe when I'm in your arms."

He could understand why she would say that, but she was wrong. She wasn't safe with him—not with how much he wanted her, desire rushing through his veins. His heart pounded, and his skin heated. He needed her.

But he would only hurt her. So he gently tugged her arms loose and forced himself to step away from the bed, to step away from his bride.

She sat up, and her hair tumbled down around her shoulders. Those thick tresses tempted him to tangle his fingers up in that silk—to tip up her mouth for his hungry kisses.

His body tensed with need. But he ignored his needs and focused on her. "Go back to sleep. You must be exhausted."

She touched her fingers to the bandage on her forehead. Nikki had told him that Sharon had needed ten stitches to close the wound that she'd been so upset had bled on his mother's wedding gown.

She shook her head. "Not anymore. How long did I sleep?" She gazed around the cabin as if trying to figure out where he had brought her. Since she had slept most of the trip, she had no way of knowing.

"You didn't sleep long enough," he said. Because awake and tousled from her slumber, she was too damn sexy—even in the hospital-gift-shop T-shirt and pajama bottoms Nikki had bought her. She also looked too young and innocent for him.

He took another step away from the bed. But that damn cabin that he'd thought such a safe place to hide was too small for him to escape temptation. Her scent filled the space; she smelled like sunshine and rain. She was a paradox—like sexy innocence.

"Are you mad at me?" she asked, her voice shaking a bit as if she was afraid of him now.

He shook his head. "Absolutely not." He couldn't imagine being angry with her. "You're the one who should be angry with *me*."

"Why?" she asked with confusion.

"I promised I would protect you," he said. He closed his eyes and saw again that SUV crash into her side of the car—saw all the glass explode around her as the car rolled over and over across the asphalt. "And I failed you…."

Soft hands touched his face, drawing him out of that nightmare. She stood before him now, on tiptoe, so that her beautiful face was nearly level with his. "You didn't fail me," she said. "You saved my life." She leaned forward and brushed her lips over his. "You saved my life…."

He had tried to resist her. He had tried to control his desire. But she had come to him. So he kissed her back. He kissed her with all the passion and desire burning in his heart for her.

She wrapped her arms around his neck and clung to him, her feet off the floor. So he walked with her backward—toward the bed. Then he laid her down, and when she pulled him down with her, he didn't resist. He covered her body with his. And he never stopped kissing her.

She teased him with her tongue, sliding it over his lips. He sucked it into his mouth, and then he kissed her back that aggressively—driving his tongue inside her mouth.

She moaned and tugged at his shirt. He had lost his torn tuxedo jacket sometime ago. Now he pulled off his holster and dropped it and the gun next to the bed within reach. She was already working his buttons loose when he just pulled the pleated shirt over his head and dropped it onto the floor, too. Then he lifted her T-shirt and peeled it off.

Her hair tangled around her face and shoulders, and he smoothed the thick tresses with his hands. Beneath the plain T-shirt, she wore a strapless white lace bra through which he could see her nipples.

"You are so beautiful," he said in awe.

She shook her head. "You don't have to do that…."

"Do what?"

"Lie to me."

His pride was hurt. "You think I'm lying to you?"

She nodded.

"I have never been anything but honest with you," he insisted, "so when I tell you you're beautiful, I mean it."

Color flushed her face. He couldn't tell if she was pleased or embarrassed—until she kissed him again. She kept kissing him, even when he undid her bra and cupped her breasts in his hands.

Then she squirmed beneath him and moaned. She wanted him as badly as he wanted her. Her passion fueled his. He pulled away despite her clinging to him and unclasped and dropped his pants. Then he tugged off her pajama bottoms. A lace garter encircled one of her slim thighs. He'd been supposed to take that off earlier, so he did now. With his teeth. And he made sure his mouth skimmed over her silky skin as he pulled it down her leg.

Her breath shuddered out in a ragged sigh. "Parker…"

But she was wearing a G-string, too, which was all white lace. So he moved his mouth to that and slid his tongue beneath it. She squirmed again, and then she was clutching at him as he played with her with his lips and his breath and his tongue.

"Parker!" She screamed his name as she climaxed.

His body ached to join hers, so he parted her legs wider and thrust inside her. Then he tensed, worried that he'd been too rough. Emotionally, she was tougher than he'd thought, but physically, she'd been through so much, too. She was bruised and battered. Had he hurt her?

She moaned.

"Are you okay?" he asked. To him, she was perfect. But maybe he was too big for her—too much. He tried to pull back slightly, but she arched and lifted her legs, locking them around his waist.

She shifted, taking him deeper, and moaned again. "It feels—you feel—so good...."

He wanted her to feel better. He wanted her to feel more pleasure than she'd ever felt before. So he took his time, thrusting slowly and gently. And as he did, he played with her breasts, teasing the tense points of her nipples with his thumbs and his mouth. She drove her fingers into his hair and pulled his head up to hers. And kissed him.

And as she kissed him, she cried out with pleasure. And she peaked again. He joined her in ecstasy, groaning her name, as he filled her. But even as their racing hearts began to slow, he didn't release her; he kept her clutched tightly in his arms. He didn't want any space between them—he wanted her touching him everywhere.

"Are you okay?" he asked again, as he skimmed his fingertips lightly over the bandage on her forehead.

She chuckled. "I'm better than okay."

"I'm sorry," he said. "I shouldn't have taken advantage of you. You've already been through too much." And he should have been focused on protecting her. Instead he'd lost himself in pleasure—in her.

"You didn't take advantage," she assured him. "I—I wanted it, too...."

Why? Was she falling for him? Concern for her heart

clutched his heart. He didn't want to hurt her—like he'd hurt so many others.

He cared about her—more than he ever had cared about anyone else. Maybe he was even falling for her. But they were in too much danger to think about forever—to believe in happily ever after. And even when the danger passed, he couldn't give her the future she deserved—one without heartache and pain.

He didn't want her to fall for him, didn't want her to grieve for him someday like his mother had his father. But then, his mother had never regretted her life with his father; she had loved the years they'd had together, the family they had made together.

He and Sharon and Ethan were family. Could he really be a father? A husband?

Only if he survived....

Chapter Fifteen

Sharon's hand shook as she lifted her finger toward the security panel. She could do this….

The judge's body was gone. It had been transported days ago in the coroner's van to the morgue. Not that it would take an autopsy to determine what had killed her. Her neck had been brutally broken. She shuddered over the violent way her former employer had died.

A strong arm wrapped around her shoulders and the warmth of his body chased away the chill. As always, she felt safe in his arms. But she couldn't believe what they had done, that they had consummated their marriage. Maybe it had all just been a dream….

But he touched her now, comforting her. With the comfort came the memories, of how he had touched her all over. Goose bumps lifted on her skin, and she shivered. But she wasn't cold—not with his arm around her.

"You coming back here was a bad idea," he said. "You've already been through too much tonight."

"Last night," she corrected him, because the sun was already up. It had come up while they had been lying in bed together, still wrapped in each other's arms.

She would rather be here than back there, embarrassing herself more. She had thrown herself at him. He had caught her, but he was a playboy, so he would have caught any woman who had acted like she had.

"And you couldn't have come back here without me," she reminded him.

He shook his head. "I can now. Nikki shut down the security system."

Because there was no one to protect anymore….

He pushed open the gate. Crime-scene tape was strung around the estate and they stepped over it.

"Even though you could have gotten inside without me, you wouldn't know where to look," she pointed out.

"Look for what?" he asked.

She shrugged. "Whatever someone else was looking for the night Brenda was killed." If only she knew what that was…

"Someone was looking for something at the bodyguard's apartment, too," Parker said. And he shuddered. That crime scene must have been gruesome, too.

She was glad she hadn't been with him then. But she wished she hadn't been in the interrogation room, either, with Detective Sharpe.

"They must have been looking for whatever he was supposed to have taken from Brenda's," she surmised. "You think he killed her?"

He nodded. "She scratched his hands and arms."

Brenda would have fought. She had been a fighter; it was one of the things Sharon had admired most about her.

"You said her laptop was missing," he remembered. "I didn't see it at the bodyguard's place, either."

"Books were ripped apart," she said as they stepped inside the house again. She shivered. Maybe it was just because nobody had turned off the central air yet, but it was colder inside the house than it had been outside. "They weren't looking for her laptop in a book."

Parker nodded. "True. And everything was torn apart at her bodyguard's apartment—even the pillows from his couch. So what were they looking for?"

"Flash drive," Sharon replied. "Brenda didn't trust computers." She really didn't trust anyone, thus her need for bodyguards. But then, her murder proved she hadn't been paranoid; she'd been right—especially since Parker believed it was her bodyguard who had killed her. "She constantly backed up her work."

"Work?" he asked. "Are you talking about her court cases or that book she was writing?"

"She wasn't working in the courts," she reminded him. "She had taken her leave to work on the book. When she asked me to proofread it, Chuck was here."

"That's why someone would think that you might know what's in her book. Do you have any idea what was in it?" Parker asked.

"I never got the chance to proofread it," Sharon replied. "I only know what you know about her. I don't know what else she might have written about." Sharon had been envious of the life the older woman had led, of the successes she'd had. But she wouldn't have killed her over it. "Who would have killed her over her own life?"

Parker shrugged those broad shoulders that just hours ago Sharon had clutched as their bodies joined together. She had never felt such pleasure, had never felt so special. But that was just because Parker was an excellent lover; he was notorious for his skills. He had made her feel special, but she doubted it had been special to him.

He didn't love her, but despite thinking she would be immune to his excessive charms, she had foolishly fallen for him. She loved her groom—her husband. And that was why she had insisted on coming back to the judge's house. Parker was doing his part to make them safe; she had to do hers.

"Maybe she wasn't writing about just her life," Parker remarked. "Maybe she was including other people's lives—lives that had either impacted or had intersected hers."

Sharon shrugged. She couldn't see Brenda writing about someone else.

"I know she was self-involved," Parker said, as if he'd read her mind. "Boy, do I know she was self-involved. I still can't believe she didn't tell me about Ethan—that she used me."

"She chose you," Sharon told him. "She respected you. She thought you were a good man." And a good-looking one, too. "That you had integrity and intelligence and charisma." Brenda wasn't the only one who could see all those special qualities in Parker Payne.

But he shrugged off her compliments as if he didn't believe her.

The night before, he had forced her to accept his compliments, so she pressed him. "It's true. You are all those things." And so much more.

"I doubt Brenda wrote about me," he said. "Good things wouldn't drive someone to commit murder. She must have written bad things about someone to make herself look better."

That was something that Brenda would have done.

Following his logic, Sharon added, "Maybe she revealed some secrets she knew."

"Some secrets someone doesn't want revealed."

Sharon checked the usual places Brenda would have

stashed a flash drive. Her desk drawer. The pockets in her empty laptop bag. But someone else had already checked those. And Brenda had been too smart to hide a flash drive someplace where someone would have found it.

So Sharon searched the unusual places—the dirt in the plants and the trim around the doorjambs. Parker followed her lead, but they came up empty-handed.

"What do we do now?" she asked. "If someone had already found it, they wouldn't still be trying to kill us—would they?"

Parker shrugged. "They might if they think we know what's on it. Chuck heard her asking you to proofread the book."

"He also heard her telling me to take Ethan and hide for two weeks and that if I hadn't heard from her to bring you…" Her face flushed with embarrassment for Brenda. But she needed to tell him everything.

"To bring me Ethan," he finished for her.

"She didn't call him by his name," she admitted. "She told me to trust only you—no one else—and to bring you the *package*."

He cursed. "She called my son a package?"

She sighed; she didn't want to speak ill of a dead woman. "Brenda wasn't particularly maternal. I knew what she meant, but Chuck might have been confused."

"He might have thought you were bringing me something else," he said. "Like the flash drive. And that was probably what he'd told whoever had tortured him before he died."

She gasped in horror. "He was tortured?"

He nodded. "He must not have wanted to put you in danger." He touched her face. "I don't blame him for wanting to protect you."

That was why he had married her. "But I don't have the flash drive," she said. "She didn't give me anything to give—"

He held up his hand, silencing her as he reached for his weapon. Then she heard it, too—the knob turning and the front door opening…

Someone had either come to search the mansion again or they had followed them here to kill them.

"Returning to the scene of the crime again," a cocky voice remarked as Detective Sharpe stepped inside the den. The rookie cop was close to his side, like a dog on a short leash. Both of them held their weapons, both barrels pointed at him.

Parker didn't reholster his weapon. Not yet. His heartbeat hadn't slowed even after he had identified the intruders. In fact, it had quickened. He moved forward slightly, trying to step between Sharon and the questionable lawmen.

"What about you?" Parker asked. "Why are you here, Sharpe?"

"I have someone watching the place."

It was pretty obvious who that someone was—his nervous sidekick. "Why?"

Sharpe waved his free arm to indicate Parker and Sharon.

"You were looking for us?" And Parker's heartbeat quickened even more.

Sharon's breath audibly caught, too. She didn't trust the detective any more than he did. "Why were you looking for us?" she asked.

"You didn't give your statement about the accident last night, Ms. Wells," Sharpe said.

Parker snorted. "That was no accident. That was an attempt on our lives."

"Yet the two of you are alive and four other men are in the morgue," Sharpe said. "Seems like wherever the two of you go, people die."

Maybe the detective should have taken that as a warning because Parker didn't dare lower his weapon yet, not when both of theirs were still raised.

"Those men tried to kill us," Sharon said. "Parker saved my life." She drew in a deep breath and added, "And it's no longer Ms. Wells. It's Mrs. Payne."

The detective chuckled, but he didn't seem particularly surprised. "I guess I owe you both congratulations." He focused on Parker again. "Especially you," he said, "since now that you've married her, she doesn't have to testify against you. She can invoke spousal privilege."

"You can't hold him responsible for what happened last night," Sharon defended him. "Those men were going to kill us."

"Or so you claim," the detective replied with that snide smile Parker wanted so badly to wipe off the man's pasty face.

"I claimed it, too," Parker said, "when I gave my statement to the officers who were at the crime scene last night. They believed me. They had already talked to witnesses who had either been on the road or in the houses by the scene."

Sharpe shrugged. "Those officers know you," he said. "They worked with you or your brother or your father, so they want to believe what you're telling them."

"They're good cops—honest cops," Parker defended the men. He couldn't say the same about Sharpe and his sidekick.

"The feds sent an agent to investigate the River City P.D.," Sharpe shared. "To make sure there is no more corruption than your father's partner."

Parker narrowed his eyes and studied the men. They were obviously nervous about that fed's arrival. "My father's partner had been retired for many years. His conduct—long in the past—wouldn't have triggered an internal-affairs investigation, let alone a federal investigation. What the hell's going on in the department?"

And who had reported it? Judge Brenda Foster? Maybe she had sent that flash drive to someone in the bureau or the Justice Department. Was that what she had been writing about—police corruption?

Sharpe shrugged but didn't lower his gun. "Maybe they're investigating you."

Parker snorted again. "I'm no longer with the department."

"But you and your brother still have friends there—too many friends that might look in the other direction and cover for you," Sharpe said. "That's why I wanted to speak to you myself."

"Why not call me down to the station?" Parker asked. "Or go by the offices of Payne Protection to find me? Why track me down here?"

"I figured you would come back," Sharpe said, "to the scene of perhaps your first crime…."

"Criminals really don't return to the scenes of their crimes." Sharon spoke now. "I've studied enough court cases to know that's not true." She narrowed her big eyes and glared at the detective. "*You* know we're not criminals."

Almost too casually Sharpe asked, "Then why did you come back here?"

The guy was such an idiot that he thought everyone was as stupid as he was. But Parker had had enough of the games, so he answered honestly. "I expect for the same reason that the two of you showed up here."

"What reason are you talking about?" Sharpe asked, the snide smile slipping away to reveal his obvious nerves as sweat beaded above his upper lip.

"You're looking for the judge's flash drive," Parker replied.

The rookie glanced up at Sharpe, who betrayed himself with a widening of his eyes. Sharon had been right about the judge backing up her book on a flash drive, and that drive was exactly what someone was looking for.

He just hadn't expected that someone to be Detective Sharpe. What secrets could that kid have to hide? His incompetence? His ignorance? Those secrets had come out the minute he had opened his cocky mouth. But was there something else? Something he was worried that the fed might uncover in his investigation?

But even if the judge had dirt on Sharpe, the young detective didn't have enough money to offer the reward that had been offered for Parker's and Sharon's murders. He was the son of a single mother, who was the chief of police's younger sister—not heir to millions like Sharon.

"What flash drive?" Sharpe asked. "I don't know what you're talking about…"

Parker chuckled. "You know exactly what I'm talking about. I can see it on both your faces. Too bad I never played poker with either of you. I feel like I could have made some money off you." He turned toward the younger cop, who was obviously more nervous as his gun began to shake. "Is that what you're getting out of this? Money?

Were you supposed to kill me the other night—at the bodyguard's apartment?"

The kid shook his head, but his face flushed a bright red, revealing his guilt.

"Could you have done it?" Parker wondered. "If my brother hadn't shown up, could you have pulled the trigger?"

Maybe he did it to prove a point or maybe because Parker had scared him too much, but the kid squeezed the trigger now. And a shot rang out....

SHARON FLINCHED. But no bullet struck her. Then she turned toward Parker, and he stood straight yet. There was no blood spreading across his white shirt. "Did he hit you?"

Parker shook his head. "Guess I shouldn't have worried about you hitting me the other night."

Sharpe snorted his disgust. "Obviously you don't have to worry about him, but I'm a much better shot."

Or he was actually a killer, and the rookie hadn't been able to bring himself to actually kill. That was why he had missed. Not out of incompetence but decency. At least she hoped he had some decency. She had no such hopes for Sharpe.

Scared that he was about to pull the trigger now, Sharon screamed. "Wait!"

The detective paused and focused on her, waiting for her argument. She had hated the mock trials in law school. Put on the spot, she had always choked. Maybe that was why she hadn't passed the bar; anytime the pressure was on, she failed. Except for last night...

She had cut Parker out of his seat belt and helped him escape the wreckage. But the bravest thing she'd probably ever done had been making love with him and falling in love with him. And because she loved him, she would do anything to protect him. "Don't you know that Brenda always made several backup copies? I'm sure her lawyer received one upon her death."

Sharpe shook his head. "I already talked to her lawyer. How do you think I found out about you getting guardianship of her kid?"

"You looked that thoroughly for her flash drive," Parker remarked.

And she knew what he was thinking. If Sharpe had looked that hard, he would have found it—if it were to be found.

"You wasted your time," Sharon said.

"You just said she backed up everything," Sharpe reminded her.

"Yes, but if she only made one flash drive, I already have it." It was obviously what everyone thought, or there wouldn't have been a reward for her murder.

"Give it to me, then," Sharpe ordered, and he turned the gun on her.

As she stared down the barrel of his weapon, she swallowed her nerves and continued her bluff. "I have given that flash drive to someone else," she said.

"Who has it?"

"Logan has it," Parker answered for her. "And if anything happens to either of us, he'll open it."

Sharpe laughed. "Nice try. You wouldn't have been here looking for the flash drive if you actually had it."

"If we don't have it," Parker said, "why has someone put out the hit on us?"

Parker had flustered the young officer again because he kept glancing from Parker to the detective as if he didn't know whom to believe or whom to trust. Sharon tried to catch the kid's attention, so that she could silently implore him to help them. But like most of the men she'd met, he never looked her way.

Sharpe shrugged. "Maybe because they think you know something about the book she was writing."

Sharon exchanged a quick glance with Parker. She had been right; it was all about the book. She nodded. "Of course I know about the book," she replied. "Brenda asked me to proofread it."

"So you read it?"

She hesitated because she had never been able to lie. But she could stall. "She's not done with it yet." And if that were true, it would never be finished now. "She started it on her maternity leave and just took vacation to complete it."

"Have you read it?" he repeated.

"Not all of it," Sharon lied. Not any of it. "But I had the flash drive, so of course I looked at it."

"What is the book about?" Sharpe asked.

"It's Brenda's memoir," she replied. "It's about her life… and the people who've crossed her path over the years."

"Which people is it about?"

She hesitated again. *Should she say cops or criminals?*

She glanced to Parker, but he only shook his head.

And Sharpe cursed. "You don't know a damn thing. You haven't read the book. So you don't have the flash drive, either—that's why you're here now. You're looking for it, too."

"Wh-what do we do now?" the young officer asked in a nervous stammer.

"I kill her and you kill him," Sharpe replied just before he pulled the trigger.

Sharon flinched again—waiting for the flash of pain, waiting for death…

There was no time—no time to tell Parker that she loved him.

Chapter Sixteen

While Sharpe had pulled the trigger, he hadn't done it as quickly as Parker had. The detective dropped to the floor. And instead of Sharon screaming, the young officer screamed and tried to steady his gun to fire.

Instead of shooting him, Parker just leaped forward and knocked the kid to the floor beside the detective. The kid screamed again and lost his grip completely on his weapon. Parker pulled it from his grasp and handed it to Sharon. He trusted her more with the gun than he did the kid.

She also bent down and retrieved the detective's weapon. She hadn't needed to worry about it. He was dead. But if Parker hadn't shot to kill, Sharpe might have struck Sharon with his bullet. Instead it had fired into the floor when Parker had dropped the detective.

"I—I thought he shot me," she murmured. And she was trembling but only slightly. She was tough. And smart. Her bluffing had bought them some time.

"Are you all right?" he asked.

"Yes, I'm fine," she said. "He didn't hit me."

Parker knew a bullet hadn't hit her. But she had to have been shaken by how close she had come to getting shot.

"Are you okay?" she asked.

"No, I'm mad as hell," he said. "I'm sick of getting shot at." The kid squirmed beneath him, and Parker tightened his grasp. The kid began to sob, his tears wetting the sleeve of Parker's shirt, as he held his arm beneath the young cop's chin. "Tell me who's behind the hits on me and Sharon."

He shook his head, or tried to, but Parker kept the pressure against his jaw. "Sharpe told me I had to help him, that I had to…"

"Kill me?" Parker asked.

He tried to nod.

But Sharpe had no reason to kill him—unless he had just needed the money. "Who was paying Sharpe?"

The tears kept coming, and the kid just shook his head. "I don't know. I don't know…."

Parker believed him. The rookie officer wasn't going to be able to help them find out who was behind the hits. So Parker eased back a little, still keeping the kid on the ground. Then he took out his cell phone but hesitated before punching in 911. Could he trust them?

But he had no choice. He wanted the young officer arrested. Maybe the kid would reveal more to authorities than he had revealed to Parker. But he doubted that the young man knew anything else. So he punched in the numbers and said, "I want to report a—"

Before he could get out the words, the door burst open and armed officers rushed into the mansion. Sharon held the guns. "Drop them," he told her, just as a bald-headed officer did the same.

They might use her holding the guns as an excuse to shoot her. She bent over and dropped them onto the ground next to the detective's body.

"On the ground! On the ground!" An officer shouted out the order.

Parker dropped onto the floor, too, and Sharon lay down next to him.

"Hands behind your heads!"

He locked his fingers behind his head, and Sharon followed his example. But maybe he shouldn't have obeyed any of the commands. No matter how many officers had rushed the house, maybe he should have tried to fight them. Because now he was down, and helpless to protect Sharon and himself....

And if these cops were as dirty as Sharpe and the rookie, they were dead for certain—execution-style....

ON THE OTHER side of the bars, Logan shook his head. "I always knew it would come to this someday," he said. "I knew I'd wind up bailing you out of jail."

Parker glared at him. "If you bailed me out, why haven't they let me out yet?" He rattled the bars.

"I paid the bail," Logan insisted. "So you better show up to court."

"For what charges?" Parker scoffed. "Defending myself? Sharpe was going to kill Sharon."

"Then it wasn't self-defense," a deep voice remarked.

Parker and Logan both turned toward the person who walked down the aisle between the holding cells. In the dim light, he looked like Cooper, but his hair must have grown out some. Had he bailed out Parker, too?

"It wasn't self-defense," Logan agreed. "It was defense of another person. He was protecting his wife."

"A court will determine that," the other man said.

It wasn't Cooper. His hair couldn't have grown out that much. But he had the exact same blue eyes, the exact same features, and he was probably about Cooper's age. Maybe younger because he didn't have as many fine lines on his face but a deep furrow between his dark brows.

"You're not Cooper," Logan said, and his eyes widened with shock. He must have done the math, too. If this man was younger than Cooper but obviously a Payne…

"Who the hell are you?" Parker asked. He hoped a figment of his imagination. This guy couldn't be real. It wasn't possible…. He reached through the bars and pinched Logan to see if this was real.

And Logan yelped and glared at him. "What's wrong with you?" But from the look of shock on his face, the same thing was wrong with him. He was as floored as Parker was.

But just because the man looked like them didn't mean that he was really related to them. The theory was that everybody had a twin in the world; of course, Parker already had one. So who was this guy?

Ignoring their interaction, the man replied, "Federal agent Rus."

"Russ?" Parker asked. "Don't you have a last name?"

"Rus is my last name," the agent replied. "Nicholas is my first name."

Their father's name…

The guy couldn't look that much like him and Logan and Cooper and not be a Payne. But their father had been an only child. So this guy couldn't be a cousin. Then that made him evidence of something Parker would have never believed: his father's betrayal. He couldn't deal with that right now—not with everything else going on in his life. Not with his life and Sharon's being in imminent danger.

"Who the hell are you?" Parker repeated.

"I'm here to investigate the River City Police Department," he said. "I'm acting as IA." Internal Affairs.

"Then you should know that Sharpe was dirty," Parker replied. "If I hadn't killed him, he would have killed me and my wife."

"As I said, a court will determine that, Mr. Payne."

"So you're not dismissing the charges?" he asked, incredulous. "That rookie cop was bawling his eyes out and announcing his guilt to everyone who would listen." That was why he was surprised that he and Sharon had even been arrested and booked. There should have been no charges. "*You* wanted us arrested," he realized.

"There can be no appearance of favoritism just because you're a Payne."

"Are *you?*" Logan asked, his voice gruff with dread and outrage. He had obviously come to the same realization that Parker had: their father had betrayed their mother. Their mother, who had loved and mourned the man for so many years…

"My name is Agent Rus," the man repeated.

"But are you our father's biological son?" Logan persisted.

The man shrugged. "I don't know. And I don't care. It doesn't make any difference to me."

But Parker suspected that Agent Rus cared very much and had made this persecution personal. He probably resented the hell out of his father's legitimate children. Pain grasped and twisted his heart.

How could his father have done this to their mother? It would destroy her to learn of his betrayal.

"I paid my brother's bail," Logan said. "Why haven't you released him?"

"I wanted to talk to you first."

"You wanted to rub it in our faces," Logan remarked, his usual cool composure slipping.

"Rub what in your faces?"

The fact that their father had not been the man they had always believed he'd been. How could he have betrayed his loving and loyal wife?

Parker was glad now that he hadn't confessed his feelings to Sharon. Knowing what he knew now about the man he had spent his whole life idolizing and respecting, he had proof that he couldn't be a good husband or father—not when Nicholas Payne had failed at it.

Sharon deserved better than him. She deserved better than a Payne.

SHARON HAD THOUGHT she'd met all the Paynes. And they had all been so nice. But this man—despite looking so much like Parker—was nothing like him. He wasn't warm and protective. He was accusatory and cold.

"Who are you?" she asked, confusion muddling her mind. She wrapped her fingers around the bars, gripping them. "I don't know you…."

All the Paynes had been so warm and welcoming to her. This man's eyes—the same sparkling blue as the rest of the Payne males—were icy. He looked about Cooper's age, but his hair was longer and his face meaner.

"My name is Nicholas Rus," he replied. "I'm a federal agent on loan to the River City Police Department."

He was the man that Sharpe and the young officer had mentioned—the one sent to clean up the police department and flush out the corrupt cops.

She breathed a sigh of relief. "That's good. You know, then, that Sharpe was a killer."

"Who did he kill?" he asked.

"Well, I don't know for certain but maybe Brenda Foster's bodyguard." She gripped the bars more tightly to still her sudden trembling. "And he would have killed me if Parker hadn't shot him first."

"Parker Payne has shot a lot of men over the past couple of days," the agent remarked as if making a casual observation. But there was suspicion in his blue eyes.

"Men who were trying to kill us," she said in defense of her husband.

"The convicts, maybe," he said with a nod of agreement, "but a detective and an officer…?"

"Sharpe was a criminal, too," she said. "And so is that young officer." The kid wasn't dead. In fact, he had confessed his involvement and Sharpe's guilt to the other officers who had arrived at the scene.

"Isn't that why you're here?" she asked. "To investigate the police department?"

He shrugged his shoulders, which were as broad as Parker's. He looked exactly like a Payne. Who was he really? Was it Cooper or Logan playing some game with her?

Could she trust anyone anymore? She couldn't trust the police—Detective Sharpe had proved that to her. And this man made her wonder if she dared to trust a Payne. How could he look so much like them but act as cold as a stranger?

"I'm here to ask you some questions," he said.

"I've already been questioned." And then she had been booked and charged on suspicion of everything—murder, manslaughter, interfering in a police investigation. Would she ever get out? Would she ever see Ethan again?

Her arms ached to hold her little man. But he was not the only one her arms ached to hold….

She shouldn't have insisted she and Parker go back to the judge's house this morning. She should have stayed in bed with her husband, in his arms...

She had been afraid then of falling in love with him and embarrassing herself. But she'd already learned twenty years ago that there were far worse things than embarrassment. There was death. And she and Parker had barely survived this latest attempt on their lives.

"I'm here to ask you about the flash drive that Brenda Foster gave you," the agent continued.

She had been right not to trust him. All anyone cared about was that damn flash drive. "If Brenda gave me a flash drive, it's been destroyed."

But *had* it been destroyed? If Brenda had given her a flash drive, she would have put it where she thought Sharon would find it. And suddenly she knew exactly where it was. Brenda hadn't just referred to Ethan as a package; she'd included his things.

The man tensed. "What do you mean?"

She couldn't trust him with the truth, especially not when she might endanger more innocent people. And no one was more innocent than Ethan and Mrs. Payne.

"It would have been in my things," she said, "my things that blew up in the hospital parking lot after someone detonated a bomb in my car." But there was one thing she'd had with her in the hospital—one thing that hadn't blown up. It had to be there....

He nodded, as if he remembered hearing about it. Or maybe he remembered setting that damn bomb. "So there's no way of knowing what the judge actually wrote—what might have been on her laptop or the mysterious flash drive?"

Sharon shook her head. "I don't know. She asked me

to proofread it when she was done, but then she sent me away to hide with her son. And I never saw any of her book." She glared at the man. "So nobody has any reason to try to kill me or Parker Payne."

The man's mouth curved into a very slight smile, which would have been unnoticeable except for the faint warming of his eyes. "I'm not here to kill you, Ms. Wells. I'm here to release you. Someone's paid your bail."

Parker. Or his family. They hadn't forgotten about her. But she didn't see any of them when the holding-cell doors slid open. Instead, she saw an older man waiting for her in the hallway. The agent walked away without another glance at her or at the stranger who had paid her bail.

"Sharon," the older man greeted her. "It is so wonderful to see you again."

Again? When had she seen him last? She cocked her head, trying to place the man with the iron-gray hair and dark eyes.

"The last time I saw you was at your grandfather's funeral. I am—I was—a friend of his as well as a colleague." He extended his hand. "Judge Albert Munson."

She nodded. "Of course. It's great to see you again." Heat rose to her face with embarrassment that she'd been arrested. Her grandfather would have been mortified. "Well, maybe not under these circumstances."

"And I expect I'll see you soon at another funeral," he said. "Brenda Foster was also a colleague of mine as well as your employer," he explained. "Your grandfather should have asked me to hire you as a law clerk. You would have been safer working for me."

But then she never would have met Ethan and fallen in love with the little man and with his father. "I learned a lot from working for Brenda," Sharon said. A lot about how to love and what was important.

Family. Even though that family wasn't hers….

"But thank you for posting my bail," she said. "I will repay you as soon as I can get to a bank. I lost my ATM card and checkbook when my car was destroyed."

But maybe she hadn't lost what everyone was looking for—well, nearly everyone….

He nodded. "I have heard about the troubles you've been having."

Well, that was obvious. How else would he have known she was at the police station? He appeared to be nearly as old as her grandfather. Was he still on the bench?

She hadn't paid much attention to any judges except Brenda since she'd started working for her. "It'll all be over soon," she assured him. "I just need to speak to my husband."

She started out of the holding-cell area, toward what she assumed was the lobby, but the judge caught up with her and grasped her arm. Despite his age, his grip was surprisingly strong—almost painfully so.

"He hasn't been released," the judge said.

"Well, then I'll wait for him," she said. "I'm sure his family has paid his bail." He would have called them, or someone in the police department would have called his brother Logan for him. There were people they couldn't trust in the department—like Agent Rus—but there were also people who knew and respected the Payne family.

"How do you know it will all be over soon?" he asked.

She turned back and noticed the desperation in his dark eyes. And she realized whose secrets Brenda had been going to reveal in her book….

She shook her head. "I don't know…."

"You're lying," he accused her. "Don't perjure yourself, Sharon."

And then she felt it. Not only was he grasping her arm, but he was also pushing a gun into her side. She recognized the coldness of the metal barrel.

How had he gotten it inside the police department?

She glanced around, looking for help. But the agent who looked so much like Parker and his brothers was gone. The only person standing around was a young officer who opened a door for the judge—a door to a back alley. That was obviously how the judge had gotten the gun inside—with this officer's assistance.

"Help me," Sharon implored him as the judge pulled her into that alley.

But the officer just lowered his head and stared down, uncaring that he was probably sending her to her death. She had been bailed out, not ordered to be executed. Why wouldn't he help her?

"You're behind everything," she said. "You're the one who put out the hit on me and Parker."

"Maybe I should have let you wait for your husband," the judge replied. "Then I could have killed you both—together."

"Parker doesn't know anything," Sharon said. "He's never seen the flash drive."

"But you know…."

"I just figured it out now," she said. "Brenda never showed me any of her book. How did you even know she was writing it?" Brenda had been too smart to announce her intentions to the dirty judge.

Munson chuckled. "As you know, she treated employees like dirt. So her bodyguard had no reason to be loyal to her."

Parker would have been. She never should have fired him. But if she hadn't, Ethan wouldn't have been born, and Sharon couldn't imagine a world without him. Or without Parker…

"Chuck told you?"

The judge nodded. "He saw some of her research and offered me the information for a price."

"And you had him kill her and steal the laptop," she realized. "But then you had him killed, too."

"Before he died, he admitted that you were going to proofread the book for her," he said. "And he also revealed—under duress—that you were supposed to bring a *package* to Parker Payne if you hadn't heard from the judge. Horowitz had a soft spot for you, Ms. Wells. He didn't want to put you in danger."

The bodyguard had looked at her as everyone else who knew about her mother had—with pity.

"I used to, as well," the judge admitted. "You went through a lot as a child and then you had to put up with His Honorable Judge Wells."

She shivered at the coldness in the judge's voice and from the memory of her grandfather's coldness.

"But my soft spot hardened," Albert Munson continued, "when I learned that you know too much."

She shook her head. "I haven't seen the book. I haven't even looked at the flash drive."

"But you know where it is."

She sighed and nodded. Then he opened the passenger's door and shoved her inside the car. As he went around the hood to the driver's door, she tried her handle, but it was locked.

The judge glanced back toward the police department, as if considering. Then he opened the driver's door and slid behind the steering wheel. "Parker Payne really doesn't know anything about the flash drive or the book?"

"He thinks Sharpe was behind everything," she lied. She wasn't a good liar, but she was getting better at it since she was doing it to protect the people she loved.

Parker already knew that Sharpe hadn't had the money to offer the outrageous reward the judge had. But how had Judge Munson had so much money? she wondered. Her grandfather had been well-off, but most of that had been his and his wife's family money. Not just what he had earned as a judge and a law professor.

"Then Payne isn't as smart as Brenda thought he was," Munson remarked. "Your grandfather would have been disappointed that you married beneath you."

"My grandfather was always disappointed in me," she replied. But she didn't care what he thought anymore—which was amazing because even after he'd died, she had been trying to please him. That was why she had tried to become a lawyer. For him. But she didn't care about the past anymore.

She cared about the future. The future for Ethan and Parker. She needed to protect them…even though it was probably going to cost her her life….

Chapter Seventeen

Anger coursed through Parker's veins, making his blood pump fast and hard. He wasn't mad about the federal agent or even about being arrested, though. He would deal with all that later. Right now he was worried about his wife. "Where the hell is she?"

He couldn't protect her if she wasn't with him. And God knew they both needed protection—even in the police department. He had finally been released from the holding cells, but now he paced the lobby, refusing to leave until they released his wife, too.

Logan shrugged. "I've asked…."

But nobody had answered his or Parker's insistent questions. At least the desk sergeant hadn't and neither had the officers milling around. So he walked up to the desk again. "I want to talk to Agent Rus."

Behind him, Logan cursed. He obviously hadn't wanted to see the agent again. Maybe, like Parker, he wanted to forget that Nicholas Rus even existed. Apparently their father must have because he had died fifteen years ago without ever mentioning that he had another son, one around Cooper's age.

"I can't believe I am willingly walking into a police station," a male voice remarked.

And a female laugh rewarded his witty remark.

Parker understood why Logan had cursed when he turned around. Logan was rushing up to their mother, whom Garek Kozminski was escorting into the lobby.

"But then, you know I would do anything for you, Mrs. Payne," Kozminski told her, oozing his usual smarmy charm.

And *Parker* was the playboy?

He was a happily married man. Or he would be when he knew where on earth his wife was.

He was happy? Images flashed through his mind—images of him and Sharon making love—and he realized he had never been happier or more connected to another human being. Not even his son.

"Where's Ethan?" was his first question for their mother, though.

"Cooper and Tanya are watching him," she replied. Then her eyes widened with surprise as she peered over Parker's shoulder. "Or so I thought...."

"You asked to see me," a deep voice said from behind Parker.

He flinched. Even his mother had mistaken the agent for one of her sons. There was no way she wouldn't realize who he was.

She gasped. "You're not Cooper...."

"How the hell many Paynes are there?" Garek remarked. Logan punched his shoulder in reply.

Parker wanted to wrap his arms around her—wanted to protect his mother like he wanted to protect his wife. But she pushed him aside so that she stood in front of the agent. Then she reached up and cupped his face in her hands just as she always did her children.

But this man wasn't her child....

Didn't she realize that?

"You're Carla's son, aren't you?" she asked.

He didn't pull away from her touch even as he nodded. "You knew...?"

"I knew about your mother," she said. "I didn't know about you until right now." Tears overflowed her warm brown eyes, rolling down her cheeks.

Parker wanted to wipe them away. But before either he or Logan or even Garek Kozminski could reach for her, Nicholas Rus closed his arms around her. Then, his deep voice gruff with emotion he hadn't yet revealed himself capable of feeling or showing, he said, "I'm sorry...."

"You have no reason to be sorry," she said, as she closed her arms around him and hugged him.

"I should have done something so you wouldn't have been so surprised." He pulled away from her, evidently embarrassed by what Parker suspected was an uncharacteristic display of sentiment. "I should have warned you...."

To his credit, Agent Rus probably hadn't counted on her showing up at the police department. Neither had Parker.

"You don't need to be here," Parker told his mother. "I've already been bailed out. I'm just waiting to find out why Sharon hasn't been released."

"She has been released," Rus replied.

"But I haven't been able to pay her bail," Parker said. "Did you dismiss the charges?" He didn't care about himself; he cared only about Sharon. She hadn't even pulled the trigger; he had.

Rus shook his head. "Not yet, but I am working on it."

Did that mean he believed them? That they had only acted in self-defense?

"Then how did she get released?"

"Someone else paid her bail," Rus replied in a slightly patronizing tone.

But the agent didn't know that Sharon Wells had no one. Her family was gone, and the one person who may have been her friend had been brutally murdered.

"Who?" Parker asked.

"Judge Albert Munson," Rus replied. "He said he was a friend of her grandfather's."

"Al is a friend of mine, too," Mrs. Payne remarked. "He's the judge who helps me get the marriage licenses issued without the waiting period."

Panic clutched Parker's heart. "Did he issue mine and Sharon's?"

She smiled and nodded. "Of course. He was very happy to do it, too."

No doubt he had been because then he had known when and where they were getting married, and he had been able to set up the ambush that had very nearly killed them.

"Good ole Judge Albert is everyone's friend," Garek chimed in, "especially criminals'. The assistant D.A. informed me that Munson is the judge who either threw out or reduced the sentences of those guys Parker took care of and quite a few more...."

So there were more criminals out there with a debt owed to the judge. Or had they already paid him? Was that what Brenda had had on him—what she'd written about in her missing manuscript?

"Where is she?" Parker asked. "Where did she go after you released her?"

Rus shrugged. "When I left, she was talking to the judge. She was thanking him for bailing her out."

He was a friend of her grandfather's. She probably would have left with him without ever realizing the threat he posed. But why would she have left without Parker?

Hadn't last night meant anything to her? Maybe he shouldn't have been so concerned about her falling for him. Apparently she hadn't even cared enough to stick around to make sure he got bailed out.

But it didn't matter whether or not she loved him. He loved her. And he was going to damn well make certain nothing happened to her.

"Give me the keys to your car," he ordered Logan. His hand shook slightly as he held it out.

"You don't know where she is," Logan pointed out.

"I'll find her," Parker said.

"It's not safe for you to be running around out there alone," Logan said as he held on tightly to his ring of keys. "I'll drive you."

Logan wouldn't drive like Parker would—with the urgency necessary to find his wife before the judge hurt her. "You can ride along with me," he offered, his hand still held open between them, "but I drive."

The second Logan reluctantly handed over the keys, Parker was gone. He didn't have a minute to lose. He had to find his bride....

PARKER WOULD HAVE no place to look for Sharon. She had no apartment anymore. Not even a car. And since he didn't know anything about Judge Munson, he wouldn't look for her at his estate, either. So Sharon talked the judge into driving her back to Brenda's house.

And even if Parker didn't come looking for her like he hadn't at the police station, there might be someone else around—one honest officer at the scene—who would come to her aid.

"It's not here," the judge said. "I've had too many people search this house for it to still be here."

She wasn't about to tell him where it really was—not even when he raised his gun and pressed it to her temple.

"Don't play games with me, little girl," he threatened her. "You brought me here because you thought there might be crime-scene techs or officers here."

But she had been wrong—as the judge had known or he wouldn't have brought her there. Everyone was gone. Only she and the judge stood inside the mansion where two people had already died. Was she about to be the third?

If only she could somehow get word out to Parker...

To warn him...

"It wouldn't have done you any good if there had been officers here," he continued. "Didn't you see the one at the station? He is on my payroll along with so many others."

She would have shaken her head but for the gun pressed to her temple. "There are honest cops, too," she insisted. "Cops you haven't been able to buy. And Parker will know who they are. He'll take the flash drive to them."

The judge snorted. "He might if he had it. But we both know he doesn't have it."

"He does," she insisted. "That's why I couldn't wait to see him—to find out who was behind these attempts on our lives. Now I know it's you...."

The judge shrugged. "It's not like you'll live to tell anyone anything," he said. "And even if you did, they would never believe you—not without the flash drive. I am as widely respected as your grandfather was."

She doubted that. If he was really known for his integrity, her grandfather would have had her clerk for this man. But Judge Wells had never really mentioned him.

"I'm even friends with your mother-in-law," Munson said with a chuckle. "She came to me for your marriage license. If not for me, you wouldn't be Mrs. Parker Payne."

So that was how those men had learned where she and Parker were the night they'd married....

He laughed again. "Not that you're going to be much longer...." From the corner of her eye, she saw that he moved his finger along the gun toward the trigger.

Was he going to kill her here?

Would Parker find yet another body in this house?

An odd ring, more of a chime, rang out—distracting them both. Sharon's phone had blown up in her car, and she hadn't had time to find a replacement. Maybe if she had, Parker could have traced it and found her.

But she had no way of leading him to where she was. She had no way of leaving a message for him to find the flash drive, either. If she tried, the judge would see it, and she couldn't endanger Ethan and Mrs. Payne.

The judge fumbled the ringing phone from the pocket of his suit jacket. "Don't try anything," he warned her. "Or I'll splatter your brains right now." He cocked the gun.

She swallowed hard, choking down her fear. She didn't want to die, but she saw no way out of her situation. No way to survive...

"Hello?" the judge answered, his voice full of suspicion. He must not have recognized the number on the caller ID. Then he chuckled. "Parker Payne, your wife and I were just discussing you."

He must have clicked the phone onto speaker because then she could hear Parker's voice, gruff with concern and anger and fear. For her?

Did he care about her? Did he love her? Or was he only being a bodyguard?

"Munson, you better not hurt her or I will not only give this flash drive to the feds but to all the media outlets, too."

The grin left the old man's face, and his eyes darkened with anger. "You are not the one who should be threatening me, Payne."

"I have what you want," Parker said.

"I thought she was lying," the judge admitted, "when she said you had it…."

Had Parker found it? Or was he bluffing like she had earlier?

"Sharon would never lie," Parker said. "She doesn't have it in her. She's a good person who's already been through too much in her life. She is the granddaughter of your friend. Don't hurt her."

"Looks like I have what you want, too, Payne," the judge replied with a sly glance at Sharon.

"You do," Parker said.

But he must've still been lying. He couldn't want her—not for more than the night before. He couldn't want her forever.

"Then perhaps we can work an exchange," the judge offered, as if he was being magnanimous. "Meet me at my estate in an hour, Payne. Alone."

"I won't give you anything if she's already dead," Parker warned him. "You better not hurt her…."

"I won't." The judge offered what for him was a pithy promise. Then he hung up the cell. "I won't kill you," he assured her, "until your husband brings me that flash drive. Then I'll kill you together."

He acted as if he were doing them a favor. But then, maybe he was. Sharon had spent so much of her life alone. But she would still rather die alone than have Parker die with her. But it was too late; she had no way of warning him that he was about to walk into a trap.

Chapter Eighteen

If only Parker had been able to figure out where the real flash drive was…or if it even still existed. There had been so many explosions; it could have been destroyed in any of them. But because he hadn't been able to find it, he walked into the judge's mansion with a blank one and hoped like hell he could bluff as well as Sharon had.

He held tightly on to it, refusing to give it up like he had his gun and his knife and his phone to the guards at the police station. Guards? He recognized some of the men as officers from the police department but most of them, like Garek had said, from Wanted posters. Or men who'd been on those posters previously…

How had no one else figured out what Brenda had? That Judge Munson had to have been taking bribes all this time. How many criminals had he thrown out cases against or set free before they had served their sentences?

Several of them surrounded the estate. Too many for him to overpower alone.

Judge Munson's estate was four times the size of Brenda Foster's, and an assortment of antique and classic cars were lined up in the circular driveway. The judge had obviously been living beyond his means, so he had found a way to supplement his income.

Two armed men pushed Parker down a wide hallway, lined with an Oriental runner, to a room in the back of the mansion. It was some type of solarium filled with plants and wicker furniture. Tied to one of those wicker chairs, Sharon looked fragile and fearful.

Rushing forward, Parker dropped to his knees beside her. "Are you all right?"

"She's fine," the judge answered for her. He stood in a corner of the solarium, a gun in his hand. With his iron-gray hair and complexion, he could have been a statue—he was that rigid and unemotional. "Where's the flash drive?"

"Don't give it to him," Sharon said. "He's going to kill us anyway."

The judge chuckled but didn't deny her claim. He obviously thought he had set a trap for Parker. "So you might as well give me the flash drive and get this over with."

Sharon shook her head. "Not yet. You were my grandfather's friend," she said. "So have some mercy. Let me talk to my husband."

"I wasn't really a friend of your grandfather's," Munson admitted. "In fact, I hated the man so much I only showed up at his funeral to gloat."

"He wasn't a good man," Sharon admitted. "He was rigid and disapproving. It was not easy being his granddaughter."

"Trying to get my sympathy?" Munson asked with a heartless chuckle.

Parker suspected that she was actually telling the truth—that her grandfather had not been an easy man to live with or please. And she had been a traumatized, vulnerable young kid when she had come to live with him and her grandmother. His heart ached for all the pain she had endured at such a young age. He wanted to hold her.

"Let us have a minute," Parker implored him. He wanted to talk to her, too, to assure her that he would figure a way out for them—that he already had a plan in place.

"Now, your mother I have always liked," the judge admitted. "Penny Payne is a good woman, when so few women are really good."

She was a better woman than Parker had even realized because she had spent the past fifteen years mourning a man she knew had betrayed her. With *Carla...*

"Then do it for my mother," Parker said, "since you're going to break her heart." Not that her heart hadn't been broken before—more times than he had ever known.

"Give me the flash drive," the judge demanded. "And I'll let you talk...."

Parker hesitated for just a moment before handing over the blank drive. The judge closed his hand around it and tightened his grasp on his gun. But then he took the flash drive and headed over to where a laptop sat open on a small table in the corner of the sun-filled solarium.

Parker crouched down next to Sharon and reached for the thin rope binding her wrists to the arms of the wicker chair. If only they hadn't taken his knife...

"I want you to know something," Sharon said.

Was she going to tell him how she felt about him? His heart quickened. But his attention was divided. Once the judge realized the flash drive was empty, he might start firing. Parker had to protect her; he struggled harder with the ropes, trying to loosen them. But he was only cutting the strong, thin rope into her delicate skin.

She flinched. "I want you to know how much I love..."

She drew his attention from the judge to her beautiful face. Her eyes were so full of fear and distress and another emotion.

Love?

She finished, "…Ethan."

Of course she loved the little boy whom she had cared for since his birth. Of course she wanted Parker to know that.

"I love him so much," she continued, "that I never even minded lugging that diaper bag everywhere with me." And her eyes spoke to him, passing the message along….

The flash drive—the real one—was in the diaper bag. The diaper bag that his mother had taken along with the baby.

The judge glanced up. "What a touching goodbye." Then he cursed. "There's nothing on this damn flash drive. You brought me an empty one!"

"You really thought I was stupid enough to bring you the real one?" Parker asked. "I know you intend to kill us. You wouldn't have put out the hit on us—and upped the reward—if that hadn't been your intention all along."

"Trying to get a confession out of me?" the judge scoffed. "I had my men check you for a wire. You're not wearing one. Do you think either of you are actually going to survive to testify against me?"

Parker shrugged. "If we don't get out of here within the hour, the flash drive will go to someone I actually trust in the police department—someone you can't buy." He didn't know if there was anyone he could trust within the department anymore—not after he had learned his father's partner had betrayed him. And now that he had learned his father had betrayed his mother…

The judge snorted in disbelief of Parker's claim. And he narrowed his eyes and studied Sharon. "Why did you tell him about the diaper bag? Is that where the flash drive is?"

The man was smart. Too smart.

"That diaper bag was in this house," he said. "Penny brought it with her when she got me to waive the waiting period and issue your marriage license." He stood up and turned toward the door, probably to summon one of his henchmen to send after their son.

Sharon gasped in fear, and she struggled against those ropes even harder.

"It's not in the diaper bag anymore," Parker said. "I found it already and took it out."

The judge shook his head. "Nice try. I don't even have to send someone to get her. I can call your mother and summon her here to show off that grandbaby of hers again. She'll be happy to do that—happy to bring along the bag."

Parker shook his head. "And you'd be wasting your time. I took it out already and I read everything that was on the flash drive."

"Prove it," the judge challenged him. "Tell me what's on it."

"I know that Brenda wrote about your taking bribes to throw out cases," he replied, "or at the very least to reduce sentences."

The judge tensed and the color of his face turned grayer than his hair; Parker's bluff was actually on the money. Because the judge had been all about the money....

"You saw it," the judge conceded. "You have it."

"Not on me," Parker said. "I gave it to my brother, who'll turn it over to someone we trust."

"That's the problem," the judge said. "You can't trust anyone." And he lifted his gun again. "I don't trust you, Payne. I'm not sure if you really read what Brenda wrote about or you just guessed it. Either way, you and your bride are going to die."

THE JUDGE WAS going to kill them. Sharon knew it now. She had hoped that somehow Parker would save them as he had so many times before, but she shouldn't have relied on him to protect them. She should have protected him and Ethan; he had already missed so many milestones in the boy's life—his first smile, the first time he had rolled over, his first crawl. He didn't deserve to lose any more.

Sharon whispered to Parker, "I'm sorry."

"You have no reason to be sorry," he assured her.

She had regrets, though. Regrets that he had come to her rescue—or tried. But that was the only thing she regretted about her time with Parker Payne.

"I know it's too late," she said. There was so much she wanted to tell him, that she wanted to share with him. But now whatever chance they might have had to make their marriage work was gone—like they would soon be.

He shook his head and squeezed her hand, offering her comfort right until the end. His efforts with the ropes had loosened them some but not enough for her to tug her wrists free. "Shhh, it's going to be okay."

But it wasn't. They were going to die. At least Ethan would have family, though—family who loved him like she loved him and his father.

Tears stung her eyes so painfully that she couldn't blink them back. She could only let them fall, like she had fallen for Parker Payne. "But I want you to know that I love you."

"Now, that was touching," the judge bitterly remarked. "Are you going to say the words back to her, Payne?"

Parker ignored the older man and stared at her. His blue eyes, those gorgeous blue eyes, filled with regret.

She had known he hadn't returned her feelings. But seeing it on his face…

She was so embarrassed and scared and disappointed that she couldn't look at him anymore. She closed her eyes.

"Sharon—"

But whatever he had been about to say to her was lost as the shooting began….

The shooting outside the estate distracted the judge enough that Parker managed to step between Sharon and the gun pointed at her.

Parker flinched, waiting for the gun to go off. But the judge just continued to hold the weapon. Maybe he was more used to others doing his dirty work than doing it himself.

"What the hell's going on?" he asked. But he wasn't even looking at Parker; he obviously didn't expect him to know.

But Parker knew that the gunfire throughout the estate was Payne Protection Agency coming to his and Sharon's rescue just as he and Logan had planned. They must have overpowered Munson's motley mix of dirty cops and convicts by now.

The judge glanced toward the door and gasped. Parker followed his gaze and gasped, too. The man standing in the doorway with a gun wasn't a Payne—at least not a legitimate one—although he looked exactly like one.

"Agent Rus," Parker murmured. "What the hell are you doing here?"

The judge tightened his grasp on the gun, obviously uncertain whose side the federal agent was on; he wasn't the only one.

The agent grinned, an expression of which Parker wouldn't have thought him capable. "I'm here to collect the reward," he said.

And Parker's guts tightened with dread. "What?"

"They're both still alive," the judge pointed out.

The agent held up a small piece of plastic. "The flash drive. I suspect this might be worth more than the two of them combined."

"What do you know?" the judge asked.

"A few days before Payne here killed him, Detective Sharpe told me everything," the agent replied. He snorted derisively. "Not sure how such an idiot made detective in the first place."

The judge's eyes widened in surprise. "Sharpe talked?"

"You didn't think he would?"

"Given the amount of money I was paying him, I thought he would keep his damn mouth shut." The judge sighed. "I should have known better than to trust him. I should know better than to trust anyone."

And it was obvious he didn't trust Agent Rus yet.

"Where did you get that?" the judge asked with a suspicious glance at the flash drive. He probably thought it was as empty as the one Parker had brought him.

Parker was afraid that it wasn't. And his guts twisted with fear over how the agent might have come to possess it.

"Mrs. Payne walked into the police department and handed it right to me," Rus replied. "She found it in her grandson's diaper bag."

That was why his mother had come down to the police

department—not to bail him out, but because she had found what everyone had been looking for. Of course, she probably hadn't known it was what everyone was looking for—just that it was suspicious to find in a diaper bag. Or, knowing his mother's curiosity, she may have opened and read the files on it.

"Did you hurt her?" he asked. He didn't care that the bastard was armed; if he'd hurt his mother any more than his mere existence already had, Parker would take him out with his bare hands like the bodyguard had Brenda.

Rus shook his head.

"Did she see what was on it?" the judge asked.

Rus shook his head again. "She has no idea what's on it." His grin flashed again, making him look even more like Cooper. But he was nothing like Parker's marine brother, who had put his life on the line for years for his country. "But *I* looked at it," he said. "I know what's on it."

Parker had always thought the dirtiest cops were the ones who investigated other cops—like Rus was doing for the feds. At least he hadn't been wrong about that.

His eyes narrowed with suspicion, the judge asked, "What was all the shooting we just heard? What happened out there?"

The fed uttered a condescending chuckle. "You didn't think Parker Payne would really come here alone, did you?"

It obviously hadn't occurred to the judge that Parker hadn't walked alone into his trap. He wasn't the idiot that Sharpe had been. Regrettably, neither was Nicholas Rus.

"That family travels in a pack—" Rus snorted "—like wild dogs."

Parker silently cursed the loss of his weapon because he wanted to use it on Rus. Badly.

"His brothers are out there?" Munson asked.

He nodded. "They were. Even the little sister was—she must have trailed after them."

Nikki had tagged along to the estate even though Parker hadn't wanted her along. And neither had Logan. But she had insisted on helping, and he hadn't wanted to waste time arguing with her. Now he wished that he had....

Horror and fear struck Parker's heart, and Sharon gasped, choking on a sob. She hadn't known them long, but she had obviously already come to love his family like her own. They had been hers—for a little while.

They had been his all his life. His mother had already lost his father; she couldn't lose all of her children, too. Maybe Rus was wrong; maybe his family had survived. Parker had to get to them, had to figure out how to help them.

The judge was concerned, too—about himself. "How are we going to clean up the mess?" he asked Rus.

"What about the guy you hired to place all those bombs?" Rus asked. "Can't he set up another little explosion?"

"There were actually a couple of guys that set those bombs," the judge replied. "But he—" he gestured toward Parker "—killed them in the street."

Rus shrugged. "I have a military background. I was deployed in Afghanistan." Like Cooper had been, but Cooper was a hero. Rus was a killer. "I'll set the bomb."

"Not here," the judge vehemently replied.

"You have to," Rus insisted. "You'll never clean it up enough that a crime tech couldn't find blood or DNA."

Sharon gasped again, as if she couldn't breathe. She wept for his family.

Parker felt sick. He wouldn't have involved his family if he hadn't believed that they would all survive. This was his fault—all his fault.

The judge's voice cracked, as if he was close to tears, too, as he said, "I've worked too hard for my estate—everything I've done I've done to keep this place."

"It's just a house," Rus said dismissively. If he didn't care about possessions, why had he killed for money?

"It wasn't just about the house," the judge said. "It was about the money and prestige, which I needed to keep my wife."

Rus glanced around as if looking for Mrs. Munson. "Is she here?"

He wasn't going to find her.

Parker pushed aside his pain to focus on their conversation, to force himself to find a way out for him and Sharon.

The judge shook his head. "In the end, the money wasn't enough for her."

Parker opened his mouth to correct the fed's misconception about Mrs. Munson. He had recalled what had become of her. But a gesture from Rus stopped him.

The man shook his head, as if commiserating with the judge. "So you took all those bribes and she still left you?"

The judge nodded. "I took dirty money—money from criminals to either throw out the cases against them or reduce their sentences."

"But your wife didn't leave you," Parker said, unable to hold his tongue any longer. "She was killed."

The judge laughed. "Do you think I would let her

divorce me after everything I'd done for her? She wasn't going to take anything else from me."

"So you had one of those criminals kill her?" Parker asked the question now. He wanted to know how long this man had been a killer.

"Hell, I did that myself," the judge said. "Right here in this solarium and had that dim-witted Sharpe kid help me clean up the scene. Too bad he's dead."

"I'll do your dirty work," Rus said. "But I want more than that reward you offered."

Parker had no choice. He had to act now or he'd miss his opportunity. It didn't matter if he got shot as long as he gave Sharon the opportunity to escape. He knocked her chair to the ground, hoping that the wicker might break or crack and loosen the ropes that he had been unable to undo.

And then he vaulted himself at Rus; he had to overpower him or die trying. But something struck his jaw, and darkness filled his vision. He fought to remain conscious so that he could protect Sharon, so that he could tell her that he loved her....

Chapter Nineteen

As Parker's eyes rolled back in his head, Sharon screamed. Was he dead? She struggled against the ropes and finally they were loose enough that she slipped her wrists free of the bindings. Then she crawled over to Parker's side and cradled his head on her lap. At least she had told him that she loved him….

His pulse flickered beneath the skin of his throat. He wasn't dead. Yet. But she doubted it would be much longer before this man—this man who looked so much like Parker—killed them both.

The judge stared at Parker on the floor. "So what do you want?" he asked Rus. "What do you want as your reward for killing these two and cleaning up the mess? How much is this going to cost me?"

Sharon shuddered as the federal agent grinned. How could he have killed a whole family and been so smug about it? If he was that heartless, there was no way that he was really a Payne.

But then the man replied, "You can keep your money, Judge. My reward will be you behind bars, Your Honor—for the rest of your life."

She had forgotten the judge still held his gun—until

he fired it—right into the federal agent's chest. The man dropped to the ground next to her and Parker.

The judge shook his head with self-disgust. "Should have known I couldn't trust a Payne. Even a bastard one has more integrity than intelligence."

Then he turned the weapon on Parker and Sharon. But Parker was no longer unconscious on her lap—he was leaping up and vaulting toward the judge. The gun went off again, the shots echoing throughout the room, shattering the glass walls.

Parker flinched. But he didn't feel the unmistakable burn of being struck by a bullet. Or maybe he was too numb with pain over the loss of his family to feel it. But were they really lost?

Footsteps pounded against the slate tiles of the solarium floor. He glanced over his shoulder to see Logan and Cooper rushing into the room. If they'd been hurt, they wouldn't have been able to move with such speed.

"You guys aren't dead," Parker remarked with a sigh of relief.

Logan shook his head. "No..."

But, remembering all the shooting, Parker bet some other lives had been lost. "Where were you, then?"

"We had to revise the plan," Logan said.

The judge squirmed beneath him, fighting him for the gun. Parker smacked the older man's wrist against the ground until the Glock skidded across the tile floor. Cooper grabbed the weapon.

Without his gun and his authority, the judge was just a pathetic old man. And as he realized and accepted that, his shoulders began to shake with sobs. Parker rolled off him and turned back toward Sharon.

She was sitting up and appeared to be unharmed. But

she wouldn't look at Parker; her attention was focused on the one person who had been hurt in the room.

Parker knelt beside the prone body of the man who looked so much like him and his brothers. The federal agent's eyes were closed.

Rus had saved his life. But what had it cost him? His own?

Parker asked, "Can you hear me?"

"Yes." The federal agent coughed and groaned and sat up. "Yes, but only thanks to this bulletproof vest, courtesy of River City P.D. I knew I never should have come here."

Parker would have agreed a short while ago, but the man had saved his and his family's lives. Maybe Rus wasn't the outsider Parker had thought him; maybe he could one day think of this man as his brother.

Rus fumbled with the buttons on his shirt. Then Velcro ripped as he opened the side of his vest and reached beneath it. Had he been hit? He grunted and squirmed and remarked, "Hope the impact of the bullet didn't short out a wire."

"You were wired?" the judge asked as Logan and Cooper helped him to his feet. He was an old man but, aware of how dangerous he was, they both held on to him.

"Yeah, I got it all on tape," Rus told the judge.

"That was the reason you revised the plan," Parker realized. But he was surprised Logan had taken orders from anyone, let alone Rus.

Logan shrugged. "Without the wire, it would have just been his word against yours and Sharon's."

And Munson was a respected judge. Or he had been....

Parker turned back to Rus. "Did you have to make me think my family was dead?" He had never been so devastated in his life.

"I had to make him trust me enough to talk," Rus pointed out. "And explain all the shooting…"

Parker sighed and nodded acceptance.

"And I got everything we need," Rus reminded him as he patted his vest.

Parker turned back to the murderous judge. "There will be no case thrown out or reduced sentences for you."

It was over. It was finally over.

Parker heaved a sigh of relief and turned toward Sharon. But only the broken wicker chair lay on the floor where she had been sitting; she was gone.

"What happened to my wife?" he asked. While he had been checking on Rus to make sure he wasn't dead, she must have slipped away.

"She met Nikki in the doorway," Cooper replied. "And they took off."

Had they told Nikki to stay outside the room until the judge was disarmed? Or hadn't she wanted to come any closer to Nicholas Rus?

She must have been devastated to meet their half *brother.* No one had idolized their father more than she had. That explained why Nikki had left so abruptly.

Why had Sharon? Was she hurt? Or in shock again after everything she'd endured?

Where had his bride gone?

SHARON'S ARMS TREMBLED as she clutched the baby close to her heart. Ethan had already claimed it for his own. She hadn't realized she had had more love left to give until she had fallen for Parker, too. But then, for so many years, she'd had no one who had wanted to accept or give her love.

Neither did Parker, though.

He had been so horrified when she'd confessed her feelings for him. Her face heated with embarrassment as she remembered the look on his face, the regret. To save them both from further embarrassment, she had to leave before he came to see his son, too.

But her arms refused to budge from around the baby. She had gone so long without holding Ethan that she couldn't release him. His warm little squirmy body gave her comfort. He was all right....

His breath hitched and then raggedly shuddered out with relief.

"He missed you so much," Mrs. Payne remarked as she reached out. Sharon thought she'd been reaching for her grandson, but instead her palm skimmed across Sharon's cheek. "Are you all right, honey?"

"It's all over now." Thanks to Parker. And to the man who looked so much like a Payne. Who was he?

"I knocked over the diaper bag earlier today and the flash drive fell out," Mrs. Payne shared. "I didn't want to pry into your life, so I didn't look at it. But I wanted to get it to you in case it was important."

It was far more important than she had realized.

"So you gave it to *him?*" Nikki asked. "You trusted something that important to *him?*" She had driven Sharon to Mrs. Payne's, but she hadn't said much in the car. And she hadn't said a word since arriving at her mother's. Hollow-eyed and pale, she looked as devastated as Sharon felt.

"I was going to give it to Sharon," Mrs. Payne reminded her, "but she had already left the police department."

Because the judge had bailed her out. She shuddered

even now, remembering how easily he had led her out of the police station at gunpoint.

If not for Parker and his family, she would have been dead. She never would have been able to hold Ethan again. But she wasn't sure that she would be able to again....

"And when Parker realized she was in danger," Mrs. Payne continued, "he was too upset to listen to me."

"Or were *you* too upset?" Nikki asked. "Wasn't it a shock to see *him?*" She had obviously been shocked to learn she had another brother and she was still in shock.

Mrs. Payne sighed. "This is neither the time nor the place to discuss this...."

Because Sharon wasn't family.

When Parker had put that ring on her finger, she had fooled herself into thinking their marriage was real, that his wonderful family might become hers. But now she was more alone than she had ever been. She had no one anymore.

"Sharon's a Payne, too," Nikki said, inclusively. "She deserves to know what's going on, too."

Sharon shook her head. "It's fine. Really," she assured Nikki. "I—I just wanted to see Ethan."

She had no right to their secrets—not unless she had Parker's love. And she didn't. If he'd had any feelings for her, he would have reciprocated her declaration of love—especially then, when they had been about to die.

"Thank you for bringing me here," she told Nikki.

Mrs. Payne's soft yellow farmhouse with a wraparound porch was as warm and inviting as her little white wedding chapel. She could imagine Parker and his brothers and sister growing up here. She could imagine Parker sneaking kisses on that porch swing with whatever girl he had been dating that day....

She doubted his relationships had ever lasted much longer than that. Their marriage had barely lasted a day. But the night...

Her skin warmed at just the memory of the heat of his kisses, his passion....

She had been a fool to think that she—awkward, inexperienced Sharon Wells—had ever had a chance with a playboy like Parker Payne.

Nikki nodded. "I didn't want to stick around there and watch *him* play hero anymore. We didn't need him interfering. We'd had it all under control...."

Mrs. Payne turned her attention to her daughter. "Honey, don't be angry with him. It's not his fault...."

Tears glistened in Nikki's eyes. "No, it was Dad's...."

Mrs. Payne reached for her, but Nikki whirled around and ran out of the living room. She didn't stop on the front porch but kept running to where she had left her car parked in the gravel driveway.

"Will she be okay?" Sharon asked.

Mrs. Payne nodded. "Of course. She's stronger than she knows—certainly stronger than her brothers realize."

"Does she have another brother? Is Nicholas Rus her half brother?" Sharon asked then flushed with embarrassment at her nosiness. "Forget I asked—"

"He is a Payne," the older woman admitted with a heavy sigh. Suddenly lines appeared on her beautiful face, and she actually looked her age. "My husband used to be an undercover cop just like Parker had been when he'd been with the River City Police Department. Nick—my husband—got really caught up in an assignment and with a witness who had been in danger...."

Was that what had happened with her and Parker on their wedding night? Had he just gotten caught up in the moment, in the danger? Was that why he'd made love to her?

Tears sparkled in Mrs. Payne's warm brown eyes. "He didn't know that she was pregnant…."

"I'm sorry," Sharon said. Her heart ached for the woman's pain even as her own heart filled with it.

Mrs. Payne blinked back her tears, obviously embarrassed. "It's fine…."

"I shouldn't have asked," Sharon said with her own embarrassment. "It's none of my business."

Mrs. Payne wrapped her arm around Sharon's shoulders. "Of course it is. You are family now."

Sharon shook her head. "No. My marriage to Parker was never real."

"You have a marriage license that proves it is," Mrs. Payne insisted.

"Considering who issued it, I'm not sure that's true anymore," Sharon reminded her. "But that's okay. It was never meant to last—only to protect Ethan." She forced herself to pass the little boy into his grandmother's arms, but he clutched at her hair, tangling it around his pudgy fingers. She teared up, but not over the pain of him tugging at her scalp. But over what she had to do, which was walk away.

"He's safe now…."

"It's really all over now?" Mrs. Payne asked.

Sharon nodded. It was all over. Her marriage. Her involvement in the Paynes' lives. It didn't matter that Brenda had appointed her Ethan's guardian; she wasn't his family. He had an amazing family that would care for him no matter what. Today had proved that to her—how they had all been there for each other, including the man they hadn't even known was a brother.

The Paynes took care of their own; they would take care of Ethan.

Sharon drew in a deep breath, bracing herself, before she replied, "Yes, it's all over now. And it's time for me to leave."

Chapter Twenty

Parker had a tight knot of fear and dread in his gut and he didn't know why. It was all over. Even the judge had known it was over and had confessed everything, as if that might make amends for all the evil he had done, for all the innocent lives that had been lost because of him.

Parker pushed open the door to the house where he had grown up, and that knot eased slightly when the little boy in his mother's arms smiled at him as if he knew him, as if he was beginning to love him as much as Parker already loved him.

Parker stepped closer, and the little boy reached out for him. Long strands of caramel-colored hair dangled from his pudgy fingers. And that knot eased even more. "Sharon's here?"

He took the little boy from his mother, welcoming his slight weight and his warmth. Ethan smelled like sunshine and rain, like Sharon.

His mother shook her head. "She's gone…."

She said it with a finality that had that knot tightening in his gut again.

"Where? How?" She had no car, no place left to go. "Did Nikki take her somewhere?" he asked since his sister's car wasn't parked in the driveway.

Mom sighed. "No. Nikki left first...."

He heard the distress in his mother's voice, and cradling his son with one arm, he slid his other one around her shoulders. "She's not upset with you."

"I'm not so sure about that," she replied, her voice cracking with emotion.

"It's not your fault...." That their father had an illegitimate son. "It was his."

"Is it your fault that Sharon left?" she asked him. "Because I can't believe that she would leave...."

"She's really gone?" he asked. That knot tightened so much that he couldn't draw a deep breath. He shook his head. "She wouldn't leave Ethan."

She loved that little boy so much. She had also said that she loved *him.* But he hadn't said the words back to her. It was his fault.

"She thinks he doesn't need her because he has us," Mrs. Payne replied. She shook her head as if she found the idea as ridiculous as he did.

"That's crazy," Parker replied. "He loves her like she's his mother."

As if in agreement, the little boy shook his fist full of those strands of hair. Parker could not blame his son for wanting to hang on to her. Sharon Wells Payne was an amazing woman—a strong, loving woman.

"Do you love her?" Mrs. Payne asked.

Parker shook his head.

"You don't?" she asked, her voice full of shock as her eyes widened.

"It doesn't matter what I feel for her," he explained. "She'll be better off without me."

"Why would you say that?" she asked. "The danger is past, right? The judge has been arrested?"

"Yes." Thanks to Nicholas Rus. "He'll go away for the rest of his life, at least." He would be serving time with criminals. But the only ones of them that he had put behind bars would have been the ones unable to afford his bribes. Parker couldn't imagine they would be very happy or forgiving.

His mother's usually smooth brow furrowed with confusion. "Then why in the world would you think she would be better off without you?"

"Do you know why I never intended to get married and have kids?" he asked her.

She nodded. "Because of how we lost your father..." She gently touched his cheek. "You always acted the silliest of all the kids, but I think that's because the loss of your father affected you the most."

"It affected *you* the most," he said. "And I didn't want to do that to my wife. I didn't want to leave someone behind to mourn me like you did Dad." And now, knowing what he did, he was surprised that she had. He was surprised that she had been able to forgive him at all.

"That's crazy," his mother said, dismissing his fears as easily as she had when he'd been a kid afraid of the boogeyman in his closet.

"You don't know that anything will happen to you," she said. "You could live to be an old man."

Like his father should have....

He shrugged. "No, but the protection business is about protecting other people, not ourselves."

"The past two weeks you have been in more danger than you ever were on the police force or as a bodyguard," she pointed out with a shiver of residual fear. "You had a price on your head."

"A big price," he admitted with a shiver of his own.

Garek and Milek had promised to get out the word that there was no way anyone could collect that reward with the judge in jail for the rest of his life.

"And you survived these past few weeks," she pointed out. "You're a survivor. We all are...."

He nodded in agreement. She was right. Cooper had survived a few deployments to war-torn countries. Logan and he had both survived numerous attempts on their lives.

"But dying is not the only way I might hurt my wife," he said.

Her hand stilled on his cheek. "What do you mean?"

"Of all of us kids, I'm the most like Dad." He reminded her of what she had always told him. Now he finally understood why she had thought that. "I'm a playboy. I'm not husband or father material."

But his arm tightened around his son. He *wanted* to be, for Ethan and for Sharon.

"Sharon will be better off without me." Because she had fallen for him, just as he had feared she would, he could hurt her so badly...like his father must have hurt his mother.

Her hand moved again and softly struck his cheek. "You're an idiot."

"Just another way I'm like Dad," he bitterly remarked. "I can't believe he cheated on you." And that she must have forgiven and taken him back since Nikki was younger than the federal agent.

Her breath shuddered out in a shaky sigh. "He regretted that so much. It happened when he was undercover. He had gotten so caught up in the assignment. And he was in so much danger. He and Carla both were. If he hadn't acted his part completely..."

Parker nodded in sudden understanding. "He could have given himself away."

"He told me right away." She shuddered. "I was already pregnant with Cooper. And I loved him so much...."

"So you forgave him?"

"On one condition," she said. Her voice cracked as if that condition had cost her.

He lifted a brow and waited.

"That he would never go undercover again," she said. "He went back to being a uniformed officer. And that's what killed him. My one condition..."

"Mom..."

"If he hadn't been in uniform, he wouldn't have had a partner—the partner who betrayed him." Tears streamed down her face. "It's all my fault."

He tightened his arm around her. She must have spent the past fifteen years blaming herself for her husband's death. No wonder she had mourned him so much. "Mom, it's not your fault. None of what happened was your fault. Not his cheating and not his death."

She leaned against his side, and her tears wetted his shirt. "When I told you that you were the most like your father," she said, "I meant that you are protective and loving. I forgave him for what happened, but he never forgave himself. He spent the rest of his life making it up to me and loving me. He was the best husband and father, and you will be, too, Parker."

"But what if I...?" He couldn't even say it; he would never even consider cheating on Sharon. He loved her too much to ever want another woman.

His mother must have seen it dawn on him because she smiled. "Go find your bride," she urged him.

But he didn't know where to look for her. She had no

car. No house. No job. She had nothing to keep her in River City…but him and their son.

He passed Ethan back to his grandmother and kissed the boy's forehead. "I'm going to go find your mama," he said. "And bring her home, where she belongs."

With their family…

SHARON HAD SPENT most of her life alone, so she didn't know why it felt so strange to her now. She didn't know why her new apartment was so quiet and empty….

She had once appreciated silence in order to study. But she didn't care to study now. She had no intention of trying to pass the bar again. She had only studied law in order to please her grandfather, but she should have known there would have been no pleasing him—even when he'd been alive. There was definitely no pleasing him now.

But she couldn't please herself, either…or she would be back with Ethan. She would be holding her little man. But she would also be begging Parker for his love. And she had begged for love for too much of her life. She wanted it given freely to her.

She dropped one of the pillows she had bought onto the couch and stepped back. The orange looked good against the chocolate suede. Maybe she could become a decorator.

But it didn't matter what she did to the apartment; it would never be a home like Mrs. Payne had made for her family. But Sharon didn't have a family….

She glanced down at the ring on her finger, the ring Parker Payne had slid there when they had said their vows. She needed to take off the gold band. It wasn't as if their marriage was real….

That was why she hadn't contacted a lawyer yet to start divorce proceedings. She doubted anything Judge Munson had signed would prove legal. Of course, it had been only a couple of days since she had kissed Ethan goodbye. A couple of days that she had filled with finding an apartment and buying a car and clothes. She'd intended to stay so busy that she didn't miss the little boy or his father.

But it hadn't worked. They were both forever on her mind. She grabbed the pillow and wrapped her arms around it. But it wasn't warm and squirmy like her little man. Or hard and hot like her big man…

They weren't hers, though. They had never really been hers.

Tears stung her eyes, but she blinked them back. Then she breathed a sigh of relief when the doorbell rang. Whatever delivery had come was certain to distract her from her self-pity. But when she opened the door, the reason for all of her pain stood on her doorstep.

He looked so handsome—even with dark circles beneath his blue eyes and his black hair tousled as if he'd been running his hands through it. He also looked angry. And his words confirmed it. "I am so damn mad at you."

"Why?" she asked, stepping back as he pushed his way inside her apartment.

He slammed the door behind himself and followed her, backing her up until she ran into the new sofa. "I thought you loved Ethan."

Tears stung her eyes again. "I do. Of course I do. Is he all right?"

"No," he said.

And panic struck her heart. She had thought the little

boy would be safe and happy with his family. "What's wrong? What's happened to him?"

"He misses you," Parker said.

She closed her eyes to hold in her tears. She missed him, too—so very much. "He's so young," she pointed out. "He'll soon forget all about me."

"What about me?" he asked with such forlornness that she opened her eyes and stared up into his face.

He was so handsome that it wasn't fair. How could she have not fallen in love with him? She wasn't as weak as everyone always thought her, but she wasn't strong enough to resist a man like him.

"What about you?" she asked, unable to understand his question.

"I miss you, too," he said.

"You'll forget me, too," she assured him. She was actually surprised that he hadn't already. That he hadn't already moved on to the next woman—one far more beautiful and carefree than his bride.

He shook his head. "I've been going crazy trying to find you. I was worried that you had left town, maybe even the state."

"Agent Rus told me that I might need to testify at the judge's sentencing hearing." She had gone down to the department to give her statement. Seeing the agent looking so much like Parker had been hard. But she'd wanted to do the right thing. Had the agent? "Did Rus tell you where to find me?"

Parker cracked his knuckles. "With a little coercion…"

"You didn't fight with him, did you?" Not over her. They needed to build a relationship, not destroy the tenuous bond they'd formed over the judge's arrest.

He sighed. "That pain in the neck loved it, loved to see me beg."

"You begged?" she asked. And now she was totally confused. First by his anger and now by the look in his eyes. They were so intense, so focused on her.

"Are you going to make me beg, too?"

"For what?" If he wanted her, she was powerless to resist him. Since she had opened the door to find him on her doorstep, her pulse had been racing. And her skin was hot and tingling just from the touch of his gaze....

His eyes were such a bright blue—like his son's. She had always been a sucker for those eyes.

"For you," he said. "For another chance..."

"Another chance?" She hadn't realized they had ever had one.

He stepped closer to her, so that his body brushed against hers. "Tell me you love me again."

Now her skin heated with the flush of embarrassment, and she shook her head.

"So you only told me that because you thought you were going to die?" he asked, his voice gruff with disappointment. "Not because you really have any feelings for me?"

"What does it matter now?" she asked. He didn't return her feelings.

"I thought you were only saying them because you thought you were going to die," he said. "And I was sorry that I couldn't let you know that I hadn't come alone, that Logan and Cooper were waiting for their chance to come to our rescue."

She didn't know what to say. Should she admit that fear had had nothing to do with her admission? That she really loved him? But if he had come to her only out of pity…

He continued, "But then Logan and Cooper didn't come in…." And he shuddered as he must have recalled those horrible moments they'd believed they were dead.

"Your other brother came to the rescue," she reminded him.

He flinched as she said it, so she lifted her hand and touched his chest, her palm over his heart. It pounded hard and fast as if he was in danger.

"I'm sorry," she said. "Sorry that you didn't know about him."

He shrugged. "Nicholas Rus is a Payne—whether he wants to be one or not."

So there were other issues with the federal agent. But Parker shrugged and focused on her again with that intense gaze.

"What about you?" he asked. "Do you want to be a Payne?"

Her breath caught, but she refused to let herself hope. "What are you asking me?"

"You haven't started divorce proceedings," he said.

She shrugged now. "Do I need to? The marriage isn't real."

"Yes, it is," he said. "Because he was a judge at the time he signed it, the license is valid. What about the marriage?"

"We're safe now," she reminded him. But she hadn't felt safe even though the federal agent had assured her that everyone knew they could no longer collect any reward for her murder. She had only felt safe in Parker's arms. "For our safety and for Ethan's were the only reasons we got married."

"And you're going to let me just have Ethan?" he asked. "You're not going to fight me for him?"

"You're his father," she said. "I'm nothing but his previous nanny."

The anger was back, darkening his blue eyes. "You're everything to that little boy." He touched her now, cupping her face in both his hands. "And you're everything to me, Sharon. I love you, and I want to spend the rest of my life with you."

She froze, unable to comprehend what he was telling her. Nobody but her mother had ever said those words to her, and that had been so long ago that she'd forgotten how they'd sounded, and how it felt to hear them. "You what?"

"I love you," he said. And as if he knew she couldn't understand his words, he proved his love with actions. He kissed her—gently at first and then with all the passion that he had on their wedding night. And then he laid her down on the couch and made love to her body.

In the frenzy of movement, she didn't even notice when he took off her clothes; she realized only that she was naked beneath him. And he was kissing her…intimately… while his fingers teased her peaked nipples. She squirmed as pressure mounted inside her; her skin tingled and heated from his touch. She wanted him so much—wanted the pleasure she knew he could give her. Then he sucked on her most sensitive place, and that pleasure came, overwhelming her so that she screamed his name.

And he filled her, thrusting inside her—joining their bodies. He wasn't as gentle as he had been on their wedding night, when he'd been worried that she was hurt from the collision. He made love to her now like a man overcome with desire.

She clutched him with her arms and her legs, matching his thrusts until she climaxed again—with him. And as he filled her with his pleasure, he kept declaring his love again and again.

Panting for breath, she sank deeper into the cushions of the couch, and he gently pushed her damp hair from her face. Then he stared into her eyes again, as if trying to let her see inside him—into his heart and soul.

"I will keep professing my love until you believe me," he promised.

"Don't stop even then," she said, as tears stung her eyes and began to run down her face. "Don't ever stop telling me."

Because she hadn't heard those words in so long....

He must have realized when she had heard them last because he kissed her damp eyes and murmured, "I'm sorry, sweetheart. So sorry you didn't get the love you deserved all these years. But I will spend the rest of my life making it up to you. You have my love and Ethan's. And our entire family loves you, too."

She was so overwhelmed with happiness that she just clung to him and cried happy tears. And finally when she could catch her breath again, she told him, "I love you. I love you so much."

"Then you will stay married to me?" he asked hopefully. "You will be my wife and Ethan's mother and Penny's daughter and Logan and Cooper and Nikki's sister?"

"You are giving me so much," she said. Everything she had always wanted. A family. "I have nothing to give to you...." Except for money, but she knew him well enough to know that money didn't matter to Parker Payne.

He shook his head. "Sweetheart, you have given me

everything. You are *everything* to me. You are my life. And I want to spend the rest of it with you."

She wrapped her arms around his neck and pulled him down for her kiss. "I love you."

She had probably always known that she would fall for her playboy protector, but she hadn't realized that he would fall for her, too.

But then he was telling her again—just as he had promised—over and over. "I love you."

She looked forward to hearing those words for the rest of their lives together.

* * * * *

"He was in my bedroom."

The cushion beside her sank and her balance shifted as George sat down. "I believe you." He pulled both her hands between his and gently rubbed them.

His simple statement of faith in her sanity swept out the cobwebs of self-doubt and touched her bruised heart.

Curling her legs beneath her, Elise pushed herself up, looping her arms about George's neck, knocking him into the back of the couch. "Thank you."

He folded his arms around her, flattening one hand against her spine to anchor her to his body. He pushed aside the jacket's collar and threaded his fingers into the short hair at her nape to massage the tension in her neck.

"You're okay. You're safe now. No one's going to hurt you."

KCPD PROTECTOR

BY
JULIE MILLER

Published in Great Britain 2014
by Mills & Boon, an imprint of Harlequin (UK) Limited,
Eton House, 18-24 Paradise Road, Richmond, Surrey, TW9 1SR

ISBN: 978-0-263-91367-5

46-0814

Harlequin (UK) Limited's policy is to use papers that are natural, renewable and recyclable products and made from wood grown in sustainable forests. The logging and manufacturing processes conform to the legal environmental regulations of the country of origin.

Printed and bound in Spain
by Blackprint CPI, Barcelona

USA TODAY bestselling author **Julie Miller** attributes her passion for writing romance to all those books she read growing up. When shyness and asthma kept her from becoming the action-adventure heroine she longed to be, Julie created stories in her head to keep herself entertained. Encouragement from her family to write down the feelings and ideas she couldn't express became a love for the written word. She gets continued support from her fellow members of the Prairieland Romance Writers, where this teacher serves as the resident "grammar goddess." Inspired by the likes of Agatha Christie and Encyclopedia Brown, Julie believes the only thing better than a good mystery is a good romance.

Born and raised in Missouri, this award-winning author now lives in Nebraska with her husband, son and an assortment of spoiled pets. To contact Julie or to learn more about her books, write to PO Box 5162, Grand Island, NE 68802-5162, USA or check out her website and monthly newsletter at www.juliemiller.org.

To Pam Jones-Hamblin and Jenny Simons—
two sisters who compete to see who can
read my books first. Too much fun!
And what a lovely compliment.
I'm happy to be a part of the competition.

Chapter One

"Elise? I need—"

"Right here." As soon as the lacquered black door between their offices opened, Elise Brown was on her feet, carrying the file from the corner of her desk over to her boss, KCPD Deputy Commissioner George Madigan. "Crime rate statistics for the downtown area over the past three years. I also checked the Farmers' Almanac for the last time Kansas City had record temperatures like this and forwarded stats on the dramatic rise in reported crime incidents for that summer to your laptop. I pulled up similar stats on the increased number of 9-1-1 calls during power outages."

"And my dinner—?"

"Done. I called the restaurant and moved your reservation this evening back to eight o'clock. Your appointment will meet you there."

George's firm mouth cocked into a wry grin, deepening the lines beside his steel-gray eyes as he opened the folder. "You might at least let me finish asking my questions before you hand over the answers."

George Madigan didn't ask—he gave orders—but Elise didn't mind. She tipped her face up to his and smiled. "Just being indispensable."

"That you are. I swear you could do this job without me. But I wouldn't manage the other way around. Thanks." He dropped his gaze to the information he held, thumbing through the pages, already engrossed in his work.

Elise smiled at the crown of his dark brown hair. It was short and thick and peppered with shots of silver that only added to the mature air of masculinity that oozed from every pore. Not that she cared one whit about how the man looked or what he oozed. All she cared about was this job and the way George valued her as a trusted associate.

There were no miscommunications when her boss spoke. No flirty double entendres she had to evaluate and dodge. No favors or blackmail or anything that could leave her feeling like a fool for not clearly understanding what was being asked of her.

She appreciated the mutual respect in their working relationship, and had no intention of muddying the waters by wishing there might be a little more charm to his authoritative demeanor or wondering how a full-blown smile or belly laugh might soften the life experience sculpted into his angular features.

The deputy commissioner and KCPD had taken a chance on her when her confidence had been so close to rock bottom that she wasn't sure she even deserved a job in the corporate world again. Working as an executive assistant for one of the top administrators in the department, she was rebuilding the self-assurance that had been shredded at her last full-time position. Fixing her bruised heart and shattered trust in men were projects for another day. For her, the job was enough. It was everything. It had to be.

"This is good stuff," George praised. "These numbers should help make my case for allocating more funds."

"You hired me to be knowledgeable, efficient and to anticipate your needs."

To make her point, she flipped the page to point out the totals he was searching for and nodded toward the office behind him where five people sat around a cherrywood conference table, engaged in a heated discussion studded with phrases like "We're already short staffed," "Not my responsibility," "How much?" and "Would you go there without a cop around for miles?"

Elise didn't even need to drop her voice for privacy. "Emergency budget meeting? Complaints from the union about freezing salaries instead of paying overtime? The most vocal person in the room is Councilman Johnson. Ergo, you want to be armed with the information showing a direct correlation between hot weather and a higher crime rate, and how putting extra uniformed officers on the street during peak power demands will counteract that danger."

A dark eyebrow arched as he looked up from the file. "Ergo?"

Elise met his gaze and shrugged. "So you can shut up Mr. Johnson."

That earned a chuckle from deep in his throat. Okay. So the man did possess a little charm. "You're onto me. Did anyone ever tell you that you'd make a good detective?"

Elise looked beyond the wide shoulders of his blue dress shirt to see the medals and commendations framed on the wall behind his desk. Her boss's day might be filled with administrative duties now, but there was no doubt who the real detective was here. "I function much better behind the scenes than I do on the front line, sir."

His square jaw tightened momentarily. But before he snapped the folder shut and gave voice to whatever thought had crossed his features, a light knock on Elise's office door diverted her attention across the reception area.

"Hello?"

"Excuse me, sir." Elise crossed the taupe carpet to meet the deliveryman hidden behind the extravagant bouquet of yellow roses at the hallway door. "Yes?"

"Is this the deputy commissioner's office?" a winded voice asked.

"It is."

"Finally. Do you know how far I had to carry these things?" When the twentysomething man poked his head around the tall glass vase, his ruddy cheeks and forehead were dotted with perspiration. She also noted that he was wearing a visitor's badge around the sweat-stained neck of his brown uniform. Good. That meant he'd been cleared at both the ground floor and the security desk at the eighth floor elevators, and she didn't need to screen him as any kind of threat to the higher-ups at KCPD.

"Has it topped a hundred degrees out there yet?" Elise asked, reaching for the electronic signature pad he pushed toward her. Since a heat wave was bearing down on Kansas City for its third straight week, it was a topic of conversation friends and strangers alike could share. She hoped her friendly smile might improve the man's mood.

But she got little more than a weary grunt in return. "I just need you to sign for these, ma'am."

Understanding how a heat index of one hundred and ten and humidity that was nearly as high could make tempers and frustrations flare, Elise quickly wrote her name. “Could I get you something cold to drink? Some ice water?”

The man’s grim expression relaxed as he traded the vase for the keypad. “I’ve got a cooler in my van in the parking garage across the street. But thanks.”

“Looks like Commissioner Madigan has a special admirer.” Elise hefted the over-the-top bouquet into her arms. Had George won some award he hadn’t mentioned? Been seeing someone during the few hours he wasn’t in the office?

“They’re for you, ma’am.” The deliveryman glanced down at his keypad screen. “You’re Elise Brown, right?”

Surprise warred with confusion inside her at the unexpected gift. “For me?”

“Yes, ma’am. Enjoy. And stay cool.” The man was all smiles as he walked away.

Elise touched her nose to one velvety blossom, cautiously inhaling its cloying, perfumey scent as she counted. Eleven, twelve…twenty-three yellow roses, complete with golden ribbons, baby’s breath and a cut-glass vase—for her?

The flowers grew unbearably heavy. *Twenty-three roses. One for every day we’ve been together.*

“Easy.” Suddenly, a strong hand cupped beneath hers, taking the weight of the glass. “We don’t want a flood on the carpet.”

A flash of blue danced into Elise’s peripheral vision a split second before her boss’s crisp voice startled her from her momentary paralysis. She backed away a step and hugged her arms securely around the vase. “I’ve got them." She turned and carried them to the corner of her desk. "Thanks."

The flowers might be a different color, but the similarity…twenty-three? Elise breathed in deeply, clearing the troubling thought from her mind. It wasn't possible. The florist had simply miscounted. Or the deliveryman had stolen one for his girlfriend. This was just a coincidence and she'd overreacted. That part of her past was over and done with.

Dead men didn't send flowers.

But who would?

Shuffling through the stems and greenery, Elise searched for a card that wasn't there. She pulled the empty plastic clamp from the vase that should have held the sender's name or a message for her, and hurried out into the hallway. "Wait a minute," she called after the deliveryman. "Who are these from? There's no card…."

But he'd already disappeared around the corner by the elevators and security desk. She could either kick off her heels and run after him, or solve the mystery on her own. And since Nikolai was dead… With another steadying breath, Elise had made her decision. *Ease up on the paranoia. There's a rational explanation. Figure it out.*

But when she turned around, she froze, her path blocked by George Madigan filling the doorway. His sturdy forearms were exposed by his rolled-up sleeves, and their tanned strength formed an impenetrable barrier folded across the front of his chest. "Did I miss your birthday?"

Although he wore no gun, his badge was right there, clipped to his belt, its polished blue enamel and extra brass chevrons indicating he had the right to stop her and ask any questions he wanted in this office. Elise tipped her face up to his narrowed gray eyes. Was that suspicion she saw there? Curiosity? Concern?

She knew that George Madigan on a mission could be an intimidating thing. His devotion to the department, his single-minded determination to solve problems, made him a force to be reckoned with in city and departmental politics. But the idea of him turning that perceptive intelligence and laser beam focus on her was as unnerving as it was thrilling.

And that made those little ripples of awareness stirring her blood far too dangerous.

Tempting as it might be to share her fears with her boss, Elise nixed the idea. Her problems were her own. She understood George Madigan well enough to get her job done, and that was as far as their relationship needed to go. Mixing work and personal was definitely a bad idea.

"Elise?"

Oh, snap. How long had she been staring at the loose knot of his tie?

Despite the air-conditioning that cooled the building's temperature to a tolerable level, Elise suddenly felt hot. She brushed aside a short dark wave of hair that clung to her damp skin and tucked it behind her ear before scooting around the file he fisted in one hand. "My birthday's not until September."

Two months away. Elise set the card holder beside the vase and sorted through the ribbons and greenery again. She found one broken stem being held upright by sprigs of baby's breath and the oversize bow, but still no card.

A queasy sense of unease turned in her stomach. Nikolai had sent her twenty-three red roses after he'd gone back to Russia. A thank-you, apology and *do svidaniya* all in one. But Nikolai was dead. Murdered by her former boss Quinn Gallagher's father-in-law when Nikolai had dared to threaten Quinn's daughter.

"I know it's not Administrative Professionals' Week. I marked that on my calendar." George followed her to the desk and reached out to finger one of the blooms. "These are unexpected."

It wasn't a question.

"Yes," she conceded, wishing she could mask her emotions as well as her boss could. "They're definitely a surprise."

The only men in her life were her father and her poodle mix, Spike, and neither one was the flower-sending type. Her mother was the one to remember special events, but nothing was happening in Elise's life today, or even this week. She hadn't completed the renovations on the Victorian home she was restoring, so any celebration of that was premature. Successfully housebreaking the dog hardly merited all these flowers. And the last man she'd gone out with certainly had no reason to send such a gift. Although they'd once shared a college romance, she'd made it clear to James this past weekend that she was only interested in friendship now that he was back in town after spending several years working abroad.

After her disastrous track record of unrequited love and getting involved with the wrong men, she wasn't interested in any kind of relationship.

Elise startled at the warm hand on her arm and looked up into George's eyes. "What's wrong?"

She jumped again when the telephone rang. Shaking off his touch and any further speculation about the roses, she leaned across her desk and picked up the receiver. "Deputy Commissioner Madigan's office. This is Elise speaking."

There was a long pause on the line, and then she heard, "Did you get them?"

The hushed, breathy voice was barely audible.

"Excuse me?"

"I got them special. Just for you."

Suddenly feeling too shaky to stand, Elise sank onto the edge of the cherrywood desk and turned her head toward the mysterious bouquet. "Who is this?"

The phone was pried from her grip by a stronger hand. "This is Deputy Commissioner Madigan of KCPD. Who—?"

The click of the call disconnecting was loud enough for Elise to hear. When she jerked her head back toward the sound, her gaze was filled with George's paisley tie and broad chest. That chest came even closer, almost folded around her, as he reached behind her to hang up the phone.

Elise pushed to her feet, curling her toes inside her pumps to steady herself, when she realized she'd nearly turned her nose into the inviting haven of the older man's crisp shirt and body heat.

But George didn't move. He stood there, feet planted like tree trunks to the floor, watching her reaction. "What's going on?"

Rubbing at the goose bumps revealed by her sleeveless dress, Elise shrugged off her confusion about the flowers as well as that sudden and inexplicable urge to take shelter against her boss's chest. "I have no idea."

George tossed the file onto her desk and quickly inspected the bouquet. "You don't know who these are from?" He didn't give her time to answer. "Did you recognize the caller on the phone?"

Elise shook her head. "I think it was a man's voice, but he was whispering. I could barely hear him. I would have thought it was a wrong number, but he…asked about the flowers. At least, I think that's what he meant. He didn't actually say 'flowers.'"

"I didn't catch a company logo on the deliveryman's shirt. Did you?" George was already headed for the hallway before she realized his intent. "I'll check with Shane at the front desk to see if he remembers the uniform. He should have logged him in, so we can at least get a name and who he works for. Then we can call and find out who ordered them."

Elise hurried after George, stopping him with a hand on his arm before he got out the door. "You don't have to go to all that trouble."

"Clearly, not knowing where these came from has upset you." He turned to face her. "I may spend my days balancing numbers and taking meetings, but I'm still a cop. I know when something doesn't smell right, and I remember how to track down a lead."

"But there's no crime here, Commissioner. And it's not your job to take care of me." As easy as it would be to let him find answers for her, Elise knew he had more important things to worry about than her self-conscious paranoia about mysterious romantic gestures. "If anything, I'm supposed to take care of you. I'll talk to Shane before I leave this evening." She nodded toward his office. "Besides, you're keeping the councilman and precinct chiefs waiting, and with this weather crisis, tempers are already shorter than usual. You need to return to your meeting."

"You're sure?" He glanced down at the spot where her pale fingers still clung to his tanned, muscular fore-arm.

Feeling her cheeks heat with embarrassment, Elise snatched her fingers away from the lingering contact and went back to her desk. "These could have been delivered to me by mistake. I'm probably just making trouble for myself by worrying about it."

It was a flimsy excuse, and George wasn't buying it. "The price of that bouquet is an awfully expensive mistake to make. Plus, the deliveryman called you by name."

This wouldn't be the first time she'd had to deal with an unwanted suitor or suffer the repercussions of a re-lationship mistake. She didn't have a good track record with men. But she certainly didn't want the boss she respected, and whose opinion of her she valued, to find out what a failure she was in her personal life. Whether this was someone's pathetic attempt to worm his way back into her good graces, a poorly timed coincidence or just a bad joke—she didn't want her problems to ever become a concern for George or the deputy com-missioner's office.

Elise's gaze landed on the stack of pink message pa-pers on her blotter. She circled the desk to pick them up and hand them to him. "You have three messages to handle when your meeting is done. Denton Hale has phoned twice. He wants a private meeting without the other union reps regarding possible staff cuts." Run-ning interference between her boss and disgruntled of-ficers and citizens was part of her job, and Elise had no problem doing it. Still, she felt a pang of sympathy, knowing how difficult a police officer's job could be without having to worry about money. "If we don't get extra funding from the city, some of the officers and support staff are going to be laid off, right?"

"It's a possibility," he answered honestly. "The city is pouring a lot of money into their infrastructure right now. I hope we can keep the personnel budget in check through attrition and simply not hire replacements for this year's retirees. I pray that's enough to avoid a strike. Hale isn't the only police officer worried about his job."

Elise nodded her understanding. "But he seems to be more worried than any of the others. He's pretty chatty on the phone. I said I'd have to discuss it with you before I scheduled it."

"Elise. What's wrong with the flowers?"

Without answering, she moved on to the next message. "Cliff Brandt from the city power district says his people have received more threats in response to the brownouts and power outages. He wants to know the result of this meeting as soon as you do. He's reluctant to let his people go out on calls unprotected, especially at night. And Mrs. Madigan said it was urgent that you return her call by five."

George was smart enough to see her diversionary tactic for what it was. But he played along, respecting her unspoken request to let the mystery of the flowers drop. "Don't stick my nose into your business, right?" Familiar lines bracketed his mouth again as he sorted through the messages. "Schedule Hale for tomorrow. Get Brandt on the phone for me in thirty minutes—it'll help me wrap up this meeting." He tucked the notes into his shirt pocket. "And Courtney's my ex-wife, not Mrs. Madigan. She gave up the right to use my name a decade ago when she said she couldn't be married to a street cop anymore. Any clue what she wants this time?"

Elise's attention shifted from the troublesome flowers to the weary sigh in George's tone. "A street cop?"

"I know. Hard to imagine, isn't it? I keep my sidearm locked in my desk and carry home budget reports instead of case files." He buttoned his collar and straightened the knot of his tie, although he didn't touch the rolled-up sleeves. "But I did my time in Vice and Narcotics once I made detective. I got into administration because I thought the desk job would make her happy. Turned out I had a knack for paper pushing and bottom lines so I stayed with it, even after she left."

Elise frowned, surprised to hear faint echoes of resignation and regret in his voice. "You still wear a badge. You're still KCPD. A lot of people in the department count on you to do your job—even if your ex-wife doesn't appreciate that."

George nodded at her show of support, even as he dismissed it. "There was more than my job wrong with our marriage." He picked up the folder he'd set down without elaborating any further. "When Court calls back, and she will—since she dropped Madigan, she must want something pretty badly—you can refer to her as Ms. Reiter."

"Yes, sir."

"Commissioner Madigan?" Henry Johnson's voice was shrill and impatient, calling from his office.

George's chest expanded with a deep breath. He checked his watch. "It's almost four o'clock. Why don't you close up shop out here. As soon as I wrap up this meeting and connect with Cliff Brandt, you can head home early. I'll lock up."

Although Elise appreciated the kind gesture, and knew she needed to go home to let Spike out into the backyard for a romp, the otherwise empty expanses of her torn-up house with its two overworked window air conditioners didn't seem particularly inviting right now. What if that phone call hadn't been a mistake and exactly twenty-three roses were meant for her? What if that ghostly voice was leaving a message on her personal answering machine or voice mail right now?

Even the unlucky coincidence of these flowers coming from James or some other old boyfriend wasn't exactly comforting. That meant her "no thanks" on a relationship hadn't registered, and that she had another long conversation, if not an outright confrontation, to look forward to this evening.

Right now, work—and the confines of her nicely appointed, if slightly humid, office—seemed more of a solace than the paint cans, phone calls or potential surprise visits that might be waiting for her at home.

"If it's all right, I'd like to stay here—I need to type up the notes for your speech at the annual officers' retirement luncheon."

George groaned. "That damned speech. If Commissioner Cartwright-Masterson wasn't expecting her first grandchild…"

Elise smiled and shooed him toward his office. "The commissioner wouldn't have asked you to take her place on the podium if she didn't trust you to represent her and the department in stellar fashion."

"That doesn't mean you need to stay late just to make me sound good at the banquet. I'll work on it. You get out of here and enjoy the AC someplace where you actually have to put on a sweater because it's so cold."

Instead of laughing at what she assumed was a joke, she offered him a half-truth. "Sounds tempting, but… I'm getting out of an unwanted date tonight with an old friend. The excuse I gave for not meeting him for dinner was that I had to work late. Do you mind?"

George arched one of his dark brows in a skeptical frown. "Maybe that unwanted date is who sent the flowers. Could be he's trying to change your mind."

"It won't."

"You should still ask him."

Elise considered the possibility. Maybe she would give James a call. But later, so he wouldn't think she'd changed her mind about his dinner invitation. "I'll check with Shane first and call the desk downstairs if he doesn't have the florist's name."

Shaking his head, George headed for his office. "Fine. I'll alibi you out. Tell Mr. Unwanted that your boss is an old curmudgeon who works your fingers until they bleed and doesn't allow you a personal life."

Elise smiled at the self-effacing comment and watched him walk away, idly noting that there was nothing old or curmudgeonly about the way his shirt hugged his powerful build. And though she knew he was more than a dozen years her senior, the lines beside his eyes and salt-and-pepper hair only added to the air of seasoned authority and masculinity he wore like a second skin. There was no mistaking George Madigan for a boyish college sweetheart or a duplicitous charmer who'd prey on her vulnerable feelings to get what he wanted from her. He was an old-school, straightforward, get-the-job-done man's man.

After an unintentional betrayal that had nearly cost her former boss at Gallagher Security Systems and his family their lives, Elise knew she was lucky to have this job. And although Quinn Gallagher claimed he didn't blame her for any of the mess that had nearly destroyed him, Elise knew she could have saved him a lot of trouble if she'd been thinking with her head instead of a broken heart. Turning in her resignation to the man she'd loved but could never have had been the right thing to do. But picking up the pieces of her life again hadn't been easy.

With that kind of personal and professional track record, Elise was grateful to have this well-paying, well-respected position doing meaningful work for the department and Kansas City. The deputy commissioner's faith in her had done more to heal her self-esteem and rebuild her trust in men than any self-help book could. That's all she should be focusing on. Noticing that George Madigan was an attractive man, noticing anything more than him as a fair leader and kind friend, could only lead to the sort of trouble she didn't need in her life.

So she ignored those little frissons of awareness that warmed her blood and sat down to work. "Thank you, sir."

He paused at the door, exhaling an audible sigh before glancing over his shoulder at her. "It's 'George' when it's just you and me talking. Okay? 'Sir' makes me feel like an old man."

Not a chance.

But before Elise could do something foolish like tell him he was a fit man in his prime, Henry Johnson shouted from his office again. "Deputy Commissioner? Today?"

With a smile that was part relief, part sympathy, Elise shooed him on his way. "You'd better not keep him waiting any longer. You want to win his support, remember?"

George paused with his hand on the doorknob, looking as if he had something more to say. Instead of speaking to Elise, though, he opened the door. "I got the file I needed, Henry. Now let's compare the costs of prevention strategies versus…"

When the door closed behind him, Elise turned to her computer and pulled up the memos he'd sent her for distribution and started proofing and addressing them. With the discussion on the other side of George's door now muted, she worked in relative silence for several minutes.

But the bouquet was casting a shadow over her work space, drawing her attention away from her keyboard and screen. Maybe she should take the time now to walk down the hall to chat with Shane Wilkins, the floor officer. Or maybe she could spare a few minutes to call James. Or her parents. Do a little investigating on her own.

Elise rose in a huff and picked up the heavy glass vase to move the roses out of sight on the counter behind her desk. "Or maybe I should just get my work done and deal with you later. I know a nice hospital where you'll be very happy and greatly appreciated," she said to the flowers as she set them down.

With that much of a plan in mind, Elise sat down to finish the memos and save them for George's final sign-off in the morning.

Do you like my gift?

The breathy whisper seeped into her thoughts to distract her again. Who else knew that her murdered mobster lover had sent her twenty-three roses, thanking her for the unintended pillow talk regarding her former employer, making a mockery of the way she'd given her heart and body to him? Or was this just an unfortunate coincidence that she was turning into something more sinister?

Lots of people got roses every day. Red ones, pink ones, yellow ones—any color of the rainbow for any occasion or no reason at all. They didn't mean anything other than "congratulations" or "get well" or "thinking of you."

So why did it feel as though someone was looking over her shoulder now?

Elise spun her chair around and gazed at the hated gift. Then she picked it up and set the vase back on her desk.

Better to keep the things that worried her in plain sight than to let them sneak up and nearly ruin her life again.

Chapter Two

"Sorry, Spikey."

Elise laughed at the furry black bullet that shot out from beneath her spirea bushes as the first spray of water from the sprinkler hit the tiny white flowers and dark green leaves. The dog was in her lap the moment she climbed up onto the new wood deck and stretched out on the chaise lounge, demanding a tummy rub and some kind words to make up for being splashed.

"Maybe you shouldn't bury your treats out there. If you'd chew them up when I give them to you, instead of hiding them in the yard, you wouldn't risk taking an impromptu bath when I turn on the water." Elise rubbed the dog's soft, curly hair a few seconds longer, then kissed him on his head and set the miniature poodle/terrier mix on the deck beside her. "It's still too hot for a cuddle, though, you brave little toodle face. You'd better scout out the perimeter before we turn in for the night."

With a soft tap to his rump, Spike scooted down the steps and followed his nose into the grass. Elise would be happy if the warm wind shifted and misted some of the water over her bare legs, shorts and paint shirt, but not the dog. She grinned, watching Spike circle along the fence, avoiding the spray while he reclaimed his rawhide chew from beneath the bushes.

Truly relaxing for the first time today, Elise picked up the icy glass of tea on the table beside her and flicked away the condensation before taking a long drink. She touched her damp palm to the nape of her neck before leaning back to enjoy the peaceful retreat of her backyard at twilight. She figured the reprieve would last about five to ten minutes before the mosquitoes found her. But by then, she'd be heading back in to finish cleaning up from the evening's renovation work.

She took another leisurely sip, purposely letting the moisture from the glass drip onto the front of her dad's old button-down shirt and trickle beneath the placket to her hot skin. The soft, worn cotton was stained with all the colors of her remodel, including a splash of dark blue from the shutters she'd been painting for the living and dining room areas this evening.

Once, she'd dreamed of restoring a home like this with her former boss, Quinn Gallagher, and raising a family together in the big house and spacious backyard. But Quinn, a widower who'd needed his trusted assistant to fill in as babysitter, comforter and sounding board, had fallen in love with someone else. And the need that Elise had hoped would blossom into something more had vanished in the span of a few hectic, dangerous days, leaving her reeling and alone. Easy pickings for Quinn's business associate, Nikolai Titov, who had said all the right things and made her feel wanted…and then used information she'd inadvertently shared to not only ratchet up his plot to destroy Quinn's security empire, but to murder Quinn and his daughter. Fortunately, Quinn's new wife, a rifle-toting member of KCPD's premier SWAT team, had been there to save them both.

A familiar knot of guilt and regret twisted in Elise's stomach. While she couldn't fault Quinn and his daughter for claiming happiness and moving on with their lives, there'd been no one but her parents to help her pick up the pieces of her broken dreams two years ago. And she'd been too humiliated to share everything with them. She hadn't even shared all the details with the counselor who'd evaluated her before qualifying for the job at police department headquarters. How foolish or desperate did a woman have to be to have an affair with a man, and not know until he sent her flowers from the airport as he was leaving the country that he didn't feel anything for her at all—that he'd only been using her?

Eric and Susan Brown had known something had changed in their daughter after that. They'd helped her make the down payment on this run-down Victorian with good bones in a quiet neighborhood south of downtown K.C. They'd encouraged her to dip into her savings for new appliances and updated wiring. They'd set her up on a couple of dates and said they understood when Elise bowed out of seeing those perfectly nice men a second or third time.

It was just her and Spike and a lot of hard work now. Hardly her dream life. Quinn and his wife were raising a family, all right, but Elise wasn't any part of it. After Quinn and Nikolai, she didn't want a man in her life. It hurt too much to love the wrong person, to believe in something that wasn't really hers. She couldn't trust a strong shoulder to lean on, even if it did smell of crisp cotton and musky man.

An image of George Madigan's stern countenance

drifted into her thoughts. Turning to him for grounding comfort had been so tempting this afternoon. A full-fledged smile from the man would probably awaken the hormones she kept in careful stasis inside her. And she could guess that a man in the prime of his life like George would definitely know how to use that firm, masculine mouth to kiss a woman.

"Really?" Alarmed by the sudden drift of her thoughts, Elise put the glass to her own lips, mentally warning herself to chill. She knew the hazards of a workplace romance better than anyone.

She shouldn't wish that she had more hugs and laughter and love in her life. She had her job at KCPD and her own place that was gradually transforming into a thing of beauty. George needed her to keep his life and office running efficiently, not speculate about kissing him. After a hundred years of use and neglect, this house needed her to care for it. Her days were full. Both jobs were as rewarding as they were exhausting. She'd adopted a wonderful dog from a shelter to keep her company. She didn't have to depend on anyone. She didn't need anything more.

She shouldn't want…more.

A drop of ice-cold water fell from the glass and splashed her thigh near the fraying hem of her denim shorts, startling her from the depressing quagmire of her thoughts. "Oh. Wow."

She hadn't gone to that dark place for a while, and hated that she'd allowed the loneliness to creep into her head the moment she'd stopped for a break. Must be the flowers she'd received at work and deposited at St. Luke's Medical Center afterward for distribution to needy patients. The gift reminded her of that horrible time, that was all. It didn't mean she still had to wallow in the past.

Dismissing any remnants of longing or dissatisfaction, Elise wiped away the rivulet of water on her skin and swallowed the last of her tea. Swinging her feet down to the deck, she sat up on the edge of the chaise lounge and peered over the railing to find the dog before heading inside. "Spike?"

Just as she put her lips together to whistle, he let out a high-pitched bark and charged through the yard, heedless of the spinning water that dampened his hair as he ran past. He was sounding the toodle alarm, barking at something or someone at the side of the house.

Elise set down her glass and stood. "Spike! Shush!" With the last fingers of daylight leaving the high, cloudless sky a muted shade of gray, she could guess it was around nine o'clock. Some of her older neighbors were probably trying to settle in for the night. "You'll wake someone." She clapped her hands to divert his attention. "Spike!"

But fifteen pounds of ferocious guard dog wouldn't be silenced.

Elise hurried down the steps and followed him to the chain-link fence to see what had alarmed him. But when she saw the tall blond man walking up the sidewalk to her backyard gate, she slowed her steps. Her guest might look handsome enough in his pressed jeans and polo shirt, but he wasn't necessarily welcome. "James."

"Is it safe?" James Westbrook tucked the skinny sack he carried beneath one arm and knelt down to hold his hand flat against the fence to let Spike sniff and lick his palm. "Hey, big guy. Remember me?" Spike's barking quieted with the recognition of a familiar scent. But his long tail curled between his legs and he darted behind Elise when James reached over the top of the gate to pet him. "I guess not."

As he pulled back to his side of the gate, Elise brushed her hair off her forehead, although that was probably the least messy thing about her ratty painting attire. She noted with annoyance that James's well-gelled hair was barely moving in the bursts of wind swirling dust and dirt through the air. "What are you doing here? It's late."

"I rang the doorbell, but no one answered."

Elise glanced up at the steady hum of her bedroom air conditioner, sticking out from the window above the back door. She hadn't heard anything. Of course, the sprinkler made a little bit of noise. And she'd been neck deep in self-pity for the past few minutes, too.

But wouldn't Spike have heard the doorbell? Or the slam of a car door? Maybe that's what had alerted him in the first place. If so, James had decided pretty quickly to come to the backyard rather than wait on the porch for her to answer.

Despite the ninety-degree heat that lingered, Elise shivered with an uncomfortable sense of déjà vu. Since the debacle of Nikolai, she never had liked surprises. And now she'd had two in the same day? She tipped her chin up to assess James's unexpected arrival. "What are you doing here?" she repeated. "You got my message, didn't you?"

"That you were working late?" He adjusted the slim glasses he wore and smiled. "I thought you meant at the office. If I'd known you were painting tonight, I'd have gotten some takeout and come over to help." He glanced down at the gate between them, then pulled off the sack to reveal the bottle of wine he'd brought. "May I come in? It's a cabernet sauvignon, like we drank back at Mizzou."

Another gift.

Perhaps not as significant as twenty-three roses, but unsettling, all the same.

"James," she began. Elise inhaled a deep breath, clearing the *Go away* from the tip of her tongue and summoning a polite explanation. Not that she really owed him one. But bitchiness just wasn't in her nature. "I did work until about six. Then I had errands to run. By the time I got home, it was too late to meet you anywhere. So I changed into these old clothes, zapped some leftovers in the microwave and went to work on the shutters."

"What do you do for fun, Lise?"

Trying not to bristle at the pet name he'd given her when they'd been dating, Elise gestured toward the pale gray siding and white trim. "Reclaiming this house is fun for me."

"No. That's rewarding," he corrected with a teasing smile. "Sounds like you're avoiding me." He raised the wine bottle again. "Could be why I felt like I needed to bring a peace offering."

Guilty feelings surfaced, then eased out on a breathy sigh. "It's not you, James," she assured him. "It's me." And a screwed-up love life, a little lack of confidence and nary a spark of the attraction a younger, more innocent Elise had once felt for him. "I'm flattered by your attention, but I'm just not interested in a relationship right now."

"I get that." He dropped his hand to the gate, but she still made no move to open it. "You and I broke up a long time ago when we graduated from college and I took that job in Korea. But we're still friends, right? We share history. I've been back in the States for a couple of months now, but Kansas City doesn't feel like home yet. I find I'm still thinking in a foreign language. I make wrong turns in the neighborhood where I grew up. Landmarks have changed or aren't even there anymore." He slid his hand over to rest on hers. "Can you blame me for seeking out a familiar face?"

Elise pulled away from the warmth of his fingers and bent down to pick up the dog. It was an obvious wall of defense she was putting up, but Spike didn't seem to mind. The dog licked her jaw a couple of times before settling into her arms and Elise smiled, even as James's faded. "What about your father?" she asked. "Isn't he retired now? Won't he spend time with you? There's a Royals game on TV tonight."

"To be honest, I was hoping for some younger, prettier company than Dad. You and I could watch the game." He slipped the wine bottle back into the sack and held it out to her. "I promise to keep the evening perfectly platonic."

The streetlamp in front of her house flickered on and grew bright. Even if she trusted James's promise, the hour was late. She had to be at work early in the morning. "To be honest, I was getting ready to clean up and go to bed."

His eyes narrowed behind his glasses before he sighed and shook his head. "Once upon a time you and I talked about getting married, Lise."

The regret in his tone cooled the air around them. She'd admit that there were some good memories between them. But that was all they were—memories.

There was not one pang of hope or regret when she looked at James now. "We were practically kids then. You wanted to see the world, and I'd snagged that internship at Gallagher Security Systems. We just weren't meant to be."

"You turned that internship at GSS into a career, didn't you. I bet you were making good money there." He folded his arms over his chest, eyeing her like the businessman he was. "Why'd you leave that kind of success and take a job with the city?"

Her smile faded. She rubbed her fingers along the soft warmth of Spike's flank, buying time to compose herself before deciding on the appropriate answer. She wound up using the same vague truth she'd given in her interview with George Madigan. "Money isn't everything. There was nothing more for me at GSS. I wanted new surroundings. I needed a new challenge."

"Turning this into a showplace isn't challenging enough?" He pointed to the painter's tape lining the glass inside the dining room windows. "Are you sure I can't help you do something here?"

Elise looked at his hands, which were pale and pristine compared to the stained fingers with which she was petting the dog. He wasn't really into home repair work, was he? "I've made enough of a mess for one night. I'm really tired."

"Maybe another time?" He put up his hands in placating surrender before she could answer. "Strictly as friends. I don't know why you're so gun-shy about rekindling things, but I won't put any pressure on you. Like I said, I'm just looking for someone my age to hang out with until I get my feet under me again."

"How about I invite you over the next time I have a big piece of furniture to move."

He laughed, and the awkwardness between them eased a little bit. "Deal." He thrust the wine over the top of the gate. "Here. You'd better take this."

Elise backed away a step. "I couldn't."

"Of course, you can. It's a gift."

If he was hoping she'd invite him in to share a glass, then he'd be in for a long wait. Still, she sensed he wasn't going to move until she accepted the so-called peace offering. At least she knew who was giving her this gift. She wrapped her hand around the neck of the bottle.

"Thank you." *Ask him. Why not?* Clearing up the mystery would go a long way toward improving her chances of getting a good night's sleep. "Did you send me flowers at work today? There wasn't a card attached, and the officer at the front desk said he didn't find one, either. I haven't had a chance to check with the florist yet. It's a bit of a mystery."

"You used to like it when I sent you flowers." He grinned. "Remember? A daisy or a rose? To commemorate any little event—acing an exam, the start of spring break…" He grasped the rail at the top of the gate and leaned in. "Thanking you for a special night?"

Yes. Those had been sweet and romantic and fitting for the young couple they'd once been. Not the point. "The flowers I got today weren't cheap."

He snorted. "That cabernet wasn't cheap."

"James, did you—?"

"I can see I'm not getting anywhere with you tonight." He shook his head, then adjusted his glasses, glancing skyward before zeroing his gaze in on hers.

"Keep an eye on the weather. We're under a tornado watch until midnight. I wouldn't want you or the pooch there to get hurt. Good night."

And then he was striding away.

Her mouth opened to call after him to clarify his response to her question, but Elise wisely snapped it shut. Better to just let him leave. "Good night," she muttered.

Were straight answers really so much to ask for? Elise plopped Spike down on his feet in the grass as James walked to the curb where he'd parked. A black-and-white police car cruised past on its regular rounds for the night, giving her ex the impetus to climb behind the wheel and start the engine when he hesitated at the open door, no doubt readying another argument as to why she should rethink sending him away.

Elise waited for James to pull into the driveway behind her car and back out in the opposite direction to leave the neighborhood, and then she turned off the water and picked up her glass. "Come on, boy. Here, Spike."

The dog bounded up onto the deck and followed her into the house. He danced around her feet while she locked the back door and headed into the kitchen. She hit the light switch with her elbow, flooding the room with light before setting the wine on the granite counter and rinsing out her glass. She turned on the radio to get an update on the possibility of dangerous weather, got Spike a treat from the jar next to the sink and set about her nightly check of the doors and windows on the first floor.

She secured locks and pulled window shades and makeshift curtains, listening to the jingle of Spike's tags as he lapped up a drink of water in the kitchen.

She stopped for several seconds in front of the living room air conditioner, unhooking the top couple of buttons on her paint shirt and cooling the perspiration on her skin before turning it down for the night. Moving into the foyer, the growing noise from the wind cruising through the leafy trees outside and knocking twigs and other debris against the house fully registered. Elise paused with her fingers on the front door's dead bolt.

She could hear the dog in the kitchen at the back of the house.

Her breath hitched in her chest at the disquieting thought that crossed her mind. Praying that she'd be proved wrong, Elise quickly returned to the living room and turned the AC unit back on high. The light in the foyer flickered at the sudden drain on the neighborhood's overtaxed power grid as the machine roared to life and the cold air blasted her again.

Noisy enough. She couldn't hear Spike anymore.

Then she opened the red front door and reached outside to press the doorbell.

The instant the bell chimed, Spike barked and came running from the kitchen. He barked again, eager to greet or warn off their visitor.

"Shush. It's okay, sweetie. It's just Mommy testing a theory."

But the yapping and squealing continued until she picked him up and pushed open the storm door to show him no one was there. Greeted by a wall of summer heat and uncomfortable suspicion, Elise crossed the porch, mentally timing how long it took her to reach the railing at the edge of the house.

Elise hugged the dog against her shoulder, patting his back as if burping a baby. "He lied to us, Spike."

Such a small slip of the tongue. Maybe nothing more sinister than a clichéd response.

I rang the doorbell.

No way had James stood on her front porch, announcing his arrival. He would have needed to sprint down the steps and around the side of the house to the back gate to reach her before Spike heard the bell and sounded his alarm. But James had strolled up the walk. His breathing had been perfectly normal, without a drop of sweat visible anywhere.

Glancing up and down the street, Elise peered into shadows beyond the streetlights but saw nothing out of sorts. The only thing that wasn't right was the portentous wind that made her clothes instantly stick to her skin again, and the nagging suspicion about a man who claimed to be her friend.

Why would James lie? What was the point of sneaking around her house? And when she'd asked him about the flowers, he'd never actually confirmed sending them. Or denied it.

She'd gotten rid of the roses. She'd gotten rid of James.

But she couldn't get rid of the feeling that her life had taken a very weird, very unsettling turn.

GEORGE HEARD THE hurried rhythm of a woman's high heels tapping across KCPD headquarters' marble floors behind him.

"Hold the elevator, please."

Even if he hadn't recognized the voice, he would have pushed the button to hold the doors open. It was the polite thing to do. But he did recognize Elise Brown's articulate, slightly breathless tone, and his blood suffused with an instant warmth.

"Thanks." Elise tilted her head and smiled as she darted into the car and moved to the railing behind him.

He knew it was wrong to identify his assistant by the warm contralto pitch of her voice. And he shouldn't be familiar with the faint whiff of tropical fruits that emanated from the soft waves of her chin-length hair as she breezed past him. His gaze dipped down to the navy blue heels she wore without hose, a choice made in deference to the forecasted triple-digit temperatures, no doubt. While a part of him admired the sensible concession to the summer heat wave, George's chest constricted and he resolutely averted his eyes.

He wasn't admiring her sensibility. He was imprinting the curve of her smooth, tanned calves beneath a hemline that brushed the top of her knees to memory, coming up with another completely inappropriate, equally unmistakable way to identify Elise Brown.

Yeah, his life would be a heck of a lot easier if he wasn't so observant of little details like that—especially where his executive assistant was concerned.

Pushing the button for the eighth floor, George tempered the quickened pace of his breathing and made sure his commander-in-chief expression was in place before he turned to greet her. "Good morning, Elise."

He might have hit fifty, but he wasn't dead. He was single and he was a man. Couldn't blame a guy for noticing an attractive woman. Still, it wasn't quite protocol to charge up with this rush of energy just because she'd smiled at him, just because he got to spend a few moments alone on the elevator with her clean, fresh scent. He felt more awake, more alert, than he had a few seconds ago. And he hadn't even had his first cup of coffee yet.

She tucked her sunglasses into the modest neckline of her sleeveless dress and brushed a swath of nut-brown hair off her cheek. "Good morning, sir."

Way to kill the buzz. It was one thing for the men and women he outranked at KCPD to refer to him with the respectful title. It was something else again for the woman he worked with every day of his life to call him sir. Hearing that from Elise, no matter how well intended, always made him feel like one of her father's friends or a Dutch uncle. It was easy to squash any perky urge to smile now.

The doors drifted together and the elevator made a slight bounce before starting its ascent. "It's George, remember?"

"I'm sorry. Good morning, George."

"No need to apologize. I'll just keep reminding you until you get it right," he teased.

Only, she didn't seem to get the joke. Her blue gaze darted up to his before she suddenly needed something from her flowered purse and focused her attention there. "Of course."

While he was careful about crossing the line into anything that could be construed as sexual harassment, there was no harm in being friends. Yet Elise seemed to shoot down every overture of appreciation or concern that could take them to being more than polite acquaintances who shared the same connected office space.

Even yesterday afternoon, when the delivery of those flowers had clearly upset her, she hadn't opened up one bit. Maybe a small stab of unprofessional jealousy had made him linger in her office longer than he'd intended.

She'd lit up at first, once she found out the bouquet was meant for her, and he'd been curious enough to find out what kind of man she was dating who could turn her serious, practical head like that.

But even when Elise's smile had changed to a frown, and her troubled thoughts had been written on her face, she hadn't been interested in sharing a thing. She hadn't even wanted him to dust off his rusty investigative skills and make a few quick inquiries to find where the bouquet had come from for her.

The elevator continued its familiar climb, but there was little familiar about Elise's oddly distracted behavior this morning. She pulled a ring of keys and fobs from her bag and clutched them in her fist, staring at them. Tugging back the front of his suit jacket, George propped his hands at his waist. "Is everything all right?"

"What?" Her eyes locked on to his, telling him one thing before she stuffed the keys back into her purse and told him something else. "Oh. I couldn't find the spare key I leave on my front porch after I walked the dog this morning." She patted her purse. "I like to use it so I don't have to carry all these and be weighed down. Don't worry. We got in through the keypad by the garage door. That's why I'm running a little late today."

Uh-uh. She wasn't dismissing the confusion he'd read in her gaze. Not this time. "Are you worried someone stole the key?"

The corners of her mouth tightened as she fixed the smile on her lips. "I probably locked it inside the house the last time I used it and forgot. I didn't have much time to look."

George valued Elise as his assistant. His office had been a chaotic mess after the previous assistant retired.

Elise had come in, quickly grasping the old information management and communication systems and updating them in ways that made his job easier, and made the entire deputy commissioner's office a model of professional efficiency that other administrative departments were now copying.

But he'd been friends with each of his partners over the years. He'd gotten to know officers and staff alike. He knew the names of their children; whether they were football, baseball or basketball fans, or if they were even into sports at all. He knew what their favorite places to eat were and what issues they might be struggling with on the job or off the clock.

Elise went to great lengths to keep her personal life out of the office. He knew the names of her parents from her personnel file, but had never met them. And other than noting she wore no wedding ring and kept no pictures except one of a small black poodle on her desk, he couldn't confirm whether or not she was in a relationship with anyone.

As stormy as his marriage to Courtney had been, he'd always kept a memento of her on his desk or in his wallet. And now that they were divorced, he had family pictures from his nephew Nick's wedding on the shelves in his office, as well as a group photo from his twenty-fifth reunion at the University of Central Missouri on his desk.

But Elise? No pictures. No personal touches. Just the dog in her lap in one five-by-seven photo, and an invisible wall that said *Keep Out.*

George butted in, anyway. "Something's upset you again. Something more than a misplaced key." He shifted his stance, feeling the elevator slow its ascent. "What is it?"

For a few endless seconds, she tilted her cornflower-blue eyes up to his, giving him a glimpse of the turbulent emotions darkening their depths. Feeling an instinctive urge to respond to that unspoken plea for help, George stepped closer and reached for her.

But the elevator jerked to a stop. Elise blinked her gaze from his and moved to the front of the car. "I'm okay," she lied.

The doors slid open and the chance to help was lost.

A lanky cop with dark blond hair that needed to see a comb rose from his chair behind the eighth floor security desk to greet them. "Good morning, sir. Morning, Elise."

"Wilkins." George slipped his hands into the pockets of his slacks, not sure what to do with the fingertips that itched with frustrated anticipation at the interrupted moment on the elevator.

Elise hurried across the lobby ahead of him to swipe her ID badge over the computerized card reader that Officer Wilkins set on top of the desk. Her serene smile was firmly in place as she looped the ID lanyard around her neck. "Hey, Shane. How are you today?"

The young uniformed officer hooked his thumbs into his utility belt and pulled his shoulders back. "Fit and fine. Ran my five miles this morning."

"In this heat?"

Shane laughed. "That's why I do it before dawn. No matter what the weather does to us, I have to stick to my training if I'm going to place in KC's half marathon on Labor Day weekend. It's only a few weeks away."

Elise gave an exaggerated groan. "I barely want to

walk out to my car in this heat. I admire your persistence and dedication."

The younger man winked at her. "I try."

George swiped his card and then clipped it to his belt beside his badge. He was out of smiles this morning and ready to work. "Is Commissioner Cartwright-Masterson in yet?"

Shane rightly turned his attention to his superior officer. "No, sir. Do you want me to tell her you're looking for her when she checks in?"

George shook his head, hating that he was in such a mood. "No. I'm just curious if there's any news on her son Seth's baby yet. I know she wants to take a few days off then, but I'm hoping to get a little heads-up before it happens and the extra workload kicks in."

"If I hear anything, you will, too," Shane assured him.

"Thanks." Elise was already heading around the corner into the hallway that led to their offices. Running away from him and his questions, it seemed. Whatever she'd been about to share in the elevator had been locked up tight inside her again. He'd be a smart man to respect her privacy and forget his concern. He'd be a smarter man to take care of the people he was responsible for. He flattened his hand on top of the counter, demanding Shane's undivided attention. "In between screening visitors, you ought to apply some of that 'persistence and dedication' to studying for your detective's exam. You got your degree in May, right?"

"Yes, sir. Finished it in three years instead of four. And that's while I was working full-time."

With that kind of drive, Shane was probably frustrated getting stuck on guard duty at KCPD headquarters. "You know I'll put in a good word for you with the promotions board as soon as you pass the exam."

"I appreciate that."

George nodded. Sometimes, it was nice to have clout and be able to make a difference in a deserving person's life. "Have a good one."

"You, too, sir."

And sometimes that clout didn't do him a damn bit of good. George followed Elise to the reception area and the suite of offices at the end of the hallway. When he nudged open the door to her office, he was instantly hit with the sickeningly sweet smell of roses filling the air. And in the split second he wondered if a woman really was impressed with that stinky kind of excess, he plowed into Elise's back.

"Whoa." Before he sent her flying across the carpet, George grabbed her by the shoulders and kept her from falling. "Is there a reason why you stopped in the middle of the room?"

"They shouldn't be here."

And that's when he realized she was frozen. In more ways than one. Her upper arms felt like ice beneath his fingers. He couldn't seem to help rubbing his hands up and down her chilled skin, trying to instill some warmth. He looked over her shoulder to her desk and the yellow roses that had transfixed her, and this time, he wasn't budging until he got an answer. "Explain."

Elise never averted her gaze, never took a step away from him, so George never let go. She eased a sigh out on a deep, stuttered breath, then inhaled again before answering.

"It bothered me that I didn't know who sent the roses, so I dropped them off at St. Luke's on the way home last night. They're too much and I didn't want them." She hugged her arms in front of her and shivered in his grip. "I got rid of them."

George stepped up beside her to get a better look, dropping a steadying hand to the small of her back. "You're certain these are the same?"

She nodded, recoiling a bit against his palm. "Cut-glass vase. There are only twenty-three roses, not twenty-four. One stem is broken. He brought them back."

George quickly verified her description and began formulating possible scenarios to explain this twisted prank. Judging by her behavior in the elevator, he could guess this wasn't the only worrisome puzzle Elise had been dealing with.

But how much of the story was she willing to share? How hard would he have to push her to get to the truth? And were her troubles any of his damn business?

Yes.

This was a threat to his office. A breach of security at the highest ranks of the police department. Besides, seeing cool, calm and collected Elise Brown rattled like this—to see his right arm, his executive partner being hurt this way—felt personal. They were a team. And nobody messed with his teammates. He'd had his partners' backs for years when he'd worn a uniform or cleaned drugs and thugs off the streets. Even though his gun was locked in his desk drawer, he was still a cop. He couldn't allow this kind of thing to happen in his office, not on his watch. Not to Elise.

"I'll take care of it," he said, turning her back out of her office. The fact that she didn't argue with him was as much of a red flag as the creepy reappearance of the bouquet. Something was seriously wrong here.

George led her to a couch in the reception area before marching down the hall to have Shane get a list of everyone who'd been on this floor in the past twelve hours, as well as any cleaning and maintenance staff or personnel who had master keys. He'd make sure every last one was accounted for. He'd make this right.

Or else he'd never be able to shake the memory of Elise trembling against the palm of his hand and murmuring to herself, "He brought them back."

Chapter Three

Missing keys. Unwanted gifts. Unanswered questions.

Elise was beginning to wonder if someone was trying to gaslight her into thinking she was nuts. Or maybe she really was going crazy.

George had removed the flowers before she reentered her office that morning. And though she was curious to know what he'd done with them, she was more relieved to have them gone.

He'd made a couple of calls on his cell phone. No one at the medical center remembered seeing her the night before. And the clerk at the information desk said she'd handled too many deliveries to recall any one particular bouquet of roses.

Elise watched George pace in and out of their office suite, keeping an eye on her and warning her to stay put, even after she'd come to her senses, reined in the fearful paranoia and assured him she was fit for duty. She was nearly an hour behind brewing coffee and sending out the daily correspondence before George and Annie Fensom, a petite, dark-haired woman from the crime lab, exited Elise's office and her boss had declared she could go in.

Although Elise recognized Annie from the wedding

photos in George's office, she knew the CSI hadn't answered his call to take care of family business. She'd come with her lab kit and left with a kiss on the cheek from her uncle-in-law and a promise to try to identify the "numerous prints" she'd found in and around Elise's desk. Not that Annie was holding out much hope, she'd overheard. There were no fingerprints on the vase itself, not even Elise's, indicating the glass had been wiped clean. And any prints around the room could be attributed to the KCPD personnel, maintenance staff and registered guests who came in and out of the office on a regular basis.

The deputy commissioner had ordered Shane to bring her a bottle of water, and then put him to work compiling a list of everyone who'd been on this floor between the time they'd closed up shop the evening before and when Shane had reported for duty this morning. Shane had offered to make a second list of anyone in maintenance or other departments who had keys to access the building offices, earning him some brownie points with the deputy commissioner for his thorough thinking.

While she was glad George had been there to keep her sane and upright when she might have done something stupid like burst into tears or hurl the vase out the window to the sidewalk below, Elise knew it was important to renew her independence and resurrect the emotional walls that kept her boss at an impersonal distance again. She wouldn't turn over her trust to a man simply because she needed someone, the way she had with Nikolai. And she couldn't sit around and do nothing while everyone else around her worked—especially when it was her problem they were trying to solve.

It had taken two friendly assurances, and finally

a third "Go" that was a little more terse, to convince George to leave for his lunch meeting.

Frankly, Elise was glad to have an hour of quiet while she ate her lunch at her desk and got her day back on schedule and her head back where it needed to be. She'd already sent out two memos with the wrong date this morning before she caught her mistake. Not that being a day off would cause anyone any grief, but the police department prided itself on getting their facts straight, and, as a representative of KCPD, so did she.

Quiet. Focus. Normal routine. Those were the things she needed to get her day back on track.

Quiet, she'd managed by staying in the office instead of joining her coworkers in the break room. Typing and filing and organizing were about as routine as her job could get.

But focus? Elise had turned on a small fan to disperse the lingering odor of the roses that had filled the room, but she was having a harder time dispelling the clean, masculine scent of George Madigan that seemed to permeate every inch of carpeting and upholstery in the adjoining rooms. Or maybe his was just a unique fragrance that had burned into her memory when she'd leaned into him this morning.

She could rationalize that the remembered scent was a mental association that had to do with strength and security. Thinking of her boss as a man who made her feel safe was perfectly reasonable. But there was nothing rational about wishing she could burrow into that heat and strength and enticing scent, and simply forget about the weird happenings of the past two days. If she wasn't careful, that need to feel safe, that latent awareness of an attractive man, might blossom into an emotional connection, into those feelings of trust and desire that had been her downfall more than once in her life.

Elise drank a long sip of iced tea through her straw and wished she'd opted for hot coffee so that the strong smell of brewed java could drown out the imagined scent of George Madigan that lingered in her nose. No matter. By sheer strength of will, she would override her hormones and emotions and concentrate on the job at hand. She needed nothing more, and she wanted nothing less. Right?

"Right."

Popping a baby carrot into her mouth, Elise printed off the draft of the speech she'd typed for her boss and stood to pick up the papers from the printer on the credenza beneath the window. She swallowed the carrot and crunched her way through another before sliding the speech into the folder she'd prepared and carrying it into George's office.

Elise studiously ignored the picture of George and his sister's family behind his desk as she set the file on the blotter. But after seeing her just a few hours earlier, Annie Fensom's wedding gown drew Elise's eye. The CSI and George's nephew, Nick Fensom, made a striking couple with their dark hair against the lacy white gown and gray tuxedoes adorned with bright red boutonnieres.

But it was the distinguished-looking man standing behind the groom and his mother that kept Elise's attention. She'd walked by those pictures dozens of times every day for the past few months. How had she never noticed that before? She reached out and touched her fingertip to the glass over George Madigan's face. "You're smiling."

Without even thinking, Elise smiled, too. The relaxed expression on George's face was so compelling, so rare, that she wondered just what it would take to see that handsome grin again.

But just as quickly as the intriguing challenge registered, Elise pressed her lips into a frown. "Idiot."

Would she never learn her lesson?

The telephone on George's desk rang, startling her. A word cursing her own foolishness slipped out before she picked up the receiver. "Deputy Commissioner Madigan's office," she snapped.

"Elise?"

Every raw emotion and dangerous thought in Elise's head short-circuited at the familiar tenor of the caller's masculine voice. "Mr. Gallagher."

"Really?" She heard a wry laugh. "You haven't called me that since the first day you worked for me. Don't tell me George or KCPD is insisting on that kind of formality." Quinn Gallagher, a wealthy inventor and the CEO of Gallagher Security Systems, was teasing her. "You and I are old friends."

Friends. Right. Her heart had been far too slow to understand that little distinction in their once close relationship. Funny how talking to the man she'd loved and lost could turn her light lunch into a rock at the pit of her stomach. Still, she'd moved on with her life. And, if nothing else, she prided herself on being the quintessential professional. "Hi, Quinn," she answered with a rueful smile. "How are you?"

"Happier than I've been in a long time."

"How's Miranda?" she forced herself to ask.

"Still can't get that woman to cook a decent meal. I thought when she got pregnant some kind of natural domestic instinct would kick in." He sounded younger, energized, blissfully content, as he always did when he talked about his wife and daughter. "Fortunately, she knows all the best take-out places, and she and Fiona have been setting up picnics on the living room floor this past week."

Any pangs of jealousy Elise felt were beaten back by the guilt of knowing she'd nearly cost her former boss this second chance at love and the family he was enjoying now. "Sounds like fun."

"How are you?" Quinn asked.

"Loving my work," she answered honestly. "And the house is halfway done. The kitchen and bathrooms have been redone and the exterior is all painted."

"I know that house is your therapy, but I wish I could tear you away from it. Are you sure a raise wouldn't convince you to come back to GSS?" His generous salary had enabled her to afford the extensive remodel in the first place. "I'm still having a hard time breaking in my new assistant. Working with you was so easy. I think you could read my mind. You spoiled me for anyone else."

"You're too kind, Quinn." But their working relationship had never been the problem between them. "The commissioner's out at a lunch meeting. May I take a message?"

Quinn's teasing tone sobered. "This is a subject I'd rather discuss in person. Soon, if George has got a half hour for me in his schedule."

Elise clicked the mouse on George's desk and pulled up his appointment calendar on the computer screen. "What should I tell him it's regarding?"

"Alexsandr Titov."

Her legs turned to jelly at the unexpected answer, and

Elise sank into the plush leather chair behind George's desk. "Nikolai's brother?"

"The same. Did you ever meet him?"

"Only over the phone." Alexsandr had called her from Lukinburg, the night of Nikolai's murder. *What can you tell me about my brother's death? Did your jealous husband do this to him?* Apparently, he'd found her name on a hotel receipt in Nikolai's bloody jacket pocket. For a moment, Elise couldn't catch her breath. "It was a brief chat."

And not a particularly friendly one.

Quinn continued, "Since you knew Nikolai, you may want to sit in on this meeting, too."

"Me? Why?"

"Alexsandr is here in Kansas City, according to my sources. Staying in a hotel downtown near Embassy Row."

Only a few miles from this very office. She had no husband. She'd had nothing to do with Nikolai's death. Still, the news of Alexsandr Titov setting foot on Missouri soil felt like a threat. "Do you know why he's here?"

Words like *payback* and *revenge* came to mind.

Quinn laughed, but there was no humor. "That's the million-dollar question. Since Nikolai's death, his younger brother, Alexsandr, has been rebuilding Titov Industrial. He's had pretty good success selling military rifles and ammunition in the Far East. Kansas City is a big import/export area. He could be here legitimately, trying to expand his business."

The words on the computer monitor had blurred. Elise blinked them back into focus and searched for a free block of time on George's calendar. "Or he could be as big a criminal as Nikolai was."

"Exactly why I want to give George and KCPD a heads-up. Since he handles equipment and munitions purchases for the department, I wanted to make sure he isn't spending any money on a dummy corporation that's laundering money or selling arms illegally the way his brother did. And..." Quinn paused again.

"What?"

"The deputy commissioner has a perfectly legitimate reason for investigating Titov Industrial as a potential resource. I want to know if Alexsandr's visit has anything to do with Nikolai's death."

Guilt stabbed through Elise. "Your father-in-law killed him."

"Vasily might have used his mob connections to eliminate Nikolai after he tried to kill my daughter and destroy GSS. But you and I both know that Nikolai's hate ran pretty deep. He blamed me for his business going under and his son's death. And he turned you into an unwitting mole." Until she came to her senses and gave testimony to the police and FBI that helped get Nikolai deported back to Lukinburg...and a waiting assassin. "I don't know if it's the same for his younger brother or not. Like I said, he could be in the KC area for legitimate business reasons."

She'd never met Nikolai's younger brother, but if one Titov could break the law and take advantage of a heartsick woman to gain access to procedure codes and personnel files, it wasn't a stretch of the imagination to believe another Titov would be willing to terrorize her or use her for some nefarious purpose.

Maybe he'd send twenty-three roses just like Nikolai had.

Or steal the key to a woman's house.

Guilt wasn't the only emotion churning through Elise's stomach now.

She pulled the receiver from her mouth to muffle her strangled gasp. Was Alexsandr plotting something to make her pay for his brother's death? Or was this yet another creepy coincidence her suspicious imagination was turning into something more dangerous and disturbing than it really was?

"Elise?"

With too many questions and no answers, and no one to calm her fears, Elise went back to the one thing that had never failed her. Work. Tucking the receiver between her shoulder and ear, she typed Quinn's name into the computer. "Would tomorrow morning work for you?"

"That'll be fine. See you then."

Elise replaced the receiver in the phone cradle, holding on until she heard the voices in the other room. She pushed the chair back from the desk and stood, but not before George Madigan filled the open doorway.

"What's wrong?"

Stone-gray eyes locked on to hers, and Elise nearly answered the concern written there.

But the shrill voice of common sense interrupted before she gave in to temptation.

"It's not as if I'm asking you to do this for a stranger." The curvy blonde who made frequent appearances in the deputy commissioner's office nudged George aside and walked into the room. She picked up a file folder from the desk and, after an exasperated sigh, fanned herself with it. "Ken Biro was your partner. You'd think you could help with a simple birthday party."

"Good afternoon, Mrs. Mad—Ms. Reiter." Elise corrected her greeting to the boss's ex-wife, tipped her chin to a relatively confident angle and crossed the room to return to her desk. "Quinn Gallagher just made an appointment for tomorrow morning to discuss Titov Industrial and potential munitions contracts with the city," she reported to George. "I marked your calendar. I'll bring in the file with the negotiations transcripts to review for your two o'clock. The retirement banquet speech is on your desk."

Elise quickly slipped by him out the door, but he grabbed her hand as she passed, forcing her to stop and turn. George's steely eyes silently demanded an explanation, but it was the warm brush of his thumb across her knuckles that almost had her spilling the details about her connection to Alexsandr Titov and the potential threat he represented.

"Good afternoon, Elise." Courtney Reiter's gaze had zeroed in on the clasp of hands between boss and assistant.

Telling herself she was glad for the blonde's dismissive tone, Elise snatched her hand away and hurried back to her desk.

Muttering a curse beneath his breath, George strode into his office. He plucked the file from his ex-wife's grasp and set it back on the desk. "I thought this conversation was over, Court. You never even liked Ken. Why is this such a big deal?"

Courtney's voice grew louder as she approached the door. "Ken has been a part of our lives for years. Just because we fight like cats and dogs on occasion doesn't mean he isn't my friend, too. In fact..." The blonde waited for Elise to look her way before she smiled sweetly...and closed the door.

Well, that message was clear as crystal. *Stay out of my business.* Though whether the older woman's warning stemmed from an arrogance that relegated Elise to being the hired help who needed to remember her place, or a more possessive streak of jealousy at seeing George and Elise holding hands, was less clear.

The click of the door left Elise feeling chilled and alone. Could Alexsandr Titov really blame her for his brother's murder? After all, she'd been Nikolai's victim. He'd swept her off her feet and she'd fancied herself in love with him. She'd even slept with him because she'd been that desperately lonely and he seemed to care. But once she found out how he'd used her to gain inside information on Quinn Gallagher and GSS, she'd willingly labeled him a criminal and provided a deposition against him.

What would she have done if Courtney Reiter hadn't laid claim to George's time and attention? Would Elise have turned into that broad chest? Spilled her guts? Confessed how a previously unacknowledged, forbidden attraction had simmered to the surface with the intensity of the summer heat wave?

Elise folded her hands together in her lap and rubbed the spot where George had held her. The firm clasp of fingers. The gentle stroke of his thumb. She could still feel his touch on her skin. She could vividly remember those brief moments of being sheltered, cared for. She could see herself wanting, needing, falling for the man.

"Please, George. Do this for me," Courtney pleaded on the other side of the door.

But Elise had no right to make any such demand on his time and caring. Wisely ignoring those tempting ideas, Elise put her hands on her keyboard to update the budget report. Although she didn't envy the one-sided argument she could hear through the closed door, she was relieved that George's ex-wife was demanding his attention. Let him solve Courtney's problems. Let him be a rock for someone else. Elise couldn't depend on her boss to comfort her or save her or whatever it was she thought he could do for her right now.

If she'd quit getting herself into trouble, she wouldn't need any man to save her.

Several minutes passed, long enough for Elise to get three pages of new data entered into the budget report. The uncomfortable opportunity to eavesdrop on the room next door went away as the voices quieted into a civilized conversation. George was either able to calm his ex, she was beginning to see reason or both.

Elise had managed to immerse herself in her work again when a man cleared his throat from the hallway door. Looking up, she smiled. "Officer Hale."

A quick glance at the time and the calendar confirmed the uniformed police officer was here for a scheduled appointment. "Ma'am."

She circled the desk to shake the officer's hand and gestured to the seating area of her office. "Could I get you a cup of coffee? Or something cold to drink?"

"Water if you have it." Denton Hale took a seat once Elise brought him a bottle of water from the minifridge and sat. Although his short-sleeved uniform was neatly pressed, the dark marks at his armpits indicated he was taking a break in the middle of a work shift. He opened the bottle and drank half of it before capping it and thanking her. "That hit the spot. My partner and I recently got our shift transferred to your neighborhood.

At least I think it's your part of town—I saw you walking your dog there."

"Could be. Spike and I are out every morning and most evenings."

"The older residential districts seem to be getting hit pretty hard with brownouts and transformers going off-line." The middle-aged cop toyed with the brim of his hat, as if nervous about coming up with more conversation. "Have you had any power outages yet? Our electricity went out a couple of nights ago. We all ended up sleeping on the screened-in porch."

"That sounds like a fun adventure."

"The kids liked it, although the camp cot's a little hard on my back these days."

Knowing Denton Hale was here to discuss possible salary freezes and staff cuts—maybe even his own job or that of his friends—with the deputy commissioner, Elise did her best to put him at ease. No sense adding to his stress. "We've had a couple of outages, but nothing that lasted for any length of time. I run the air-conditioning just upstairs at night, and turn it on low during the day—enough for my dog to manage the heat. I'm trying to do whatever I can to help conserve energy."

"Yeah. I guess it's been pretty rough. We followed one utility worker out on a call this morning. Somebody had vandalized his work truck. Painted a message on it I wouldn't want to repeat."

Elise shook her head. "That's terrible. It's not like this weather is the city's fault. I guess tempers are shorter when the temperature is higher."

"Yes, ma'am. That's been my experience." After an

awkward pause and another long drink, the police officer pointed toward George's door. "Is he in?"

Elise took his empty bottle and brought him another water. "Mr. Madigan's appointment is running a little longer than he anticipated."

Denton Hale shoved his fingers though his brown hair, finally relaxing a bit, and grinned. "I think I've had more conversations with you on this couch, waiting for the commish to talk negotiation strategies, than I have with my wife the past couple of weeks."

Elise smiled at the joke. "Budget time does that, I think. Lots of meetings, lots of waiting."

"You're easy to talk to, I guess."

"Thanks."

"I bet you're putting in extra hours, too. What does your boyfriend think of that?"

"My boyfriend?"

"A pretty lady like you must be taken." He took another drink before pointing to her. "I didn't see a ring, though."

Although she smiled, Elise suddenly wasn't feeling as welcoming as she had a moment earlier. "No boyfriend. Never married."

"That's a shame." A split second later, Officer Hale's cheeks reddened and he put up an apologetic hand. "Wait. Girlfriend?"

Shaking her head, Elise stood and checked her watch. She had no problem with small talk to make a visitor more comfortable about waiting for the deputy commissioner. But today wasn't a good day for her to be the main topic. "If you'll excuse me a moment, I'll remind Mr. Madigan that you're here."

She picked up the negotiations file from her desk and knocked softly on the black door.

"Come in."

As soon as George responded, Elise nudged open the door. He was sitting on the front edge of his desk, holding a box of tissues for his ex-wife, who was dabbing at tears. Despite a tug of sympathy, Elise quickly quashed any urge to ask if everything was okay. "Your two o'clock is here, sir. Denton Hale from the officers' union?" She handed him the file. "Here are the transcripts you wanted."

George opened the file and stood, flipping through the pages. He frowned. "You have to go now, Court. I have work to do."

"What else is new?" With another sniffle, she apologized for her sarcasm. "I'm sorry. Of course, you do. You're an important man." Courtney rose, tossed the soiled tissues into the trash and smoothed her blond hair into place. She smoothed the skirt and blouse she wore, too, before tilting her red-rimmed eyes up to George. "You're okay with this? You promise you'll help me?"

"It doesn't make much sense to me, but..." He closed the folder and nodded. "I promise. But this is it, Court. I haven't been your husband for a long time now. You've got to learn to stand on your own two feet."

"I will." Courtney Reiter stretched up onto her toes and kissed his cheek. She would have kissed his mouth if he hadn't turned his head at the last moment. "Thank you."

George groaned as if he'd heard that promise before, and wiped the pink lipstick from his skin as Courtney breezed past Elise and out the door. "We need to talk," he said to Elise, reaching around her shoulder to push the door shut behind her. He held up the folder between them. "This is the wrong file."

"What? No, I'm sure I..." She pulled it from his grip and read the label. Budget Notes. "I'm sorry. I must have grabbed the wrong one. It's a simple mistake."

"If you made mistakes, it would be. But you don't." He held the door firmly in place when she reached down to open it.

Elise held her breath, thinking it was an accident that she'd been caught in the space between the door and George's chest.

But there were no accidents with this man. He flattened his palm on the wood beside her head and leaned closer, dropping his gaze to match hers. "Talk to me. You're scaring me, Elise. I don't like it when I don't have the answers I need. Tell me what's going on. Did something else happen?."

"Something else? No, I... No." Her breath rushed out as she braced her hand on his chest to push him away. "Denton Hale is waiting. I think he's on a shift break, so I'm sure he doesn't have long. And I need to...get the transcripts."

George's skin was warm, his muscles firm beneath the crisp ecru cotton. When she felt the strong beat of his heart leaping beneath her palm, Elise realized she was doing more lingering than pushing, but couldn't seem to break away from the tempting intimacy. He probably didn't even know how all this closeness and concern was affecting her. Or maybe he did.

He covered her hand with his before she could make herself escape. His fingers splayed over hers, infusing her with warmth from both his body and touch. "We need to discuss this, too."

The quiet depth in his tone, along with his firm touch, made his message perfectly clear.

"What 'this'? There is no 'this.'" There couldn't be. Knowing he felt something, too, would only make it that much harder to keep a professional distance from him. She hugged the folder to her chest and pulled against his grip. "We're coworkers, George. Friends, at best. I respect you tremendously, and I'm grateful for the job, but you're not the kind of man I want to get involved with."

"What kind of man do you think I am?" His eyes darkened like granite and his hand fell away. "Don't answer that." Giving her the space she'd asked for, he retreated to his window overlooking the north edge of the city. "Get me the right file and show Hale in."

It was on the tip of her tongue to call him back. To tell him none of this was his fault—to admit how easily she could fall for him. She wanted to explain her screwed-up track record with men and how her best line of defense was to avoid giving in to any of this attraction or that need. But Elise knew a smarter plan of action was to overlook the sting of his words, accept his dismissal and scoot on out of the room.

She opened the door to find Denton Hale standing next to the chair behind her desk. He'd been slightly stooped over, but pulled up as soon as he saw her. Odd. Elise crossed the room to roll her chair back into position and reclaim her personal work space. "Did you need something?"

He spun his uniform cap between his hands, nervously covering for whatever he'd been up to. "I was just trying to double-check when my appointment was. I have to report back at three."

"Sorry for the wait. The deputy commissioner will see you now."

"Dent?" George called. "Come on in."

Officer Hale's brown-eyed gaze danced over her face for a moment before he heaved a sigh. "Sorry. I know I seem a little uptight about gettin' in to see Madigan. But I need this job. My family depends on me."

Now why did that apology sound like some kind of threat? Would she ever trust what a man said to her again? "I'm sure they do."

With a nod, he circled around her desk and closed the door as soon as the two men shook hands.

Squeezing the back of her chair as if she needed its support to stand, Elise warned herself to get a mental grip instead. She dropped the budget file onto the desk and sat down to straighten it. Yes, the appointment calendar had been moved, but so had a couple of other things. And her screen saver was no longer on, meaning Officer Hale had either bumped the mouse in his brief search, or he'd clicked it on purpose to view something on her screen. While she did keep both a written and electronic record of the deputy commissioner's appointments, the only thing on her screen was the budget report she'd been working on.

Had Denton Hale seen the paragraph about salary freezes pending evaluations for officers with poor performance reviews or reprimands in their files? Was he truly in fear of losing his job? What did Hale's service record with the department look like?

With suspicion already pumping through her blood, Elise clicked off of the report and brought up the link for KCPD service records. Just as quickly, she backed out of the system. If Denton Hale did have something in his file that targeted him for extra scrutiny and job probation or termination, it wasn't her business.

After all, she didn't want KCPD or anyone else looking too closely into her past mistakes, either.

ELISE TURNED OFF the motor of her car and reached across the seat to retrieve her purse and the pumps she'd exchanged for tennis socks and walking shoes after work.

Home. The dark red door of the gray-and-white Victorian welcomed her like a familiar sanctuary. She climbed out of her Explorer, but paused for a few moments as the hundred-degree heat and matching humidity crept over her skin, pricking open pores and sapping what energy she had left. She tilted her gaze up to the heat lightning sparking in the distant sky beyond her rooftop. There wasn't a cloud above or an answering rumble of thunder. So no break in the weather this evening.

The silent violence in the evening sky felt appropriate. Ominous and hopeless somehow. She'd become a lightning rod for suspicious people and unexplained events. She hadn't forgotten the returned roses or the missing key.

Bringing her gaze down, she studied the windows and doors, making sure nothing looked out of place. The flowers wilting on the porch needed a good soaking, but they hadn't been moved. There were no footprints in the grass, no packages left on her front steps. Maybe the key disappearing had been a fluke. As upset as she'd been with James's visit last night, she could very well have simply misplaced it and not remembered.

The only way she was truly going to know if a thief or vandal had stolen the key and broken in was to march up those steps, unlock the door herself and give the house a thorough search.

Fisting her keys in her hand and steeling herself with a resolute breath, Elise slammed the car door.

Spike barked an instant mix of excitement and welcome. Only it wasn't the muted sound of the dog announcing her arrival through the window from the back of the couch. This was louder. Clearer. Closer. What the…?

"Spike?" Elise turned toward the sound. He was outside. "Spike? Spike!"

She heard the jingle of his tags hitting together before she saw him dash around her neighbor's hedge and run to meet her.

"Spikey?" Elise dropped her shoes and scooped him up as he leaped into her arms. She kissed his head and hugged him tight, alarmed by his panting and how hot his little body felt against her chest. "How did you get out?" She checked the rapid beat of his heart and looked into his dark brown eyes. "Are you okay, sweetie? Have you been out all day? Did I…?"

She swung her gaze toward the house. Surely she hadn't left him in the backyard in this heat. With no water? Had he climbed the fence or dug underneath it to escape? And she never let him out in the front without being on a leash. "I know I put you inside."

But she'd been out of sorts and running late this morning, so she must have forgotten him. She seemed to be forgetting a lot of things today. What was happening to her?

A lick on her earlobe, demanding more petting and less thinking, cut through Elise's confusion. She scratched his belly and tried to shake off that nagging sense that she was losing it. "It's just you and me. I'd never forget you."

Yet here he was, running through the neighborhood, waiting for her to come home.

"Come on, sweetie." She moved the toodle to one arm and bent down to pick up her pumps. She didn't care that they'd gotten scratched on the concrete. She was fighting hard to stop second-guessing herself and stay in the moment. "Let's get you something to drink."

Instead of going straight up the front steps, though, Elise carried the dog around the side of the house to the backyard. "Good."

She'd gotten at least one thing right today. The gate was still latched. She opened and closed it behind her, carrying the panting black dog up onto the deck. Pulling her keys from the outside pocket of her purse, she quickly glanced around the yard for possible escape routes. There were no holes in the dirt or gaps in the fence that were readily visible. But she'd investigate the hidden places behind the bushes and landscaping later. Right now, she needed to get Spike into the air-conditioning with a wet towel and some cool water to drink. He didn't seem bleary-eyed and shocky. Hopefully, he'd stayed in the shade or made himself at home with a friendly neighbor. But she wasn't taking any chances with her dearest companion.

Elise inserted the key into the back door, feeling another glimmer of relief to discover the knob and dead bolt were both securely locked.

Once inside, she carried Spike straight to the kitchen and set him down in front of his water bowl. While he greedily lapped up the reviving liquid, Elise set her things on the counter and turned on the faucet to wet down a kitchen towel. “Feeling better, sweetie?”

Spike nosed the food in his dish—a good sign that he wasn’t feeling the ill effects of the heat, she hoped—before going back for another noisy, messy drink. Elise turned off the running water and wrung out the towel before stooping down to wrap it around the dog. “Easy—”

A loud noise banged overhead.

Spike barked a warning and lurched from her grip. But Elise grabbed him before he could get away from her. She picked him up, wet towel and all, and hugged him against her racing heart. “Spike?”

Elise looked up as the dog tipped his nose to the ceiling and barked again, a cautious little yap followed by a squeal of alarm and a high-pitched growl in his throat. It was enough of a distress signal for Elise to push to her feet. She grabbed her keys from the counter, looped her purse over her shoulder and retreated toward the back door at the sound of footsteps on the floor above her.

Footsteps running from her bedroom.

Someone was in her house.

Chapter Four

"Ma'am, I'm sorry. I just don't see any signs of forced entry." Denton Hale pointed to the television, jewelry box and smart tablet on Elise's dresser and bedside table. "And you yourself said that nothing's been taken."

Elise's head was throbbing with too much stress and a lack of food. She held herself together by hugging her arms tightly around her waist and glancing over at Spike, who was curled up next to the pillows on her bed. She schooled her patience and tucked her hair behind her ear before turning back to the uniformed officer and articulating every last word. "He was in my house. I heard him running down the stairs and out the front door."

She'd said the same thing a dozen times in the past half hour, to both Hale and his partner. She'd said it when she'd met them at the front sidewalk, said it again in every room they'd gone through together. A man was in her house. She was certain it had been a man by the heavy tread of his step.

A man who sent her flowers and stole her key?

Or some other threat, altogether?

"You didn't get a look at this guy?" Officer Hale asked.

"No. I didn't want a confrontation with him in case

he was armed or wanted to hurt me." If the man hadn't made a noise… If Spike hadn't barked… She rubbed at the goose bumps dotting her bare arms and tried to block out the horrible what-ifs swirling in the back of her mind. Harming her could very well have been what the intruder had wanted since theft didn't appear to be the motive. "I called 9-1-1 on my cell and went to the Kecks'—the retired couple next door."

"The front door was locked when we came in, Elise. May I call you that?" She didn't care. She just wanted him to believe her. "None of the locks have been tampered with, and there are no broken windows."

"So he locked it when he ran out. I told you the key was missing."

"Are you sure?" Officer Hale pulled his gloved hand from where it rested on his thick utility belt and touched her elbow. His eyebrows arched with a sympathetic smile. His tone patronized as if she was an imbecile—or a desperate woman who was making this all up to get some attention. "It's there now. You opened the box in the flowerpot and showed it to me. Remember?"

Why not just pat her on the head and say, "There, there"? Elise jerked her arm away and took a step toward her closest ally. "Spike and I both heard him."

Hale shrugged, sounding exasperated with her seeming lack of reason. "Unfortunately, I can't take the word of a fuzz mop."

Apparently, he wouldn't take her word, either. "I'm not lying. He could have taken the key and made a copy," she argued, still looking for a reason to explain what she knew to be true.

"I didn't say—"

"Elise!" After a quick rap on her front door, a deep, clipped voice bellowed from the foyer below.

With a woof, Spike sprang to his feet.

"George?" She swung her head toward the sound of the deputy commissioner calling her name through the rooms on the main floor.

"Ma'am, wait." Officer Hale put his arm out to block her rush toward the bedroom door, but Elise skirted around him. "We don't know who—"

"I do. G… Commissioner? What are you doing here?"

Spike hurried down the steps after her. The broad back of George Madigan's navy suit jacket turned to reveal an open collar and that inviting chest. At the last second, common sense reined in Elise's relief, and she stopped herself from running straight into his arms, denying herself the haven of security he offered.

But he clasped her shoulders anyway, his slightly rough hands making contact that shot through her skin like a bolt of lightning, exciting frayed nerves and weakening a resolve that couldn't handle many more demands on it. "I heard your address on the scanner driving home. I called Dispatch to verify that you'd reported an intruder. Officer Boyd just let me in." Although he lowered the volume of his voice, there was no less authority behind it. "Are you okay?"

Denton Hale loomed up like a shadow behind her on the stairs. "I didn't know you two were…" The tone of the officer's voice snapped to attention. "The scene is secure, sir."

Without asking permission or apologizing for startling her, George tucked Elise to his side, draping an arm around her shoulders to keep her snugged against his solid flank. "She works for me, Denton. That's all you need to know. But it doesn't matter who she is. Get outside with your partner, Boyd, and double-check that everything's secure, from the basement to the attic. Don't forget her car and the garage, too."

"Her car wasn't here when the alleged intruder—"

Elise snapped her gaze up. "Alleged?"

She felt a squeeze on her shoulder as George moved them out of the uniformed officer's path to the front door. "Do it. Canvas the neighborhood, too. Get statements from anyone who saw anything around Miss Brown's house today. Ask if there have been any other break-ins or suspicious activity in the area."

"Boyd is already doing that."

"Good. Then you'd better get out there and help him. There are a lot of homes on this street."

"Yes, sir." Denton pulled his cap from his rear pocket, squeezing it in his fist before turning to Elise. "Ma'am, if anything I said or did—"

"Now." George dismissed Hale before he finished his apology. As soon as the door closed behind the officer, George tugged Elise into step beside him and crossed through the arch into her shrouded living room. "So what did he say or do to upset you?"

"He took my statement."

"And?"

Elise's feet didn't seem to be moving under their own power. "I don't think he believed me."

George may have muttered a curse. But whether it was aimed at Officer Hale or the cluttered state of her house, she couldn't tell. Other than a pause to orient himself to the drop cloths and sawhorses in front of the fireplace, George led her to the furniture that had all been stacked against the opposite wall. Even a small black dog sniffing around his feet didn't slow him down or alter the purpose of his stride. "Don't you generate any heat, woman? It's a hundred degrees out and you're freezing."

He shrugged out of his jacket and wrapped it around her. Elise shivered at the shock of his scent and lingering body heat sliding over her chilled skin.

"There was a man in my house." She sounded like a worn-out recording.

"I know." George pulled the paint tarp off her sofa and tossed it to the floor. He unloaded the two end tables she'd stored on top of the cushions before he took her hand and urged her to sit.

"I think he let Spike get out the door when he came in. Or else he put him out on purpose." It was the only scenario that made sense. If any of this made sense. Elise clutched the suit jacket together over her dress, shaking at the knowledge of what could have happened to her if she'd met him face-to-face. "He was in my bedroom."

The cushion beside her sank and her balance shifted as George sat down. "I believe you."

"Even if there's no evidence?" Elise glanced up to see if he was simply trying to placate her the way Officer Hale had. "The doors were locked. And nothing's missing."

"You may have scared him off before he had a chance to take anything. And a barking dog changes a lot of intruders' minds." He pulled both her hands between his and gently rubbed them. "Besides, you're too cold for me to doubt you. That means you had a real shock. It happened."

George Madigan's matter-of-fact tone did more to make her feel safe than two armed police officers and a robotic sounding dispatcher had. His simple statement of faith in her sanity swept out the cobwebs of self-doubt and touched her bruised heart.

Curling her legs beneath her, Elise pushed herself up, looping her arms about George's neck, knocking him into the back of the couch. "Thank you."

"For what…?" After a momentary hesitation, his chest expanded with a deep breath, meeting hers. When he exhaled, there was no more gap between them. He folded his arms around her, flattening one hand against her spine to anchor her to his body. He pushed aside the jacket's collar and threaded his fingers into the short hair at her nape to massage the tension in her neck. "You're okay. You're safe now. No one's going to hurt you."

Elise turned her cheek into the soft rasp of his evening beard stubble, feeling the vibration of his deep voice against her ear. Her own fingertips brushed against the dark silk of his hair as she rode each measured breath on his chest, absorbing his heat. George was solid and real. There was no mistaking this vital, caring man for a figment of her imagination. "I almost wish they would."

"Hurt you? I'm going to disagree with that idea, if you don't mind."

"But all this is making me think I'm going crazy. There are too many things that I can't explain." He took the edge off her raw nerves with his calm voice and soothing massage. "I'm not crazy. I'm not."

"What do you mean by 'all this'?" His fingers stilled when she shook her head, reluctant to answer. He unwound her arms from his neck and let her slide down onto his lap. Pulling the jacket back over her shoulders, he urged her grasping hands to settle at the lapels. Once she was holding the coat together at her neck, George brushed the hair off her forehead and pressed his lips against the spot. “Talk to me.”

It was the gentlest of kisses, and maybe the most dangerous. Because, while a lingering kiss to the forehead was soothing, patient, kind—the caress also gave her a glimpse of what George’s lips might feel like against hers. They were firm. Masculine. Pure, incandescent heat. She had a feeling that a man of his experience might know exactly what to do with those lips, too.

Elise’s breath locked in her chest at the desire suddenly humming between them. Her fingers slipped from the jacket to the starched crispness of his unbuttoned collar. “George?” she breathed.

“Beats sir.” For a split second, his gray eyes locked on to hers. They were so close, she could read every hue of granite, smoke and steel in the irises there. Then his gaze dropped lower, to her mouth, and a deep-pitched groan rumbled beneath her hands.

George dipped his head, touching his mouth to hers, kindling a slow, liquid fire in Elise’s blood that chased away the chill of doubt and fear. The kiss was as tender as the graze across her forehead had been. A simple meeting of skin against skin. At first.

When she didn’t resist, George’s lips urged hers apart. His warm breath rushed in to mingle with hers. Elise’s fingers fisted in his shirt. Her tongue darted out to sample the smooth, male plane of his bottom lip, and his own tongue forced hers back to taste the soft skin inside her mouth. The cold she’d felt moments earlier shattered with bursts of heat inside her belly and at the tips of her breasts.

It was, by far, the most potent, most surprising, most spontaneous response she'd ever had to a man's kiss. Every place they touched—her lips, her earlobes and neck where he held her against his mouth, her fingers clinging to the muscles of his chest, her hip and bottom nestled against his thighs—was on fire.

And that's when the alarm bells went off inside her head and she knew she had to stop. She eased her grip on George's collar and pushed at his chin, leaning back when he moved to resume the kiss. "What are you doing?" she asked on a throaty whisper.

George's fingers tensed before he untangled them from her hair. "I'm more rusty at this than I thought if you have to ask."

She'd loved Quinn Gallagher with hopeless devotion. She'd given herself to Nikolai Titov out of loneliness and lust. But this was different. She'd never felt this alive, this desired, this needy in a man's arms before. And if anything frightened her, it was the knowledge that she could very easily fall for George Madigan—for the wrong man—all over again. "I…I can't. We can't."

"My mistake." His eyes shuttered as he moved his hands to her waist and lifted her off his lap. Elise landed on the seat cushion beside him, catching herself before she tumbled back into his side.

"No. I was a part of that as much as you were. I'm sorry. I wasn't thinking for a minute there. I was just… scared." She pointed to his grim expression, then to her own shaky smile. "Boss, assistant—remember?" He might think she was quoting departmental protocol, but reminding herself of the hazards of getting into a relationship with this man was more a matter of her own emotional survival. "I shouldn't have encouraged you—"

"What else has happened besides the intruder and the mystery of the roses?" George's tone was as sharply articulate and impersonal as it had been hushed and indulgent moments earlier.

Although the worst of the spooky chill that had numbed her of self-sufficiency and common sense had dissipated inside George's embrace, Elise reluctantly shrugged his jacket off her shoulders. She folded it neatly in her lap to return to him, fearing it was too much of an imposition to reject his kiss, yet still ask for his comfort. "George. It's not you. It's—"

"What else has happened?" So they weren't going to talk about that kiss. Because this, whatever it was, didn't—couldn't—exist between them. She'd said as much to him this morning. George rolled up his sleeves, literally and figuratively transforming himself into work mode. He nodded at the dog sitting at his feet, staring at them as if he wanted the people to make room for him on the crowded couch. "So this is the guy on your desk at work. What's his name?"

"Spike."

"Is he friendly?" Elise nodded, holding out the suit coat to return to him.

Instead of accepting the jacket, George reached down with one hand to scoop up the miniature poodle mix and set him on her lap. Spike immediately curled up on George's jacket and made himself at home. Elise would have tried to protect the coat if George wasn't already scratching the spoiled dog around his ears and making an instant friend. She tried to ignore the warmth of

George's hip and thigh butting against hers. She tried to make sense of the mature, no-nonsense cop wooing her closest ally. She tried to dismiss the confusing emotions warring inside her.

George was her boss, fourteen years her senior, a workaholic like herself. He carried weighty responsibilities on his shoulders. Responsibilities she'd sworn to support. Not the man she would have chosen to be so viscerally attracted to.

It was her talent to form relationships with the wrong men. And while she believed George was a good man, he wasn't the man for her and she would certainly get hurt again.

He was her friend. There were few people she trusted so implicitly. She didn't want to screw that up.

She needed him to ground her in the current, crazy chaos of her life with his decisive words and stalwart support.

She wanted him to kiss her again.

George caught her staring at him when he lifted his stony gaze to hers. Understandably, he misread her silence as a reluctance to share the details of the past few days. "If you won't talk to me, then tell Spike what's going on."

The man was dead serious. Elise dropped her gaze from those probing eyes and stroked the silky curls of Spike's hair. "I can't explain any of it."

"Yes, you can."

Boss. Friend. Security. George Madigan was all those things. It was enough.

And with nothing more than a relaxed little dog binding them together, Elise talked. She told George about the significance of twenty-three roses, how her affair with Nikolai Titov had lasted twenty-three days before he'd been deported to Lukinburg and was murdered. He already knew about Titov's vendetta against her former boss, Quinn Gallagher, but he listened patiently when she told him how she'd unwittingly given Titov and his hit squad access to information on GSS Security and Quinn's personal schedule. And though she'd never met Aleksandr Titov, the fact that Nikolai's brother had come to Kansas City was a little unsettling. She talked about the house key and how the police officers had found it in its box as if the thing had never gone missing at all. She talked about the dog greeting her in the front yard, and the crash and footsteps they'd heard upstairs. She reminded George that no one else had seen the key missing or heard the weird phone call in her office. No one could prove that the very same bouquet she'd taken to the hospital had been returned to her desk or she hadn't left Spike outside herself or that there had ever been an intruder in her home.

When she was done, Elise hugged the dog against her chest. "At least you're okay, sweetie. You could have been hit by a car, running loose like that. Or gotten heatstroke."

George moved to the edge of the couch, turning to face her. "Someone's trying to scare you."

"They're succeeding."

"Any idea why? Could someone be trying to discredit you for some reason? Got any old boyfriends you've ticked off?"

She shook her head. "That's the scariest part—I have no idea why these things are happening to me. I mean, what's the point?"

George pushed to his feet. "You haven't been yourself the past couple of days. If nothing else, these mind games have disrupted the efficiency of my office."

Elise cradled Spike in her arms and stood. "I'm sorry."

"I'm not worried about you doing your job. Even on your worst day you get more done than any assistant I've had." He picked his suit jacket up off the floor and shook it open. "I'm throwing out a possible motive. Budget shortfalls and increased demand for trained personnel don't make me a popular man."

"I would never let anything happen that could impact KCPD or the deputy commissioner's office." She wouldn't betray the people she worked with ever again. "After what happened with Quinn Gallagher, I keep my job and my private life separate."

"You and Quinn?" He paused in the middle of buttoning his shirt cuff. His gray eyes zeroed in on her. She hadn't confessed to unrequited love and heartbreak. But maybe George was reading between the lines of the story she'd told. "That explains a lot."

Maybe it was all the explanation he needed to dismiss that kiss. Maybe she should dismiss it, too. But he'd seemed so…insulted that she had.

"George. I truly am…attracted to you, and I value our friendship. But there are a lot of reasons why we can't—"

But Elise never got to finish. Her front door opened and James Westbrook stormed in. "Lise? Baby, what happened? Are you okay?" He brushed off the police officer who tried to stop him. "Let go of me."

Denton Hale caught James firmly by the arm this time and pulled him back into the archway. "I'm sorry, sir. Since you were here, I didn't think to relock the door. I saw him from across the street and tried to stop him before he got in. He says he's a friend of Miss Brown's."

James jerked his arm free and took a step closer. "I am a friend. Lise, tell them."

George took his time shrugging into his jacket and adjusting his cuffs, planting himself in the middle of the room's narrow pathway. James would have to climb over paint cans and sawhorses if he wanted to get any closer to her. "Is Miss Brown expecting you?" he asked.

"No," Elise answered. "Why are you here?"

"Lise!" James's gaze darted from Elise to George and back to her. With a noisy sigh, he stayed where he was and held up a bundle of letters and ad flyers. "Your mailbox was open out front. So I brought it in for you. What's with all the cops?"

"Answer her question," George insisted.

Concern morphed into anger in James's expression. "I'm not talking to you."

"Answer…the question."

"I knew you were upset last night so I came over to take you to dinner and apologize. As friends." James negated the sincerity of his apology by glaring through his glasses at her around the jut of George's shoulder. "Who is this guy? Is he why you've been avoiding me?"

Elise touched George's arm to nudge him over a step so she could stand beside him. When her fingers lingered against the summer-weight wool of his sleeve, James's gaze landed on the spot and she quickly pulled away. "Someone broke in, but nothing was taken and I'm not hurt. This is the man I work for at KCPD, George Madigan. Deputy Commissioner, this is James Westbrook."

James seemed to calm down as if the hot air of his

temper was a balloon that had suddenly popped. "Oh. Your boss. Good to meet you."

Although George shook the hand James offered, he was already backing James toward the foyer. "I'll walk you out."

But when they reached the door, James splayed his fingers at the waist of his pressed jeans and held his ground. "Is there some reason why I can't stay? We can order a pizza. We don't have to go out."

Elise followed the three men into the foyer. "I'm really tired, James. I'd be lousy company."

There was a momentary glitch in the diplomatic charm of his blue eyes. "I'll take a rain check, then." He handed Elise her mail, palmed Spike's head and leaned in to kiss her cheek. "Be sure you lock your doors. I wouldn't want anything to happen to you. Call you tomorrow?"

Whatever. She had no energy left to say even a polite no. "Good night, James."

With an order to Officer Hale to escort the unwanted guest back to his car, George pushed the door shut, leaning against it and crossing his arms. "He's the guy I alibied you out for, isn't he."

There was no avoiding that probing gaze. "We used to date. Years ago. We went our separate ways by mutual agreement."

"Does he know that? That you're not interested?"

"He's lived overseas for several years. Now that he's back in Kansas City, he doesn't know that many people. He's just looking for companionship." George's eyes never wavered, never blinked. Elise bristled with a shot of defensive anger. "You don't think James is behind this craziness, do you? He's more likely to pester me into saying yes to him than he is to terrorize me."

Those broad shoulders lifted with a shrug. "I've dealt with crazier scenarios. Maybe he thought you'd get scared enough that you'd turn to him for comfort."

"James doesn't make me feel safe. You…"

The moment of anger passed on a noiseless sigh and Elise dropped her gaze to the middle of his chest. She'd already shared way too much of her personal life for the impersonal relationship she claimed to want.

"I do." George straightened away from the door, nodding as if she'd spoken the words out loud. "Okay. Then here's what we do. Call someone to change this lock first thing in the morning. I'll post a black-and-white unit outside tonight."

"The city can't afford to dedicate a unit just for me. You don't have to do that."

"Yes, I do. It's my job to allocate funds and personnel where they're needed most. They're needed here tonight." She recognized that tone, the one that said *I'm in charge and what I say goes.*

"No." Whether she was really thinking about the common good or if she was distancing herself from the temptation of letting this powerful man take care of her, of letting him become even more involved in her life, she wasn't sure. But she protested, anyway. "Think of the resentment. Officers like Denton Hale are already worried about their next paycheck. With the increased power demands, the city is struggling to make ends meet. You can't just order someone to babysit me because a few weird things have happened. The police have more important jobs to do right now."

"A trespasser in your house is a real crime, Elise."

"But attacks on utility workers are more important."

"You're important." With her arms full of dog and mail, he reached out to brush aside a loose wave of hair that had fallen over her cheek. "All right. I'll work something else out. But I need you to be safe, Elise. You're too valuable to me."

As his assistant. As the fuel that made his office run so successfully. It was a lovely compliment. Yet oddly disappointing. Still, Elise summoned a smile for him. "I'll see you tomorrow at work."

His fingertips lingered behind the shell of her ear, and for a moment she thought he might do something sweetly reassuring like kiss her on the forehead again. Instead, he scratched the dog's head one more time. "Keep an eye on her, Spike."

When the dog nuzzled his hand, the man almost smiled. But that wasn't George Madigan's way. He opened the door and listed off directions just like he did at the office every morning. "Bring that spare key into the house and lock this when I leave. Call me or 9-1-1 if you see or hear anything else that's suspicious. If something seems off to you, it probably is."

"Yes, sir."

He arched a dark eyebrow. "Not funny."

Elise smiled. Because it was her way. And while they couldn't admit to this attraction or discuss that kiss, she was grateful that he'd been here for her this evening. "Thank you for everything. I'll be careful. Good night, George."

"Good night, Elise."

She watched him stride down the porch steps to his silver Suburban, stopping to have a word with Denton Hale and his partner. George looked up and down the street, probably verifying, like her, that James had driven away. When he looked back at her, Elise set Spike down on the floor. She pulled the key box from the flowerpot and went back inside to lock both the knob and dead bolt.

Then she turned on the porch light, letting George know she was following his instructions and was secure inside. She watched at the front window until Hale and his partner left in their police cruiser and George climbed inside his SUV.

Feeling drained from tip to toe, Elise kicked off her shoes and carried the mail to the kitchen. The light in the foyer flickered when she cranked up the air conditioner to cool the first floor. After shutting off the extra interior lights to conserve electricity, she set the end tables back on the sofa and covered them all with the paint tarp, erasing the reminder of being held in George's arms.

She could do this. She had Spike for company. She didn't need a man in her life, certainly not George Madigan with his surprising tenderness and chivalrous protective streak. Tomorrow would be a normal day. Maybe she'd even get lucky and the temperatures would break and the city would get some much needed rain.

A girl could dream, couldn't she?

Too tired to fix a meal, Elise nonetheless wound up in the kitchen. She couldn't take anything for her headache unless she had food in her stomach, and if she didn't eat, the throbbing would only get worse. So she tossed Spike a rawhide chew to nibble on while she grabbed a yogurt cup and half of a chocolate bar from the fridge. With only the light from the range hood to illuminate the shadows, she sat down on a stool at the island's granite countertop to force a few bites down her throat and sort through mail. A couple of bills, summer sale notices from local merchants, a postcard from her parents vacationing in Glacier National Park and one envelope that had neither a return address nor a familiar business logo. She slit open the envelope and pulled out the letter.

Elise's spoon clattered onto the countertop. Suddenly, the air-conditioning was working very, very well.

> I hate it when you make me angry, Elise. I wasn't pleased to see you give away my roses. That's why I brought them back. When I give you a gift, I need you to treasure it the way I treasure you. I forgive you this time, but don't make that mistake again.
>
> I Love You.

"Who...?" she whispered, tossing aside the letter. The stool toppled over when she hopped off and backed away from the disturbing message. Elise barely heard Spike's startled yelp through the haze of fear and madness clouding her brain. When her back hit the wall behind her, she cried out as if an unknown hand had touched her shoulder.

But the start was enough to clear one thought in her head.

"George." *Call me. I need you to be safe.*

Screw practicality and relationships that shouldn't be.

Elise dumped her purse onto the counter, digging out her phone and racing from the kitchen to put as much distance as she could between herself and that anonymous letter. Searching through the numbers as she and Spike climbed the stairs, she touched George Madigan's name and put the phone to her ear.

She dashed straight into her bedroom and opened the top drawer of her dresser to pull out a pair of socks. Her home should feel like a sanctuary, not a padded cell. She intended to put on her running shoes, hook Spike to his leash and go out into the steamy night air because even the suffocating humidity was preferable to the hazards sneaking their way inside her home.

George's number rang once.

Elise pushed the lingerie around in her drawer. Her socks were always on the left-hand side. Her cash-filled envelope of fun money was still stashed beneath them. "What…?" She was imagining the subtle shift in things.

She shoved the drawer shut as the phone rang a third time and she opened the second drawer. Elise rifled through the contents there before opening the next two. This wasn't right. Why wasn't this right? She glanced over at the empty laundry basket by her closet. Everything had been neatly folded and put away. Everything.

"Oh, God." She pressed her fist to her mouth to keep from retching. Then she pulled open the top drawer again and tossed everything onto the bed. *One. Two. Three. Four.*

She'd counted to five when the phone stopped ringing. "George!"

"What's wrong?"

"I need you." Forgetting her socks and shoes, she staggered back to the landing and sat on the top step, hugging her knees to her chest, turning her head at every creak and groan of the big empty house. Something slammed in the distance, jerking her in her seat. "Please come back."

His clipped voice was deep, urgent. "Is someone there?"

"I don't know what's happening to me—" She screamed at the loud pounding on her front door.

Spike dashed past her, barking at the commotion at the front of the house. The bell rang, over and over. "Open the damn door!"

"George?"

"Hang up the phone and open—"

Elise was already running down the stairs. "How did you get here so fast?"

She left her phone on the newel post and attacked the locks. She could hear George shouting through the front window now. "I was parked out front. I volunteered for guard duty tonight." She flung open the door and he marched inside. "What's going on?"

"I don't know." Elise walked straight into his chest. Circling her arms beneath his jacket, she burrowed her cheek into his shoulder and held on tight to his familiar, welcome strength. His chin settled at the crown of her hair and his arms folded around her, pulling her snug against his hardness and heat, absorbing every shaking molecule of her body.

"I was on the phone, recruiting some backup to help keep an eye on things, or I would have answered your call sooner."

"Just shut up and hold me."

"I am holding you." His fingers tunneled into her hair. The buttons of his shirt crushed into her skin beneath her dress. And still, she snuggled closer. "Honey, you need to talk to me."

"In the kitchen." She felt his body shift and she curled her fingers into the back of his shirt, keeping him with her. "He sent me a letter. He said he loves me."

"Who?"

"I don't know." She sniffed back a silent sob. "That's not all. When he was in my bedroom…there is something missing. Nothing significant. I didn't even notice it at first."

A curse grumbled through his chest. "Tell me."

Elise felt so chilled and dizzy, she didn't think she'd still be standing if George's arms weren't around her.

"He stole a pair of my panties."

Chapter Five

"I'm not asking you to do this."

The tremulous pulse along Elise's pale jawline sent George a different message. This gas lighting campaign was taking a toll on her. "You think this is going to go away on its own?"

She'd had sixteen messages on her answering machine by the time she got around to listening to it last night. All untraceable, all saying the same thing in a breathy, toneless, increasingly drunk or distressed voice. "I love you." Sixteen times. Sixteen counts of harassment at the very least.

No, this wasn't going away on its own.

"But to get other people involved when we're already blurring the lines between work and—"

"It's not up for debate, Elise. Something needs to be done."

Unsure whether those tired eyes were flashing anger, fear or annoyance at his peremptory end to her subtle warning reminders, George braced his fists on the sill of his office window and looked up into the clear blue sky. Not even ten in the morning and the sun was already cooking the city.

But as this blast of summer neared its breaking point,

Mother Nature was already showing signs of her temper with some pretty violent weather. From Oklahoma up the state line into northeast Missouri, they'd already had three tornado watches in the past two weeks. Torrential rains out west had caused flash flooding and runoff that was filling up rivers and streams that had been dry arroyos through years of drought, and now all that extra water and debris was flowing into the Missouri River. The Missouri, in turn, cut through the middle of K.C., bringing humidity to the city, drawing nightly lightning storms like a magnet, taunting them with the promise of rain that dried up before it ever reached the parched earth. Something bad was brewing in the heart of the Midwest. It was going to hit them hard.

And George had a feeling that Kansas City was going to be smack-dab in the middle of whatever was coming. Despite the stress of the past few weeks, he trusted that KCPD, other first responders and the citizens of K.C. themselves, would rise to the occasion to get through the coming crisis.

A storm was already brewing in his executive assistant's life. And whatever Elise Brown had to deal with, he was dealing with it, too. She was his right hand, the smiling face who greeted him every morning, the patience and caring that tempered his worst days and made the high-pressure issues he had to deal with seem practically routine. And because he needed her, he needed to do this for her.

Protect the city. Protect the department. Protect the office. Protect her.

George glanced over at the brunette waiting dutifully beside his desk and wished to hell he could do even more to ease the tension that kept her smile flatlined and her posture ramrod straight this morning. "Put the call on speakerphone. We all need to hear this. If you think it'll be too much for you, you don't have to stay."

"I'm staying." With a quick breath that sounded as if she was gearing up for battle, Elise punched the flashing button on his phone and placed the receiver in its cradle to make the conference call happen. "Dr. Kilpatrick? Elise Brown here again. I have the deputy commissioner here, as well as Detective Nick Fensom and his wife, CSI Annie Fensom."

George turned back to the room, nodding his thanks to his nephew and niece-in-law for answering his early morning call for a little off-the-record help. The woman on the phone was a friend who worked as a departmental psychologist and criminal profiler for KCPD. "I'm here, Elise. Good morning, George. And I know Nick and Annie well. We worked together on the Rose Red Rapist task force."

Nick looked like the detective George had once been, with his badge hanging around his neck over his black T-shirt and his sidearm holstered to the belt of his jeans. "Mornin', Dr. Kate." He reached across the space between the two guest chairs and batted at one of his wife's dark brown curls, pulling her attention from the taunting love letter she'd been studying. "Annie says 'hi,' too."

"Engrossed in some piece of evidence, I imagine," Kate teased.

Annie's cheeks dotted with embarrassment before she returned the paper and envelope back to the plastic bag George had sealed it in and peeled off her examination gloves. "Yes, ma'am. Good morning."

George's chest expanded with an impatient sigh.

Enough pleasantries. "Kate, did you get a chance to read a copy of the note I had Elise fax you this morning?"

"I did." Understanding the urgency of the situation surrounding Elise, the police psychologist got down to the business of offering the professional evaluation George had asked for. "One anonymous letter isn't much to go on. But with the gifts and break-in that you mentioned, and the fact that he took a souvenir, it's creating a disturbing pattern. I can give you a general idea of the type of man who may be behind it."

Kate Kilpatrick's clinical description of recent events seemed to hit Elise like a blow to the midsection. As she hugged her waist, George rolled his chair around the desk to her. When the stubborn thing wouldn't sit immediately, George touched her elbow. Damn. The stalwart facade and show of independence were costing her. But as soon as he rubbed his hand up her arm to instill some warmth into her chilled skin, she pulled away from even that impersonal contact and sat.

"I didn't realize there was more than one kind of stalker." Elise picked up her laptop from the desk and set it on her lap, opening a file to take notes or doodle or busy herself with whatever it was she suddenly needed to do besides interact with him.

"Yes, there is," Kate replied, probably unaware of the tension on this end of the call.

But Nick's raised eyebrow and glance toward Elise told George that his nephew seemed to think there might be something more prompting this meeting than protecting one of the department's professional assets.

Ignoring his nephew's curious perusal, George folded his arms across his chest and sat on the front edge of his desk. "So what did the note tell you about this guy, Kate?"

"The *I*'s the sender uses in every sentence could indicate an egocentric dysfunction," the psychologist said. "That means the sender lacks an objective perspective of the world around him."

"Explain," George said.

"He probably functions reasonably well in society—he can hold a job and have relationships. But he projects his feelings and values onto others, and assumes they think and feel the same way."

"Sounds pretty arrogant," Nick commented.

"Most psychopaths typically are."

"Psychopath?" Elise murmured. Her fingers stilled over her laptop keys. "How would I attract a psychopath?"

George curled his hands into fists, quelling the urge to push past the distance and decorum Elise had insisted upon in the light of day, and go to her. "Bottom line, Kate. Is a perp who fits this profile dangerous?"

Her lengthy pause wasn't terribly reassuring. "He may see disagreement as a personal insult—even as an attack. And that could make him angry."

Nick grunted a curse that matched his own. "Let me guess, he takes that anger out on the target of his affection?"

"It's possible," Dr. Kilpatrick agreed. "With a lesser degree of dysfunction, he'd probably simply turn his attention to someone else who feeds his ego. But if this guy has become obsessed with a particular target, then yes, he could definitely be a threat if he feels she's disrespecting him or cheating on him."

"Cheating?" Elise's voice was stronger.

"Yes. Take a married woman, for example, if he was fixated on her, then he'd see her normal relationship with her husband as cheating. He'd want to punish her for that perceived betrayal."

"Oh, my God."

Exactly what he'd been afraid of. George pushed away from his desk. He was good enough at pulling the right people together to get a job done, but physically protecting Elise would require a different strategy. "Thanks, Kate. I appreciate the input."

"Before you hang up…" George paused with his hand over the phone. He'd been ready to do just that. "Elise is your assistant, isn't she?"

George stuffed his hand into the pocket of his tan slacks. "She is."

"Not to throw a wrench into your fact-finding meeting, but have you considered the possibility that your perp may be a copycat? This is pretty textbook stuff thus far—I've discussed this same unsub profile in classes I've taught at the university. Heck, you can read it online if you know what to look for." Dr. Kilpatrick was as thorough at her job as he'd hired her to be. "Think about your office, George. This perp could be targeting Elise as a means to get to you."

Elise's gaze shot up to his. "I would never—"

"I've considered it." George silenced the protest Elise had made more than once the night before. Whatever her ex-boyfriend Nikolai Titov had done to screw with her head to gain access to Gallagher Security Systems info, the damage he'd done to Elise's self-assurance was unforgivable. He didn't doubt her loyalty to him or KCPD for one moment. But the thought that Elise believed she was so weak willed that she'd betray him or the sensitive information in this office bothered him more than the fear of an unknown stalker that raised goose bumps along her soft skin. "We're still in the process of gathering facts to see if we need to launch an investigation. Thanks, Kate."

"Anytime. Stay safe, Miss Brown. Goodbye, everyone."

With Elise's distracted focus turned down to the screen of her laptop, George reached across the desk to disconnect the call himself.

The shadows under her pretty blue eyes indicated the restless sleep she'd had. Even though George had spent the night on the couch in the construction zone of her living room to offer some degree of security, and she'd had that pint-size guard dog upstairs to keep her company, Elise's bed had rattled overhead as she'd tossed and turned. And when she couldn't fight her troubled thoughts any longer, she'd gotten up and turned on lights and spent an hour or more opening closets and drawers and moving things around in muffled noises that sounded suspiciously like cleaning house…or taking inventory to make sure nothing else had been touched or taken by the intruder.

Fueled by the aching frustration in his gut, George had lain awake most of the night, too, deciding exactly what he should do to help. Elise's problem wasn't something he could fix by writing a report, negotiating a compromise or issuing a statement.

This was old-school. She needed someone to stand between her and the nut job who was stalking her. She needed a man in her life. A bodyguard. She needed a cop.

More than anything—more than he should—George wanted to be that man.

But his years behind a desk had made him soft. Sure, he passed all his physicals and kept in shape, but when was the last time he'd run after a perp and taken him down? He'd grown more cerebral, less instinctive. The sidearm he'd strapped onto his belt this morning felt heavy against his hip. He hadn't taken the lead on an investigation since he'd left the Narcotics division. He was used to giving the orders, letting his team make things happen while he watched the budget, supplied the equipment and approved the manpower they needed to do their job.

Elise's intelligence, caring patience and endless legs gave a man plenty to notice and appreciate. But there was something more than the dark caramel hair and undeniable efficiency that had gotten beneath his hardened exterior. For years he hadn't cared about anyone on this gut-deep level. He loved his sister and her family. He cared about Courtney being happy. But he hadn't wanted anything like this for himself for a long time. There was a vulnerability about Elise Brown that had awakened some basic primal need in him. He hadn't even thought about falling in love again, about being with a woman for something more than companionship. But Elise had him thinking.

That forbidden kiss.

Those tight embraces.

I need you.

What was he supposed to make of a woman who called him with a panicked request like that and clung to him like a second skin, yet pushed him away and quoted departmental protocol if he overstepped the lines of friendly concern or, God forbid, tried to get ahead of the slimy psychopath who'd made her so afraid?

George's chest expanded with a deep breath. Being a frontline cop wasn't the only skill that had gone rusty on him. Elise's fingers were moving over her keyboard again, and she seemed completely oblivious to his assessing gaze and uncharacteristic introspection.

"Uncle George?" Startled from his thoughts by his nephew's voice, George reached up to massage the tension beneath his collar before slowly turning, masking any reaction. Nick had pulled out his notebook and pen, ready to work. And if that was suspicion narrowing the blue eyes that looked so like his sister's, it had better be aimed at finding answers for Elise, not reading anything into George's long silence. "I said, do we have any suspects?"

Propping his hip on the edge of his desk, George turned his attention to the family he'd called in for help with this unsanctioned investigation. "Here's the plan. Annie, I need you to do your scientific magic and find out who sent that letter."

"I can swab the seal and stamp for any DNA trace, but I won't make any guarantees. If he's not in the system, I'd need more evidence to confirm a match. And this guy seems to be making a concerted effort to remain anonymous." Annie carefully placed the sealed evidence inside her kit and locked it. Her explanation included Elise, drawing her back into the conversation. "I didn't find any prints in your bedroom or on that vase except for your own. Even if there are prints on this letter, we'll have nothing to compare them to, making it difficult to even know if it's the same guy."

"It has to be," Elise said.

"He's smart," George conceded. "I wouldn't be surprised if he's wearing gloves."

"Anyone wearing gloves would stand out in this heat, wouldn't they?" Elise suggested. "We could look for that."

"If we get a visual on him, yes. But I'm hoping we can ID this guy before he ever gets that close to you." George turned to his nephew. "Nick. Compile a list of all the men in Elise's life—everyone from family friends to men she's dated to casual acquaintances."

"I'm already working on it," Elise said, turning her laptop around to show them a screenful of names. "I started with my dad and worked my way down to the kid who bags my groceries at the store. I put asterisks next to a couple I thought might hold some kind of grudge against me—"

"Like Westbrook?" George asked. Preppy-boy with the glasses had acted as if he had some sort of proprietary claim on Elise last night, which put him at the top of George's suspect list. Of course, he'd still been mentally stomping out the residual embers from that incendiary kiss he and Elise had shared when Westbrook had stormed in, so he was pretty sure his objectivity had been in question. "Anyone else?"

Elise shrugged. "I can't imagine that James would want to hurt me, and I don't know anyone that I've insulted or angered like Dr. Kilpatrick suggested, certainly not intentionally. In a lot of ways, I live a pretty unremarkable life. And what if it's someone I haven't thought of, or don't even know?"

Nick pointed to her computer. "I'll give you my number. If you send me that list, it'll give me a place to start running background checks, at least."

Nodding, Elise set to work organizing the list and

attaching it to an email. But a second later, she raised her head. “What about Alexsandr Titov?”

“Who’s that?” Nick asked.

George could guess what she was thinking. “He’s the brother of that European mobster who went after Quinn Gallagher and GSS a few years back—blamed Quinn for his son’s death. Elise worked at GSS during that time.”

Nick whistled between his teeth. “You were caught up in that mess?”

George interrupted before Elise could answer or confess to the collusion she blamed herself for. “Quinn’s on his way over here to discuss his suspicions about why Alexsandr is in Kansas City.”

“His timing is a little hinky, considering what’s going on with Miss Brown. Is he connected to a foreign mob, too?” Nick shook his head and jotted a note when George didn’t answer. “I’ll find out.”

But Elise refused to avoid the subject George had tried to protect her from. “It’s the same thing his brother, Nikolai, did to me when I worked for GSS.” She set her laptop on the desk and stood, clearly agitated by her thoughts. “Oh, not the threatening love letter and creepy stuff. But, seeing me as the weak link and preying on that.”

“The weak link to what?” Annie looked from George to Elise as they faced off. “Are you talking about what Dr. Kate said? If our unsub is a copycat instead of some pervert psychopath?”

Elise tilted her eyes up to George. “I would never betray you or this office. I would never jeopardize the work KCPD is doing or reveal any kind of sensitive information.”

"I know you wouldn't."

"I did it before."

"No." Forgetting their audience, George took her by the shoulders, holding on tighter and dipping his face closer to hers when she would have twisted away. "You didn't. Nikolai Titov was a selfish bastard who took advantage of you when you were hurting. He used you."

"I'm hurting now, George. I'm frightened, and I don't know how to make it stop." Her hands settled at his biceps, ready to push him away, but somehow curling into the cotton of his sleeves instead. "What if I make the same mistake again? I wouldn't mean to, but I could. It may not be Mr. Titov. It could be someone else who wants something. The budget negotiations are going to determine who gets to keep his job and who's going on probation. Aren't there plenty of officers who'd like to have the inside scoop on that? The city's on edge with this heat wave—what if someone wants to take advantage of the emergency response procedures we have in place to rob a bank or commit some other crime when your officers are focused elsewhere? I have access to that information, just like you do."

"Elise, I trust you."

"Maybe you shouldn't."

"Elise—"

"It's nearly ten o'clock." She smoothed the wrinkles she'd made in his shirt—one stroke, two—before snatching her fingers away and quickly picking up her laptop. "I'd better go out to my office to meet Quinn for his appointment. He's usually very prompt."

"Ma'am." Nick stood when she headed for the door. "We'll get this guy."

Elise paused with her hand on the doorknob and

looked over her shoulder to Nick and Annie. Her smile might not have reached her eyes, but it was there. "Thank you for your help."

Then she was gone and the barrier of an office door had been resurrected between them. George couldn't help but notice he hadn't been included in that thank-you. Maybe he was the one who should be worried about his sanity if he was still thinking there could be something more than a professional relationship between them.

"She's wound up pretty tight," Nick said, tucking his notebook into his back pocket. "Do you think this stalker is going to hurt her?" George's brooding silence was answer enough. With a nod, Nick bent down to pick up Annie's investigation kit. "We'll get to work."

"Sorry to chase you kids out, but I've got a meeting." His eyes were burning by the time he blinked and tore his gaze from the door to shake his nephew's hand. "I'll hear from you later?"

"I'll make it priority one today."

"Same here." Annie stretched up on her tiptoes to give George a hug. "I'll call with whatever results I get from the lab."

He hugged the petite woman right back. "Thanks. I know I'm asking a lot of you both to volunteer your time to help the old man. I don't need to remind you that until we find more concrete evidence, this isn't an official investigation."

Nick shrugged off the apology. "You're family. You're the reason I became a cop. It's what the Madigans and Fensoms do…old man."

Annie swatted Nick's arm and scooted him toward the door. "You're not old, Uncle George. And Elise is very pretty. Her pupils dilated when you two argued. I think she likes you, too."

"We're just friends."

Nick grinned. "Don't tell me you didn't notice those legs going all the way up to her neck."

"Nicolas," George warned.

"Nick!"

Nick threw his arms out in protest, smiling down at Annie. "What? You get to tease him about the looks he's been giving her, but I don't?"

Annie pointed. "You open that door right now. We've got work to do."

"All right, all right. I get it. Their relationship is as unofficial as the investigation."

"There is no relationship."

"Uh-huh." Nick flipped George a salute and opened the door. "Getting to work now. I'll have something to report by the end of the day."

The young couple left George's office, bickering back and forth in heated whispers, but holding hands and bumping shoulders together like the newlyweds they were as they exited into the hallway.

Well, hell. No wonder Elise was so adamant about keeping their own relationship professional and platonic. He'd already crossed some invisible barrier if Nick and Annie could spot the tension radiating between them after spending barely thirty minutes together. George planted his hands on his waist and stood in the middle of his office, willing the rawness inside him to go away.

As the line between boss and man blurred, George admitted that he wanted Elise with a fury he hadn't felt for any woman since long before he and Courtney had started to splinter. He liked holding her, feeling her sleek curves and soft skin pressed against him. He loved how her fingers snuck past that careful reserve of hers and latched on to him with a surprising passion. He wanted to kiss her again. Hell, he wanted to strip off those sensible dresses and kiss a lot more than that sweet mouth. He'd felt more alive, more like the man he used to be these past few days than he'd felt in years.

But he needed her to feel safe and confident and sure of her world again.

Elise would be the one risking her career if they got involved. If the board of review demoted or fired her for breaking KCPD protocol, she could claim sexual harassment and sue the department. Not that he thought Elise would be so vindictive and lie about an affair, but he didn't want her to go through a hassle like that. She didn't deserve it. Especially, with the nightmare she'd gone through with her previous job.

"Suck it up, Madigan." He had to keep it square in his head that Elise only needed his help, not his heart.

He could live without a special woman in his life—he'd done it well enough since his divorce. But he couldn't live with himself if anything happened to Elise Brown—at a stalker's hand or because of his own selfish desires. He needed to rope in his libido, get a grip on these burgeoning emotions and be what Elise needed him to be. A cop with considerable influence. Her protector. Nothing more. And certainly nothing less.

With his resolve firmly in place, George straightened the knot of his tie and strode out to Elise's office where he could hear friendly voices greeting one another.

Some resolve. He walked out to find Quinn Gallagher, invention genius and wealthy entrepreneur, lifting

Elise onto her toes in a tight hug. Yep, that was definitely a stab of jealousy that hit him in the gut when her feet touched the carpet again and Elise beamed the big smile she'd denied George all morning.

George and Quinn were good friends who'd done a lot of business dealings together to benefit the department and Kansas City. Quinn was a happily married man—George had attended the wedding and even wished him well. But yeah, he wished that hug and smile had been for him.

Understanding the departmental rule forbidding romantic entanglements between police officers and their direct subordinates far better than he'd like, George crossed Elise's office with his hand outstretched to greet his friend. "Quinn. I was looking for another crisis to add to my list today. So what's raised a red flag about Alexsandr Titov coming to town?"

SETTING THE BLACK steel gun down on the counter beside the empty magazine that had housed fifteen bullets, George removed his noise-dampening headphones and pushed the button to bring up the paper target at KCPD's indoor firing range. The attendant had already gone home, and with C shift out on patrol or working at their desks in their respective precinct buildings, George was alone in the building's basement.

Good thing, too. He grunted a curse as the paper outline of a full-grown man flapped to a stop. He was all over the place with his shooting. He'd clipped an ear, hit three belly shots and landed the rest of his bullets on the picture's extremities—nice, if all he wanted to do was give a perp an interesting scar. He counted fifteen holes. At least all his shots had hit the paper. The eye doctor had promised him reading glasses in the near future, but the more likely culprit for his sad performance was simply a lack of being out in the field and practicing his skill as often as he once had.

"You used to be better than this, Madigan," he grumbled.

He sent the target back and reloaded the Glock's magazine. He used to have better hunches about suspects, too. But he was no closer to knowing who was terrorizing Elise than he'd been this morning. Quinn Gallagher had given him an interesting theory about Alexsandr Titov. Although the Lukinburg native had no known ties to organized crime in his country, neither had his brother, Nikolai, until Quinn had closed the ammunition production factory Nikolai had run for him. Arms smugglers who'd used the factory's shipments to transport their contraband around the world had kidnapped and killed Nikolai's son in an effort to coerce him into reopening the plant. Nikolai had come to the U.S. supposedly to urge Quinn to reopen the plant, when in reality, he'd come to take revenge on the man he blamed for his son's death.

Was Alexsandr really in Kansas City to rebuild a business empire and restore his family's good name? Or was he, like Nikolai before him, here to avenge his family? Quinn had arranged a lunch meeting with Titov tomorrow, ostensibly to hear his pitch for working with GSS again and selling the goods produced in his newly opened factory to KCPD. But George and Quinn both were hoping to come away with a more accurate reading about Alexsandr, and whether or not he held a grudge against Quinn, his wife or Elise.

If Titov was legit, then that left a whole city full of

potential nut jobs, resentful employees and desperate crooks who might be targeting Elise.

Yeah, he was doing a real whiz-bang job of keeping her safe.

George loaded the magazine into his gun and slipped the first bullet into the firing chamber. He was ready to put his headphones back on and yell, "Firing fifteen," when he heard the footsteps on the floor behind him.

"Target practice?" Some of the tension eased from George's shoulders as his nephew, Nick Fensom, strolled into the firing booth beside him. "I noticed you were carrying this morning. Haven't seen that for a while."

George set his gun on the counter, with the barrel facing away from them both. "Since the department is short staffed right now, I'm heading over to Elise's to park out front and keep an eye on her house tonight. Figured I'd better be armed with more than a big cup of coffee if I was going to do her any good. Didn't want to push my luck on recruiting more volunteers."

"Uh-huh."

He eyed the deceptive nonchalance in Nick's muscular frame as Nick leaned an elbow on the counter and peered downrange to assess George's lousy performance. "Do you have a report for me?"

"How is this thing with Elise Brown not personal for you?"

George groaned. Nick must have inherited his smart mouth from his brother-in-law's side of the family. "Let it go, Nick. She's closer to your age than she is to mine."

"So? She's an adult, isn't she?"

"She's understandably rattled by this anonymous maniac who thinks he's in love with her. Or who's pretending to be, at least." He propped his hands at his waist, shrugging off his nephew's fishing expedition. "If she's got this paternal thing going where I can use my experience and influence to make her feel safe, then that's what I'll do for her."

"That is the biggest crock of—"

"What did you find out today?" There. George's paternal tone was sharp enough to get Nick to straighten and pull his notebook from his back pocket. But he was still grinning.

"Well, her dad's clean. He's vacationing in Montana as we speak." He waved off George's pointed look and got serious. "Nobody else on the list she gave me popped up as an obvious suspect. No mental illness, no major crimes. Nobody on the special victims unit's watch list."

"What about Westbrook?"

Nick flipped a page in his notebook and scanned the information. "He moved to Korea right out of college. Climbed the corporate ladder pretty quickly. Last job was VP of finance with an international firm of lawyers in the Czech Republic. He's got money in the bank, rents an apartment downtown and bought two season tickets to the Chiefs this fall, so he's planning on staying around for a while."

George tugged at his rolled-up sleeves and folded his arms over his chest. "Any clue why he came back to the States?"

"The translator's English wasn't that good, and I know zero Czech, but I got the idea a romance soured on him. It sounds like the woman might have died. I could make out the word *accident* but not the details."

Since Westbrook shared history with Elise, George supposed it made sense for the man to try to rekindle whatever he'd once had with her. He didn't like that Westbrook wanted Elise to be a solace for his grief, but it made sense. The emotional upheaval could even explain his short temper. "I may talk to Kate Kilpatrick again tomorrow. I wonder if it's plausible for a man to fixate on another woman as a means of coping with a traumatic loss."

Nick slipped the notebook back into his pocket. "I didn't know K.C. was the place where middle-aged hearts came to heal."

Not this again. "Are you referring to me?"

Nick shrugged. "I don't need to be as smart as Annie and notice dilated pupils to see you've got a thing for Elise. It's the first time I've ever seen you this involved with a woman since Aunt Courtney."

Involved. He supposed there was no resolute will or ignoring of facts that could make this thing go away. George raked his fingers through his hair and released a weary breath. "I kissed her."

"Aunt Court?"

"Elise."

"Now, that's more like it." Nick reached over and clapped him on the shoulder, congratulating him. "Did she kiss you back?"

"It was a heat-of-the-moment thing. She'd just gotten a good fright."

"Even in the heat of the moment, you don't make out with someone you have paternal feelings for." Nick was grinning like the Cheshire cat. "She's into you."

"She's made it clear that she doesn't want to be into me. I have to respect that. And I have to respect departmental policy about having a personal relationship with a subordinate."

"You know, you've been divorced from Courtney for ten years. You're a grown man, you're unattached—it's okay for you to have a fling."

"Elise is not the kind of woman you have a fling with."

Nick's knowing nod belied the hushed maturity in his voice. "It's also okay for you to find someone and be happy again."

"There are rules to follow."

"Screw the rules."

George slapped his hand down on the counter. "I am the deputy commissioner of a major metropolitan police department. I'm your boss. I'm her boss. I don't have the option of forgetting the rules."

"Wow." Nick didn't even bat an eye at the rare burst of temper. "That's what they mean by 'it's lonely at the top,' eh?"

George shook his head. "How does Annie put up with you?"

"Slugger loves me. And she knows I love her. I took a bullet for her, George, and I'd do it again. Yeah, we both have blue running through our blood, and it isn't always easy. But we try not to bring our cases home with us, and we make it work." He enunciated that last line to let it sink in. Nick seemed to think there were options for a workplace romance that George knew damn well didn't exist for him. And while George wished he still had that young man's optimism in him, Nick picked up a set of headphones, turned the light on the target at the end of his lane and pulled out his own weapon. Cradling it in his hands, he urged George to pick up his gun and do the same. "The Glock 9 mil is heavier than the gun you used to carry. Aim down a quarter of an inch or so, and the kick will get you right on the target."

George put on his headphones and took aim beside his nephew.

"We won't let her get hurt."

At least there was one thing they could agree on.

George nodded beside him and squeezed the trigger. "Firing fifteen!"

Chapter Six

Pitsaeli's on the Plaza was well-known for its Italian cuisine, its fine wines and its busy lunch crowd. It wasn't known for its fritzing lights or questionable air-conditioning.

Elise finally gave up pushing her salad around the plate and picked up her napkin to fan herself.

"In Lukinburg, we do not have this unseasonably hot weather." Alexsandr Titov's accent was as melodic as his brother's had been. Noticing her distress, he signaled their waiter and had him top off her glass of ice water. "The sun is bright there. But between the sea and mountains, we have cool breezes. And the air is dry."

Perhaps even more handsome than his older brother had been, Alexsandr's European manners and genteel decorum might have charmed her a couple of years ago. But while she nodded her thanks, she honestly wished George and Quinn would wrap up this meeting and let her step outside onto the Plaza's wide sidewalks to search for an American breeze.

Titov hadn't told them anything useful. He'd apologized more than once for his brother's actions, assured them that his new import/export company was completely legit, and that he was expanding into more than just ammunition manufacturing. He'd even invited George to have KCPD conduct an investigation into his books and business practices. It wasn't as if an intelligent businessman would come right out and ask them for inside information, and since this was a first meeting, it would be inappropriate for Alexsandr to do more than hint that he'd like to become a subsidiary of GSS and sell his defense and survival products to KCPD and other contracts in the Midwest.

Elise had been invited along to today's meeting for one purpose—to see if she recognized Titov's voice or anything else about him that seemed familiar. Unless she could get him to whisper "I love you," or provide a sample of his handwriting, however, there was no way she could confirm that he was the man who'd called her office, left those creepy messages or invaded her home.

And she couldn't bring herself to ask if he knew about the twenty-three roses Nikolai had sent her before his death. She wasn't sure which was more unsettling—having no clue who had developed this obsession with her, or knowing the man terrorizing her was sitting right beside her in a public restaurant.

The lights on the walls flickered again. Elise gasped when they went out for nearly half a minute. For a few seconds the entire restaurant was silent, with only the clinking and clanking and Italian curses coming from the kitchen.

"So sorry, everybody," a thickly accented Italian voice shouted from the kitchen alcove. "I am Arturo Pitsaeli, your host. It is just a blown fuse. We shall have it fixed in moments."

In the spirit of patience and cooperation, the patrons all seemed to be holding their breaths. Soon she heard the drone of electricity surging through the building again. The lights popped back on, and there were cheers from many tables and the crew in the back.

A hand patted her knee beneath the tablecloth and Elise jumped a second time.

"Afraid of the dark?" Alexsandr asked.

After catching the questioning look in George's eyes across the table, she tucked her hair behind her ear, subtly masking the shake of her head, indicating she was all right. "I didn't think I was. Just startled."

She crossed her legs and pulled away from the lingering, unwanted touch as Alexsandr winked a blue eye at her. "One of the items Titov Industrial is developing is a more powerful portable generator. One could run this restaurant during a blackout. Three could run this entire city block." She didn't relax until she saw both his hands on top of the table again. "Perhaps that is something you could use a demonstration for today, yes?"

"Perhaps," she agreed, although she'd warn George and Quinn to stay away from doing business with this man. Her recommendation had nothing to do with business and everything to do with the fact that Alexsandr had just taken his charm over the edge into Creepy Land. She'd like nothing better than to end this meeting and never see another Titov again. And whether it was the language barrier or his propensity to combine business with pleasure, Elise thought the direct approach might be the best way to get the answers they needed from this man. "I don't suppose you know how many roses your brother sent me before he left the country, do you?"

"What?" Alexsandr shook his head. "Nikolai sent you flowers?" He twisted his pinkie ring on his left hand and smiled. "You were very special to him, no?" Elise's left hand fisted around her napkin when he caught the fingers of her right hand and lifted them to his lips for a kiss. "I can see why even my hardheaded brother was charmed by you."

That was no answer at all. Of course, if he did know the significance of twenty-three roses and how they might frighten her, he'd hardly admit to it, would he? She was definitely out of her element on the front line of an investigation like this.

Elise pulled her hand away as quickly as was polite and picked up her purse. "If you gentlemen will excuse me, I need to visit the ladies' room."

All three men rose to their feet when she stood, but she only saw George's stony-gray eyes narrowed with concern before she shook her head and hurried through the path of tables and past the wait stand to the back hallway where the restrooms were located.

After the woman in the stall beside her left, and Elise was alone in the quiet, windowless room, she breathed a noisy sigh of relief. She washed her hands and splashed cool water on her face and neck. Grabbing a towel to blot her skin dry, she looked at herself in the mirror. "Oh, my."

The sleeveless navy blue coatdress and silver jewelry looked as chic as the day she'd bought them. But no amount of style or makeup could negate the haunted look on her face. She hadn't looked this sleep-deprived since finals week at college. At least those late nights had served a useful purpose. This bone-deep fatigue, the wariness that shadowed her eyes, felt like someone's nefarious plan to wear her down until she caved in to whatever her stalker wanted from her…or she lost her mind.

She quickly tossed the paper towel and opened her purse. Hopefully, a touch of coral lipstick would make her look a little more normal. No wonder George was so worried about her, calling in favors from detectives, crime scene investigators and criminal profilers to solve her little problem. He probably thought she was on the verge of losing all competency as the most trusted member of his staff…and if something didn't change soon, she just might.

Last night she'd showered and gone to bed, thinking exhaustion would claim her and allow her to sleep. But a constant feeling of being watched, of someone lurking in the shadows outside her securely locked windows kept her tossing and turning. Spike's sotto voce growling and suspicious woofs at every little noise hadn't helped her relax, either.

Until she realized there *was* someone watching.

When she peeked through her curtains, she recognized the silver Suburban parked away from the streetlamp outside. As soon as she saw that George Madigan was sitting inside his car, that he was the uninvited presence making her so paranoid, she'd hooked Spike up to his leash, marched outside in her robe and pajamas and kindly asked him to leave.

"You're scaring me."

"Not my intent." He'd climbed out of the car as soon as she'd flipped on the porch light, and met her on the front sidewalk.

When he clamped his hand over her arm and tried to steer her inside, Elise planted her feet. "It's not your responsibility, either."

"It is in more ways than you know."

"What does that mean?"

"It means I'm not going anywhere."

Once she could see it was an argument she wasn't going to win, Elise invited him inside to spend another night on her Chippendale couch. No sense sweating inside his car on the warm summer night, or running his engine all night long just to have air-conditioning. And if she knew exactly where he was, she wouldn't be questioning the presence in the shadows, either.

She didn't suppose her tailored sofa was big enough for the broad-chested man, nor soft enough to be very comfortable to stretch out on. But she hadn't offered him a guest room upstairs, and he hadn't complained.

In fact, he seemed to be making himself right at home in her house. Although he'd stripped off his jacket, shirt and belt to sleep, he'd placed the gun that he hadn't worn before yesterday beneath the pillow she'd brought down for him.

Her sleep had proved equally fitful as she adjusted to having company in the house. She'd heard him moving around through the house, checking locks, warming up his coffee in the microwave, tussling with Spike when he'd trotted downstairs to check on the noises. Elise wished she could be just as curious and carefree as the dog and go down to George, too. Maybe he'd hold her again. Maybe they'd kiss. Maybe they'd just talk. Maybe then, she'd feel safe enough to let sleep claim her.

Elise drew the lipstick across her mouth, remembering the sensuous pull of George's lips across hers. She remembered every look, every touch.

There were other desires at work, too, plaguing her sleep—the hunger for a man whose masculinity and confident strength were such an integral part of him that he made her feel utterly feminine. It would be easier to fight that forbidden attraction once this mess was cleared up and she could have her normal life back and take care of herself again.

She capped the lipstick and put it away in her purse, just like she had to put away any fantasy she might have about her boss. In another job, in another life, she could see how good she and George might be together. But this was the life she—

The lights in the bathroom suddenly went out. "Oh!"

Elise froze. It was much darker back here than it had been in the dining room, where a bank of windows facing the street had compensated for the blown fuse. Elise heard shouts and the crack of dishes breaking from the kitchen on the other side of the wall, and a rising din of complaints from customers and staff alike. The power must be out throughout the restaurant again.

With her vision struggling to compensate for the near blackout conditions in the restroom, Elise fumbled in the darkness to find something familiar and wound up gripping the edge of the sink, anxiously waiting for the lights to come back on. She waited and waited. A body banged into the hallway wall, and she jumped. A tray of silverware crashed to the floor and someone cursed.

"Why aren't the lights coming back on?" Elise whispered. The air in here was quickly growing stale without the vents and air-conditioning on to filter out the scents of potpourri, oven fumes and something faintly moldy in the background.

Arturo Pitsaeli was shouting again. "Please, everybody, stay in your seats. My apologies. Free gelati for everyone. Please. Sit."

But it didn't sound as if people were listening. Dozens of footsteps and chairs screeching across the terra-cotta tile floors sounded more like people were panicking—or were furious, at least, about the new delay in their lunch break.

The entire fuse box must have blown. This was a complete power outage.

She needed to get out of here. She needed to get to some light.

Elise reached forward until her fingertips butted against the mirror. Turning to her left, she headed toward the exit, trailing her fingers along the smooth glass to orient herself. When her fingers grazed across rougher plaster, her hip bumped into the trash can, knocking it against the wall. She reached out to grab it, but before she could stop its wobbling, the bathroom door opened and a sliver of murky light took the room from opaque to merely dark. "Hold the door, would you? Trust me, it isn't any better in here."

No one answered.

"Hello? Is someone there?"

The blast of noise from the restaurant muted and the blackness returned as the door softly closed again. Maybe whoever had tumbled into the wall outside had accidentally knocked the door open, without coming inside at all.

Elise shook her head and inched forward.

But other senses were arguing with her useless vision. She halted, inhaling a quick breath, imagining a whiff of musky heat in the air. Perspiration? Not hers.

Her pulse thundered in her ears at the deafening silence and she recoiled half a step. "Who's there?"

No reply.

Was her imagination working overtime to create a threat that wasn't there?

Was that…? Yes. The deep, rhythmic whisper of someone breathing.

She wasn't alone.

And her company wasn't talking.

"Who are you?" The darkness swam inside her head and she stumbled back against the sinks. "Answer me!"

Chapter Seven

"Answer me!"

"Elise?" She squealed at the sharp rap against the bathroom door and gave up her blind search for the phone in her purse. The door opened and a broad figure was silhouetted in the dim light. "Are you in here?"

"George?" Relief was so intense, it made her lightheaded. "Watch out. There's someone—"

The beam of a small flashlight swung into the room and bounced off the mirror, temporarily blinding her. She turned away.

"Elise!" His familiar grip closed around hers, pulling her to the door. "Let's go. It's Crazy Town out here."

"But—"

"Now."

Squeezing George's hand, she held on as they jostled their way through swarming people and moving chairs. Waiters carried trays with free desserts, patrons tried to pay their checks and depart, and a few, possibly, simply departed to be chased down by the hostess and by Arturo himself.

"Quinn will cover the check," George announced. "I want to get you out of here."

Compared to the pitch-black bathroom, the dusky

twilight out here was hard on her eyes. She squinted her lids against the growing brightness as they neared the front windows. But she couldn't forget the smell and the sound in the restroom. She tugged against George's forward momentum. "Where's Mr. Titov?"

"He got a phone call. He was heading to the front door to take it when the lights blew. To be honest, I don't know where he ended up."

Elise planted her feet and got him to stop. "What about the man in the restroom?"

"The what?"

She raised her voice to be heard above the chaos. "There was someone in there with me. I think it may have been him."

"Titov?"

"I don't know. He never said anything."

There was no need to explain why she'd be concerned about company in the restroom. George's eyes hardened like granite and he quickly reversed course. "Come on." When they reached the back hallway, he pushed her against the wall and bent his knees to bring his face even with hers. "Wait here. Don't move." Although she couldn't read his eyes in the shadows, there was no mistaking the frustrated sigh that matched her own. Before she could even thank him for believing her implausible story, he leaned in and pressed a hard, quick kiss against her mouth and pulled away. "Right here," he reminded her. "I'll be back."

Her hand had barely landed on the silk of his tie before he was pulling his jacket back, drawing his gun, leaving her. "This is the police. I'm coming in."

Opening the door, he pushed it all the way around to the wall, ensuring no one was hiding behind it before bracing his wrists together to point his gun and flashlight in the same direction. Sweeping the light back and forth, he went inside and disappeared into the darkness.

Elise's fingers drifted back to touch the tingling stamp of caring and promise that lingered on her lips. She held her breath, praying as hard for George to find the silent intruder as she was for him to avoid any kind of confrontation that could get him hurt.

She tried to tune her hearing to pinpoint the soft breathing she'd heard before, but it wasn't easy. The more she tried to concentrate, the more distractions there were. The chef was herding his sous chefs and waitstaff out of the kitchen with a flashlight while Arturo Pitsaeli pushed by her in the opposite direction, carrying a broken wine bottle and muttering in Italian. Greenish security lights had come on, casting a weird glow over all their faces, obscuring their expressions into distorted masks.

"Empty. I checked every stall." George holstered his weapon as he shooed the last waitress out of his path. "Checked the men's, too. There's no one there."

Another mystery she couldn't explain? "But he was there. I didn't imagine it. I smelled him."

"He could have easily lost himself in this crowd or slipped out back through the kitchen." George leaned in close enough for her to read the seriousness of his expression. There was no confusion or pity there, only a sense of urgency. "I think distance from here is our best protection right now." He snatched her hand and she willingly hurried into step with him as he led her back into the restaurant. "Let's go."

They reentered the throng that seemed to grow more crowded and less friendly by the second. She was tall in her high heels, but not tall enough to see over George's shoulder or around the patrons standing so close to her. They hurried closer to daylight with every step, but even as Elise's eyes adjusted, there were too many people and too much movement to focus on any one face.

"Maybe it was just one of the waitresses catching a moment of quiet away from the dining room. It may not have been Alexsandr. Or any man." That was the explanation she was going with when George pulled her through the front doors onto the sidewalk outside. She instantly squinted against the bright sun and reached into her bag for her sunglasses. But when she released George's hand and someone pushed her into a mother trying to negotiate a stroller and a crying child through the crowd, she decided it was safer to keep moving with the tide of people pouring out of storefronts and eateries. "Sorry," she apologized, catching the woman's diaper bag and hooking it securely back over her shoulder.

The sidewalk was packed. Not just with the usual spate of summer tourists coming to see the historic Mediterranean architecture, fountains and works of art, but shoppers, lunchtime guests like themselves and personnel from the local businesses. Doors were closing. Gates were coming down over storefront windows. The outdoor dining tables at Pitsaeli's took up half the sidewalk, creating a bottleneck of pedestrians who all seemed to be heading toward the parking lot and garages beyond the next intersection. And where the side streets crossed the wide boulevard, traffic lights were blinking on backup power and a jam of cars was blocking the crosswalks.

George lifted the woman's stroller past the fence surrounding Pitsaeli's sidewalk café, accepted her thanks, then pulled Elise back into step beside him. "Don't talk yourself out of what you saw."

"But I didn't see him. Even when you opened the door that first time, he could have been behind it. She could have been. No one could have—"

"Stop it. I know you. Practical. Levelheaded. Resourceful. I don't think you imagined it for one moment."

"But I haven't been myself lately. You know that, too."

With a grumbling curse, he pulled Elise around the fence as well, into a small pocket empty of humanity for the moment. George stretched his neck above the crowd and looked up and down the street, assessing the situation before pulling out his cell phone. "This is a madhouse. Electricity on the whole block must be out."

He punched in 9-1-1, but they couldn't wait there long. With the hundred-degree temperature, the stucco reflected even more heat. If dots of perspiration were already beading between Elise's breasts in her cotton dress, then George must be boiling in his jacket and tie. Nodding as if he'd read her thoughts, he took her hand again and led her back into the flow of people.

The press of pedestrians was almost suffocating. Despite the slippery heat of their adjoining palms, Elise laced her fingers with George's and held on tighter while he made a call to Dispatch. Raising his voice to a commanding timbre to be heard over the din, he identified himself and ordered street patrol and backup crowd control as well as the utility department into the area pronto.

Spotting a familiar uniformed officer beside his black-and-white cruiser across the street, Elise walked the next several steps on tiptoe and pointed. "That's Denton Hale's partner, Gary Boyd. We can get them to help."

"Good idea." Shifting course, George pulled her around a bronze statue and flowers decorating a planter in the middle of the wide sidewalk.

But her grip loosened as they jostled through the crowd. Someone stepped on her heel. "George?"

With a hop, she tried to keep the leather pump on her toes. But someone elbowed into her side, knocking her off balance, and she lost both George's hand and her right shoe.

"Wait." In a blink they were separated by a family rattling off panicked directions to each other in Chinese or some other Eastern tongue. Panicking a bit herself, she bent down to pick up her shoe. But a man's foot lumbered past, kicking it away into a trample of feet. "Hey!"

"Elise?" She heard George's shout and straightened back up.

She bobbed up and down as the crowd carried her farther from the sound of his voice. She caught a glimpse of his distinctive silver and brown hair and raised her hand over her head so he could see her. "I'm over— Ow!"

A hard shoe ground her bare toes against the concrete. Pain shot through her foot and she nearly toppled over.

"You stupid—"

A gloved hand snagged hers. A voice whispered against her nape. "I'll save you, Elise."

That voice.

"No!" Elise stumbled as the hand dragged her back through the crowd. "Let go of me!"

But the moment she spun around and would have seen his face, he released her or she was knocked free. Several people surged between them, blocking her view. She caromed from one person to the next, some cursing her, some helping, all keeping her from the truth.

"George!" She finally threw herself against the wall of the nearest building. Limping on one shoe, protecting her injured foot, she hugged the wall and inched forward.

When a hand clamped down on her shoulder, she screamed. The crowd retreated from the shrieking woman the way a line of ants swerved to avoid a puddle. But the hand on her arm stayed put. She clawed at the grip.

"Easy. Easy, Miss Brown. Whoa. Are you okay?"

Elise froze. It was a full voice, not that creepy whisper. Blue uniform. Black gloves tucked in front pocket. Bare fingers against her skin.

Panic rushed out on a quick breath and she tilted her chin up to read the apology in Shane Wilkins's green eyes. "Elise?"

"Shane? Thank God it's you."

"I was eating lunch at the sub place down the street when the lights went out and I heard the all call..." His gaze dropped to the ground. "Ma'am, you're bleeding."

The scrapes on her foot were inconsequential. "A man grabbed me. Where's George...the deputy commissioner?"

"Elise!"

He pushed through the edge of the crowd and she threw her arms around his neck. "George!"

"I've got you." His arms latched around her back like

a vise and he carried her back to the wall before setting her down. "What's wrong?"

When her feet touched concrete and his hands settled at her waist, she hung on to his lapels and kept him close. "He's here. He just grabbed me."

"I grabbed you, ma'am." Shane threw up his hands in surrender, apologizing again. "Sorry I startled—"

"No. In the crowd… I felt… He said…" Elise peeked between the two men, searching for a face she didn't know in an overwhelming sea of faces. George's body was braced around hers, but she could feel the bumping and pushing.

He brushed aside the hair that stuck to her cheeks. Maybe they were damp from heat. Maybe they were damp from tears. Either way, those stone-gray eyes didn't seem to like what they saw. "We're getting out of here. Can you walk?"

Elise managed a jerky nod before George tucked her to his side. She willingly wound her arm around his waist beneath his suit jacket, clinging tightly to the belt beside the holster he wore. What little strength she had left ebbed into his and he half led, half carried Elise straight into the swarm of pedestrians. His body was a shield that protected her from figments of her imagination and the crazy mash-up of hot, sweaty bodies filing past.

"Wilkins, can you take point and get us across the street to the parking garage?" George didn't wait for a confirmation before his shoulder shifted beneath her cheek and he waved to another officer on the scene. "Hale, we need your help."

The ground suddenly dropped from beneath her feet and she clutched at George's chest. When her bare foot grazed against hot asphalt, she understood that George had lifted her to step off the curb and carry her across the street. She felt a hand on her elbow and turned. Denton Hale's face swam in and out of focus above his blue collar. Maybe she was suffering delirium from heatstroke.

"Is she all right?" He looked from George to her as he helped her cross the street. "Ma'am, you look mighty pale."

"She'll be fine." With a boost onto his hip, George took her full weight and climbed over the concrete median. "Wilkins. Clear that entrance. I'm on the first floor, third row in. Hale, get those cars out of the intersection."

"Yes, sir." The officers answered in tandem, rushing away in a blur of blue and a hail of shouts and whistles.

"This way, sir." Shane waved them forward, scattering the people gathered at the entrance to the parking garage. "Move along. This is a police emergency. Coming through."

The relative coolness when they reached the shady side of the boulevard revived Elise a little. "I can walk," she offered.

"I know." Although he eased her feet down to the ground, he never relinquished his hold around her waist or slowed his pace. "My car's back there."

"Got it, sir." After George hit the remote to unlock it, Shane opened the door and George lifted her inside behind the steering wheel.

A sharp whistle drew her attention to the street. "Let's move it!" Denton Hale tapped the hood of a car and waved it on through the intersection, clearing the lane in front of the garage exit. When his gaze met hers through the windshield of George's Suburban, he touched the brim of his cap in a salute to her and Elise nodded her thanks.

Meanwhile George was dismissing Officer Wilkins. "You'd better go assist with crowd control, son. Make sure that utility truck gets through."

"I will, sir. Ma'am." He, too, acknowledged Elise before jogging back to the entrance.

"You have good people working for you."

"I do." When George climbed in behind the wheel, Elise scooted across to the passenger seat. The effort seemed to drain the last bit of energy out of her and she sagged against the tan upholstery. Her eyes felt gritty, unfocused. George reached over to pull her purse off her shoulder and drop it to the floorboards at her feet before starting the engine and turning on the air. "There's only one employee I'm worried about right now."

"He touched me. He was in the bathroom with me when the lights went out. And in the crowd, in those few seconds you and I got separated, he grabbed my hand and…" She looked down at her hand as if it were an anathema. "He whispered my name."

She was vaguely aware of George sliding across the seat. Or maybe he was pulling her closer, because he lifted the offending hand onto his thigh and rubbed it between both of his, blotting out the memory of another man's touch. "Can you describe him for me? Do you remember anything about him?"

She'd heard. She'd felt. But she hadn't seen anyone. A tear spilled over and burned a path down her cheek.

"I'm not crazy. He was there."

"It's okay. We'll figure it out." He wiped away the

tear with the pad of his thumb and leaned in to kiss her temple. "We'll find the answers we need."

But when he pulled away, Elise felt a moment of such profound loss that she snatched at his jacket to keep him beside her. She palmed his tie and collar and the strong column of his neck before grasping his jaw between her hands. She looked deep into those handsome eyes, traced the firm line of his mouth with her thumbs, slipped her fingers through the silky salt-and-pepper of his hair and came back to frame his warm skin again. "You're real, aren't you, George? I see you. I can touch you. I hear your voice."

"Yeah, honey, I'm real." The lines beside his eyes deepened as he offered her a reassuring smile. His chest expanded with a steadying breath before he brushed aside a lock of her hair and tucked it behind her ear. He turned his lips into her palm and pressed a ticklish kiss there. "Do you feel me? Do you feel this? I'm right here. And I'm not going anywhere."

He wiped away the next tear that fell, and the next. And then he stroked the pad of his thumb across her mouth, urging it to open, giving her a taste of her own salty tears when her tongue darted out to soothe her sensitized lips. If this tenderness was a figment of her imagination… Her eyes filled with sorrowful tears. "George? I need…"

With a groan that vibrated through the air between them, George leaned in to replace his thumb with his mouth. His lips moved deliberately over hers, sampling, healing, demanding. He thrust his tongue into her mouth, giving her a taste of the rich cappuccino he'd drunk after their meal. He threaded his fingers into her hair, branding her with his hands and mouth as he angled her head back against the seat and moved his body into hers.

The encompassing heat seeping into every pore shocked her to her senses. With an answering hum in her throat, she slid her fingers across his crisp hair to clasp them behind his neck and pull herself further into his kiss.

She opened deeply for him, danced her tongue against his. Catching her bottom lip in a soft nibble, he held her in place as he dragged his hands from her hair, skimming them down her body. Her small breasts leaped beneath the lace of her bra and her properly tailored dress to thrust into the heat of his palms. And when his thumbs teased the tips into hardened pearls, she cried out at the arrows of pure wicked heat firing deep into the heart of her.

George moved his lips to the gasps and hums in her throat, and discovered a sensitive bundle of nerves along her collarbone that elicited a low, keening cry. "Your skin is so soft and pretty," he murmured, kissing his way up the side of her neck to capture a lobe and its silver earring between his teeth.

His skin was tempting, too. Like fine sand beneath her fingertips in some places, like smooth silk in others. Always warm to the touch. And far too covered up.

Eager to explore his body, Elise fought with his tie. She slid the knot down his chest and unhooked some buttons on his shirt, slipping her hands inside to singe her fingers on the musky heat of his chest.

When he reclaimed her mouth, she willingly gave him everything he asked for. He slid his hand along her thigh and hooked it behind her knee to pull her into his chest, forcing her to wind her arms around his neck and straddle his lap. His lips continued to work their magic against her mouth and skin, kindling fires with every kiss and sweep of his hands. And if he wanted to do something about the bulge swelling behind his zipper, she wouldn't stop him.

This man was her lifeline to sanity, her feelings for him the only thing that made sense in her senseless world.

This was the passion that had been simmering beneath the surface of protocol and past mistakes for too long. These were the emotions that went far beyond friendship and respect. This was the want, the need, the love she felt for this man.

The love she shouldn't feel.

The love that would surely guarantee her another broken heart.

The love that was as overwhelming and fragile and impossible to hold on to as the certainty she would walk away from this mess with her wits intact.

"George," she whispered, dragging her mouth from his. "We need to stop. You know we shouldn't… I'm okay now."

"Maybe I'm not." He hugged her to his chest for several moments, each of them breathing deeply, quickly.

She could feel his heart thumping against her breast as strongly as she felt her own. Her thoughts were clear now, and she was aware enough to know that she'd climbed into his lap in a public parking garage, giving in to a desire that simply couldn't be. She was also smart enough to know that the terror hounding her might be at bay for the moment, but it was by no means gone from her life.

Easing her grip on his neck, Elise leaned back to

frame his face and give that handsome mouth one last kiss before she crawled off him and back to her seat. "We can't do this, George. As much as I want to, I can't. There are too many things that could go wrong…."

"Too many ways you could get hurt." He tucked a mussed lock of hair behind her ear and nodded. "Hurting you is the last thing I want to do."

He slid back behind the steering wheel, taking a few moments to straighten his clothes, although he ended up pulling his tie off completely and leaving the top button of his shirt open. "You make me feel like I'm twenty again." He shook his head and shifted the car into Reverse. "And sometimes like I'm a hundred and twenty."

She hugged herself, trying to calm all the nerve endings still sparking with the electricity of their embrace. Yes, George was older than she was, but she'd never considered him old. His age had never been the reason she'd kept her distance. "If a crazy woman's opinion matters, I'd say you're just right."

That earned her half a laugh and a little less guilt.

"Buckle up, Goldilocks." He pulled a magnetic light from beneath his seat and stuck it on the roof of the car. Then he punched the siren a couple of times to clear a path and pulled the big vehicle into the bumper-to-bumper traffic as if they were the missing piece completing a puzzle.

Elise was emotionally exhausted and physically weary. Her scraped-up toes were throbbing and the loss of George's abundant body heat left her feeling chilled. And despite Denton Hale waving them on through the intersection, she felt trapped. She was a prisoner in her beloved city, at the mercy of a man who seemed to know her every move and delight in staying one step ahead of her. He knew where she lived, where she worked, where she ate and, quite possibly, how much the man beside her meant to her.

If her stalker's plan was to wear down her mental and emotional strength and make her vulnerable to whatever influence he wanted to have over her, then he was succeeding. If he thought he was having some twisted kind of relationship with her, expressing true love, then he was even sicker than she felt at the moment.

Despite another *whoop-whoop* of the siren and the flashing lights, there was still a logjam of pedestrians and traffic, making it difficult to get out of the Plaza area.

"Do you think he did this?" she asked, glancing out the window at the thinning crowd and dark, closed-up businesses.

"Caused the power outage and the panic?" George nodded to Shane Wilkins as the young cop held up a line of traffic so they could pass. Had he or Hale or anyone else seen that make out session in the front seat of their boss's car? Would they dare gossip about it? Would George care if they did? Should she care about compromising her position in the deputy commissioner's office any further? "At the very least he was following you and took advantage of the opportunity. I'll call Cliff Brandt to have him tell me exactly what caused the lights to go out and have Nick check alibis on Alexsandr Titov and James Westbrook."

"I'll mark it on your calendar as soon as we get back to the office."

"I'm not taking you to HQ, Elise."

She glanced across the car, seeing the look that allowed no argument on his stern features. No. She didn't suppose she was in any shape to do her job right now.

"You're safe," George assured her, reaching across the seat to squeeze her hand. "We'll get through this. Together."

She nodded and held on tight, not quite believing him.

Chapter Eight

Elise drew the thin brush along the groove in the window's top casing, evening out the white trim that would frame her navy blue shutters. After this second coat dried, she'd be ready for hardware and installation. She held on to the top of the stepladder and leaned back to evaluate her work.

"Are you going to do this all night long?"

Back in her own house, amongst her own things, with her own familiar routine, Elise was feeling a sense of relatively peaceful normalcy, considering the afternoon she'd had, and didn't startle at the low-pitched voice teasing her. She even smiled when she turned to see the deputy commissioner of KCPD leaning against the archway into the living room, with his fingers hooked into the front pockets of his faded jeans. Those gray eyes were focused on her bare legs beneath the edge of her cutoff shorts, well south of the face he was communicating with. Spike, who had traitorously seemed to prefer making friends with their new guest than spending time with her, trotted past George into the room and jumped onto the couch.

"Are you going to stay on your phone all night?" she teased right back. "Is that how you spend all your evenings after a full day at work? Doing more work?" She glanced over to the black dog, pawing at the protective tarp and cushions beneath to make himself a comfy bed. "Good grief, you've even worn out Spike."

George's gaze dutifully kicked up to hers and walked into the room. "I offered to help."

Maybe having George Madigan in her home was beginning to feel a little too normal. She'd never seen him dressed so casually before. But when she'd come downstairs in her paint shirt, shorts and flip-flops two hours earlier, he'd changed into a pair of wrinkled jeans and a gray KCPD T-shirt pulled from a duffel bag in the back of the Suburban he'd parked in the driveway behind her Explorer.

He was still wearing his gun and badge, still moved with the same authoritative bearing—still looked like a man in charge. But this version of her boss was one who was a little more approachable, one who could patiently clean and bandage a scraped foot, and didn't seem to mind Chinese takeout at the kitchen counter for dinner, or a dog napping under his chair while he sat in Elise's home office across the foyer to make phone calls.

Realizing she'd been staring as overtly as he had, Elise turned back to the window to dab at a couple more spots. The man who'd rescued her from that madness this afternoon, then nearly seduced her back to her senses, had been heroic and irresistible, larger-than-life and strictly off-limits. But the man strolling through her living room tonight didn't seem like the forbidden boss in a suit and tie. This guy seemed like someone she could meet anywhere, a man whose sense of duty, caring and sexy confidence would have turned her head instantly. This was a man she would have willingly looked forward to spending time with and getting to know better.

That made her attraction to this George Madigan even more dangerous than the man she had already fallen for. Elise knew how to follow rules and do what was expected of her. She wasn't so certain about following her heart and trusting fate to lead her to a happily ever after.

She wiped her brushes on the rag hanging over the top of the stepladder. "It's good therapy for me. Fixing up things, taking care of them. It makes me feel like I'm accomplishing something worthwhile. I like the idea of preserving something that was once important to someone else. It's good, honest work, the physical activity gives me time to think and, of course, I love the beautiful results."

George's hands closed around her waist to help her down. "There's nothing broken about you, Elise."

"So now you're my therapist, too?" She moved away from both his distracting touch and discomfiting words, kneeling down on the drop cloth to put the two brushes into a tin can she'd saved.

"I'm just a man who calls things like I see them." He handed her the rubber mallet from atop the sawhorses after she'd replaced the lid on the paint can. "You've had bad things happen to you, but that doesn't mean it's your fault they happened. You don't have to fix everyone and everything because of some penance you think you owe."

She hammered the can shut with a little more force than usual. "So what makes me such a magnet for the weirdos and users of the world, then?"

"You're bighearted. You put others before yourself. You're too kind to not listen to a problem or try to help."

Elise picked up the can and pushed to her feet. "In other words, I'm a doormat."

"In other words—" he plucked the can of paint from her hand and set it on the sawhorse table "—you're a kind, caring woman who sees where she can make a difference in people's lives, and does."

Not fair. She valued his appreciation of her efficiency and dedication on the job—she needed him to respect her abilities there. But between her experience with Nikolai and this crazy stalker, she was barely keeping her personal life together. Getting to know this surprisingly tender, supportive side of the tough, no-nonsense man she worked with every day was making it even harder to remember they should never be more than friends. "I appreciate you volunteering to keep an eye on the place, sir. But I don't need a pep talk."

As expected, George bristled and backed away a step at her use of the formality. It felt like a cheap shot, but if she didn't learn to keep her distance from him soon, she never would.

"Sorry if I overstepped the boundaries of your hospitality, Miss Brown." Miss Brown? Was that rankling punch in the gut how calling him sir made him feel? Elise's gaze shot up to his, but George's eyes had hardened like stone again. He propped his hands at his waist beside his gun and badge, reminding them both of the real reason he was here. "I spent most of my time on the phone with my nephew and the crime lab tonight. According to Nick, Titov's only alibi is that he was stuck in the crowd at the Plaza, like us, until his driver picked him up around 1:35 p.m. Westbrook says he was at the ball game at Kauffman Stadium, but Nick is looking for more than a ticket stub to prove it. The game lasted over three hours, so that would be plenty of time to leave and get to the Plaza and get back to his seat."

Elise slipped back into assistant mode, although she wasn't sure where the glum mood was coming from. This professional relationship was all she wanted with George, wasn't it? "And the power outage? Did Mr. Brandt have any answers for you?"

"There was a transformer that blew the power grid in that area. His preliminary analysis indicates something was misaligned and it couldn't handle the peak demand. But whether that misalignment was human error or deliberate sabotage, he can't tell yet."

"I don't suppose there's good news from the lab, either?"

George shrugged. "Annie pulled a DNA profile off the envelope flap, but she hasn't found anything to match it to yet."

"Can she expand her search worldwide? Maybe Mr. Titov's profile will show up in a foreign database."

"Or Westbrook's. You said he worked abroad for several years." She nodded. "I've already got her working on it." Then George's chest expanded with a deep breath, a sure sign she wasn't going to like his next bit of information. "Our perp has upped his game. Sending gifts and love notes isn't enough for him anymore. Now he wants to make contact."

Elise hugged her arms around her waist, staving off a sudden chill. "Your garden-variety sicko. How did I get so lucky?"

"If Titov or Westbrook or whoever was trying to get to you this afternoon, then their plan failed. I don't know if that was an attempted kidnapping or something worse. But since isolating you in an unruly crowd didn't work—"

"He'll try again."

George simply nodded.

Since there was nothing more to discuss that wouldn't hurt one or the other's feelings, or make Elise feel they were no closer to identifying the man whose twisted idea of love was poisoning her life, she picked up the can with the paint-filled brushes and circled around George. "It's getting late. I'd better clean my brushes and clear up some of this mess so you have a place to sleep tonight."

Spike hopped off the couch and followed her through the kitchen into the garage. Despite the cool formality that had resumed between them, George followed her out to the utility sink. While she washed out the brushes, he and the dog inspected the storage shelves and the antique furniture and doors waiting to be stripped and restained or painted. Those were projects for cooler weather when she could open the garage door for plenty of ventilation.

But while Spike flushed out a black cricket to do battle with, George tapped his fingers against the old glass in the door to the backyard. The whole thing shook in its frame when he jimmied the knob.

"I don't suppose I should tell you that's an antique," she cautioned.

He pulled a paint-chipped oak dresser in front of it to reinforce the exit. "And I don't suppose I should tell you that even your little poodle monster there could break through this door if he wanted to. It's not secure enough."

"An intruder would have to get through the door into the kitchen, too."

He shook his head. "That one's not any better. We should have replaced all the locks when you got the front door changed."

Elise's chin dropped to her chest in a weary sigh. "Are you trying to make me feel safer? Because you're failing miserably."

He didn't answer until he stood right beside her. "I have never lied to you, Elise. And I'm not going to start now." He turned off the water and rescued the brushes that were long past clean, shaking them off and hanging them up on the hook over the sink. "I don't know what we're up against exactly, yet. But I'm doing everything I know how to keep you safe." He turned on the water again and picked up the bar of soap, sudsing it up before he pulled her hands beneath the warm spray and cleaned the stains from her fingers. "I'll admit that I'm a little out of my element—I've been pushing papers for too long. I'm not sure I'll see the bad guy coming."

"George, I didn't mean that you weren't capable—"

"Hush." The warmth from the water and his gentle, purposeful hands were taking the edge off her fears and fatigue. "I'm old enough I don't need my ego stroked. I may be a step or two slower than I once was. But I'm smarter. I'm a hell of a lot more patient. And I guarantee you that, no matter what happens between you and me, I will never give up until this guy is caught or dead and out of your life. I want my old friend back."

By the time he'd turned off the water and was reaching for paper towels, Elise was resting her head against his shoulder. "I'll keep fighting, too."

"We make a good team. Always have." He dipped

his lips to kiss her temple. "Don't let him get into your head. We're gonna beat this guy." George moved away when she took over drying her own hands. "I'll check the rest of the house, make sure everything is bolted down for the night."

Elise nodded. "I'll put Spike out for his nightly constitutional. If he doesn't run around and stake things out now, he'll be waking me before dawn to relieve himself."

"I don't want you outside by yourself."

Elise nudged him toward the kitchen door. "All I'm doing is opening the door to the deck and putting him in the backyard. He can run around for a few minutes while I make up one of the guest rooms upstairs. Unless you prefer the hard couch?"

"Wherever you're most comfortable with me is fine."

She'd be most comfortable with everything going back to the way it had been before she'd gotten those twenty-three roses. But since that wasn't an option, Elise called Spike and they followed George into the house where he locked the door behind them. "Spikey, *outside?*"

Understanding the word that meant checking smells and running free, the dog charged straight to the back door and danced in anticipation until Elise turned on the porch light and opened the door. A gust of wind blew some flying dust into her eyes, stinging them shut. By the time she blinked them clear of the debris, Spike had leaped down the steps into the grass and disappeared into the darkness beyond. She caught the tendrils of hair whipping about her face and tucked them behind her ears, holding them in place while she turned her gaze up to the sky. The stars were dim dots of light behind the clouds that moved quickly across the sky, and the moon was nonexistent.

Rain would be a welcome respite after so many days of record-setting heat. But the yawning moans from the thick branches of her elm trees catching the wind warned her that it wasn't any gentle, reviving rain headed their way.

"Do your business fast, sweetie," she said as another, cooler gust rippled through her baggy paint shirt.

Retreating from the gusting breeze, Elise stepped back inside and locked the door behind her. She jogged up the stairs and turned on the radio in her bedroom, cranking the volume to hear the weather report while she gathered sheets from the linen closet and went into the room next to hers to make up the bed.

"…tornado watch until 1:00 a.m." The announcer talked about cold fronts pushing high pressure systems out of the area as well as other scientific data. Elise attuned her ears to the most pertinent information. "…80 percent chance of rain tonight…possibility of severe weather tomorrow."

Elise turned on the ceiling fan to draw cooler air from the window air conditioners. By the time she'd fluffed the last pillow and set out a fresh towel for George, the announcer had moved into his public service announcement spiel. "The city power district and emergency response teams recommend stocking up on batteries, flashlights, portable lanterns and other supplies. In the event of a tornado, go to your basement or to the innermost, windowless room—"

Elise shut off the radio and headed back down to let Spike in. Having grown up in the Midwest, she knew the safety procedures by heart. As she passed the archway at the bottom of the stairs, she looked in to see George pacing beside her desk, on his cell phone again. Judging by the snippets of conversation on his end, he knew about the coming storm, too, and was verifying that KCPD's emergency teams would be ready to respond if needed.

When he paused midconversation to make eye contact, she pointed down the hallway to the back door, indicating her destination. With a nod, he returned to his conversation and Elise smiled. The people of Kansas City were in better hands than they knew with men like George Madigan in charge of their safety. She was lucky that he'd made it his personal mission to keep her safe, too.

Knowing he had everything he needed to do his job, just like at the office, Elise left him to his work.

This time, she braced herself for the wind when she opened the back door and whistled. "Spike? Come on in, boy."

Lightning flashed in the clouds overhead, lighting up the backyard for a split second. She waited in the doorway for several seconds before whistling again. "Here, boy!"

Thunder rumbled in ominous portent of the coming storm. "Spike?"

Normally, the dog ran in as soon as she called, anxious to be rewarded with a treat or a tummy rub. Maybe the wind was carrying her voice away from him. But that's what those sharp ears were for, weren't they? "Spike? I've got a treat."

Lightning strobed within the clouds, briefly illuminating the trail of tiny red paw prints crossing back and forth across the deck. Elise shivered with the answering thunder. Where was the dog? "Spike!"

She ran to the railing and peered into the shadows beyond the deck. She heard a snuffling noise off to her right and caught a glimpse of movement beneath the spirea bushes. "Spike?"

Elise hurried off the deck. "Sweetie, are you okay?"

The dog was digging furiously in the dirt. She dropped to her knees and reached beneath the bushes. She slipped her palm beneath his chest, intending to lift him away from the prize he was burying. But when she touched his warm belly, she felt something wet and sticky in his hair. "Sweetie?"

She pulled back her hand. The lightning flashed.

Blood.

Elise screamed.

Throwing herself belly down in the grass, she reached beneath the bush to grab her beloved pet and pull him into her arms.

"Elise!"

She heard loud steps on the deck behind her. Elise rolled onto her bottom, cradling Spike in her arms, stroking his back, checking every limb. He scooted up her chest to lick her chin. His heart thumped rapidly beneath her hands. But there was enough blood to turn his black coat a muddy brown. "Sweetie, what happened? Where are you hurt?"

"Elise? Damn it. I told you not to go outside." She saw the silhouette of a man with a gun in her peripheral vision and instantly recoiled. A light swept through the backyard, but the bright beam settled on the bundle in her arms and George was kneeling beside her. "What happened?"

Recognizing their savior, she grabbed a handful of George's T-shirt and pulled him closer, leaving a red handprint on the cotton, and probably one on her own cheek, too, as she wiped away tears. "We have to help him. That creep's done something to Spike. There's so much blood."

George tucked the gun into the back of his belt and cupped his hand beneath her elbow to help her stand. "Come on. We have to get you back in the house. Wait a minute." He swung the flashlight to the ground and went down on one knee. He pulled a crumpled piece of paper from the dirt where Spike had been burying it. "What the hell?"

Elise tugged on George's belt. "Hurry. We have to get him to the vet."

"Right. Inside." With the first drops of rain pelting them, they ran back into the house.

Elise went straight to the kitchen, snatching her purse off the counter and heading for the front door. "Can you drive? You're parked behind me."

"Elise, wait." George met her in the foyer, pushing the door she'd just opened shut and turning on the light overhead.

She reached for the knob, but George blocked her path. "Damn it, George, he could go into shock."

He swiped a finger across the stain on his shirt, then touched it to his tongue and spat it out. "Let me see the dog."

"Fine. I'll drive." She gently lay Spike in George's arms and pulled out her keys. But he still wouldn't budge.

"He's not hurt. It's red paint. Like your front door.

Honey, it's paint. He's fine." Spike braced his front paw on George's chest, leaving two more prints. George pulled each leg up and squeezed his paws. There was no squeal of pain, no sign of lethargy, no visible wounds. "See? Just four dirty paws in need of a bath."

"I don't understand." She dropped her purse on the floor and swept her hands over the dog, petting, double-checking. Elise's world rocked on its axis. She'd been so certain Spike was hurt, so devastated that the man from the Plaza had abused her pet, maybe even tried to kill her most loyal friend. But now it was some kind of sick joke? "How did he get into the paint? I keep it in the garage when I'm not using it. And I haven't had the red out for months." She pulled a torn shred of paper from the clasp on Spike's collar. "What's this?"

George folded his hand around hers, heedless of the paint they were transferring. "I need you to sit down."

"Why?" She looked up into George's eyes. Lightning flashed through the windows behind him, and he didn't so much as blink. He knew something. "What is it? Did he do this to Spike? Was he here?"

He nodded toward the stairs. "Sit."

"No. Tell me." She saw the dusty piece of paper stuffed into the front pocket of his jeans. Elise pulled it out before he guessed her intent.

"Elise."

"This was attached to Spike's collar." The torn scrap in her hand fit the missing corner of the paper the dog had been burying in the yard. She read the note. Elise's world swayed and George's strong hand guided her to the stairs where he sank down beside her on the second step. The last bit of fight left in her surrendered.

Next time, the blood will be real. You should have listened to me. I don't want to hurt you or the things you love, but I need you to understand how much you hurt me. I saw you kiss him. I can forgive you a second time. But never again. You and I have something special. Once we are together, I'll make you understand.
I Love You, Elise.

A boom of lightning shook the walls, but she barely heard it. "Here." She pushed the note into George's hand. "This is evidence. You'll need to give it to your nephew. I assume you'll be calling him."

"Elise?"

She had nothing left. No energy. No hope. No fear. No memory of love or happiness or relief or regret. There was work to do and responsibilities to manage. But she felt…nothing.

She scooped Spike from George's arms and hugged him against her chest. "Give him to me. I'll go start a bath."

GEORGE STOOD IN the darkness on the second-floor landing, looking through the doorway into Elise's bedroom to watch her sleep. Or try to, at least.

She'd left the lamp on beside her bed and was dozing in fitful starts on top of the quilt, touching the dog, who rested against the curve of her stomach, each time she awoke. Even the storm that cocooned the house in a steady drumbeat of rain and cooled the humid temperatures to a tolerable level couldn't coax her into a restful slumber.

He wasn't in much better shape. It was tearing him

up inside to see her like this—a pale, numbed automaton who couldn't even dredge up a smile for the spoiled mutt she loved so much.

George had changed into the button-down shirt he'd worn earlier in the day and tossed his paint-stained T-shirt into a plastic bag in case there was any useful evidence on it the department could use. He scraped his palm over the stubble of his late-night beard, masking a weary sigh before turning to his nephew. "Has the storm washed away any chance of finding this bastard?"

"There's no trail to follow. No cars in the neighborhood that don't belong here." Although he'd hung his KCPD rain slicker on the hook inside Elise's back door to dry, Nick's wet hair was slicked to his scalp and dripping tiny dark circles on the shoulders of his black T-shirt. "I bagged the paint can I found under the bushes. It's the same brand as the others in the garage."

George suspected as much. "He probably took that, too, when he broke in before."

"I'll have Annie check the can and the letter at the lab." Like George's, Nick's voice was barely more than a whisper. "There were depressions in the grass that looked like shoe prints—bigger than mine. Looks like he came into the yard through the side gate." Nick tucked his phone back into the pocket of his jeans. "I took a picture of the shoe prints, but anything else out there is a puddle of mud now. He probably lured the dog out to him with the treats we found underneath those white-flowered bushes, then attached the note to his collar and dumped the paint on him to freak her out."

"It worked. She's exhausted, but she wouldn't take a sedative." Elise was lying in there in the same baggy paint shirt and cutoff shorts she'd had on earlier. Spike had been thoroughly bathed and was drying off on her clothes and quilt top. "She just wants to hold the dog."

Nick squeezed a hand over George's shoulder. "Well, then you try to get some rest. I'm parked out front. I'll keep an eye on things for a while. I called Spencer, too." Nick's partner had just been promoted to lieutenant and would probably be moving into more administrative duties like George soon. But until then, he couldn't think of two better detectives to back him up on any case. "Spence is going to track down where Alexsandr Titov and Westbrook have been this evening. He's coming over after that, too, to help keep an eye on things. We'll make sure nothing else happens tonight."

"Thanks, Nick." George tore his watchful gaze away from Elise long enough to give his nephew a hug. "Tell Spencer thanks, too."

After patting each other's backs, Nick pulled away. "Spence asked me why you didn't call him in sooner. He thinks of you like family and would have volunteered his time on this investigation in a heartbeat."

George shoved his hands into the pockets of his jeans and nodded. "I know. At first I was trying to respect Elise's request to stay out of it. When I realized I had to get involved, that I was losing her to these mind games, I knew we were short staffed and I couldn't assign anyone to an unofficial case—not with tempers so high around the department and money so tight." His shoulders lifted with a weary sigh. "And maybe part of me wanted to see if I could still be the cop I needed to be without calling in any favors at all."

"I don't see you missing a beat, old man. The evidence we've got against this guy is starting to stack up. Terroristic threats, attempted kidnapping, burglary. All we need is the perp to match that DNA to, and you can put this guy away for a long time."

George grunted a wry laugh. "All we need..."

Another beat of silence passed. "You want to tell me again how this isn't personal for you?"

George glanced down at the young detective beside him. Maybe not so young anymore, because Nick's instincts were right on target. "It's personal."

After a decisive nod, Nick headed down the stairs like a man on a mission, disappearing into the darkness of the house's first floor. A few seconds later, George heard the downpour of rain and rumbles of thunder when the front door opened and locked again, leaving him and Elise alone in the house.

George stood there in the shadows several seconds longer, absorbing the quiet of the rain and the night, letting Mother Nature's healing power seep into his blood and smooth the rough edges of his protective anger before he moved to stand in Elise's doorway. From the bandages on her bare toes to the waves of dark hair that had kinked up with the rain and fanned over the pillow behind her head, Elise Brown was a thing of beauty. He'd probably been half in love with her for a long time. But the rules and regulations had never let him think of her as anything more than the woman his office couldn't live without.

Now he was trying to resolve himself to the fact that he, the man, couldn't live without her, either.

"I could hear you out there, talking." Elise's voice was soft, but not drowsy. Still, she never lifted her head from the pillow. "Is Nick going to stay?"

George stepped into the room, winking to the dog when he raised his head. Spike settled right back down against Elise, as if the dog was smart enough to know what the reassurance meant, or he was simply that comfortable with having George around. "He's parked out front. He and his partner will watch the house tonight."

"Good. I hope you can get some sleep, then."

She still had her back to him, but George wasn't making any secret of his intent. He untied his shoes and toed them off. "Neither one of us can afford another night without much sleep."

"I know."

He unhooked his belt and removed his gun and badge, setting them all on the table beside her bed before turning off the lamp.

"I'm not sleeping next door, Elise." He sat on the edge of the bed, resting his palm on the curve of her hip. The fact that she didn't startle at his touch spoke to her fatigue. Or maybe to something else.

"I don't want you that far away. I need you to stay."

"I need to stay," he echoed in unison.

At last, she rolled onto her back and looked at him. In the flashes of light from the storm outside, he could see the crystallized remnants of tears that had dried on her skin. "Don't be my boss tonight, okay? Just be George Madigan."

With a nod, he lay down beside her on top of the quilt. She turned onto her side and he circled his arm around her waist, pulling her close, spooning her back against his chest. Her bottom nestled against his groin and their legs tangled together. George found a comfortable spot for his head on her pillow, and wrapped both Elise and her dog in his arms.

A shared sigh of rightness, of finally being where they needed to be, merged them tightly together, with only the clothes they wore keeping them apart. “I want to fight this guy, George,” Elise whispered. “But I don’t know if I’m strong enough.”

“Tomorrow you will be. We’ll both be strong enough.”

George kissed her neck, then buried his nose in the silk of her hair and let sleep claim them both.

Chapter Nine

Elise pushed her hair off her face and opened her eyes to the sunshine glowing behind the curtains on her windows. The deep, dreamless sleep was hard to shake off, and it took her a few moments to orient herself.

Her bedroom.

The sun was up.

Rain stopped.

Heat wave had returned.

Her arms were empty.

Instantly waking to full alertness, she patted the bed beside her. "Spike?"

"Shh. He's okay."

When she tried to roll over, the vise around her waist anchored her in place. But the deep whisper against her ear was clear—as was the explanation for her body being so toasty warm.

"Don't worry." George's lips stirred the hair at her nape. His husky morning voice hummed into her ear. "Nick is walking him outside. I had him give Spike some fresh water and food, too."

Spike was okay. She could drift back to sleep.

Or not.

Was there a cell in her body that wasn't suddenly aware of the man holding her?

George was spooned against her back. She could feel his chest pushing into her with every breath. She felt soft denim against the bare skin of her leg, his muscular thigh draped over both of hers, their toes touching.

His hand was tucked possessively beneath her shirt, his fingertips teasing the elastic that curved beneath her breast, her palm layered over his on the outside of the old cotton shirt that still smelled faintly of wet dog. Even now, she matched her fingers to his, as if she'd welcomed the intimacy of his warm hand on her skin and was holding on to keep him from moving away.

Had they slept together like this all night?

Elise pulled her hand away. "I'm sorry. I didn't realize I was that much of a cuddler."

"I'm not complaining." When she shifted to put some proper distance between them, his fingers splayed across her belly and his grip tightened. "But don't move for a couple of seconds, okay?"

"Need a minute to wake up?" She studied the sunshine creeping in behind the curtains to warm her delicately striped wallpaper. "It's going to be hot again today. After only one night of rain. It'll probably make the humidity even worse. I wonder if we'll get those storms the weatherman predicted today." When she realized she was rambling like a nervous schoolgirl, she reminded herself she was a full-grown woman and should start acting like it. With her brain more awake than it had been a minute ago, she started considering the possible reasons for George's request. Her first instinct had her tugging at his wrist and trying to sit up.

"I'm sorry. Did your arm go to sleep? I've been lying on it all night, haven't—?"

"Elise—"

"Is something wrong…?" But her squirming only drove her bottom into the juncture between his thighs and she felt the unmistakable bulge of his arousal butting against her. Elise went still. "Oh."

But suddenly, every nerve in her body tingled in anticipation, chasing away the last dregs of her heavy sleep.

George moved his hand to the jut of her hip to gently force a little distance between them. "I don't know if I was trying to save you from embarrassment. Or me. Nothing has to happen. I just need a minute to…get comfortable again."

"You don't want something to happen?"

His chest-deep groan stirred the hair at her nape. He pressed a soft nip to the juncture of her neck and shoulder, and every eager nerve seemed to rush to the spot. "This is what we need to discuss," he whispered against her skin, his very breath another caress that raised goose bumps across her skin. "Oh, I don't just mean the obvious reaction I'm having to you. But how good we are when we're together. At the office. As friends. When we're close like this. Somewhere along the line, you turned being indispensable into being…irresistible."

Elise reached down to lace her fingers together with the hand on her hip. "I thought you were the irresistible one."

"Now you're just stroking an old man's ego."

A touch of ire blended with the desire waking inside her. Keeping their fingers entwined, she lifted his hand from her shorts and carefully adjusted herself to roll over onto her back and look up into gray eyes that had darkened into granite this morning. "I wouldn't do that. One, I don't see an old anything—I just see a man. And two, you said you'd always be honest with me. It goes both ways, George. Why wouldn't you expect me to be honest with you? I always thought you were..." She cupped the side of his jaw, rubbing her palm against his morning beard stubble that was a handsome mosaic of tawny, dark brown and silver. What was the right word? *Distinguished? Powerful?* "...sexy."

He propped himself up on his elbow beside her, arching an eyebrow in doubt. "Explain."

She lifted her fingers to trace the eyebrow's curve. She traced the straight line of his nose and the square shape of his jaw before sliding across the impeccable sculpt of his lips. His hand slipped beneath her shirt again, settling at the nip of her waist while she explored each compelling angle.

"You're confident. Accomplished. So comfortable in your own skin. Do you have any idea how empowering, how hot it is to have a man like you interested in someone like me?"

"Someone like you?" His voice had dropped a note in pitch, grown husky.

Her gaze lowered to the placket of his shirt where she unhooked one button, then two, blazing a trail along skin that was rough, smooth, ticklish and always warm beneath her fingertips. "Anyone else would think I've gone nuts these past few days, but you keep saying you believe me."

"I do. I've seen the evidence of his cruelty."

"I'm complicated, George." She loosed another button and slipped her hand beneath the cotton to palm the firm plane of his chest and feel the muscles quiver beneath her touch. "I'm so worried about making mistakes and hurting someone I care about again that I stop relationships before they have a chance to begin." She inhaled his uniquely clean, masculine scent and got a whiff of something else that made her blush. "And I smell like dog shampoo this morning."

He laughed, catching her hand before she could pull it away, holding it against the taut male nipple and the beating heart underneath. "Maybe I think Eau de Spike is hot."

It was Elise's turn to laugh. She was shaking with the freedom of his honest humor, loving how the shared laughter eased the lines of stress on his face, when he dipped his head and stopped up her laughter with a kiss.

Instantly, the atmosphere in the room shifted. Humor gave way to hunger as Elise wound her arms around George's neck and he pulled her more firmly into the heat of his body. By heaven, did this man know how to kiss. Tenderly. Passionately. Seductively.

He wasn't bad with his hands, either. While his lips roamed over her jaw and earlobe and temple, he unbuttoned the front of her paint shirt and spread it open on top of the quilt. His mouth followed the path of his fingers, touching, tasting, stroking, praising as his sandpapery beard tickled and his warm tongue soothed.

"You have such soft hair." He nuzzled her ear, pushed aside the worn collar and teased the sensitive bundle of nerves at the base of her throat. "These long legs? Let's just say I'm glad you like to wear dresses." He squeezed her bottom and drew his hand along her thigh as he kissed his way down to the curve of her breast.

"You have miles of cool, creamy skin that I can't seem to stop touching."

"I won't stop you." Elise pushed his shirt off his shoulders, ran her fingers through his silky, sleep-rumpled hair, touched whatever she could reach. He was all hot, all muscle, all man.

He squeezed her breast and captured the beaded tip in his mouth, wetting the lace of her bra and making her ache to feel his tongue on her skin. "Don't tempt me."

Elise curled a leg around the back of his, pulling his weight partially on top of her. "Would this help?"

George lifted his head, squeezed his eyes shut and groaned before levering himself above her and rubbing his hard thigh against the seam of her shorts. She dug her fingers into his shoulders and held on as shock waves of desire rushed straight to her core at the feel of him there.

His eyes were dark with passion when they opened again. Every muscle in his body was rigid with the effort to retreat. "Ah, hell, Elise, I want to be inside you so badly I can't think straight."

She gradually found her voice again. "Then don't think. I want the same thing. It feels right."

He dropped a kiss on her tender lips. "Yeah, but, honey, I haven't done this for a while. I'm a little out of practice."

"Your parts all work, don't they?"

"Obviously." The pressure nudging between her thighs left no doubt of that. "But my style—"

"I don't need style, George. I need you." She worked the last buttons of his shirt free and found the snap of his jeans. His skin quivered beneath her hands as she gently unzipped him. "I need the man who always tells me the truth. The man I never have to doubt. Please. Just…"

"Just what?"

She paused with her hands at his hips, pushing his jeans and shorts out of her way. "Take me away from this nightmare for a while. Make me feel normal and healthy and brave."

"Brave?" He stroked her hair off her forehead.

"Brave enough to feel something and want someone—and not be afraid that there's a penalty attached to caring." She thought she'd feel a hesitation, an inner voice warning her to stop. But everything about this moment felt right. Everything about George felt right. "I need to know what it's like for a real, flesh and blood man to want me. Just for me. That is what you want, right?"

With a nod, he lowered his mouth to reclaim hers. "No hidden agenda. No conditions. Just you. I want you."

And then there was an eager bumping of hands and limbs as she helped George shuck his jeans and briefs, and he pulled her shorts and panties off to join them on the floor. He unhooked the front clasp of her bra and pushed it aside before squeezing and tonguing the sensitive tips into throbbing, tight beads. Elise mimicked the same exploration on him, loving the musky smell of his skin as she found each taut male nipple with her lips.

They were still half dressed on top when George pushed his hand down between her thighs and palmed the pressure building there. She bucked beneath the force of his hand, and bucked again when he slid two fingers inside to test her slick readiness for him.

"George," she gasped as she raised her knees and he settled himself between them. "Now."

He cursed against her breast, then kissed the spot. Apologized. "I don't have any protection."

She wrapped her legs around him, holding his hips in the cradle of hers when he would have pulled away. "I'm on the pill. Do you have any health issues?"

"No. You?"

"No." She caught his face between her hands and lifted her mouth to reclaim his. But he quickly took over the kiss, driving her back into the pillow, driving her weight into the bed, driving himself deeply inside her.

He held himself like that for several seconds while her body adjusted to welcome his, while her breasts pillowed beneath the weight of his chest, while her arms wound around him to hold him close.

"Are you good?" he whispered against her ear. She couldn't answer. She didn't want to talk. She just wanted to feel again. "Elise?"

She nodded, tightened her legs around his buttocks to open herself more fully and urged him even deeper. Who needed sexy words or seductive style when a man's desire for her was this straightforward, when he knew where to touch a woman. Where to kiss. What to… His fingers found that sensitive nub between them as he thrust inside her and she arched against him, gasping at the power of her release.

Elise soared to a place where the world made sense, where she was everything a woman should be, where the nightmare could no longer reach her, where she was safe, in George's arms.

When he drove into her one last time with a husky groan and found his own release, she knew, without a doubt, that she loved this man—that anything she'd once felt for Quinn Gallagher or Nikolai Titov or even

James Westbrook was a pale comparison to the humbling emotions George Madigan had awakened inside her. This was the right man, the only man, for her.

They collapsed into each other's arms and dozed together, skin to skin, sated and whole, her energy spent, her spirit stronger than it had been for months. And yet, her future was still uncertain.

If only George wasn't the one man she couldn't have. Was she willing to lose the job that had given back her confidence and self-respect? Would George be willing to give her up at KCPD and let his office return to the slow-moving machine it had once been?

Did he even want the same things she wanted? Or was this blissful morning together a job perk for a man who would do his duty by her, but who wouldn't appreciate the complications of an ongoing commitment outside of the office? Apparently, there was still a lot more of *this* they needed to discuss.

But later. If she had a later.

She snuggled closer to the heat and strength of George's body, fearing this perfect morning might be the only one for them.

The alarm woke them a half hour later and the rest of the world demanded their attention again.

ELISE HAD TURNED on two lamps in her office, in addition to the overhead lights, to compensate for the turbulent gray clouds rolling in and blotting out the sun outside. With every bolt of lightning, the lights flickered. With every answering boom of thunder, she jumped inside her skin.

But as long as the power was on and her computer was working, she could finish typing the final draft of

George's banquet speech while he was on the phone with Commissioner Cartwright-Masterson. The commissioner's daughter-in-law, Rebecca, had gone into labor during the night. With her son, Seth Cartwright, in the delivery room, and the rest of their extended family in the hospital waiting room, Rebecca had given birth to a daughter named Sydney.

Elise was glad for the numerous phone calls coming into the office, with meetings to reschedule, reporters to appease until an official statement could be issued, and friends and coworkers to update on the latest news from the top floors of KCPD headquarters. If she had any fewer calls to manage, any fewer reports to file, any fewer memos to send, she might have time to drive herself mad.

The worries that did creep in when her mind wandered could easily derail the normal routine she was clinging to this morning. She had an armed detective named Spencer Montgomery dog sitting Spike and watching her house for her. She'd fielded a call from Annie Fensom at the crime lab which hadn't offered much hope. They could approximate a shoe size on her stalker from the picture Nick had taken in her backyard. But unless they could compel every man in Kansas City with size twelve feet to give a DNA sample, there was still no way to identify the man who'd sent her those sick I-love-you messages.

The weather outside seemed to echo Elise's mood today. For a few wonderful minutes, she'd been happy and content in George's arms and the sun had been shining. But as the storm gathered force and the skies darkened at noon, her thoughts kept going back to all the reasons why she and George Madigan might never have more than this morning. First, there was the difference in their ages. She didn't think fourteen years was an issue, but it seemed to bother him. Then there was his position of authority over her. Her need to do the work she was so good at in order to prove her self-worth and redeem her past mistakes. Her scary track record with choosing the wrong men.

And if any of those obstacles weren't enough, she came with the extra baggage of a mysterious psychopath who said he loved her, but promised violence if she did anything he deemed a mistake.

Like making love with George and silently giving him her heart?

Those were probably two pretty unforgivable mistakes in the eyes of the man who would harm an innocent dog and terrorize a frightened woman.

The thunder shook and a new, terrifying thought turned Elise's gaze toward George's office door.

I don't want to hurt you or the things you love.

Would he hurt George? With every contact, the creep found new and more devious ways to terrorize her. He'd nearly broken her completely by making her think he'd attacked Spike. If he went after George or her parents or anyone else she cared about, she might never recover from the emotional destruction. How could she fight an enemy who preyed on her mind and emotions and refused to reveal his identity?

Lightning flashed in the bank of clouds overhead and thunder rattled the windows and furniture almost immediately. The tiny hairs on the back of her neck stood straight on end. Whatever new threat was coming was nearly on top of them.

The telephone rang and Elise let out a tiny yelp. Cursing her own skittishness, she inhaled a steadying breath and picked up the receiver. "Good morning, Deputy Commissioner Madigan's office. This is Elise."

"Good morning, Elise. Garrett Cho here."

"Deputy Commissioner Cho. How are you?" She eyed the greenish tinge of the squall line moving beneath the charcoal-gray cumulus clouds. "Hope you're battened down someplace safe. Looks like we're going to have a gully washer."

"At least. I don't think an umbrella will do us any good today." The deputy commissioner in charge of facilities management was always a friendly conversation. She smiled through the next thunderclap despite the tingling at her nape. Something about working in a high-rise building, that much closer to the root of a storm, always made it seem more intense. "I understand we're in for a temporary shuffle in command over the next few days. Commissioner Cartwright-Masterson's a grandmother?"

"Yes, sir. Deputy Commissioner Madigan is on the phone with her right now, going over the final details. She's taking a full week off to help her son and daughter-in-law adjust to being new parents."

Cho laughed. "We can run the department while she's gone. I'm not worried about that. And you can assure George that all of our precinct storm shelters are fully supplied and ready for whatever hits us today. But I'm more interested in the baby details. We had a pool going, you know."

Elise grinned as the second light on her phone went off. George's conversation with Commissioner Cartwright-Masterson had ended. She could transfer this call to him, but she knew he had plenty on his agenda already and decided to handle this social call herself. "Sydney Cartwright weighed in at seven pounds, fourteen ounces, and she arrived at 7:15 a.m. How'd you do?"

"Well, since I'd put my money on a baby boy—not very well. But as long as the mother and baby are fine, I shouldn't complain about losing five bucks." She could hear the teasing in Cho's voice. "Unless George won the pot. Then I'm complaining."

"I couldn't tell you that, sir. But I'll let him know you're thinking of him." A rock slammed into her high-rise window and she nearly jumped out of her chair. "What the…?"

Not a rock at all. A chunk of frozen rain. Dozens of hard, icy pellets hitting the windows. Hail.

"Elise?" Cho's tone was suddenly one of concern. "Are you all right?"

She steadied her breathing. "It's hailing here. The noise of it startled me, that's all."

"I'm north of town so the storm hasn't hit here yet." His voice grew as businesslike and commanding as she'd ever heard George's. "I'd better hang up and call my crew chiefs, make sure the facilities are all secure. People go nuts when the weather's bad. Thanks for the update."

Nuts. Yeah. Maybe the intense, unusual weather pattern was the reason her world had turned upside down this week.

"You bet. Goodbye, sir." George's door was open by the time she hung up.

"Anything important?" he asked, striding to her window to watch the hailstones collecting on the ledge outside. "Some of those are golf-ball-size. It must be pretty windy out there to keep sending the rain back up to the clouds."

Elise rose to stand beside him, although she seemed to jump every time one of those tiny missiles hit the window. "That was Garrett Cho—asking about Commissioner Cartwright-Masterson's granddaughter and assuring you his team is ready to deal with the storm and its aftermath."

"Good." The window fogged when he released a deep breath. With the subtlest of movements he reached across the few inches separating them and brushed the back of one finger along her arm up to her shoulder. "Goose bumps. From the storm or something else?"

He might hurt the things you care about.

As much as she wanted to turn into that caress, she knew it was wiser to cross her arms and pull away. "We really shouldn't. Not here."

The gruffness returned to his tone. "You didn't answer my question."

And she wouldn't get a chance to. Her phone rang and Elise returned to her desk. Recognizing the line that lit up, she answered. "Hey, Shane. What's going on?"

"Hey, Elise—I mean, Miss Brown—um, there's a James Westbrook heading to your office. He doesn't have an appointment, but he told me he's here to see you, not the deputy commissioner. He said he's a friend, so is that okay?"

"He's coming here? Now?"

Not the reaction Shane had expected. She heard his chair bang against the wall or desk as he stood too quickly. "Do you need me to come get him?"

And do what, arrest him? She didn't even know what James wanted yet. Just because she didn't want to deal with another confrontation didn't justify sending an armed police officer after him. "No. I just have other things I need to do this morning. Thanks, Shane, I'll handle it."

There was a sharp rap at the door before she hung up the phone. When she saw James's dripping clothes and fogged-up glasses, her *What do you want?* became "You're soaking wet." Elise grabbed the box of tissues on her desk and hurried across the room, pulling out several to hand to him when he tried to wipe off his glasses on his sopping oxford shirt. "Here."

"I could have swum across the street from the parking garage." He wiped his face with more tissues before putting his glasses back on and pointing to the window. "Man, it's a bear driving out there. I could barely see beyond my headlights."

Elise glanced over her shoulder, meeting George's inquisitive glare before looking past him. The hail had stopped as quickly as it had started, leaving what looked like snowfall outside on the ledge. But the wind gusted a wave of rain against the glass, washing away her view.

Ignoring both Mother Nature and the sturdy forearms crossed over George's chest, Elise urged James to the sofa before crossing to a storage closet. "I've got a stash of hand towels here. Have a seat. The leather's been waterproofed."

She wasn't foolish enough to think James had come here to discuss the weather. But she wasn't prepared for his anger to follow her across the room. "I want to know why the police stopped by my apartment and called my father to find out if we had proof that we were at the ball game yesterday afternoon. Proof! Can you imagine the questions Dad was asking me? That pesky little detective said he was even going to find out who was selling frosty malts in our section at the stadium to see if the guy remembered seeing me there."

George moved several steps closer, inviting himself into the one-sided conversation. "What did you tell Detective Fensom?"

"Why did Detective Fensom ask?" For a moment, James lost interest in Elise and drying off. Instead, he went toe-to-toe with George, dripping on the rug in front of him. "This is about me interrupting your little date the other night, isn't it. You're abusing your power, Madigan. If you're trying to force me out of Elise's life, it won't work."

"What did you tell Detective Fensom?"

James snatched the towel Elise handed him and pulled off his glasses to wipe his face and hair. "I was at the game. The Royals won. My father will tell you the same thing, and so will the guy who sold me the frosty malts."

George wasn't fazed by James's accusation or the puddle on his carpet. "And you didn't leave the stadium at all."

Shoving his fingers through his hair to comb the blond spikes back into order, James refused to answer. "I'm beginning to think that you've been lying to me, Lise.

"Lying? How?"

"You don't want to be friends. You put your boyfriend up to this harassment campaign."

"George isn't my boy—"

"I don't think you want to see me at all."

Not when he was like this. He'd never been this petulant and temperamental back in college. She never would have gone out with him if he had been. But three years of dating and almost marrying a man made him deserving of some type of explanation. "There was another incident yesterday, James. The deputy commissioner and Detective Fensom are investigating. Someone tried to…frighten me."

"Someone tried to kidnap her," George corrected, driving home the reason for his so-called harassment. A boom of thunder punctuated the danger she'd faced, and Elise shivered. He pointed to her sandals and the purple bruise and bandages on her right foot. "Someone assaulted her."

Pretty minor injury compared to the damage done to her peace of mind and any sense of security she'd once had.

"And you think it was me?" James turned his narrowed eyes on her. "That's rich." He paced to the door, then came back, pointing an accusing finger at them both. "This is just like that investigation in Europe. Having to prove my innocence when I wasn't guilty of a damn thing."

George kept pushing for answers. "The death of your girlfriend?"

"Oh, so you checked that out, too. That's why that cop out by the elevator frisked me before I could come see you." She wondered if it was grief that made him look so suddenly gray and gaunt. "Because you think I'm going to kill you, too?"

"James!" Elise's knees wobbled and she quickly sat in the closest chair. Whether fueled by anger or grief, his words cut her to the quick. She hadn't believed the man she'd once loved would want to hurt her. But she hadn't known just how much pain he'd been in, either.

George took a step toward James, forcing him to retreat without ever touching him. "Officer Wilkins was doing his job, Westbrook. We're on heightened security this week. Even if you had an appointment, he wouldn't let you just wander in here. And I'm guessing you don't have an appointment."

"I came to see Elise. Not you."

"Unless you start talking to her with some respect, you're going to be dealing with me."

James seemed to consider George's threat. Maybe he hadn't realized how vile his words had sounded. If he'd been lashing out in grief, she could forgive that. But George wasn't about to.

"You leave now and deal with my detectives," he warned, "or you answer our questions."

Making his decision, James sank onto the couch opposite Elise. "I'm sorry, Lise. You know I didn't mean that. I love you."

Not the most comforting words a volatile man could say to her right now. "You loved your girlfriend."

"My fiancée," he corrected, conveying the depth of his grief. James wadded the towel in his hands, then shook it out and folded it neatly before saying anything more. "Marta's death was an accident. Our car went off the road and hit a bridge abutment. I survived with barely a scratch because I had my seat belt on. But she didn't even make it to the ambulance."

How awful. If he'd loved Marta as much as he claimed, it was no wonder he'd taken a leave from his job and come home to Kansas City. Home was almost always the best place to heal a wound like that. "I'm so sorry."

George sat on the arm of her chair and rested his

hand on her shoulder, gently halting her from saying anything more. "Was there an inquiry?"

James nodded, his normally bright eyes looking dull and sad. "I couldn't even grieve, there were too many cops asking too many questions. Accusing me of things like staging the accident. I think if I'd died, too, they wouldn't have cared."

"Don't say that."

"You're probably thinking that I want to replace Marta with you. I don't. I know you and I were done a long time ago. But until I find someone else and can move on, I thought it'd be nice to have a friend."

She blinked back the tears that stung her eyes. Could grief and anger twist a man's psyche until he couldn't distinguish reality from the relationship he'd lost? Was James the threat George suspected him to be? A familiar face and playing on her sympathies would make a perfect disguise for a man who wanted to divert suspicion from himself.

"It's okay, Lise." James leaned forward, stretching out his hand to hers, perhaps misreading her silent tears. But she couldn't seem to make herself reach out to clasp the peace offering. "I want you to know I was cleared of any charges. You don't have to be afraid of me." Maybe he hadn't misread her at all. His gaze shifted up to George. "And your cop friend here doesn't need to sic his buddies on me, either."

The whole building vibrated with a low-pitched drum roll of thunder that lasted several seconds. And maybe it was just Elise's imagination, but the building seemed to be swaying with the wind. "Has anyone checked the weather report lately?"

James straightened. His blue eyes flickered over her,

perhaps gauging her concern, perhaps judging her for refusing to take his hand. "Something bad's coming. You feel it, too, don't you."

Elise shivered. The barometric pressure must have suddenly dropped. "I was hoping for something a little more scientific."

George patted her shoulder and nodded to her desk. "Why don't you get online—see if there are any new watches or warnings we need to be aware of. I'll show Mr. Westbrook out."

She nodded and got up, relieved to have something to do besides sit there and wonder what James's hand would feel like in a leather glove against her skin. Would there be a shock of recognition to the man on the Plaza?

"Goodbye, Lise," James called after her.

She didn't even care that he still had the damp towel draped around his neck. Until she was certain of his innocence—of any man's innocence or guilt—she couldn't afford to be too trusting or forgiving, or care too much that an old friend was hurting. "Bye, James."

Pulling up the local weather, she cringed at the swath of dark red and orange that covered a good portion of the state line—including almost all of Kansas City.

When George strolled back in, he was rolling up the sleeves of his blue shirt. "The guy tells a good story."

Elise glanced up. "Do you think James was making that up about his fiancée? He seemed so heartbroken."

"It'd be a good way to gain your sympathy and trust, which is exactly what the sleazeball who's trying to get his hands on you would do." He arched a dark eyebrow. "You weren't completely buying it, either. You wouldn't touch him."

George had noticed. That meant James had probably noticed the slight, too. "I kept thinking of the man who grabbed me on the Plaza. What if his grip felt the same?"

"All the more reason to shoo him out of here." He loosened his tie and unbuttoned his collar next, a sure sign the man was getting down to some serious work. "I told Shane to escort him all the way downstairs and keep an eye on him until he leaves the building. The kid's eager to do me a favor and get a good recommendation for making detective. Westbrook can wait in the lobby until the storm lets up."

"And if that story's legit and James's grief is real?"

"Then it upset you. And I don't like that, either."

As much as she loved having George stand up to protect her, she could already see how letting their personal feelings into their working relationship was compromising their professionalism. "You're the face of KCPD now, while the commissioner is gone. You can't put me above—"

The lights in the room blinked off and on, a sure sign the weather was getting worse. Her argument died on her lips and she stood. The windows rattled beneath another assault of wind.

"That's not good." George moved to the window, peering out into the wall of rain and darkness there. "What have we got?"

Although Elise's computer had shut down and was busy powering up again, she'd memorized the dangers swirling around them. "Thunderstorm warnings. Strong winds. Heavy rain. Several tornado watches in the area."

He drummed his fingers against the windowsill.

"What are you thinking?" Elise asked.

"An ounce of prevention…" He brought his hand back to his gun and badge at his waist. Decision made, he faced her. "We need to move downstairs. Find out how many people are on the top floors and let's send out a text and call advisory."

The boss was back. This, she knew how to handle. "Right."

She sat down at her computer and pulled up the program to issue a building-wide text and phone alert. She was pulling up a separate screen to get a list of personnel checked in on the top three floors when she heard wet shoes squeaking on the hallway's marble floor.

Elise glanced up. "Shane's not at his post to screen visitors."

George warned her to stay put at her desk. With his hand on the butt of his gun, he moved toward the open door. "Keep working. I'll check it out. Ah, hell."

Courtney Reiter came through the doorway with her arms wide-open, and wrapped them around George. "Thank God I got here in one piece."

With Courtney's wet hair and dripping yellow trench coat soaking his clothes, George took her by the shoulders and gently pushed her away. "This is not a good time, Court."

The normally stunning blonde looked almost waifish as she clung to her ex-husband's wrists. From this distance, Elise couldn't tell if it was the rain or tears that left the other woman's mascara running in rivulets down each cheek. "I could have been trapped in that elevator when the power went out. Do you have any idea how frightening that is? You know how scared I am of storms."

"What are you doing here?" With a glance over Courtney's head and a nod toward the closet, he instructed Elise to find them more towels.

"Where were you last night, George?" the blonde accused. "And don't say working because I called here as well as your cell number and you never answered. I left messages and you never called me back. Did you see all that rain we had?"

"I was aware of the storm." He draped an arm around her shoulders and led her to the hallway. "We're in the middle of dealing with round two right now, so I'm going to ask you to leave. You can wait downstairs where it's safe until the storm passes."

The woman might appear helpless, but she was definitely persistent. With a quick turn, she spun free of George's grasp and walked over to the sitting area. "The ground was so dry that the rain leaked right into the basement of our house."

"Your house, Court—"

"It's probably ankle deep by now." She sat, nodding her thanks when Elise handed her a towel. And she kept right on talking as Elise gave George a towel to dab at his sleeves and shirtfront. "I had a creek running from one of those egress windows right through to the laundry room drain. I had to move all my storage boxes up onto shelves and two-by-fours. I needed your help and you weren't..." Elise's hands must have lingered too long on the towel George pressed against his shoulder. She turned to see Courtney staring right at her. "You were with her, weren't you?"

Elise felt the stillness come over George's body and recognized the quiet anger in him. Putting the towel in

Elise's hands, he nudged her toward her desk. "Get that alert sent out. Now."

"Oh, my God." Courtney smeared mascara across her cheek as she blotted her face with the towel. "I knew there was something going on between the two of you. Isn't an affair with your secretary against departmental regulations?"

George took Courtney by the arm and pulled her to her feet. "Let it go. You and I aren't married anymore."

Smarting at the barb aimed squarely at her, Elise clicked Send, relaying the deputy commissioner's order to close down shop and head for lower floors in the HQ building. "Message sent, sir."

An accusation like George's ex had made was exactly the sort of thing that could cost Elise her job, and make it difficult to get hired on someplace else. And, being labeled the woman who ignored the rules and slept with her boss wouldn't do a whole lot for the personal reputation she'd worked so hard to rebuild.

"Good. Now make sure we've got our key files backed up and shut things down so we can head down, too."

This time, Courtney couldn't extricate herself from George's firmer grasp. "In my head, I always knew you'd move on one day. But then, for so long, you never did. I guess I took it for granted that you and I… I made such a mistake when I left you, didn't I."

After tipping his head back in a frustrated sigh, George turned the curvy blonde to face him. "We're ancient history, Court. I will always care about you, but I am never going to be in love with you again."

"Are you in love with her?"

Elise froze at her desk, hugging a stack of files to her

chest and waiting far too expectantly for George's answer. Did he love her? Even this morning, when they'd been so close and had shared so much, he'd never said the words.

Her heart plummeted to her stomach. He didn't say them now.

"I can't be at your beck and call whenever you need something, Court. I'm tired of feeling guilty about not being there for you when I was starting my career and working the streets. There's only so much penance a man can pay." He turned her toward the door. "Now go. Be a grown-up. You need to learn to face your problems. I've got my own to deal with."

When George walked back to his office, Courtney followed. "This isn't fair, you know. You're an executive now. You work at a desk. You go home every night." She pointed to Elise who quickly went back to gathering files and shutting down the computer. "She doesn't have to worry about whether or not you're coming home at all, the way I did. It isn't fair."

"I'm the same man, Courtney." George stopped in the doorway to his office and turned, plucking his badge from his belt and holding it up. "I'm still a cop. We'll never fit." His gaze drifted across the room to find Elise. He repeated the same phrase, his quieter tone turning it into some kind of vow, some kind of promise, to her. "I'm a cop."

Elise narrowed her gaze, questioning the message he was sending.

But before he explained, before she understood, he snapped his badge back into place and offered Courtney a rueful smile. "You didn't want a cop then. And you don't want one now. You wanted an executive. I've got the trappings now, but it's not me. Underneath the suit and tie, I'm still just a cop."

"No, you're—" Whatever Courtney was about to say ended with a startled shriek.

The tornado sirens went off.

Chapter Ten

A clap of thunder exploded overhead, shaking the building so badly, it felt as if a bomb had gone off. It knocked over Spike's picture on her desk and Elise gripped the back of her chair. Courtney screamed and covered her ears, collapsing into the door frame beside George. "It's so loud. I can't stand it when it's so loud."

"We need to get to the storm shelter!" George shouted above the wail of the sirens. "Emergency procedure alpha, now!"

Elise nodded. She pulled her purse from the bottom drawer of her desk and dropped Spike's picture inside. Then she opened the center drawer to retrieve her emergency two-way radio and a bracelet full of keys she slipped onto her wrist.

George took Courtney by the shoulders and pulled her to her feet. "Take the stairs all the way to the basement, Court. The men's and women's locker rooms, firing range and workout facilities are down there. Someone will show you where to go. You'll be safe."

Courtney latched on as soon as George let go. "You're not coming?"

He looked over Courtney's shoulder to Elise. "You've got your building access keys?"

Raising her arm, Elise jangled her wrist. She looped her bag over her shoulder and picked up the phone to dial the prearranged number to Cliff Brandt at the utilities office. "Everything on our hard drives is backed up to remote servers. Do you want me to put the flash drives in my purse and take them with me?"

"Negative." George left his ex-wife leaning against the wall and ran into his office to retrieve his own radio and a flashlight. When he came back he was tucking his cell phone into his pocket. "One of those lightning strikes must have taken out the cell tower on the roof. I've got no reception."

Courtney whimpered as a flash of lightning lit up the sky and the thunder retaliated with another boom. Elise put the phone on speaker mode as the utilities director answered.

"Cliff?" George leaned over her desk to speak. "I need to know if we've got any blackout areas." They both turned to the pounding of footsteps in the marble hallway. Other staff heading for shelter? George thumbed over his shoulder, urging her to join them, and returned to his call. "If there are sections of the city without televisions or working sirens, I want to dispatch units to get people to shelter immediately."

"Sir?" Shane Wilkins appeared in the doorway from the hall, his chest heaving with deep breaths. When he spotted George and Elise, he jogged into the room. "We've got to get out of here. Doppler radar spotted a rotating storm cell south of here. Heading northeast. Right for the city. Spotters on the ground already reported a funnel cloud touching down on the Kansas side of the river."

George straightened. "What the hell are you doing

up here? Did Westbrook go out in this? I want to keep eyes on that guy."

Shane turned to Elise, as if his superior officer hadn't understood the urgency of his announcement. "Look, I ran up here to let you guys know. The elevators are shut down already. We're right in the storm's path. The tornado is coming here. Downtown K.C."

"You ran up eight flights of stairs?" Elise asked, astounded by the effort he'd made to warn them.

The uniformed officer nodded. His nostrils flared as he regained control of his breathing after his wind sprint. "Cell reception is spotty. Except for Dispatch, landlines are for outgoing or station-to-station calls only during an emergency, not personal calls within the building. You guys are my responsibility. I volunteered."

Elise smiled her thanks for his dedication to his duty and squeezed his arm. "You're one in a million, Shane."

George jotted down the information he needed and ended his call. He tore off the note and handed it to Elise. "Go. Get on your radio to Dispatch and tell them to send a unit to these areas. Tell them no heroics, on my command. The officers make the announcement, then get to shelter themselves. That goes for you, too." He grabbed Elise's hand, giving it a subtle squeeze as he pulled her toward the door and released her. She stopped. He wasn't coming with her? No, he was looking up at the blond-haired officer. "Wilkins?"

"Sir." Shane snapped to attention.

George poked the center of his flak vest. "No. Heroics. I'm not planning on losing any of my men today." He held up his own radio. "You should have used one of these instead of running up here."

"Oh. Right." The younger man's shoulders sagged.

"I knew that. I guess I just wanted to see for myself that you all were okay."

"You're too young to know you're not invincible yet." Shaking his head, George tucked his radio onto his belt and pocketed his flashlight. "But I do need you to do something for me."

"Sir?" Shane's dull green eyes brightened with the chance to redeem himself in his commanding officer's eyes.

"I want you to do a room-to-room search up here to make sure the entire floor is evacuated. Radio the guards on each level to do the same and get everyone to the basement ASAP. Including yourselves. And remember, this is no drill. Be thorough, but be fast."

"I'm on it." Striding past Elise, Shane turned his mouth to the radio on his shoulder, relaying George's order.

George nearly ran into Elise when he turned back to his office. His look included both her and Courtney. "What are you two still doing here? I gave you an order."

Her worries about departmental regulations and forbidden relationships didn't seem important right now. She splayed her hand on the left side of his chest, seeking out the familiar, strong beat of his heart. "Why aren't you leaving? He said the storm was heading right for us."

George covered her hand with his, sealing this powerful connection between them. "I'm a cop, remember? And with the commissioner off the clock, I'm the one in charge. I'm going to back up Shane. Make sure all the floors are clear. Time is of the essence." Without a moment's hesitation, he leaned in and captured her mouth in a kiss. It was sweet and urgent and perfect. He raised his lips to her forehead and kissed her again before releasing her. "Don't worry. I'll meet you in the basement."

"You'd better." She curled her fingers around his tie, holding on a moment longer. "Or else, I'll come looking for you."

"Always keeping me on task, aren't you." He smiled and gave her one more hard, quick kiss, before hurrying past her out the door. "Wilkins!" he called out. "Give me your twenty." He disappeared to the left and was gone.

"You really do love him, don't you?"

Elise turned to the blonde woman. Courtney was a pale shadow of her usual beauty, with her dark gaze leaping to the window at every gust of wind. But even though her observation was on target, Elise's feelings were too fragile, maybe even too futile to admit to anyone.

"George is counting on us to do our job, Ms. Reiter, so he can do his." Although she imagined that hers was not the help Courtney wanted, Elise crossed the room and linked their arms together, pulling the woman into step beside her. "Come on. We have to get out of here."

Coaxing the frightened woman along every step of the way, Elise hurried as fast as they could to the stairwell beside the elevator. She radioed the information George requested to Dispatch and tucked her radio into her purse. With every flight of stairs, they joined more officers, visitors, administrators and support staff on their way down to the basement. With every floor they descended, the concussive noise of the wind and rain and the scream of the warning siren faded.

Elise led Courtney down the last flight of stairs into

a crowded hallway where a uniformed officer directed them into the men's locker room. Another officer there told them to find a seat against the concrete block wall near the showers.

"All these people work here?" Courtney seemed to be realizing for the first time just how many dedicated men and women worked for the police department.

"Most of them." Elise helped the other woman off with her yellow coat. While Courtney folded it up to make a cushion for herself on the concrete floor, Elise stretched up on tiptoe to scan all the faces for any sign that George had made it safely down to the shelter with them. There were a lot of people crowding into the rooms down here. "This is just the headquarters and Fourth Precinct building. Each of the precincts employs almost as many people."

"And George is in charge of all of them?"

"Until Commissioner Cartwright-Masterson comes back to work, yes." Was Courtney just now beginning to understand the responsibilities her ex-husband carried on his shoulders? Could she comprehend that he needed a partner who could be a help to him, and not a drain on his time and emotional energy? "Do you see him anywhere?"

Instead of finding that distinguished dark hair spattered with silver, she spotted a familiar head of blond hair slicked back with water—and the beige towel from her office draped around the man's neck. Elise climbed over a bench to reach him before he turned the corner. "James?"

"Lise." He stepped out of the line he'd been following and excused his way back to her.

"I thought you'd left." She hated the feeling crawling up her skin when a group she recognized from the tech squad jostled past her. Despite their apologies and a forgiving smile from her, she was developing a serious phobia about crowds of people.

"Here." James helped her get back across the bench and out of the flow of human traffic. "The siren went off before I could get to my car. An officer in the lobby instructed me to come down here."

"You mean Officer Wilkins."

"I didn't catch her name." Her? Definitely not Shane. "You mean the tall guy who escorted me out? He ran off like he had a mission of some kind."

Elise felt a tug at the hem of her dress. "Who's your friend, Elise?"

"Oh, this is Courtney Reiter. This is—" she hoped this could still be the truth "—my friend. James Westbrook."

When they shook hands, Courtney held on to pull herself up. "Nice to meet you."

James nodded. "Pleasure."

"Are you a police officer?"

He shook his head. "Financial consultant."

"Really?" Did Elise imagine the healthy color that seeped into Courtney's face? "No gun? No badge?"

"No." He released Courtney's hand and turned to Elise. "Look, I'm sorry about what happened upstairs. I guess I'm a bigger mess than I realized. I lost Marta, I left my job. I know you're going through something now and you needed me to be there and I wasn't—"

"Let's not talk about that now." She glanced around the room at all the anxious faces. The building was rattling above their heads. The sirens were still sounding their warning. "We have bigger things to worry about right now."

"May I have your attention, please! Everyone!" A black man with streaks of gray in his hair and a badge hanging around his neck shouted above the noise in the room. Elise recognized Joe Hendricks, the fourth precinct watch commander—probably the highest ranking officer in the room. Instantly, the conversations fell silent and people stopped moving to listen. "We've been keeping up on the latest weather updates. At this time, I need everyone to have a seat against the wall. If your back's not against a concrete block. Find one."

The three of them sat on the floor while Captain Hendricks gave more orders regarding radio silence except for certain officers, and head counts for staff and guests. With Courtney wedged in the middle, Elise scooted closer, allowing as much room as possible to accommodate everyone taking shelter here.

Without a roomful of voices echoing off the concrete walls, Elise could hear the wind raging above them. She wondered what kind of devastation was raining down on the city. And she worried that George was still upstairs somewhere, facing the storm head-on. And then…silence.

Elise's breath caught in her chest. Everyone in the room seemed to be looking upward, holding their breaths.

Sitting shoulder to shoulder, she felt Courtney shivering beside her. "Why is it so quiet?"

Elise hugged her purse to her chest, warding off the dreadful anticipation that twisted her stomach into knots. "The rain stopped."

Courtney raised her voice above a whisper. “That’s good, right? Now they’ll turn off that horrid siren.”

Elise shushed her. “No. That silence is very bad.”

James nudged Courtney’s shoulder with his, trying to cajole her out of her fears. “The tornado is close enough to suck up all the rain. I remember a storm like this when I was a kid growing up east of here.”

“Really?” Courtney turned her attention to James. “You’ve survived one of these before?”

“Yeah.”

“Could I…?” She looped her arm through James’s and leaned against him. “Could I hold on to you? I’m afraid of storms.”

“Sure.” When James looked over Courtney’s head, Elise shrugged.

Why not? It wasn’t as if this wasn’t already the strangest week of her life. James needed a new project to focus on—and Courtney Reiter was definitely a project. It was almost a relief to see him put his arm around Courtney’s shoulder and hug her to his side.

“We’ll be fine down here,” he assured her. “All these reinforced walls? Below ground level? We’ll be safe.”

Not all of them were safe.

“Captain Hendricks said to do an office roll call, right?” She really didn’t need anyone to answer. “We’re all here. Where’s George?”

I’ll meet you in the basement.

You’d better. Or else, I’ll come looking for you.

Something wasn’t right. As surely as she had known an intruder had violated her bedroom, a man had followed her into a restroom during a blackout and that any of a dozen different weird events had been real threats and not tricks of her imagination, she knew that George was in trouble. It was her job to take care of him, just as he'd made it his job to protect her.

"Will you look after Courtney, James? Make sure she stays safe?" She slid the bracelet of keys up her arm, tucked the radio into her pocket and pushed herself up the wall to her feet.

He nodded. "Where are you going?"

She dropped her purse in her spot so she could move quickly through the room without hitting anyone. "To the other locker room. George isn't in here. I need to make sure he's safe."

Perhaps a sharp-eyed wariness or determined purpose to her movements made others lean back or pull their feet out of her path as she stayed as low to the floor as she could while stepping over the bench and circling around several banks of lockers. But every "Excuse me" she uttered, every nod she traded, put her no closer to spying any sign of a damp blue shirt or that salt-and-pepper hair.

She'd nearly reached the exit when a concerned voice called out to her. "Elise? You need to sit down."

Recognizing the uniformed officer, she squatted down beside him. "Officer Hale. Have you seen the deputy commissioner?"

"No, ma'am."

His dark hair was wet, his shirt plastered to the flak vest he wore underneath. "How bad is it out there?"

"Bad. Nobody needs to be outside right now."

Or on the upper floors of this building. "Could you try to get him on your radio? I don't want to interfere with emergency transmissions."

With a nod from Joe Hendricks, Denton turned his mouth to his shoulder and turned on his radio. "Commissioner Madigan, what's your twenty? This is Officer Hale, badge number 1897." Static was the only reply. "Commissioner Madigan, do you copy?"

"Why doesn't he answer?"

"He could be on a different frequency. His battery's dead. He's taken shelter behind a wall that blocks his signal. Lots of reasons."

She looked to Captain Hendricks for permission, as well. "May I?"

"Do it."

Elise pulled out her portable radio. "George? This is Elise. Where are you? You said no heroics, remember?" The answering static squealed—probably from a lightning strike disrupting the electricity in the air. "Just let me know you're safe."

Still no answer. Fear squeezed her heart.

"Something's not right." She pocketed her radio and stood again. "I'm going to the ladies' locker room and the firing range to look for him."

But her ears popped with a sudden change in air pressure. She braced her hand on the wall for balance and felt the subtle vibrations in the steel-and-concrete structure. She was too late.

The roar of a freight train hit the building above their heads.

"Get down, Elise!" Joe Hendricks ordered.

Officer Hale grabbed Elise's wrist and pulled her to the floor beside him as they heard explosions of glass and flying debris overhead. "Your search for loverboy will have to wait."

Denton Hale was wearing a black leather glove.

She flashed back to the Plaza and the gloved hand that had yanked her through the crowd. Her panic was instant and terrifying. She jerked her arm from his grasp and scooted across the aisle to sit next to Joe, despite the curious frown on Hale's face. At least with the captain as a buffer between them, she wouldn't have to worry about Hale being able to hurt her.

"Oh, my God," she whispered. She swept her gaze around the room. Every single uniformed police officer in this room was either wearing gloves, or had them tucked into their utility belts.

Loverboy? Surely that snide nickname meant he was the only cop in this room she had to worry about.

She hugged her legs to her chest and kept Denton Hale in her sight for as long as possible, until the watch commander ordered them all to cover their heads.

The tornado was here.

GEORGE OPENED THE fifth-floor men's room and ran a sweep with his flashlight.

Three floors cleared.

Four minutes time.

Five persons routed from various rooms and sent down to the sublevel storm shelter.

He listened to the chatter on his radio as officers on each floor reported in and then got themselves downstairs. He and Shane were the last ones through each floor, running a quick secondary sweep. Although the back of his mind was filled with thoughts of Elise and visions that she'd made it safely to the basement without Courtney getting on her nerves or any other incident stopping her, he made himself focus on the job at hand. He couldn't be prouder of his department and the way the men and women who served under him were handling one weather-related crisis after another this summer.

And he couldn't be more anxious to confess the stunning revelation he'd made about himself, his work and his relationships upstairs in his office before the sirens had gone off to Elise. If he didn't get the chance to tell that woman how much he loved her and everything he was willing to do for them to be together, then he and Mother Nature were going to have words.

But he had a duty to this department and the entire city he needed to complete first before he could grab a little happiness for himself.

"Clear!" He moved next door to the ladies' room, but had taken only a couple of steps inside when the air pressure around him plummeted and his ears were suddenly stopped up with pain. "Ahh."

Not good.

He checked his watch. Five minutes had elapsed.

"Anybody in here?" He swallowed and yawned until his ears popped, and then he was suddenly aware of the eerie silence, broken only by the blare of the storm sirens.

Really not good.

Search time was over.

George pulled his radio from his belt. "Wilkins! Wherever you are, get to the basement now! If there's anyone left up here, they're on their own."

Fortunately, George was on the right side of the door when the row of tiny windows at the end of the stalls exploded into the room. The force of the blast threw him to the floor of the hallway. He hit hard and skidded across the floor as shards of glass pelted the marble tiles behind him like hail stones.

"Ah, hell." The roar of the wind was deafening, like a locomotive crashing at full speed into the side of the mountain. George pulled himself up onto his bruised knees and stood. A trash can beside the water fountain hovered off the floor, then flew past him and smashed into the wall. This wasn't any child's storybook with houses and dogs dropping into a colorful land.

This tornado was real.

And he was far too close to the heart of it.

"Wilkins!" That kid had better already be two steps ahead of him. George ran toward the double walls and steel doors of the stairwell, but his forward progress was more like fighting to escape the gravity of a black hole.

And then he heard the glass breaking inside the last office on his right. "Wilkins?"

The cry of pain he heard wasn't the storm and it wasn't his imagination.

"Shane!" George pushed open the door and immediately ducked his head as books and papers and a barrage of knickknacks got sucked out of the room. His tie whipped him in the face and the wind itself made it hard to open his eyes more than a squint. "Shane, are you in here? Are you injured?"

Grabbing the edge of a built-in bookshelf, George pulled himself along the front wall of the room. He was pelted with more books and debris before he reached a heavy office desk and dropped down beside it. The sturdy walnut shifted a little on the carpet, but blocked enough of the wind and flying missiles to allow him to search most of the room. "Wilkins?"

Following the sound of another moan, he crawled around the desk. Still no sign of the other officer. But his knee crunched down on a broken piece of glass, drawing his attention to the window above him.

George scanned the carpet around him and frowned. “One piece of glass?”

The floor in the bathroom had been littered with thousands. Holding tight to the desk, George pulled himself up and threw himself toward the shattered window. Bits of dirt stung his face like shrapnel, but he pushed his back against the wall and opened one eye to peer outside. He could see the funnel cloud coming up the street, more a giant cloud of flying dirt and debris than the spinning corkscrew he’d imagined. It picked up a car and dashed it against a streetlamp, bending the steel in half and shooting up sparks of electricity that were quickly swallowed by the storm.

Most important, he saw all the bits of glass wedged beneath the window frame and stuck into the concrete ledge outside the window.

George braced his forearm over his eyes and turned to verify the horrible suspicion burning in his gut. This wasn’t Mother Nature’s handiwork. Someone had deliberately broken this window.

He glimpsed a blur of blue from the corner of his eye, but it was too late to react. Something hard whacked him on the back of his head and neck, driving him to his knees. Another blow dropped him to the carpet, and in his spinning vision he saw the metal chair being thrown across the room. Probably what the perp had smashed the window with.

It had all been a trick, a perfectly plausible ruse to lure him into the room, to trap him here. Maybe even to kill him. And no one would suspect anything other than the tornado had been responsible. *Smart boy. I always knew you could accomplish anything you set your mind to.*

"You stay away from her. Elise is mine."

With the wind knocked from his lungs and his head spinning, George was too weak to stop Shane Wilkins from stealing his keys, radio and gun, and throwing them out the window.

The wind was roaring louder than his thoughts as Shane locked the door behind him, leaving George with no way to get down to the storm shelter now.

But George was a smart man, too. He rolled underneath the heavy desk as the tornado hit the building and thanked God that he was conscious and able to think.

Now he just had to live. Or else, Elise wouldn't.

Chapter Eleven

The moment the sirens stopped and Joe Hendricks gave the all clear, Elise pushed her way out of the ladies' locker room and moved upstream against a sea of people spilling out into the hallway and heading toward the stairs to assess damage and to find daylight and working phones to call loved ones.

"George?" Her worried shout was swallowed up by the mass of bodies. But, desperate to find him, to know he was okay, she shoved her way into the men's locker room to look for him. In here there were people with cuts and concussions being tended by the medics on staff and a nurse who'd been meeting her husband for lunch in the building. Careful to stay out of everyone's way as she searched, she stepped up onto the long bench between two rows of lockers and called again. "Is Deputy Commissioner Madigan in here?"

There were several nos and "I haven't seen hims," but no replies that could give her the information she needed.

The crowd of survivors was thinning out when she went across the hall to check the firing range. One woman said she'd met the deputy commissioner on the stairs, going onto the sixth floor. He'd warned her to get downstairs fast and had promised to join them once the tornado got close enough to keep him from safely clearing all the floors.

But no George. She had a sick, sick feeling that something terrible had happened. That her gun-shy caution about relationships and fears of becoming a detriment to George's office if she gave in to her emotions had prevented her from telling him the truth. She should have been braver. She should have taken the risk and told him how much she loved him.

"Where are you?" she whispered, finally joining the flow of people to get back to her purse in the ladies' locker room.

Captain Hendricks had turned this space into an impromptu command center, deploying officers to various parts of the building to check for damage, sending others on out to neighborhoods and hospitals in the area to assist and protect emergency teams there. He was being briefed by other officers and approving a statement for the press liaison. There were reports of extensive property damage already coming in, threats of flash flooding near the river and the creeks and sloughs that fed into it, hail damage and more. Everyone had a job or was awaiting an order.

No one was looking for the man in charge of it all.

"Have you found him yet?"

Elise jumped at the hand on her elbow and jerked away from Denton Hale's touch. She supposed that coming right out and accusing him of being her stalker wouldn't be the smartest move, even surrounded by a roomful of policemen and women. Better to stay friendly and act as if she didn't suspect a thing. "No. Not yet."

Denton tapped the radio on his shoulder. "I tried to hail him a couple more times once the captain gave us the all clear. Sorry, though, I'm still getting nothing but static."

She forced a smile onto her lips. "Thank you for checking."

A distant drum of thunder reminded her that the storm hadn't finished yet. But the sound of rain hitting the ground and windows upstairs was a much gentler threat, maybe even a cleansing aftermath to the tornado's fury.

But the threat was still here, standing much closer than any lightning bolt or rain cloud outside. "Do you want me to go with you to help look for him?" Officer Hale asked.

"No." She answered a little too quickly. When his eyes narrowed and looked at her like she was a crazy lady, Elise came up with another smile. "No, thank you." When Joe Hendricks called Hale over to join him, Elise backed away. "You have work to do."

Her intent was to find James and Courtney, and retrieve her purse, but she smacked into a wall of blue shirt and a flak vest.

"Whoa." Shane Wilkins reached out to grab her before she tumbled backward. But his green eyes weren't offering an apology when she looked up. His forehead was creased with concern. "Are you looking for the deputy commissioner?"

Elise's relief was short-lived. Shane would have been smiling if everything was okay. "Have you seen him?"

"He got hurt." He wrapped his fingers around her upper arm and pulled her into the hallway beside him. "I'll take you to him."

Elise glanced over her shoulder to see Denton Hale watching her as Shane, taller and broader than most of the people around him, decided to avoid the open stairs that led up to the lobby and pushed a pathway through the crowd to get to the north emergency stairwell. Once the steel door was safely closed behind them, Elise breathed a sigh of relief.

But she dug in her heels and questioned the change in direction when he turned to the first floor exit instead of continuing up the stairs. "You said we were going upstairs."

Shane pushed open the door to the noise and more natural light of the building's open lobby. Shaking her head, Elise tugged her arm from his grasp and turned toward the stairs. She tipped her head and shouted up the tall stairwell. "George?"

Everything above her seemed rock solid. A good sign, she hoped. But she'd only reached the second step when Shane closed his hands around her waist and lifted her to the floor.

She swatted his hands away. "What are you doing?"

He grabbed her wrist and pulled her toward the exit. "I'll get you out of here."

A spurt of frustrated anger made her strong enough to pull away from his grip. "I thought we were looking for George."

"Stop saying his name like that!" Shane's shout echoed off the concrete walls. "You mean the deputy commissioner?"

Elise retreated when he leaned closer and walked toward her. "Yes. I'll find him myself. You have other duties in the building, I'm sure."

She gasped when her back hit the wall. But he kept coming. "No. I'm saving you."

Elise put up her hands to brace against his chest. "I don't need to be saved."

He was leaning over her now, his handsome face red with anger. "Damn it, yes, you do. You've got a stalker. You've had a Russian mob guy try to kill you."

"Alexsandr didn't threaten me—"

"Shut up!" He slapped his hand across her face and she felt the coppery taste of blood in her mouth.

"Shane?" The übercalm that followed was more frightening than the outburst of anger had been. He squinched up his face and turned away as if he was grappling with impulses that threatened to tear him apart. Elise didn't intend to stay to see which Shane won. She slid along the wall to get away from him. "I'm going to go find Commissioner Madigan," she said in a soft, even tone.

He raked his fingers through his dark blond hair, breathing hard with the effort to control whatever sickness consumed him. She had her hand on the door lever when he turned to her with tears in his eyes. "Do you love him?"

Elise didn't know whether to lie or keep him in reality with her. She opted for reality. "Yes."

Wrong choice.

When she turned to push open the door, he grabbed her from behind and smacked her head against the unbending steel. There was no pain for a split second—all the nerves had been deadened by the blow. But while the ache blossomed and the black door and white walls spun into a sea of gray, Shane snatched her face between his hands and ground his lips over hers in a kiss.

"You're mine." He lifted her onto her toes and kissed her again. "I love you."

Elise gripped the door behind her for balance when he dropped her to her feet and backed away. He smiled down at her, as if a beautiful moment had passed between them.

But Elise wiped away his kiss with the back of her hand, taking a smear of blood that had dripped onto her cheek with it. She tenderly touched the gash at her temple, then looked down to see the black gloves that had fallen to the floor. Shane?

She couldn't think of anything to say to properly express her fear and revulsion at the terror and violence he'd put her through. "Why?"

With her vision cleared by anger, she pushed the door lever behind her and swung it open. But before she could call for help or get away, Shane pulled his gun and shoved it into her back. A death grip on her arm yanked her back against his chest and he whispered against her ear, "I'll shoot anyone who tries to help you or keep us apart again."

Then he urged her toward the building's front doors.

"Elise, are you okay?"

She turned at the sound of James Westbrook's voice. With his arm around Courtney Reiter's waist, he was helping her up the main stairs into the lobby.

Even Courtney looked concerned. "That's a bad cut."

A steel barrel jabbed beneath her ribs before she got the chance to say anything. Elise wasn't surprised at how earnest and concerned Shane sounded. "She got hit by some flying debris. I'm taking her to the first aid station."

"I thought they'd set that up downstairs," said James.

Elise looked to the double glass doors. The granite steps out front were completely blocked with the wreckage of a car and an ancient pine tree that had been uprooted from the front lawn. There were several people between them and the exit Shane had hoped for, some pointing and chatting about the damage, others dealing with the rain coming in through the broken glass.

With a quick breath and glance around him that smelled like desperation, Shane pulled her back toward the stairwell. "There's another aid station upstairs."

James nodded, his eyes narrowed in doubt behind his glasses. "Okay. Call me when you get the chance. Let me know you're okay."

"I need George." Elise mouthed the words as Shane dragged her back to the stairs. It was a plea for her life, and theirs. But she didn't risk saying anything out loud as the stairwell door closed behind them.

GEORGE SHOVED THE mountain of tangled blinds, books and furniture away from the opening beneath the desk, and made a solemn vow to buy himself a sturdy antique like this one for his office upstairs. Assuming he still had an office. And an upstairs.

The rain blowing through the broken window splashed his face and arms as he pushed to his feet and surveyed the damage. There was plenty. But the floor was solid, and the walls of this 1920s steel-and-limestone fortress seemed to still be standing.

But the building damage was the least of his concerns right now. It didn't take him long to decide that what had worked for Shane would work for him. Picking up the metal conference chair the young officer had clocked him with, George swung it against the door, smashing the wood around the lock so he could pull it open, run to the south stairwell and get to Elise.

He'd brushed aside several status reports, and inquiries into the nicks and scratches on his face and hands, and the bruise at his temple, to get downstairs to the storm shelter as quickly as possible. Although there were a few wounded refugees in the men's locker room, most of the area had been cleared out. He certainly wasn't seeing anyone with soft brown waves framing her face and killer legs organizing some kind of team and tackling a list of tasks necessary for a recovery effort.

George propped his hands at his waist and took several deep breaths, keeping his fear at bay. Fine. If he couldn't locate Elise, then he'd look for Shane.

He stopped the first uniformed officer who walked past. Denton Hale wasn't much of a go-getter on his own time, but he snapped to when George called his name. "Which one is Wilkins's locker?"

Hale led him to the end of the row. "This one, sir."

"Can we cut that lock?"

Hale called over a maintenance man with a toolbox and cut off the lock with a set of bolt cutters.

When George pulled open the metal door, he swore one choice, biting word.

Hanging from a hook at the back of the locker was a dried-up yellow rose. In the gym bag at the bottom he found a pair of lacy blue panties and a ton of pictures. All of them of Elise—waving to the camera across a parking lot, walking her dog, lounging on the deck in her backyard, eating a salad in Pitsaeli's Restaurant, standing on her front porch, hugging Spike, looking wary and afraid.

A box on the top shelf held something even more disturbing—stacks of love poems and letters, all saying variations of the same thing.

I love you.

You're mine.

We belong together.

No one will keep us apart.

When the bile in his throat receded and he could speak again, George turned to Officer Hale. "When was the last time you saw Elise?"

"About fifteen minutes ago." He nodded toward the locker room exit. "She went looking for you. Wilkins was with her."

"Shane Wilkins?"

"Yeah."

"Do you know which way they went?"

"Your last known location was upstairs. I'm sure they went that way. They headed to the north end of the building. She was worried sick about you." Hale pointed to the drops of blood on George's damp shirt. "Sir, you're hurt."

"Just a few cuts and a bump on the head. Give me your building keys." When George gestured for him to hurry and hand them over, Denton unhooked the ring of keys and dropped them into his palm. "Are you carrying a spare gun?"

"Yeah." Hale nodded and pulled a Smith & Wesson from the ankle holster beneath his pant leg.

George held it down and away and checked the loaded magazine and weight of the weapon before sliding it into his own holster. "Get on the horn and find out if my nephew, Detective Fensom, is in the building.

Tell him and any of his friends to meet me upstairs. I may need backup."

"Sir?"

George strode into the hallway, with Hale hurrying along beside him. "You want to guarantee your job, and get those lousy performance evaluations off your record?"

"Yes, sir."

"Make that call, then get your butt upstairs and help me find Elise."

ELISE COULD SENSE Shane's growing agitation with every step. When his getaway out the front door, parking garage or fire escape exits had been thwarted by crowds of people or storm damage that would require him to holster his gun and risk Elise screaming for help or making a break for it, Shane had decided to head up the stairs.

But every floor they tried to enter had cops on it, searching through rooms. Elise recognized some of the detectives and uniformed officers. A. J. Rodriguez and Josh Taylor, detectives who'd worked together for years, were on the third floor, righting desks and chairs and cubicle walls. Shane avoided a tall K-9 officer and his German shepherd peeking into a room on the sixth floor. She saw Nick Fensom's stocky figure. He was wrestling with his cell phone to get some decent reception on the eighth floor leading to George's office. But she didn't dare call out to him. The hand crushing her arm and the gun bruising her ribs wouldn't allow her to risk it.

Her lungs were beginning to ache with their steady climb. But, like a cornered animal, Shane seemed to think he had no place to go but up. When he heard voices on the stairs two flights beneath them, he forced her into double time, taking her up the last few stairs onto the roof.

When he pushed open the last door, Elise instinctively drew back from the slap of rain on her face. It was pouring outside. The air smelled of dust and ozone, but felt cleaner than the stale musk of Shane's nervous perspiration. Streaks of lightning forked across the sky, pricking the hairs on her forearms and at the back of her neck. Thunder rumbled loudly, as if a marching band was waiting on the roof to greet them.

Shane released her just once, to push aside the wreckage of a satellite dish that littered the steps leading up to the helicopter pad, air conditioners and power units that served the entire building. She'd only backed a few feet away before his gun was trained on her again. He reached down his hand to her, leaving her no choice but to join him up top.

The rain soaked her to the skin in seconds and the wind whipping through her hair made her shiver. "What are we doing up here, Shane? There's no place left to go."

"We're together." He had her by the arm again, adding five more bruises to the marks he'd already left there. "That's all that matters to me."

He ducked his head against the driving rain and hiked across the empty helipad to the concrete wall at the edge of the building. "Shane, what are you doing? There's lightning up here. I don't think it's safe."

Elise tried to pull away when he leaned over the side. "Look at our city," he said, the tone of his voice matching the drama of the sky above them. "I thought it'd be in shambles. But it's still standing. Cars are moving, see?" He pulled her to the wall, and for the first time that day, she prayed he had an unbreakable hold on her. "See?"

Elise forced herself to look. She saw broken windows and toppled trees, lines of streets with streetlights on and others that were dark—and way too much distance between her and the ground below. Magnificent view. If she wanted to die.

"Shane, you're scaring me."

"What? Why?" He let her back away from the edge, but sat down on top of the wall, pulling her onto the slick seat beside him. *Don't look behind you. Don't look down.* Shane moved his hand to her knee, where his grip proved just as effective at holding her captive as her arm had been. "I love you. And you love me. I won't let you get hurt. I'll save you."

The rain loosened the blood that had dried on her temple and cheek, and it dripped into her lap. So this was how her sorry, second-guessing life would end. "How do you know I love you?"

The wind buffeted them and the rain chilled. Shane rested the gun in his lap, with the barrel pointed at her. And he smiled. "Every day, you talk to me. Every day, you smile. I'm one in a million, you said."

She said hi to him every morning because he was the first person she'd see when she stepped off the eighth-floor elevator. She talked to him because they worked together. She smiled because…she smiled at nearly every person she met. It had become a brave mask to hide behind when she felt unsure of herself or needed a boost of self-confidence.

"We've always been friends—"

"It's more than that. Your loyalty is one of the things

I treasure most about you. I've had other people say they love me. But they didn't. They lied to me. They left.

"I've got my degree," he went on. "Soon I'll have my master's. I'll make detective and I'll be commissioner one day. And you'll be right there with me. Supporting me, just like you always have."

When he took her hand and got down on one knee, Elise nearly retched. "Shane, don't."

When tears joined the rain rolling down her cheeks, he smiled. "I love you, Elise Brown."

"Put the gun down, son. Step away from the edge of the roof."

"George!" Her relief was so intense that she nearly forgot her precarious perch. But the stony eyes boring into hers across the roof sent a warning instead of a promise.

In a flash of movement, like Jekyll and Hyde, Shane jumped to his feet and pulled Elise in front of him like a shield. Although he stood a head taller, she imagined the target he presented to the gun George aimed at him wasn't very big.

"Get back!" Shane warned, pushing his gun against her neck. "I don't want you here."

Whether he was yelling at George or the other detectives and uniformed officers she saw climbing up the stairs and taking positions beside him, she couldn't tell.

George's rock steady hands never wavered. "Elise, are you hurt?"

She sniffed back her tears as she clawed at the arm cinched around her throat. *Be brave.* This was her last chance to seize the life she wanted with no regrets or second-guessing. "Nothing serious. Yet."

"I wouldn't hurt her," Shane insisted, despite the blood and bruises and terror. "I love her."

George took two steps across the roof. "Shane, this isn't going to end well if you don't put down that gun and let her go."

How could she help? How could she make George's job easier? How could she save herself?

And then she knew. "It's all right, George. Shane and I have been talking. We're friends." She erased the tremor from her voice, blinked the rain from her eyes so she could see that face filled with so much life experience and love. "We're more than friends. He's been watching over me. I think he wants to marry me."

Shane's arm eased its choke hold on her neck. "What? What are you saying?"

"Weren't you about to propose to me?"

George was slowly shaking his head. "Elise, what are you doing?" He put out his hand to warn the other officers to keep their distance, then cradled the gun again. "Honey?"

"If this is a trick…" Shane tapped her neck with the barrel of his gun, reminding her of his control over her.

"I will never leave you." Elise petted the arm she'd dug her nails into just moments earlier. "You promised me a lot, Shane. But you have to ask. A girl likes to be asked."

She felt him nod behind her. And then, with a streak of lightning cutting through the sky over their heads, he took her hand and knelt down. But when she stepped to the side, he knew.

She'd lied.

Shane clamped his hand over her wrist, swinging

the gun toward George, and charging toward the edge of the roof, dragging her behind him. "She's mine!"

"Drop it, Shane!"

Before her knees hit the wall, gunfire rang out, drowning out the thunder.

Elise couldn't count how many bullets there were. But she felt the spatter of blood on her neck, and the tug on her arm as Shane's body crumpled to the roof and pulled her down with him.

"Elise!" George was at her side in an instant. He kicked Shane's gun from his lifeless hand before holstering his own. "What a damn waste."

Before she could get to her feet, he scooped her up into his arms and carried her away from her captor while other officers swarmed in to secure the scene.

"Put me down, George." She pushed against his chest. "Put me down."

"What's wrong? I'm trying to get you out of the rain." When she pushed again, he stopped and set her down beside the broken satellite dish at the top of the stairs. "Are you hurt?" He clasped her face, checked the cut on her head, ran his fingers along her arms, cursing at the bruises already forming there. "What did he do to you?"

Elise threw her arms around his neck and hugged him so tightly, even the rain couldn't fall between them. "This is what I need. I need you to hold me."

"Okay, honey." He sighed in relief, folding his arms around her at last. He pulled her into his chest, surrounded her with his body and rubbed his smooth cheek against hers. "Okay. I've got you. I need to hold you, too."

They stood together like that for endless moments,

cheek to cheek and heart to heart. Elise cried out her stress and fear, and absorbed George's strength. When she was spent, when she was breathing normally against him, he leaned back, his face as grave as she'd ever seen it. And then he was kissing her, hard, thoroughly. Just as quickly, he tore his mouth from hers to press a far gentler kiss beside the wound on her forehead. "Damn it, woman, I won't survive another day like this."

Elise curled her fingers into his collar, squeezing the water from it and smoothing it against his neck and chest. "Dealing with a psychopath?"

"No."

She glanced up, surprised by his answer. "Surviving a tornado?"

"Thinking I was going to lose you."

This time, Elise stretched onto her toes and kissed him, sliding her fingers into his hair and pledging with every stroke on his lips, every slide of her tongue that she was no one's but his. Elise felt the rain running against her scalp beneath her hair. She heard the thunder rumbling overhead. But all she knew was the taste and power of this man's kiss.

"Damn, Uncle George—get a room." Nick Fensom walked up beside them and squeezed his uncle's shoulder. It was a gesture of love and relief, and probably the only way he could interrupt this relationship that wasn't supposed to exist. "Does she need a medic?"

George never took his eyes off her. "Do you?"

Elise shook her head. "Not yet. I probably need stitches, but I'm not ready to go down yet." She never took her eyes off George, either. "We need to discuss *this* first."

While a smile spread across George's handsome face for her, his voice commanded Nick and the others. "Clear the roof. Get him off my building. Find the next senior officer on-site and tell him to get me a status report on casualties and damage." At the last second, he turned to Nick. "In twenty minutes."

Nick grinned. "I can buy you twenty minutes, old man."

Someone brought a morgue bag and others carried the troubled officer's body down the stairs. A few detectives snapped pictures of the scene, but it was raining too hard for them to preserve any evidence beyond the body itself. Elise tucked her head beneath George's chin and held on until they were all alone.

But it was George who spoke first.

"Twenty minutes may not be enough time to say everything I want to." In the pouring rain, with a streak of lightning dancing over the skyline that still stood tall and proud over Kansas City, George Madigan spoke the words in his heart. "For years I've been trying to turn myself into someone I'm not. Because that's what Court wanted. But you get me. I can be the man I want to be with you—the man I'm meant to be. You needed me to be that man. I'm a cop. Always have been, always will be. Okay, so I'm a cop who puts together budget sheets and personnel charts, but I'm still a cop."

"Protect and serve your city. That's you, George. I never doubted it for a moment."

With a wry laugh, he smoothed the wet hair off her face and tucked it behind her ear. "Not even when I did. You and I fit together in a way no other woman has. You make me happy. And whole again. I need you, Elise Brown."

She spoke the words in her heart, too. "I need you."

And somehow, with the way he was kissing her, with the way she couldn't let go of him, "I need you" became "I love you."

He left her mouth to lap up the cool rain from along her jaw and warm the skin there. "I know you've got a thing about dating your boss—"

"There are KCPD rules and regulations to consider." She nibbled on his chin, kissed the grooves of laughter beside his eyes. "You're a superior officer. You have to uphold them."

"I'm going to marry you even if I have to fire you. Understood?"

Elise blinked the rain from her lashes and framed his face, too, smiling up at him. "You could just transfer me to another office."

"I'm in charge of that stuff, aren't I. I could do that."

"Yes, you could."

"It might mean a cut in pay. For now. Or getting stuck with some tyrant for a boss. But I will fire his ass if he gets out of line—"

Elise pressed a finger against his lips to hush him. "Do you think money is what I want? Do you think I can't handle some grumpy old curmudgeon? Do you think there's an office out there I can't run?"

"I'm going to miss you at work, Elise." His smile faded for a moment, and the man who never minced words seemed unsure of what to say. "But I'll see you in bed every night and across the breakfast table every morning. Right?"

"Is that an official proposal, Deputy Commissioner?"

"Yes. If you'll have an old man."

"I won't." Elise stretched up on tiptoe to kiss his lips into a smile. "But I'll have you."

* * * * *

Don't miss the next thrilling installment of
USA Today bestselling author Julie Miller's
miniseries THE PRECINCT *on sale later in 2014.*

MILLS & BOON®

Why not subscribe?

Never miss a title and save money too!

Here's what's available to you if you join the exclusive **Mills & Boon Book Club** today:

- *Titles up to a month ahead of the shops*
- *Amazing discounts*
- *Free P&P*
- *Earn Bonus Book points that can be redeemed against other titles and gifts*
- *Choose from monthly or pre-paid plans*

Still want more?

Well, if you join today we'll even give you

50% OFF your first parcel!

So visit **www.millsandboon.co.uk/subs**
or call Customer Relations on 020 8288 2888
to be a part of this exclusive Book Club!

SUBS_2014